Graham, Alice
    The summer queen.

Graham, Alice
    The summer queen.

DATE DUE

DATE	ISSUED TO
SEP 15 1973	*Mrs Penyer*
SEP 15 1973	*B. Miller*
OCT 19 1973	*Kane*
NOV 3 9 1973	*Mrs. H. Miller*
FEB 2 6 1975	

By Alice Walworth Graham

❀ ❀ ❀ ❀ ❀

THE SUMMER QUEEN

❀ ❀ ❀ ❀ ❀ Alice Walworth Graham

Doubleday & Company, Inc., GARDEN CITY, NEW YORK
1973

29.734

ISBN: 0-385-05111-5
LIBRARY OF CONGRESS CATALOG CARD NUMBER 72–84916
COPYRIGHT © 1973 BY ALICE WALWORTH GRAHAM
PRINTED IN THE UNITED STATES OF AMERICA
FIRST EDITION

TO CLINTON BROOKS WHITFIELD

FOREWORD

I want to thank Mrs. M. Bridges, who was once married to Sir Benjamin Astley, and Major and Mrs. Dodd for their help when I was doing research in England. While I was there, I went to royal palaces, feudal castles, and churches. Middleham Castle and Fotheringhay have vanished, but Warwick Castle, above the town, is reflected in the Avon. Ten miles away, Astley Castle and church still stand, off of the main road, in a green and secluded spot. The castle at Ludlow is a massive ruin, but enough is left to show what it must have been when it was the great fortress guarding the marches of Wales.

Tewkesbury Abbey, with all of its tombs and effigies, some showing traces of their former brilliant coloring and gold leaf, evokes the past and the people of the past. The town still commemorates the battle that was fought close by the Abbey's doors.

Also, I heartily thank my editor, LeBaron Barker, for his help, advice, and encouragement.

Now is the winter of our discontent
Made glorious summer by this sun of York.
Shakespeare, *Richard III*, Act 1, Sc. i

The Summer Queen

"You will meet your cousins of York," Dame Joan said.

"I know their names and their ages." I counted them on my five fingers. "Edward's the eldest, he's called Earl of March; Edmund's a year younger, and he's Earl of Rutland; their sister is Margaret, then comes George, and Richard is the youngest, but I've never laid eyes on them, and don't know anything about them except their names."

"After you've met them you'll know more," Dame Joan predicted.

I turned in the saddle to look at her, wondering how she could seem so cheerful, and how she had managed to make the long journey without appearing travel worn. She had a neat compact body and a round fresh face framed in the folds of a coif which never became disarranged. A knight's widow, she was my lady governess, who had charge of me and would stay with me. So would my waiting women, but the men who had escorted us would go back to Shute Manor in Devon, where they belonged, where all of us belonged.

If circumstances had been otherwise, I would have been eager to make the journey, and overjoyed at the prospect of staying for a time in a great castle, but in this summer of 1459 war had broken out in earnest between York and Lancaster. My lord grandfather and my parents had decided to send me to Ludlow, to the Duke and Duchess of York, who had sent for their younger children and had offered to take charge of me.

My lady Duchess was my great-aunt and my godmother; she had held me in her arms at the baptismal font and had given me her own name, Cicely. Although she had never seen me since then, she had a great affection for my mother and therefore was willing to concern herself with me. Ludlow was a strong fortress, I was told, and was further protected by the Yorkist army, but I was worried about what might happen to my family and my friends, and the people on our estates.

My mother was staying on at the manor, and said that she would not be in any danger, but I was troubled. My grandfather and my father were with the Yorkist ships guarding the coast against French invasion and keeping foreign supplies from reaching the Lancastrians. The sea was always dangerous, and the peril was much greater because of this wretched war. I thought of the hazards that they might encounter and my eyes filled with tears, but my name was Cicely Bonville and I was expected to show courage.

"Yonder's Ludlow," one of the men said and pointed to the distance. I had pictured a grim fortress, but I saw walls and towers emerging from a haze of sunlight, endless walls and crowding towers covering a vast expanse of ground on a slope overlooking the Teme. I knew that the little town was clustered at the base of the castle, on the other side, out of sight. The Yorkist army was out of sight too, as it was encamped on a flat meadow to the south, where the river made a bend. I saw Duke Richard's standard flying on the keep, and along the battlements the banners of the lords and knights who had answered his summons.

A procession of carts was lumbering up to the gates, and a continuous stream of people were coming and going, some on foot and some on horseback. What caught my attention most were the shrubs and flowers planted on the slopes along the riverbank. I thought how pleasant it would be to walk along those shady paths on a summer day, down to the river's edge, and I forgot about the war.

The courtyard swarmed with people, but I saw him at once as he came toward us, and I knew who he was without being told. He was undoubtedly Edward, the Duke of York's eldest son, I said, and Dame Joan answered yes, but how did I know as I had never seen him before.

"Because they told me that he was tall—and he is. Taller than anyone else."

"So he is, and clean-made, well proportioned," she answered, watching him too.

Without seeming to hurry, he moved quickly, with a long effortless stride. The light wind flicked the folds of his scarlet cloak, and ruffled his tawny gold hair; his face, browned by the sun, had a darker tawniness, tinged along his cheekbones with an underlying healthy red. Most of all I noticed the brightness of his eyes. His smile was for me—for all of us, and he spoke first to Dame Joan, making her welcome. He thanked the men for bringing us safely to Ludlow, and turned to me. "We've been on the watch for you—you've had a long journey, you must be tired."

The warmth in his voice made me believe that we were truly welcome. Swinging me out of the saddle, he kissed me before he put me on my feet, as if I were his sister instead of an unknown child cousin.

Edward's squire, John Dynham, ran down into the courtyard to greet us, and led us to the rooms assigned to us, talking all the while, asking for news of home. The Dynhams had lands close to ours in Devon and John was an old friend I hadn't seen for years.

Later, when I went down to supper, Edward led me to my place at table. By that time, the rest of his family had greeted me. "Your family as well as mine" Edward had pointed out. The Earl of Warwick was here with his retainers. My mother was his sister—his best-loved sister, he said—and she often spoke of him, taking great pride in his renown as Captain of Calais and "the finest knight now living." To his friends and to his enemies he was "The Earl"—as if there were no others. "Love him or hate him," John Dynham had said. "He looms large in men's minds."

He had courtly manners, a knightly bearing, and when I looked at him I could see why men said that he was "born to command." Every person present seemed to love and admire him, and hang on his words—even his own father, Lord Salisbury, who

3

said of himself that he was more fitted for camp than for royal courts.

"Lord Salisbury is your maternal grandfather, be sure to show him every respect," Dame Joan had admonished me. Lord Salisbury had greeted me in his own way. "Come here, poppet—let me have a look at you," he had barked. "Why hasn't my daughter Kate presented the Bonvilles with a sturdy boy or two—or even three?"

Duke Richard had pointed out that my parents were young, and were likely to have many more children—and he had patted my shoulder.

"Doesn't look like it," Lord Salisbury had grunted. "They have had time enough, and they have only this one scrawny little she-mouse!"

I might have been downcast, but I caught Edward's eye who began to laugh. "Girls have value too—and we cherish this one," he said.

There were other lords and knights at Ludlow, but the Earl of Warwick and Lord Salisbury were the most important. The Duke and Duchess of York kept their state, sitting in armchairs, with a canopy over their heads. None of the men wore armor, and everyone present was richly dressed. For the first time in my life I had given some thought to my appearance, and had worn my best—a rose-colored gown embroidered at the neck and on the sleeves.

The windows in the great hall had been enlarged and filled with painted glass, but as the weather was warm the casements stood open, and sunlight flickered in, but on the high table the candles had been lighted in the tall silver candlesticks. Duke Richard had thick mouse-colored hair, eyebrows the same color as his hair, and though he was not handsome he had a kind face, I thought. He was hot tempered, I had heard, but warmhearted and affectionate with his children, as with me.

"Duchess Cicely was a famous beauty," my mother had told me. "In her girlhood she was known as the Rose of Raby." She was still handsome, and stately, with an air of great dignity, but

4

no longer famous for being the most beautiful girl in England. She had earned another name. According to my women, when the duchess was at Fotheringhay she assumed so much royal state and exacted so much homage that the country folk had dubbed her Proud Cis. I could see why, but as Dame Joan said, my lady Duchess had bequeathed her beauty to her children—or at least all but one of them.

My cousins of York—already I found myself watching them and listening to them. Edward was wearing a satin doublet—pale saffron—a sunny hue; it suited him, and the linen showing at the neck and wrists was of the best quality, and the most immaculate whiteness. His manners were fastidious too. He always wiped his lips before he drank wine, and he took care to keep even the tips of his fingers away from any sauce.

Next was his brother Edmund—only a year younger—and equally well-mannered. Although not so tall as Edward, he was a good height. His hair was a light yellow, and his eyes gray-blue, with a gentle expression. Those two—Edward and Edmund—had been brought up together here at Ludlow, and were devoted to each other, I was told.

A gap in years separated them from the other three, who usually lived at Fotheringhay and had been brought to Ludlow for greater safety as I had. There was Margaret—the Lady Margaret of York—beautiful in her blue gown. She was thirteen, in my eyes a woman grown, with a womanly dignity and graciousness which I greatly admired. George was ten, well-grown and vigorous; his cheeks were ruddy, his bright gold hair curled over his head and his eyes, bright and blue and clear, invited trust. I doubted if he was as guileless as he seemed.

The last and least was little Richard, who was entirely unlike the other four. He had none of their health and shapeliness and brilliant color—their radiance. He was undersized for his age, sickly, and sallow. I had never given any thought to my looks until I had seen my cousins here. In their midst, I had a fellow feeling for little Richard. Although I was scrawny, I was wiry, and had never been ill, and I might grow tall, but I had no hope of

5

being anything but dark—black hair, black eyes, with mouth and eyes too big for my face. Boys did not need to be handsome, but Richard's smallness and weak health put him at a disadvantage in learning the use of arms, and he must learn even though it would be difficult for him to handle weapons.

There was mention of Queen Marguerite. Ever since I could remember I had heard people talking of Lancaster's queen. She was French and she had brought no dower. The king was weak and witless and this Frenchwoman with her friends ruled or rather misruled England.

So poor and threadbare was she that when she had landed in England, she had no gown or mantle fit for her wear when she made her state entry into London. She had halted at Dover, until needlewomen could be sent there. They had sewed night and day to supply her with suitable attire. She was not to blame for her poverty, but she had other faults.

"King Henry's marriage to Marguerite of Anjou has brought nothing but disaster to this country," my lady Duchess pointed out.

Edward seemed to be listening to the music, but he must have heard his mother because he answered, "And has brought no joy to Madame Marguerite—yoked to such a poor witless shadow as Holy Harry. At the time of her marriage, she was the fairest princess in Europe." Crowds had lined the road from Dover to London, Duke Richard remembered, and to do their Queen Marguerite honor, Lords and Commons had worn her daisy flower emblem.

"It must have looked as if the whole population had gone a-Maying and had chosen her as their May queen," Edward said.

"The people would never choose her now." My lady Duchess spoke somewhat sharply. "They hate her."

Edward seemed unable to hate anyone.

"The people believe that sudden terror brought on King Henry's madness," Edmund said. "That he encountered Humphrey of Gloucester's ghost."

6

I could picture the king wandering down some dim passage in his palace and recoiling in dread when he saw the apparition take shape.

"There's this much truth in it," Edward answered. "A dead man does haunt the king and causes his madness—the ghost of his French grandfather, who was insane."

My scalp prickled and I looked over my shoulder. Nothing was there to frighten me, but I felt the chilling presence of unseen spectors, coming out of the past to cast shadows on the future.

When morning came I forgot my fears and the talk of ghosts. The sun came up, the sky turned blue, and below the castle and the town the river sparkled through the meadow flats. Within the walls men tramped back and forth, horses neighed, the smithy clanged, pages chattered and laughed. Below my windows, I saw a garden, bright with flowers.

After mass, I ran down a flight of steps and made my way to the garden to gather flowers while the dew was yet on them. Roses were blooming and buds were opening, in many colors. I collected the white ones, intending to make a wreath for my cousin Margaret, and if I did not tire of the work, another for myself. While I was wandering about, spying out the finest, cutting them with my dagger and stripping the stems of thorns, I heard Edward's voice, talking to George.

They were on the other side of the hedge, and I followed the path until I found an open archway in the hedge, leading to a level grassy space. As I saw, Edward was teaching his brother the use of arms, and I halted in the archway to watch them. They were practicing with blunted weapons, but as the blows could be heavy they wore steel-plated corselets. However, they didn't need helmets or other armor. Each held a shield, and Edward was showing George how to shift his to meet the thrust of sword or battle-ax.

Edward must have seen me out of the corner of his eye. Interrupting the lesson he came over to the arch where I stood and asked me if I had slept well. I answered that I had but he scanned my face. "You look somewhat pale—like your roses." He invited me to stay and watch their practice, and led me to a marble bench. He waved the sword that he held—it suited George's size, but in Edward's hand looked like a plaything.

"Come on, George, and this time we must show our skill— we have a fair demoiselle to judge us."

George had given me an offhand greeting. Now he looked around. "Fair demoiselle? Oh, you mean Cicely! What does she know about sword play? She's only a little girl—she's never seen a tournament!"

"Mind your loutish manners, George." Edward's voice was quiet, but he commanded and George obeyed.

"I meant no harm. I'm sorry if I offended you, Cicely."

His tongue was glib but his expression was sulky, and though I accepted his apology with a smile, I added sweetly that I paid no heed to children's prattle. Edward glanced at me, his face alight with laughter, then he became serious. Dropping on one knee before me, he asked me if I would do him the honor of permitting him to wear my favor in the lists.

Although I had never seen a tournament, I knew enough to draw my white veil from my head and give it to him, saying, "My lord, you do me great honor."

Edward thanked me, kissed my hand as if I were a woman grown, and beautiful—a great lady and he my champion, about to enter the lists. As he wound my veil around his arm he said, "White is better than any color, it shows in the dark."

Sitting in the shade, I watched Edward as teacher and George as pupil. After some time, Edward sent George's sword spinning and George rolling on the ground, then reached down and pulled the boy to his feet. Together they came back to the bench where I was, with Edward's arm around his brother's shoulder. In his looks, in his voice, in every way he seemed all untroubled joyousness. He returned my veil and took one of the roses that I offered him, saying how well he loved the scent of roses, and savored its perfume.

I had never met anyone who had such zest for extracting

8

the honey from the vanishing moment. He seemed to have forgotten last nights discussions and debate, forgotten any threat of danger. Then he turned to George. "You come on well—you come on boldly but you are too reckless. You must learn coolness—how to measure your opponent. Or opponents."

George listened with the respect due to his older brother, but showed a hint of impatience in his tone. "In a *mêlée*, how can any man measure each and every foe?"

Edward laughed. "Of course no man can, but find out everything there is to know about the enemy commanders, and their soldiers, and the terrain, before you fight a field." He added, "And pray for luck."

Before I knew it, I spoke my thoughts aloud. "How glad I am that all of my family are for your cause"—and plunged ahead—"because I never would, never could be your enemy!" Once the words were out I was embarrassed. Of what importance was my goodwill?

Edward took my two hands in his. "Are you so sure of what 'never' and 'ever' mean as to pledge yourself my friend through all chances and changes, and for all time?"

"I can promise—and do promise, with all my heart!"

"Then whatever happens, we are sure of each other." Edward's face was grave as he stooped and kissed me on the lips. It was a gentle, solemn kiss, sealing our vow forever.

The next day Sir Walter Devereux with his men came to Ludlow from the west country. He was able to give me news of home and to reassure me that nothing was amiss at Shute Manor.

"The war is not likely to turn in that direction," he said. "The west is the most peaceful corner of England—as long as the Earl of Devon is elsewhere."

Before I was born, this Earl of Devon had attacked the Bonvilles, although he was our near cousin. I had been brought up on tales of battles, sieges, and harryings, when the fairest shire of England had been worse than a den of snarling wolves. The private war had come to an end only because our enemy no longer had the men or money to keep on fighting. He had left Devon for London, to become a Lancastrian partisan and Queen Marguerite's friend.

So far he had not returned to his estates, and the people prayed night and day that he never would. The Bishop of Exeter denounced him as a murderer, and the citizens called him "as cruel a monster as ever befouled the earth." Since his going, south Devon had been tranquil—"largely because of my Lord Bonville's ability as High Sheriff, and his influence," I was told. I knew that in other shires great lords assembled armies under their own banners, and attacked their neighbors, while the French raided the coasts, but the turmoil seemed far away.

Then the lesser wars had grown into the large one—between York and Lancaster. When I had first heard of it, I had paid very little heed—war seemed far off from Shute Manor, but the threat came nearer and nearer, and all of my family became entangled. I knew that ties of blood and marriage bound us to the House of York, but as everyone said, "These days kinship counts for nothing." Kinship counted with my mother, and she was a zealous Yorkist. According to her, Duke Richard of York had a better right to the throne than King Henry of Lancaster.

"Perhaps," my Lord Bonville had answered, "but that's a complex matter. I was knighted by Harry the Fifth on the field of Agincourt and would be content to give my allegiance to Henry the Sixth but he's too weak-witted and weak-willed to rule."

The Bonvilles had their personal reasons for supporting Duke Richard. He was their friend and they would not be brothers-in-arms of their enemy, the Earl of Devon, who was Queen Marguerite's friend. "But there are other reasons too," my grandfather had said. "The great lords are at each others' throats, there is lawlessness and riots. We have no navy to defend our shores against invasion, the treasury is bankrupt, the people are sick of the present state of things."

Duke Richard was our only hope. He had proved his ability

when he had been Lord Lieutenant of Ireland. He had ruled justly and had brought peace—"the only Englishman who had ever succeeded in that task or ever won the love of the Irish." But Queen Marguerite was determined to crush Richard of York.

❧ Two

Duke Richard had word that a Lancastrian force was moving on Ludlow and Queen Marguerite was riding with her army. "It seems hard to believe," my cousin Margaret said when I was with her on the ramparts. Both of us were scanning the distance. It was near sundown on a fair October evening. South of the castle the river made a bend, and at the bend were flat meadows, where our soldiers were encamped, behind a barricade of earthworks.

"What do you find so hard to believe?" Edward's voice startled me, and I turned to see him standing near us. He had come so quietly that we had not heard his footsteps.

"The queen's behavior," his sister answered. "Is she with her troops?"

"We'll soon find out." Edward learned his elbows on the parapet and seemed unperturbed, even though our enemies were bearing down on us. I tried to be calm, but my heart was hammering against my ribs. "I've heard of the one the French call La Pucelle, but she was a witch," I said.

"And I've heard of Amazons," Margaret said, "but they were in ancient times."

"Only about a hundred and fifty years ago a queen of England rode with her army," Edward told us. "Like our present queen, she was French."

Margaret thought a moment. "Oh, you mean the She Wolf of France who led a rebellion."

"For the sake of her lover, one of our Mortimer ancestors. They held high revel here."

As I knew, Ludlow had come to Duke Richard through his mother, heiress of the Mortimers.

"He was the first Earl of March," Edward went on. "The first to make the white rose his device—not an apt choice for a man who earned such a dark name in history."

"Does his ghost walk here?" I asked.

"Edmund and I have lived here all of our lives, and we've never encountered any evil spirits." Edward spoke seriously but there was a glint of laughter in his eyes. "Ludlow has been almost entirely rebuilt since it was the lair of that Mortimer."

"Let him stay buried," Margaret said.

"I doubt if it's as easy to escape from the grave as some people believe. So you needn't be afraid, Cicely," Edward said, and gave his attention to the view. His face was intent and he was watching for some flicker of light different from the soft sunset flush, some quiver of movement in the distance. Then from the highest tower a trumpet spoke, and Edward said, "Lancaster has come."

Our enemies had brought a large army. I was too ignorant to know what "large" meant in military parlance, but the earl said, "We are ready for them. My soldiers held Calais, some of them are here to hold Ludlow." He was in Duke Richard's presence chamber, and the other Yorkist chiefs were listening to him for the earl's soldiers were the best trained and the most experienced in our camp.

As long as I was in the warm, well-lighted presence chamber I could be brave enough, but when I went out on the ramparts again I saw the enemy campfires glinting and glittering in the autumn night. I fully realized then that we were cut off from the outside world.

The next night, shortly after nightfall, the earl's trusted captain and his men from Calais deserted and went over to the enemy. Without them, it would be impossible to defend the castle, Duke Richard said. We lacked men and worst of all the traitor captain knew the whole plan of Yorkist strategy. The earl took an oath to hang every man of them and brought his clenched fist down on the table. "First you must catch them," Edward pointed out, "and prevent them from catching us."

The Yorkist leaders had gathered in Duke Richard's presence chamber, in a great hurry to come to a decision. Duchess Cicely took part in the debate. Servants and pages scurried in and out, bringing meat and wine and bread, the torch flames wavering then brightening as doors opened and shut.

Send orders to the loyal soldiers to leave their camp and scatter, the earl insisted, and the leaders must likewise get out of Ludlow. Duke Richard was reluctant for he was unwilling to leave the women and children without defenders. "No harm will come to us," Duchess Cicely argued, begging him to go. "We have no choice," Edward told his father, who listened to him, and finally yielded. And we, the women and children, waiting and watching, knew very well that if the men stayed they would be killed or taken prisoner.

The group around the table dispersed. John Dynham, who had been standing behind Edward, found me in my shadowy corner. No attack would begin until dawn, he said, and the black night offered a good chance for escape. He would be with Edward, and they would ride to the west. Edward came up to me. He was wearing a long black cloak with a hood drawn over his head, but no cloak could conceal him. How could he hide from his enemies? If they ever caught sight of him they would know him in any guise. Every creature in England would recognize him from what they had heard of his height and his looks.

He had made his farewells to his mother, his sister Margaret and his young brothers, then had halted in front of me. In his dark cloak he was giant tall and the hood cast a shadow over his face, but his voice was just as usual. "Take heart," he said. "Queen Marguerite won't eat you."

"I'm not afraid, not for myself," I answered, "but for you."

"We'll soon come back, with banners flying." He gave me a parting kiss. "All will be well—I promise you."

His certainty lifted my spirits. Then he was gone, and John

Dynham with him, to find their way out of the castle, out into the dangers waiting for them.

Before day, my lady Duchess led the women and children out of the castle into Ludlow town, hoping to give some protection to the people, but she was powerless to help them. Lancaster's soldiers overran the town, looting shops and houses. Soldiers swarmed into the castle, trampling the gardens to ruin, swilling the wine, destroying what they could not carry off, until the castle was stripped to the bare walls. A drunken archer passed near me, dragging a torn length of tapestry through the mud.

We were herded into the Lancastrian camp. George and little Richard walked along with an air of boldness, but boys were endowed with more courage than girls, and these boys were princes. Their sister showed no fear but she was older than I, yet if Margaret of York could seem unafraid so could Cicely Bonville.

We were abruptly halted and I looked up to see that we had reached the Lancastrian camp with its lines of tents and banners. In front of the royal tent, I saw a woman on a silvery white palfrey—Lancaster's queen, Marguerite of Anjou. Her chief captains on their war horses were ranged on either side of her, making her the center of their steel ranks. She was directly in front of me. A scarlet mantle billowed away from her shoulders and her gown was embroidered with gold. Her bodice was cut so low that the curves of her half-bare breasts were boldly exposed. I had never before seen such a display of bosom, or such pearls as she wore—a double row, perfectly matched, encircled her throat. I was near enough to see that she was a small woman, but Marguerite of Anjou was not to be measured in inches. She gave an effect of commanding beauty and majesty, but she was no young May queen.

Neither she nor any of her lords did anything to restrain her soldiers, nor did they show any pity for Ludlow's helpless people. The queen took not the slightest notice of any of us standing there—not a word did she give the Duchess of York. Her words were for the Lancastrian peer on her right. His face was always turned to her, and his eyes sought hers. His armor was thickly overlaid with gold and as he talked and laughed and gestured the bright green plume in his helmet bobbed back and forth. I made out the portcullis on his banners—for Beaufort, and someone murmured, "the Duke of Somerset." Like the queen, he ignored us.

In contrast to Somerset, the figure at the queen's left— doubtless second in command—was still and silent. His plain armor, the plumes trailing from the winged crest of his helmet, his horse, and the sweeping housings of his horse were all black, and unrelieved black. He showed a lean swarthy face, with the skin drawn tight over his bones. I asked who he was and was told that he was young Lord Clifford.

His squire held his standard, a winged wyvern, taking on a semblance of life as the wind tugged at it. Half bird, half serpent it seemed to me a malign thing and the young lord who had chosen it as his device seemed lost in the depth of some dark dream. Then I realized that he was watching not the Duchess of York, or her daughter, but her two sons—George and Richard.

The Lancastrians had only netted a useless haul of women and children. They sent us to a dreary manor in the Midlands, but did us no harm. We wondered why they kept us mewed up— perhaps because Madame Marguerite disliked the Duchess of York. We scarcely noticed the lack of comforts—food and firewood were scantily supplied—but the days and nights were long while we waited for news. Weeks went by and no word came to tell us what had become of the Yorkist lords after they had left Ludlow.

Some of our women were with us, but the other servants were in the pay of the Lancastrian government, and as we suspected them of spying on us we took care to watch our words when they were about. But my young tiring woman contrived to win over a servingboy, and he told us what he had been able to learn in the nearby village. All of York's leaders had escaped.

Duke Richard, with his son Edmund, the Earl of Salisbury, and others had reached Ireland. Edward, Warwick, and John Dynham had found haven in Calais. My Lord Bonville and my father doubtless sailed in and out of west country ports, and I could hope that my mother was safe at our manor.

Edward, with all of his preoccupations, showed his care for his young brothers; he asked the Archbishop of Canterbury to take George and little Richard into his household to continue their education, and the Archbishop persuaded the Lancastrian government to place the boys in his charge. We were glad for them, but missed their company. George was so delighted to go that he seemed to give very little thought to his mother or his sister Margaret, confined in the dismal manor house.

For months it rained without ceasing, and all we could see was rain falling, a glimpse of a dismal little village, and sodden fields. Margaret and I devoured every word of *Tristan and Isolde*, a book I had carried all the way from Ludlow castle. By the end of the winter we could describe every detail of the illuminations—and we knew the French words by heart.

On a cold day when the rain had slackened to a mizzle, two ladies came to the gates "to pay their homage to the Duchess of York" and sent one of the servants to ask if she would receive them. When I heard of their coming, I dropped my mending, rushed to the window, flung open the wooden shutter and leaned out as far as I could to get a look at the strangers. I had only a mist-blurred glimpse of muffled figures on horseback. Their names meant nothing to me.

"Have you ever heard of them?" I asked Dame Joan.

She pursed her mouth. "I know very well who they are and what they are." She drew me away from the window. "And my lady Duchess will be anything but overjoyed at their visit."

I ran back to the window. "They're riding in the gates now!"

"My mother feels bound to receive them," Margaret said, joining me at the window. "It would be unmannerly to turn them away—even if they are Lancastrians. I've heard of Lady Jacquetta—Jacquetta of Luxembourg."

"Then she's from a foreign country," I said. "Is she a princess?"

"By birth, perhaps," Dame Joan answered.

I wanted to know more, and was told that Lady Jacquetta had first been married to an English prince, an uncle of King Henry the Sixth, and had been left a widow. She had demeaned herself by making a secret marriage with a mere Woodville. When the secret was found out, it caused grave scandal. Jacquetta's jointure was taken from her, she and Woodville were driven from court in dire disgrace, and, as they were penniless, they had been forced to bury themselves in a remote manor. I pictured them gathering faggots, and living on nuts and wild berries.

"But the Woodvilles prosper now," Margaret pointed out.

"Lady Jacquetta's fortunes rose again," Dame Joan said. "She claimed to be the queen's cousin, and soon won her friendship. Then her eldest daughter—the one with her now—married Sir John Grey, a great match for the dowerless Elizabeth Woodville!"

We were summoned to the hall to greet the visitors. Lady Jacquetta and her daughter were plainly attired in dark colors without any display of jewels. They had brought laden baskets with them—wine, game, fresh-baked manchet loaves, and honey. We had not had a whiff of such fare for months, and I was afraid that my lady Duchess would be too proud to accept delicacies from Lancastrians, but she thanked the ladies for their kindness with chill courtesy.

"It's little to offer, madam," Lady Jacquetta said, and spoke of other things. The incessant rains had made some roads impassable, she said, and told us of a man and his cart disappearing —so deep was the mud. I admired her skill at gliding over all dangerous topics without touching them. Her complexion was dark, with a yellowish tinge, but her skin was smooth and unlined, her mouth was small, with full lips, her nose was small too—a delicate beak, and her eyes were black and bright and sharp.

Something in her face, her gestures, the tones and inflections of her voice struck me as un-English. Even if she had not been

Lancastrian, and Queen Marguerite's friend I doubted if Lady Jacquetta and my lady Duchess would ever have any liking for each other. Whenever Lady Jacquetta glanced in my direction I felt a kind of unease, as if she could read my thoughts but would never reveal what was in her own mind.

Her daughter was very different. She showed great deference to my lady Duchess, but seemed shy, and though she was a Lancastrian I could not think of her as an enemy. Her gentle grace of manner and her soft voice disarmed me. She was tall, I noticed, and seemed as slightly made as a young girl, but she told me that her eldest son was near my age and I was nine years old. I found myself watching her, and waiting to hear the sound of her voice. The shockheaded servingboy who came in to put wood on the fire gazed at her and as he went out kept turning to look at her.

When she was leaving, she came to me and took my hand in hers. She almost smiled and looked at me, scanning my face. In the firelight I saw that her eyes were green, a clear translucent green, slanting up at the outer corners. She wished me good fortune. "And be lucky in love," she added, in a whisper.

"Why did Lady Jacquetta come here, dragging her daughter in her wake?" Margaret asked after the two ladies had gone and we were discussing their visit.

"I can think of one reason," Dame Joan answered. "Their zeal to pay homage to my lady Duchess can be taken as a straw in the wind, and the wind is blowing for York. Lady Jacquetta is trimming her sails."

"But she's Queen Marguerite's friend!" I was shocked, and yet I could believe it of her.

"Her daughter came because she felt sorry for us," I said, remembering her caressing voice.

"Perhaps," Dame Joan conceded.

"How did John Grey's family take his marriage to a Woodville?" Margaret asked. "He could have made a better match."

"He was besotted with her, and his father yielded."

"She was lucky in love," I said, with a vague pang of envy.

❦ *Three*

In the summer of 1460, Edward and the Earl of Warwick landed in England, with an army, and won a great victory over the Lancastrians at Northampton. King Henry was taken prisoner, Queen Marguerite fled with her son, some of the highest-ranking Lancastrians were killed in the battle, and others went into exile. All Yorkists were freed and our chief lords met in London, with their families.

My parents and I were lodged in Baynard's Castle, the vast town house of the Dukes of York. It had a stern and gloomy aspect, but it was well and richly furnished, and it seemed as if all the world came to fill the halls and presence chambers. Then it was directly on the river, with the gardens behind it. From the windows we could watch the wherries and rafts and barges, watch the ships coming in to London, or sailing to foreign countries. The river was the gateway to the wide world. Best of all we could look for Edward's barge as it neared the water gate. He came every day to see his brothers and his sister, and as I was with them, I shared his visits.

As I knew, Duke Richard and the chiefs of his party were gathered in London to arrange the government of the country, and sometimes I heard discussions of plans and policies, but paid very little attention, unless the conversation caught my interest. Everyone knew that King Henry was treated with great respect, but that the Yorkists ruled. The king seemed content, and had agreed to name Duke Richard heir to the throne—ignoring the claims of Lancaster's prince. "The prince has no real claims," the earl argued. "The people refuse to believe that he's the king's son."

"He's Marguerite of Anjou's son," my father said. "Do you see her tamely agreeing to a settlement that excludes him from the throne?"

19

"I know her vindictive temper," the earl answered, "but the boy will never wear the crown." He frowned, and his straight black brows gave a cold, severe look to his face. "It would have been better if he had never been born."

I saw London's pageantry when the settlement and peace were proclaimed, and the procession wound through the streets on the way to St. Paul's. The brilliant colors flared in the sun, the trumpets blared, the crowds made a din. Behind me, some of the ladies were speaking of the king—poor crazed Henry the Sixth. He had founded a school for poor boys at Eton, and if he met any of the students he admonished them to be "good boys." He often wandered about the grounds of Windsor wearing a home-spun robe with a rope around his waist and rough sandals on his feet. As a penance he wore a hair shirt.

He had a horror of sin, particularly any carnal sin, and when some beautiful young women, scantily clad, had appeared at his court he had cried out and had hidden his face. And when the prince—Marguerite of Anjou's son—had been presented to him, he had been puzzled and amazed and had declared that the child must be the son of the Holy Spirit. Of course the Lancastrians hotly denied this account of King Henry's behavior. According to them he had recovered his sanity and had been overjoyed at the birth of a prince. They maintained that King Henry had fathered an heir. After fifteen years of a barren marriage! He was known to be impotent, so Madame Marguerite must have taken some lusty young lover to her bed.

King Henry walked in the procession, in royal robes. I wondered if he wore a hair shirt. He wore a crown, but I was unable to see his face; he shambled along with a wavering, uncertain gait. The people were sorry for him, but hardly noticed him. The earl walked ahead of him and thousands of voices shouted "A Warwick, a Warwick." Then Edward came, directly behind the king, and drew all the attention and all the acclaim. As he passed the balcony where we were, he looked up and smiled at us. He smiled at the people, and they responded with cheers and blessings. The women leaned far out of their windows and balconies to throw flowers and kisses.

With autumn, our happy time in London came to an end, and most of the Yorkist lords left the city for duties elsewhere. While I was in London, I had met the earl's wife and his two daughters, Isabel and Anne, who were staying at Warwick House, and had made friends with the two little girls. They had been pent up in Calais for several years, until the Yorkist victory at Northampton had brought them back to England. They talked eagerly of spending Christmas at Middleham, Lord Salisbury's great castle in Yorkshire.

Now that peace had been made, Lord Salisbury had set his heart on holding his Christmas at Middleham as he had in the past, with all of his family gathered around him, and he planned to offer bountiful hospitality to the neighboring gentry and the citizens of York, "in the old way of Merrie England," he said, as it was celebrated in the north. My mother had been born and brought up at Middleham, and was happy to have an opportunity to revisit her former home. I would have preferred to go back to the west country, and Shute Manor, but I held my tongue, and as everyone around me pictured Middleham in bright hues I began to look forward to my stay there.

Edward was going in another direction, to the marches adjoining Wales, perhaps into Wales, to win the people's allegiance to the Yorkist government, and to recruit men, in case the Lancastrians made any attempt to land on the Welsh coast, but at the time I was more interested in the date of his return than in his reason for going.

"If all goes well, I'll be in London again in good time for Twelfth-night," he said, in bidding me goodbye. "And you must be here too."

I was not the one who decided my comings and goings, as he knew, nevertheless I promised.

"You're certain to be back. Will you dance a gaillard with me?"

"Gladly," I answered.

My Lord Bonville and my father were detained in London, and my mother decided to wait for them. There would be no long delay in their going north, she said, but my parents decided to send me to Middleham with Lady Warwick and her daughters, otherwise my visit would be too short, and because it was well to go while the fine autumn weather held. Later in the season, the roads were likely to be miry and the journey would not be so pleasant.

Lady Warwick traveled with a large entourage, and in a leisurely way, halting at the castles and manors of our kinsmen and friends. The crops had suffered from the incessant rains of the spring and early summer, but in the Midlands, flocks of sheep dotted the hillsides and in the warm golden autumn the countryside had a smiling aspect. We went on to Middleham, which was as splendid as I had imagined it to be.

We had left a peaceful London, and on our way north had met nothing but goodwill. Everywhere the people seemed content with Yorkist rule, but as we soon learned, peace was not secure in the north. Great preparations had been made for the holy days of Christmas, and shortly after our arrival guests began coming to Middleham, but they came heavily armed, they did not linger long, and they brought troubling news. They talked of bands of marauders, who were hiding on the moors or in the hills.

These bands swooped on isolated farms and manors, burning and looting Yorkist estates, killing anyone who opposed them. If they were outlaws, and wild Scots from across the border, they were undoubtedly led by Lancastrians. Where was Queen Marguerite? After she had fled, she had first shut herself up in Harlech Castle, and from there had gone to Scotland, and was there yet, unless she had crossed the border and was inciting the raids.

The attacks grew bolder, and Yorkists suffered greater losses; the people sent to Duke Richard for help. In answer, he sent word that he was marching north, with an army. So all of Lord Salisbury's plans were changed. He would have to march with Duke Richard. As I realized, neither my mother nor any of the other ladies would visit Middleham now. In her letter to me my mother wrote of her disappointment—and tried to hide her anxiety. She was able to send the letter by the earl's courier, but I did not know when I could expect any further word from her.

The earl was too necessary to the government to leave London, and Lord Bonville was with him, but my father was in Duke Richard's army, which numbered some four thousand men. We knew this because couriers galloped to Middleham to give us news of the army's advance, and it was cheering news. As soon as Duke Richard drew near, the raids came to an end. Even better, he and Lancaster's most powerful supporter in the north, Percy of Northumberland, had agreed to a truce. To make sure that the terms would be kept, Lord Salisbury would stay in the north, with enough men to enforce order, but the rest of the army, under Duke Richard's command, would return to London shortly.

At the moment, I did not think to ask why, because Duke Richard's headquarters was at Sandal Castle, only ten miles from Middleham, and my father had written to tell me that he was among those who would march south. "This is an opportunity to take you and Dame Joan and your attendants back to London under the protection of an armed force." He would send sufficient men to escort me safely to Sandal, or come for me himself. Finally Duke Richard arranged to have Lady Warwick and her daughters ride to Sandal with me, to hold Christmas there. The little girls were overjoyed, and I was wild with excitement.

"Do you think Duke Richard will set out by the first of the year?" I asked Dame Joan, thinking that if my father and I could only ride on ahead of the first soldiers, we would be in London by Twelfth-night.

"He's quite as eager to get back to London as you," she answered. "Much more anxious in fact. With Edward away too, the city is left without an army to defend it."

"Where's the danger?" I asked, seeing none.

"I don't know," Dame Joan admitted, "but London is the prize."

"Edward will soon be there," I said. All would be well.

Sandal was built on a high ledge of rock, overlooking the little town of Market Wakefield and Calder Plain. As far as I knew, Sandal had no history, except that it was called "the cradle of the house of York." A dark stony mass against a gray December sky, it seemed to me a grim cradle, rocked by rough winds. Once within its walls, the lords of our family seemed happy to have us with them, and instead of finding women and children an encumbrance, said that without us their Christmas feast would be dreary.

My father had come himself to bring us from Middleham on Christmas Eve. As soon as I had caught sight of him riding up the steep ascent, his men filing behind him in the well-known Bonville livery, I had gone running down many flights of steps, out of the door, into the courtyard, out of the gates to meet him. Laughing, he had swung me up into the saddle with him, but I had buried my face against his shoulder and burst into tears. Why? Because it had seemed a long time since I had been with him, and I had been afraid that it would be a long time before I saw him again.

Duke Richard seemed in good spirits at the Christmas feast but he had changed since I had last seen him. I noticed lines in his face and streaks of gray in his brown hair. When he was not smiling or speaking, he looked careworn. Lord Salisbury, who was much older, had not changed at all, and perhaps never would change—at least in appearance. This time he met me without grumbling because I was a girl and not the desired "heir male."

He contented himself by pointing out that I showed no trace of his family—I was all Bonville.

I was like my father, I had his very dark eyes and heavy black hair, and perhaps something of his nature, because he seemed to understand my feelings, and encouraged me to speak frankly to him.

The barren frozen countryside made it difficult to find enough food for the army and fodder for the horses, and what was stored must not be wasted. At our Christmas feast, the fare was plain, and not many dishes were served, but we had plenty to eat and to drink. The leading citizens of Wakefield shared the feast; the poor were fed and received alms, the yule log blazed on the hearth, and to the sound of trumpets the holly-wreathed boar's head was brought in. Duke Richard drank to Lady Warwick, then to "the three young demoiselles who grace our Christmas."

The waits came, to sing and carol, and the men of Wakefield entertained us. Doubtless they played the same parts every Christmastime, and were masked and disguised as animals and Devils and Green Men. They rode their squat hobby horses, carved out of wood and painted, and scampered around the hall. One of the mummers appeared as a Wode Wose—a hairy wild man of the forest. I knew that he was only a farmer, a shepherd, or one of the townspeople, but when the shaggy Wode Wose in the ugly mask came near me, I thought what if these brutish creatures did exist somewhere in the lonely northern woodland—and one of them had crept out to mingle with the mummers?

As usual, Death was represented, with a skeleton outlined in white on a tall, thin black-clad figure. Death capered nimbly among the others, sometimes darting at them or pointing at one of the onlookers, the painted skeleton face leering.

That night, when I was in my bedchamber, I looked out of the window at the darkness, and wondered if Edward had turned toward London. He had asked me for a Twelfth-night dance, but, as I realized, Edward's tryst was not with me, it was with London.

❧ Four

Two days after Christmas, Lady Warwick, and her daughters, and her retinue left Sandal to return to Middleham, where they chose to spend the winter. I watched them until they had crossed the bridge and were out of sight. Dame Joan and I lingered on the battlements a little while, braving the cold. We were wrapped in fur-lined cloaks, the angle of the wall protected us from the wind, and the sun was shining—or what passed for the sun, although it was a small steely disk in a colorless sky.

After dark, Duke Richard and his son Edmund and his captains were discussing a message that had come during the day, from Sir James Metcalfe of Nappa Hall, which was about ten miles from Sandal. One of his shepherds, on his way homeward, had seen helmeted heads against the sky, and Sir James thought this information was worth passing on. Duke Richard was not greatly impressed.

Davy Hall, who was Duke Richard's chamberlain and had been with him many years, took the message seriously. Sir James must have believed the shepherd's accounts or he would not have sent his men at a gallop to give warning. And helmeted heads could only mean Lancastrians—where none should be.

Duke Richard had faith in the truce. "Davy, you're getting to be an old woman," he said, with a smile.

But my Lord Salisbury agreed with Davy Hall. "Heads seen at a distance against the horizon mean horsemen. It might be a party of John Grey's cavalry but he's in the Midlands."

I remembered then that John Grey was the husband of Elizabeth Woodville.

"It also might be Clifford and his horsemen," Lord Salisbury added, and Clifford was a name I would never forget. He had been in exile in Scotland, but it would have been easy for him to cross the border and hide somewhere in Cumberland, with its wild mountains and fells.

Nearly every day, a foraging party went out from Sandal to buy the necessary supplies, and sometimes had to go as far as York to find provisions. Duke Richard took care to pay a fair price, and punished his soldiers if they seized the people's goods. On the 30th of December, the foragers set off as usual. More than half of the Yorkist army was making ready to march, and must have food and fodder.

On this last day of the year 1460, the wind was rising and slate-colored clouds threatened snow. Sandal was two hundred feet above the plain, and attacked by all the four winds. The great hall was brightened by the torches set burning to dispel the shadows and a tree trunk blazed on the hearth.

Duke Richard sat down to dine at eleven o'clock, and while we dined the mummers came as they did every day—animals, Devils, Green Men, the Wode Wose, and Death. Yet this time I watched them with a sense of disquiet when they faded into the shadows.

Edmund was sitting next to me and asked me if anything ailed me. I was quite well, I told him, but I also told him a story I had just heard about one of the fishermen who had found a water kelpie in his net in the Calder River not far from Sandal. It had the face of a fair girl but with long green hair and webbed fingers.

Edmund listened with attention, but rather doubted the tale. "Edward and I used to scan every brook and river in hopes of seeing an undine," he said, and we fell to talking of Edward, and drank to him in his absence.

"Next, I will drink to you, cousin," I said, "to wish you good fortune in the coming year and in all years."

I had barely lifted my wine cup when an icy gust of wind swirled into the hall. I looked up to see the captain of the archers running to Duke Richard. An attack, he was shouting. The foraging party was under attack, on this side of the bridge. They were assailed by Lancastrian horsemen. Lancaster had broken the truce.

Someone spoke scarcely above a whisper, "Clifford."

I heard Duke Richard giving orders to go to the aid of his men, but Lord Salisbury tried to restrain him.

"We will be too late to save them," he said.

"Will we sit by and see them butchered?" Duke Richard demanded.

Davy Hall urged caution too. Stay behind Sandal's walls, and send word to Edward to come with his army, he advised.

"Davy, when you've loved me so long, how can you want to see me dishonored? If we're too late to save our men, we must avenge them!"

Duke Richard had made his decision. I left my place and went to my father, saying not a word. He looked down at me, took my hand and allowed me to go with him to the great chamber beyond the hall, where his squires were waiting to arm him. I wound my fingers through his until he gently detached his hand to put on his gauntlets. He kissed me and asked God to watch over me. I had never known such heaviness of heart.

I ran up the winding stairs and out onto the battlements, with Dame Joan panting after me to wrap a fur-lined cloak around me. Servants, pages, a few of the garrison—too old to fight—women and children watched, all of us huddled together. The clouds had lifted near the horizon and the landscape below us was harshly defined. Wakefield town was out of sight, but here was the plain, the bridge, the woods. The attackers had set the foragers' carts afire and they were still burning with a dull glow. The dark patches on the plain were the bodies of the foragers.

The Lancastrians had retreated, but not far. A mass of horsemen were lined up on the plain, near the bridge, their leader in front of the ranks. We saw him darkly outlined, and though we were too far away to read the blazonings on his banners, no one doubted that Clifford was in command. His trumpets sounded, defying York.

And Duke Richard led his army out of Sandal's South Gate. He was experienced in warfare, but his son Edmund had never seen a battle. Edmund was now seventeen years old and was expected to do his part. Over his head was York's great standard, with its royal blazonings for Plantagenet and the six white roses. The Bonville banner showed me where my father was, and our Haryngton cousins followed him. The Yorkist captains were on their warhorses, the rest of the army on foot. They left Sandal, left the high escarpment, went down to the plain, spreading out and forming their ranks.

Any fool could see Clifford's danger—he must make his escape from the Yorkist bowmen—but he held his position. His trumpets sounded, and York's answered. The clouds had thickened and lowered, had changed from gray to a smoky purple; dusk would soon come, and snow. A flake fell on the fold of my cloak, a snow rose, shaped like the roses of York's banner. The carts had burned to charred fragments, and the embers no longer glowed. Shadows blurred the dead bodies sprawled on the moorland. The arm of the forest, dark as iron, jutted out, tapering to a knife point. Clifford had become a shadow too—a sinister shadow.

Our archers sent their arrows into his lines, and his horsemen charged forward. Seen from Sandal's heights, the battle swirled into a dim tangle. Outnumbered, Clifford's force was pushed back, closer and closer to the river, but his trumpets still challenged and taunted, and seemed to draw some far-off response from the depths of the woods. Perhaps I heard an echo. But the sound was not an echo. It was repeated, shrilling through the woods.

Suddenly, the rigid outline of the trees changed, grew longer and wider, flinging men out into the open. It was Lancaster's army, coming out of the forest, eddying to encircle York's four thousand with their countless thousands. Then as the day ebbed, twilight and falling snow, falling faster and faster, veiled the plain and the battle.

The battle had lasted hardly more than half an hour, and out of our army of four thousand, few survived, and only those few who had been able to crawl into the woods, and find shelter in the trees. Some of these men were seriously wounded, and would have frozen to death if a search party from Wakefield had not found them, and brought them to Sandal. They told me that my father had been killed early. My Haryngton cousins had fallen; Duke Richard and Davy Hall who had begged him to stay within the castle, were dead. All of the Yorkist captains were dead. Knights, gentlemen, squires, archers, foot soldiers—they had been slaughtered in the *mêlée*.

Lord Salisbury had been taken prisoner and Edmund was dead. His chaplain, Sir Roger Aspall, had been with him all through the battle. Edmund had fought on until his sword had broken in his hand, but as he was near the bridge, Roger Aspall had urged him to try to escape, but Clifford had marked Edmund out and had overtaken him. Clifford's own squire had begged for Edmund's life, crying, "He is a prince's son—and may do you good hereafter." Clifford had thrust him aside, saying, "Your father killed mine and I will do the same to you and all your kin." He himself had driven his dagger into Edmund's throat.

Queen Marguerite was riding with her army, and had halted near the edge of the wood. She had watched the slaughter, and after the battle, she was still there. Roger Aspall had dragged himself to the shelter of some trees. He had seen Lancastrian soldiers carrying lighted torches, the flames sputtering in the snowfall, and they had built up a fire of logs, and Queen Marguerite was nearby —on a white horse. A hood had covered her head, but the blaze had showed him her face.

Clifford had come up to her and had brought her Duke Richard's severed head. "Madam, your war is won," Clifford had told her. At first she had seemed to draw back, but then she had looked for a long time, and laughed aloud.

"Hail, King Richard!" she jeered.

Lord Salisbury, taken prisoner, was executed at Pontefract the day after the battle by Queen Marguerite's command. She then led her army on to York, where she encamped. The Lancastrians had no further interest in Sandal. It was an empty shell.

The women cared for the wounded, and I did what I could to help. Even the smell of food made me retch, and if I dropped asleep I woke with a start. I became obsessed with the need to give my father, and the other dead, Christian and honorable burial, but was told to wait until spring. The corpses were already buried deep in snow and ice, and it would be an impossible task to reach them.

For more than a week the wind beat against the walls in a screaming gale bringing a sleet storm. Sandal was cut off from the rest of the world, but I hardly noticed the weather, until late in the night I became aware that the wind had dropped.

In the silence, I heard another sound. It came faintly but I knew what it was—wolves howling on Calder Plain.

When the storm had subsided, the people from Wakefield were able to come to Sandal again, and from them we learned what was happening within a few miles of the castle. Some of the townspeople loaded carts with their possessions, and took refuge within Sandal's walls. Barbarous Scots and all the scum of England were flocking to join the Lancastrians; bands of ruffians were roving about, preying on the countryside. Queen Marguerite and her great lords were lodged in the town, and were demanding money and men. The citizens were in a frenzy to be rid of them.

Duke Richard's fair city! I knew what great pride he had felt in its beauty, its size, its prosperous bustle, the glory of its minster, and the strength of its walls. The queen had brought trophies from the battlefield, and had decked the gates of York with the heads of her enemies. Duke Richard, wearing a paper crown to mock his claim to the throne; his son Edmund; my father; the Earl of Salisbury and his son Thomas; Sir John Haryngton, and five other knights.

Madame Marguerite, very richly dressed, had led a cavalcade through the streets to the Great Gate, and there had halted, looking up at the row of heads, and pointing at them.

In the sight and hearing of a throng of sullen people, she had boasted that she had left room for two more heads—Warwick's and the head of the Duke of York's eldest son, Edward.

The town gave thanks when Madame Marguerite and her army and all the rabble left and turned southward. They passed by Sandal and Wakefield, and as soon as they had gone from Yorkshire, Sir James Metcalfe sent his son Miles, with an armed escort, to convey me back to Middleham, to Lady Warwick and her daughters. And so Dame Joan and I, with our attendants, rode away from Sandal, and Wakefield—rode with heads bent, not looking to left or right.

At Middleham, the household was in deepest mourning. News filtered in to us that the Earl of Warwick was gathering troops and rousing the shires to send men to defend London. My grandfather, Lord Bonville, was with him. I felt that my grandfather Bonville had suffered the greatest loss of all in my father's death—an only son, an only child.

The Lancastrians had landed in Wales, with a large force; Queen Marguerite expected to join them with her great horde, and Edward had the task of keeping the two Lancastrian armies apart—without hope of any help from the earl, who could not afford to weaken the defense of London. Edward must grapple with the danger alone. The people around me were gloomy about his chances of surviving, but I was not.

❧ *Five*

In the north, 1461 brought the worst winter in over a hundred years, and all the season it snowed. Lady Warwick kept to her own apartments. Her daughters hovered around me, offering their affection, but I was unresponsive. Isabel and Anne seemed too young for me; I thought of them as children, and I was no longer a child.

Queen Marguerite's army was swollen by turncoats, Scots, Frenchmen and outlaws, and was followed by a great rabble of thieves, cutthroats and whores—more vicious than the soldiers. The queen offered as inducement to any and all who would join her freedom to pillage without restraint. The Lancastrians gutted churches, seized the gold and silver chalices on the altars, reckless of sacrilege. They carried off everything movable, raped women, even nuns, tortured anyone suspected of hiding money or goods, murdered those who resisted them or happened to displease them. They ravaged a path thirty miles wide along their line of march, and left ruin behind them.

As they neared London, we knew that the Earl of Warwick must give battle. Pent up in Middleham, we waited for news, but as time passed and he sent no word, we were sick with fear. Then we learned that the Yorkist army had come to grips with the Lancastrians at St. Albans. In the dawn of Shrove Tuesday, Sir John Grey had led a Lancastrian cavalry charge into the town. He had fallen, mortally wounded, but his onslaught had broken the Yorkist defenses, and Clifford had sabered the Yorkist gunners. The earl had tried to re-form his lines, but he had lost, and the largest army that York had ever put into the field had been wiped out. The earl had rallied a few of his soldiers—but no one could tell Lady Warwick where he was, or what had happened to him.

My grandfather Bonville was dead. The Earl of Warwick had taken his prisoner, King Henry, to St. Albans, and had given him into the keeping of Lord Bonville and Sir Thomas Kyriel, and instead of making their escape, they had stayed with the king, afraid that the Lancastrians might harm him before they recognized him. The Lancastrians had found him sitting under an oak tree, singing to himself with his guardians watching over him, and had led him to the queen. She had established headquarters at the Abbot's house, and in the evening of that day had celebrated her second great victory in the Abbot's hall, with her puppet king and her son now restored to her and her captains.

My grandfather and Sir Thomas Kyriel had been brought into the hall. King Henry had babbled of his promises to reward them for their care, but Madame Marguerite had whispered an order and her people had led the king away. Then she had seated her son in the Abbot's chair and had asked the boy what should be done "with these two men. They fought against their rightful king and are guilty of treason."

"Then let their heads be struck off," the prince had answered. He was eight years old.

Miles Metcalfe, on his way from York, stopped for the night at Middleham. "The people are aghast at the executions—against all law and justice—of two brave men. Sir Thomas Kyriel fought in the French wars. And all know how well my Lord Bonville has served this country in war and in peace."

Queen Marguerite had promised to spare London from sack, if the city would open the gates, but the executions had infuriated the citizens; they had armed themselves, locked their gates and manned the walls. So far, the Lancastrians had not attacked.

Bastard or not, Marguerite of Anjou's son was healthy and handsome. I had heard the Yorkists admit that the queen had been skillful at building up the idea of herself as a persecuted madonna, and her son as the heir cheated of his birthright. The sight of the prince had induced many a man to wear his badge and fight for Lancaster. "But she's undone all her work," Miles Metcalfe said. "The people will have none of her or the boy who talks of cutting off heads."

March brought a courier from the Earl of Warwick himself. After his defeat, the earl had rallied his remaining troops, and by leading his on little-known paths, had joined Edward, who had already defeated a Lancastrian army, eleven thousand strong, moving from Wales. Together they had marched on London, and the citizens had flung open the gates. Queen Marguerite had hesitated too long; Lancaster's army was retreating, again turning north.

In London, the earl had gathered Yorkist lords and bishops together and before a great crowd of people had asked them if they would take Edward of York as their king. They had answered "Yes! Yes!" And so, on the 4th of March 1461, Edward had worn a king's robes of state and a king's crown, and, in Westminster Hall, he had been proclaimed Edward the Fourth, by the grace of God King—and all the rest. But he must win his kingdom.

There had been no time for ceremonies. On that same day, the earl had led the van of the army out of London. Edward had soon followed. In the south and the Midlands, men were joining the earl and the young king. These were not the greatest peers, for most of them were Lancastrians, but instead the knights and gentlemen of the shires, with their retainers; yeomen in leather tunics, carrying their bows on their shoulders and a quiver full of arrows, merchants, and sober citizens. They were all enlisting under Edward's banner.

As they retreated from London, Queen Marguerite's soldiers, coming north by another route, were wreaking as great a ruin as they had before, burning hamlets, seizing everything, leaving the people without beasts to till the fields. The enemy army was coming near Middleham, with the earl and Edward following. "There will be a great battle," the courier told us. "And between York and Lancaster it's war to the death."

From then on, couriers came often. On Friday, the 27th of March, the earl sent word that our army had reached the banks of the Aire, and would cross the river to come to grips with the enemy encamped on the other side. During Friday night Lord Clifford had taken advantage of the darkness. He had led his horsemen to seize the ford at Ferrybridge and destroy the bridge. Edward had sent cavalry to intercept Clifford and regain control of the ford. So as to recognize friend from foe in the blackness, Edward had ordered each man to wear a white scarf tied around his left arm.

The Yorkists had met Clifford and his horsemen in the woods near Dintingdale, two miles from his own camp. In his black armor, he was part of the night around him. Shadow men on shadow horses, twisting in and out among the trees. Careless, or reckless, Clifford had taken off his helmet to ease his neck. At that moment, an unknown Yorkist archer had shot an arrow, and by chance the arrow had pierced Clifford's throat. So, in that March night, under the arches of the woodland he had found the pale rider on the pale horse waiting for him.

In the north the only sign of spring was rain, and on Palm Sunday, the 29th of March, the wind again brought a heavy snowfall. When we heard Mass in the chapel our breath made an icy mist. As we knew from the courier, our men had repaired the bridge and our army had crossed the Aire yesterday, to face the Lancastrians. Queen Marguerite was not with her soldiers; she and her son and King Henry were in the town of York, waiting as we at Middleham were waiting—as all England was waiting.

The Lancastrians would undoubtedly feel the lack of Clifford's leadership, the courier had said, but they had thirty thousand men. We were greatly outnumbered, and as we knew, the earl and Edward would be in the heart of the *mêlée*. I could not even form the words of a prayer. One of Merlin's prophecies ran through my head. "The crown and its power, on the turn of the hour, on the fate of a flower, will be lost and won." The red rose of Lancaster, or the white rose of York.

It was long after nightfall before we learned that the Yorkists had won a great victory. Near Towton Hamlet, the Lancastrians had massed on a ridge, and the Yorkists had taken their position on high ground, facing them. Between the two armies, the ground sloped to a depression where a stream ran and the bridge spanning it was narrow. For a time the Lancastrians had the advantages, but eventually Lord Howard had come with fresh troops for Edward. Although most of their leaders had fallen, the Lancastrians had fought on—without hope. They had died on the blood-darkened slope, in the stream. In their retreat, the bridge had given way, but dead and wounded men had fallen into the little river, choking it, making a bridge of corpses, trodden by the living as they struggled to escape.

The household at Middleham drank to the earl, and to the

young king. When news of victory reached London, and Exeter and Plymouth, I knew the bells would ring out and the people would rush into the streets, but as I listened to the story of Towton, I could not feel any joy. The sight of the herald, filthy, tattered, bloodstained, reeling from exhaustion, brought before us not triumph, but the battle itself. After he had given his account, he brushed his hand across his eyes and said as if to himself, "Dead. Ten thousand tall Englishmen."

🌷 *Six*

For three years and more I had been living quietly on my estates, mostly at Shute Manor. It had been a sad homecoming, but my mother would not permit me to shut myself up to indulge my grief. "These are your lands, and your people," she had told me. She was not the Earl of Warwick's sister for nothing. She had his gift for organizing and administering, and as she had often been left in charge of the estates, she had acquired experience. She insisted on my learning how to manage my inheritance.

Although I could never take the place of my grandfather or my father, I learned to know the custom of the manor, and how custom differed in Somersetshire from the usual and accepted pattern in Devon or Cornwall. I interested myself in my tenants and retainers, studied the best methods of tilling the soil so as to get the largest crops on the arable and the demesne lands, and was concerned with the price of wool. I could not add to the luster of my name by my valor, but I could and did continue the works of charity that had made the Bonvilles well loved in the west country.

After two years of widowhood, my mother took another husband. He was William, Lord Hastings, and the alliance was in every way suitable. As she was the earl's sister and he was one of Edward's closest friends all the world approved, and predicted that the marriage would be yet one more tie between the earl and the king. It was my good fortune to have Will Hastings for my stepfather; he gave me valuable help in all worldly affairs. Following the usual custom, I was to go in a few months to the Duchess of York to be part of her household, where I would be trained in manners and accomplishments—all that I needed to know in order to take my place in the world.

It was safe for me, safe for everyone in the west country since Edward had begun to reign. He had rid us of the Earl of Devon, who had been taken prisoner at Towton and had been executed without delay. When the citizens of Exeter heard of his death, they lighted bonfires. Marguerite of Anjou had succeeded in reaching Scotland with her son. From there, she had plotted with a few Lancastrian lords, who had rebelled against Edward although they had sworn allegiance to him and had been generously treated. But the earl and his brother besieged the rebels' castles, and compelled them to surrender.

After a time, Henry the Sixth was taken prisoner and shut up in London Tower; Marguerite of Anjou gave up hope at last and sailed for France, and by the summer of 1464 England had peace at home and abroad. In September I would make the journey to London, to join my lady Duchess and her daughter Margaret at Baynard's Castle. I was eager to see my cousins of York again, although I realized that I would find them greatly changed.

Edward had been generous to his brothers; little Richard had been created Duke of Gloucester. He was at Middleham Castle, being educated under the tutelage of the Earl of Warwick, and was said to be very happy there. George was Duke of Clarence, and was at present in London. He had his own palace on the Strand, and wherever he was he kept a great establishment, but then he had become an important person. Until the king married and had a lawful son, George was heir presumptive to the throne.

And, until the king married, his mother was the first lady of the realm. She lived retired, but she was said to wield great influence over her sons, most of all over Edward. She knew that it was his duty to make an advantageous alliance, for the good of England and the House of York. It was time for him to beget a Prince of Wales. Perhaps in her heart my lady Duchess would begrudge yielding her place to Edward's queen, no matter how royally born or richly dowered.

Edward seemed in no hurry to take a wife. In the previous reign the people said that ghosts had stalked the royal palaces, but had vanished with Edward's coming. He and his friends were young, and full of zest. They rose before dawn to hear Mass, broke their fast on meat and ale, then were off to hunt or joust or find what sport the day would bring. In the evening they rode back to feast and dance at Westminster or Windsor, made love by moonlight or starlight, and with morning were eager to set off again. Edward's horses and hounds and hawks were the envy of foreign rulers; his musicians were the best in Christendom, and when envoys from other countries came to England they were swept from one diversion to another.

"The envoys go back and report that the King of England is chiefly addicted to pleasure," Will Hastings told me, "and that the Earl of Warwick rules, but the members of Edward's council know better—and so do the people."

Edward was determined to enforce the law and rebuild the power of the crown. He often startled judges, juries, and witnesses by appearing in court and sitting on the king's bench, where no king had come in person for many a long year. Moreover, Edward rode out into the shires with his justices to find out for himself how the law was administered, and to make sure that the sheriffs and other officers of the crown were honest and impartial.

My mother and I had benefited from Edward's rule. Because his government was strong enough to protect us, we could live at Shute Manor or any of our manors with only a small garrison. Some of the great lords found fault with Edward because of his "too great familiarity with all kinds and conditions of persons." They thought it unbecoming to the majesty of a great prince, but he endeared himself to his subjects by being approachable, by his

39

willingness to talk and laugh with them, and by listening to their grievances.

He was such a king as the English people had longed for. They gloried in his military success, took pride in the beauty of his person, and made liberal allowance for his faults. There was talk of his mistresses, but no one seemed to think he was greatly to blame. Even matrons of strictest virtue were tolerant. The king was young, "hotly amorous" by nature, and surrounded by temptation. "At least our king has no inclination for unnatural vices," one gentlewoman remarked, "and he never uses coercion to get a woman to his bed." And his wild young knights were strictly forbidden to use any violence or threats to maid, wife, or widow.

As for the king's fickleness, he provided generously for his discarded mistresses, and for his bastards. What more could we expect? I listened without comment, but with a certain disappointment too. The Edward that I had once known was someone who would love with all his heart.

By the summer of 1464, the Scots had sued for peace, the French no longer dared to raid our coasts and were eager for a treaty. The Earl of Warwick was all for an alliance with France and for a long time had been working to bring it about. It would include Edward's marriage to the French king's sister-in-law. The negotiations had dragged on; Edward distrusted the Spider King of France, so did the English people, but at last all the difficulties had been smoothed out and the earl was making great preparations to sail for France and bring back the princess to be Edward's wife.

Now all the talk was of the royal marriage, and I was thinking of it while I waited for John Dynham's expected visit. He had been staying on his own lands for the summer and was coming to Shute Manor for a day and a night before rejoining the king and the court.

Although Dame Joan and I lived quietly, the families who had long been friends and allies of the Bonvilles came often—

Dynhams, Raleghs, and others. They were welcome guests, I could always turn to them if I needed their help, and their coming enlivened the household. This year I had roused myself to offer suitable entertainment to my neighbors and had more than once accepted their hospitality.

Shute was a fortified manor house, strongly built on a smooth green slope with a village at the foot of the slope and the dark woods in the distance. Village and manor house were sunlit, sheltered from sea storms by the velvet smooth downs where sheep grazed. On fair days I could look out at the sea beyond the downs, the water catching and reflecting the light. When a storm was coming the sea was a hard dark line and often after a storm spars and wreckage drifted on the waves.

As John Dynham knew, he could speak freely to Dame Joan and to me and after we had dined, I led him to the solar where we could talk together at our ease. Although September had come, the day was as warm as midsummer. The orchards were heavy with fruit and garden plots were ablaze with many colored flowers. But September meant that the Earl of Warwick would soon be sailing for France and I asked John Dynham when Edward's marriage to the French princess would take place, thinking that he would know the exact date.

"The Royal Council meets in October to discuss the king's marriage," he answered. He was sitting in the strong light from the open window, and I was opposite to him, where I could see his face clearly, and it seemed to me that he was troubled.

Dame Joan looked up from her needlework. "From all we hear, the match is as good as made."

"The earl thinks so, the Council thinks so, the Spider King of France thinks so."

"And the princess thinks so," I added, assuming that she was doubtless elated at her good fortune, and not only at the prospect of wearing a crown. If Edward had been a woodcutter, women would pant for him.

"Edward has yet to commit himself," John Dynham was still being evasive.

"He was always quick to decide," I said. "Why does he take so long to make up his mind?"

"Perhaps he has by now. I have not seen him since the spring, but then he seemed to be uninterested in the French alliance."

"Doesn't he have any curiosity concerning the princess?" I asked.

"I doubt if he had any thoughts to spare for her. He was preoccupied."

Dame Joan was quick to understand. "Preoccupied with some other woman. When the princess is our queen she can expect to have rivals."

"She has one now—a formidable rival, in my view—but please never quote me."

"Who is she?"

"She is unknown at court."

"But you know her," I said.

"By chance, because I happened to be on hand when the adventure began over a year ago. I was with Edward hunting with only a few of his men in Whittlebury Chase. Edward and I turned in another direction from the rest of the hunt and came to a grassy space where a stream ran close by and an immense oak spread its branches. Suddenly three figures took shape, moving suddenly from the shelter of the oak. They hurled themselves forward and flung themselves on their knees directly in front of Edward's horse. I thought at first it might be a trap but it was only a woman wrapped in a black mantle and a black veil. She had two boys with her, one a gangling stripling, the other very much younger."

"In God's name what were they doing there—and who was she?" said Dame Joan.

"She was Elizabeth Woodville, John Grey's widow, and she admitted she had waylaid Edward to beg him to restore some part of her sons' inheritance. The Woodvilles being Lancastrians had, of course, lost their estates but had been allowed to keep nearby Grafton Castle where Elizabeth and her sons had found shelter. She didn't deny that her husband had fought for Lancaster but she made the point that he had been killed before Edward's reign had begun. She asked nothing for herself, only for her sons, who had never been guilty of offending him. Edward kept staring at her pale face like a man bewitched, and finally he told her that she had pleaded her cause too well for him to refuse anything in his power to give. And he kissed her hand."

"Then what happened?" I asked.

"Well, after he finally left her and rejoined the hunt, Edward told his people that he intended to stay the night at his hunting lodge. Instead he returned to the lodge only long enough to change his clothes, and announced to me that he was paying a visit to nearby Grafton, and that I was to accompany him with only four attendants. Nothing I could say could stop him from venturing into that nest of Lancastrians. I was uneasy because at the time, we had proof of Lancastrian plots."

"I doubt if you could find a woman in England who would betray Edward," I said.

"In his eyes," John Dynham answered, "the woman who had waylaid him under the oak was the most innocent and defenseless creature on earth. He refused to worry about her family."

"What was your impression of the Woodvilles?" Dame Joan asked.

"I had encountered two of them as enemies in a battle, but they showed not the slightest constraint. They might have been staunch Yorkists from the beginning. Since I had last met him, Woodville's hair had turned pure silver, which had rather added to his good looks. He had a silk-smooth manner but he was a man who calculated every word and gesture! I liked his son Anthony's face—and his manner better.

"Edward assured Lady Jacquetta that we had supped but she insisted on our taking some refreshment—sweetmeats, fruit, and wine. In the castle, the rooms were almost bare of furniture—the Woodvilles had sold it as well as all of their plate and their jewels, but the lack was hardly noticeable to my eyes. The floors were covered with fresh, sweet scented rushes, greenery and flowers masked the walls, and everywhere we saw perfect order and cleanliness.

"Lady Elizabeth greeted the king, then kept to the background while her parents presented her young brothers and sisters. The boys are fine young cockerels, the girls all have beauty—I could hardly decide which one is the fairest.

"Anthony Woodville evidently knew that Edward loved music and regretted that there were no minstrels to entertain the king, but Anthony himself played the lute—very skillfully too— and his brother the viol, and the younger Woodvilles danced. The demoiselles had no jewels, but did not need them. After dancing had ended, Anthony Woodville handed the lute to Lady Elizabeth begging her to play it and sing. She made excuses saying she had long ago forgotten what she had been taught, but if the king commands—and she looked up at Edward. He answered, 'You command—I can only entreat.' The words could pass for courtly gallantry, but not the tone, or the expression of his face. He meant it.

"She veiled her eyes and turned her attention to her lute. The only song that she remembered had taken shape from the well-known legend of the undine who had loved a man—the story of the fey Melusina. Her brother Anthony had written a poem, making use of the legend, and had set the words to music.

"She had not lost her gift or forgotten her training. The rippling notes of the lute did call to mind the sound of a river and made a suitable background for the song. Watching her and listening to her, I became aware of her beauty.

"As the evening wore on, it seemed useless and needless for me to play the part of watch dog, I asked leave to withdraw, made my goodnights, and went to the bedchamber assigned to me. It was late when Edward burst in, face flushed, but not with wine, eyes blazing, and stalked back and forth, back and forth in silence until he was impelled to put his feelings into words. He had taken good care to find out if Lady Elizabeth was promised in marriage. She was not. Did she love or desire any other man? She did not, she swore—and mentioned the negotiations for Edward's marriage to the French princess. Kings marry for reasons of state, he had reminded her, not from choice. When he had met her under the oak his choice was already made.

"He had argued, beseeched, promised, and she had sighed no, but hoped that he would be angry only with her, not her family. Edward had berated her on that. Did she dare to think that he would drive such a bargain? Or that his policies depended on a woman's whims? He had restored her family as he had restored others, to bring peace. He would judge the Woodvilles as he judged others, according to their merits.

"Edward was ready to promise her anything if only she would consent to share his life, but she had murmured that his generosity had already put her in his debt forever, and that she must set a good example to her sons.

"He had assured her that she would have first place at his court, or wherever he was. In her soft voice, she had murmured, 'Your queen will have first place. I know I'm not good enough to be your queen, but I am much too good to be your mistress.'

"In the morning, when we were making ready to leave, Lady Elizabeth came out, wrapped in a white cloak with a white veil over her head. She must be some years older than Edward, but even in the clear light she looked as young and fresh as her sisters and yet when she handed Edward the stirrup cup her expression belied youth or innocence."

"Tongues must have been busy," Dame Joan said, "and are doubtless still clacking."

"There was and is talk—and grumbling," John Dynham admitted, "because Edward has been so quick to show favor to the Woodvilles, and their fortunes are rising again, but I've yet to hear any mention of Lady Elizabeth."

45

"But I don't understand," I said. "A number of people must know, or guess."

"But not why he goes to Grafton—or that Elizabeth is living there. It's a remote place, veiled by the forest. The Woodvilles are shrewd enough to guard the king's secrets and their own."

❦ *Seven*

It was a mild day in October and I had become part of the Duchess of York's household in London. Baynard Castle had immensely thick walls, but heavy hangings kept out the chill of the stone, and the fire gave light and warmth.

I was reading aloud to the Duchess from a book of devotions as I often did at this hour. As I was familiar with the book I could read on without stumbling over a word and let my thoughts drift. Since her widowhood, the Duchess of York had lived in semi-retirement, and I found her household more than ever given to piety, and more strictly ordered, but as the mother of the king, she kept royal state both at Fotheringhay and here at Baynard's Castle. Margaret was her only unmarried daughter and lived with her, but she had not yet arrived in London. In the meantime, I could not claim to find existence dull at Baynard's Castle. Peers, prelates, and foreign dignitaries thronged to pay homage to the king's mother, and were suitably entertained. But what she valued was the duty that her children paid her, their affection for her and for one another.

Since I had been at Baynard's Castle I had seen Edward once. He had swept in with George, both had kissed me, praised me, asked me why I had stayed away so long and begged me never to do it again.

"On my return," Edward had said, "I hope to see you and Margaret at Westminster—I need you both at court." A hint that he would marry the French princess and give us a queen. As he knew, well-brought-up young demoiselles were seldom seen at his bachelor court, but when he married the presence of the queen would doubtless impose more decorum, at least outwardly.

Perhaps my lady Duchess expected to keep her influence with Edward after he took a wife. "The king always listens to his mother," her ladies kept repeating.

I roused myself and tried to give my attention to the book, but before I could finish the chapter, the king was announced. I closed the book, put it aside, and rose as Edward came in. He greeted his mother with respect, inquired about her health, and spoke to me in his usual affectionate manner. He was in London only briefly, he explained, and must be on his way to Reading for the meeting of the Royal Council. I looked at my lady Duchess, waiting for her to dismiss me, thinking that today she might prefer to be alone with Edward to discuss the meeting in advance. But he took my hand and invited me to sit down, asking why I was so ready to take wing at the sight of him. I was glad to stay—now I would hear his decision. He would tell us that he would marry the French princess on such and such a day, at such and such an hour.

My lady Duchess sat stiff and straight in her tall-backed chair, and waited for Edward to speak. Her heavy black robes brushed against me, but I could not see her face; I looked instead at Edward. "Youth is proud, and youth is debonair," came to mind. His cloak and doublet were violet, deep but vivid, set off with gold and jewels; the collar of suns and roses which he had invented flashed in the firelight. The hot summer sun had made his skin brown, and lightened his hair to wheat color, and in his dark face his eyes were a brilliant blue. Usually he was glad to lounge in a cushioned chair, but this time he chose to stand without moving, and I became aware of a controlled restlessness and impatience in his stillness.

"The question of my marriage is settled," he said, "I have found a wife for myself. She is Elizabeth Woodville."

A heavy silence answered him. Faint sounds came from outside. A voice giving orders as the guard on the battlements changed; on the river, boatmen shouted to one another. It was ebb tide and the laden ships with painted sails were being drawn out to sea. Elizabeth Woodville! Her name echoed in my ears, pounded in my head. Only Edward himself could have compelled me to believe that he had spoken of marrying her, and spoken in earnest. I knew it, not from his words but from his voice and the look on his face.

It was some time before I could take in anything further as Edward confronted his mother; she had long practice in mastering any display of weakness, but I dared not look her in the face. At last she spoke, and I knew what an effort it must cost her.

"My son, you cannot seriously consider demeaning yourself," she said. "You have agreed with your cousin Warwick that you must marry to your honor and profit—and England's advancement. You can do nothing less since you have encouraged him to go so far in negotiating the French alliance."

"Encourage—no," Edward answered. "He is perfectly well aware of my reluctance. He sees only the advantages, but I have reminded him of the disadvantages of a French marriage."

"Nevertheless you knew he was making preparations to go to France, and you allowed him to go on with his plans. The French king has made lavish preparations to receive him, and is even now waiting on him."

"He needn't wait any longer," Edward told her. "The French Spider is not to be trusted. He fawns on Warwick, and intends to use him. He's trying to use me."

"Then why did you allow Warwick to go so far? Has he spent the years of your reign in feasting and wantonness? No. He's fought your enemies at great risk to himself and known toil and hardship for you and England! Is this the reward he reaps for his great services, that you should flout him and gull him?"

"I never intended . . ." Edward began.

"But by deluding him you've affronted him. He's not the man to take such treatment tamely."

Thinking of the earl's wrath, I became more and more terrified. How had Edward dared?

"I'm sorry to offend him," Edward said, "but his anger will fade. I must rule as I see fit."

"My son, you are the king, but the duty that I owe to God compels me to speak out, not as your subject but as your mother."

"Madam, you have the right to speak your mind to me whenever you see fit. I am always your son."

"It is not princely for you to marry a subject. You have nothing to gain, either in possessions, or in enhancement of your power."

"It's more in keeping with God's law when husband and wife love each other, rather than when a man and a woman take marriage vows with nothing in view but worldly advantage. If alliances with foreign princes are needed, I'll find means to make them. It would be much better for my brothers and my sister to marry into the royal houses of Europe and all parties be contented than for me to marry where I cannot love." He paused, but as his mother said nothing, he went on. "As for enlarging my inheritance through some claim in a foreign land—those expectations usually cause more trouble than profit. For the mere possibility of getting more why lose all happiness in what I already have?"

"You need the goodwill of other nations," his mother said.

"That's of no great importance as long as I have the friendship of my own."

"You are not only offending Warwick, you are giving insult to Louis of France by abruptly declining the princess. He'll bear you malice."

"My own people have never wanted me to take a French bride. They are likely to bear me all the more favor because I did not disdain to take a woman of my own country."

"Such a match for you would be like the case of a man who marries his maid servant. The world comments the maid's good fortune, but not the master's wisdom. Although between maid and master there is not the vast difference that exists between the King of England and this—widow." And the king's mother, for all her control, was unable to hide her bitterness.

Edward had listened to her with respect, and without effort

remained pleasant and courteous. His good temper seemed to me an ominous sign, showing how little influence the earl, or the King of France or his mother had over him in this matter.

"And in first marriage," his mother pointed out, "it would be more suitable for the King of England to take a virgin bride as his wife and queen rather than a widow with two sons. A Lancastrian —the widow of a Lancastrian—your enemy—the enemy of all of your house."

"Madam, I would be glad if you would take it well," Edward answered, and in the same pleasant tone added, "but I am under no person's rule—I think it's only reasonable for me to avail myself of my right to marry where I like. I'm sure that my cousin Warwick would not be so unreasonable as to think that in choosing a wife I ought to be ruled by his eyes rather than my own—as though I were a ward bound to marry at the dictate of a guardian! I would not be king under that condition—to be deprived my freedom in the choice of my marriage."

"I say nothing against her as a person, but whatever good qualities she has, the same and better can be found in other women who are more nearly your equal, my son," his mother argued.

"Let the men who want them marry them." Edward smiled as if to himself. "She's a widow, and has children—I am a bachelor and have some too, and so each of us has proof that neither of us is likely to be barren. And I hope that you will be content for I married Elizabeth Woodville last May Day."

As we expected, Edward's announcement to the Council at Reading brought forth protestations from Warwick and others and started the great quarrel with Warwick, who flung his sacrifices and his victories in Edward's face. "Who made you king? Who keeps you on the throne?" he shouted in anger. But Edward refused to be baited.

Edward set himself to appease the earl's anger, and at Reading, on Michaelmas Day, the people saw the earl, and the king's brother George, Duke of Clarence, escort Elizabeth in state to the

Abbey Church. There, before the high altar, Edward took her hand and presented her to the lords spiritual and temporal as his lawful wife. After she made her offering at the altar, the lords paid her the formal homage due to the Queen of England.

I could picture the scene in the church, with the bright sun shining in the high windows on either side of the altar, sending long bands of light across the chancel, illuminating the figures of the king and queen. But none of the angry men gathered in the church had seen any sign indicating that heaven blessed Edward's marriage. Well, he had showed himself bold enough to defy the world, and Elizabeth Woodville was the happiest and most fortunate of women, not because he had made her Queen of England, but because he loved her for herself alone.

Every household in England was buzzing with the news that on May Day the king had married Elizabeth Woodville. No one else had been present but her mother, the priest, and a boy to sing the Mass. No wonder this wedding caused a stir. Edward was the first King of England and as far as we knew the only king in Christendom to take a non-royal wife.

Edward prided himself on being "entirely English" but if he had thought that his subjects would approve of his marriage to a woman of their own country, he had deluded himself. Not only the Lords but the Commons took it with ill grace. No one seemed to give Elizabeth credit for virtue. They thought she had refused to be the king's mistress, not because she was virtuous, but because she was guileful. Perhaps more than guileful, the people thought.

Her mother boasted of her descent from a water spirit, Melusina, and it was well known that from time to time the women of that race were enchantresses. Lady Jacquetta had the reputation of being learned, and there were the whispers and hints that her learning extended to knowledge of the Black Arts. According to the talk, a mysterious person called Friar Bungay occupied a room in one of Grafton's turrets, where he studied the stars and read books in all languages. The Woodvilles claimed that he was a scholar but the people gave him the name of astrologer and sorcerer.

As rich and poor, high and low were in the habit of consulting soothsayers and astrologers, I asked why Lady Jacquetta should be blamed if she listened to the friar's predictions, but to the people, Edward's marriage was due to witchcraft.

❧ *Eight*

To please Edward, his sister Margaret went to the palace to pay her homage to the new queen, and I accompanied her, not only to please Edward, but myself. I was full of curiosity and had no intention of cutting myself off from friendship with him, or from a court which promised to be brilliant. Neither my mother nor my lady Duchess made any objection, and Will Hastings heartily approved of my going. So did Dame Joan, who advised me not to make disparaging remarks about the king's marriage, or about the Woodvilles. I took her advice and listened without comment while the people around me vented their indignation aloud, or in whispers exchanged the latest rumors.

Westminster Palace looked as it always did outside, but within it had a look of brightness and newness, for the ceilings were painted and gilded, there were hangings embroidered in gold, and highly colored tapestries. The painted glass in the windows sent jeweled light into the rooms, and showed us people in silk and satin and jewels. There were ranks of servants in livery, and any number of pages darted here and there.

My Lord Hastings had met us and escorted us to the queen's apartments, then into a room which was filled with sweet scents, from the cedar logs burning under a carved chimney piece, and from the crushed lavender and vervain spread beneath the great silky carpet that covered the floor. The ceiling was painted crimson and azure; the arras showed ladies riding through a woodland to surprise a unicorn sleeping under a tree. A tall buffet held silver plates, embossed cups, candlesticks and dishes; the chairs were cushioned, and a table held several books, bound in silk or velvet, with jeweled clasps.

This was the queen's solar, and I had the opportunity to look around me because no one else was present. Behind the curtained arch at the farther end of the room someone was playing a lute— the music had a plaintive, insistent rhythm. A narrow door, hidden behind the tapestries opened, and a boy came out. He was about my age, perhaps younger, I judged. He was tall, thin as a reed, with a pointed face, reddish sandy hair, and hazel eyes. His russet-colored doublet was the shortest ever seen, showing all of his long legs; they were well shaped, and his hose fitted without a wrinkle. His shoes ended in long points, the extreme of newest fashion.

He was presented to us as my Lord Marquis of Dorset, and I realized that he was Thomas Grey, Elizabeth's eldest son by her first marriage, and now very much at home in the king's palace. To myself, I dubbed him Renard the Fox, because of his coloring, and because of something a little sly in his expression. I could find no real fault with his manners, and yet his air of being on equal terms with as great a lord as Hastings annoyed me. With all of his flattering courtesy his appraising glances at me likewise annoyed me, although I might have imagined them. What I resented most was his rank and title, newly bestowed only because his mother was now a queen.

At his nod, a page drew back the curtain and announced us. The notes of the lute rippled into silence, and I saw Edward lounging in a cushioned chair with his arm around the woman who was sitting beside him. Again I saw her face, revealed in the firelight, and at a little distance she seemed just as I remembered her.

Edward came to meet us and seemed unchanged in his fondness for us. The queen was expecting us, he said, and led us to her. She had put her lute aside, but otherwise made no move, and waited for us to come to her. When we were near, she spoke to Margaret and Hastings with politeness, but without Edward's warmth. Taking my hand, he presented me to Elizabeth Woodville, so strangely Queen of England, as his dear cousin. She favored me with a smile, and gave me her hand to kiss, and said that she hoped to see me often at court. Edward invited us to sit down, and young Dorset placed himself behind Elizabeth's chair, where he stood watching us.

Edward was all in green, putting me in mind of Sir Lancelot, arrayed in green to go a-Maying with his love in the forest, as Edward had gone a-Maying in Whittlebury Chase. He seemed joyous, happy with her, as if he gloried in his reckless love. At first impression, Elizabeth seemed simply attired, but her pale purple gown was Genoese velvet, with a silvery bloom on the folds, the hanging sleeves were lined with ermine, and I noted the size of the pearls bordering her headdress.

I noted too how the velvet clung to her body, outlining her suppleness and grace, giving a sensuous effect, I thought, although her gown was long and trailing.

Her lips were full and red—a passionate mouth, made for kisses. She listened to Edward's every word, and watched him, sometimes stealing long looks at him from under her lashes.

"This is not the first meeting with Lady Margaret," she said to him, "or with Lady Cicely Bonville. But as it was long ago they would not recall it."

Margaret said nothing, but I spoke up. "Madam, you are not so easily forgotten." And I only told the truth.

Edward was very much interested. "But when and where did you ever meet before?"

At first I was puzzled; why had Elizabeth brought that former meeting to light? Doubtless she had made an unlucky slip of the tongue, in alluding to the winter after Ludlow's fall, when the Yorkist chiefs had been in exile, and the Duchess of York had been imprisoned in that dreary manor. However, she did not seem in the least abashed.

"Why not ask Lady Cicely how it came about?" she said, but would not say more.

I waited for Margaret to continue the tale, but she was resolutely silent, and as Edward insisted, it fell to me to describe the visit that Elizabeth and her mother had paid to the Duchess of York, how they had found their way to the manor, and had appeared with gifts of wine and other delicacies. As soon as I began, I understood why Elizabeth had mentioned the incident—it put her and her mother as well in a favorable light. As Edward now learned, the Woodvilles had showed kindness to the Duchess of York and her dependents when Yorkists fortunes had sunk low.

While I gave my account, Elizabeth's face wore a gentle, wistful expression, and brought back my first impression of her when I have believed that she had come because she had been sorry for us in our plight.

"So the queen has already proved herself your friend," Edward said, and kissed her.

Young Dorset watched me, with a sly look in his yellowish eyes, as if he understood his mother the queen very well. I could not blame her for using feminine guile, and I still gave her credit for her goodwill.

Afterwards, I thought of what I had seen and heard in the palace. Edward and Elizabeth seemed sufficient to themselves, and music had shut out London's clatter and raucous cries. Any sounds of the city came faint and blurred, just as the echo of the rough sea murmurs in a pearled and glistening shell. Elizabeth must be aware of the enmity around her, but she was safe in her royal palace, with Edward to protect her. Beyond the palace gates, Londoners spoke their minds, but only a whisper of their discontent reached her ears. And Edward was accustomed to hewing his way through opposition.

However, he did try to conciliate the Earl of Warwick. Although there was no question of Edward's marriage to a French princess, the earl's mind was still fixed on a treaty with the French king. As if to prove his unabated friendship for his cousin Warwick, and his complete confidence in the earl's skill at statecraft, Edward gave him the freedom to use his own judgment in making a treaty to England's best interest, either with the Duke of Burgundy or with the French king. In the spring, the earl sailed for France, and was received with every honor.

"The Spider of France is too embroiled with his enemies to offer more than promises and fair words," Hastings said. "Warwick will come back empty-handed. But he's gained one advantage—his stay in France will spare him from taking any part in the queen's coronation."

The Duchess of York stayed in London, but immured herself in Baynard's Castle; my mother found it necessary to go to her estates, and many of the greatest ladies followed the example, and found excuses to absent themselves.

In honor of Elizabeth Woodville's coronation, the court flowered into a brilliance never before known in England—certainly not known for centuries, it was said. Edward intended to impress the people with Elizabeth's high lineage on her mother's side, and invited her kinsmen from the Low Countries to see her crowned. The Princess of Burgundy and Luxembourg had disowned Jacquetta when she had demeaned herself by marrying a Woodville, and were unaware of Elizabeth's existence, but when she startled the world by becoming Queen of England, her uncle, Jacques de Luxembourg, came to present the Duke of Burgundy, and brought with him a train of a hundred knights.

Londoners immediately dubbed Jacques de Luxembourg "Lord Jakes," delighted that his name was so easily converted into a jibe at Woodville pretensions. (Perhaps he came and went without ever learning that in England "Jakes" was a lowly privy.) The Woodvilles eagerly seized on him as their claim to princely blood. He was a thin, nimble little man, richly dressed, and very affable—bowing and bobbing like a cork afloat. The crowds stared and jeered, but Edward took care to put London into a good humor. He renewed the city's privileges, bestowed honors on leading citizens, invited the mayor, the aldermen, the heads of the guilds, and the leading merchants to feast at the palace, and in turn dined or supped at their houses. He gave the people a varied amount of pageantry to dazzle them, and they cheered him lustily whenever he appeared.

At a banquet in the Guildhall, I was placed next to one of the young foreign knights, who wondered at the sight of the king, and his nobles mingling on terms of equality with commoners. His sovereign lord the Duke of Burgundy would never show such condescension to inferior persons, nor would any one entitled to wear the spurs of knighthood. The foreigners were agape when Edward led the dance with the buxom middle-aged Lady Mayoress, and I very willingly accepted a London merchant as my partner—a man who had traveled by land and sea to far countries.

Whitsunday fell on the 20th day of May that year, and on Whitsun Eve, the queen came from Eltham Palace to London. Whitsunday dawned bright; the bells rang, the fountains ran with red wine and white for Elizabeth Woodville's coronation, and crowds filled the streets, struggling to catch sight of her. Years ago, the people had struggled to catch sight of Marguerite of Anjou, when she had entered London for the first time.

Now her former maid of honor had taken her place as Queen of England. With the newly made knights riding before her, Elizabeth Woodville was carried through the city to Westminster Abbey in an open litter drawn by white horses, their shining manes like sea foam. Elizabeth was smiling, but it was a secret smile—not for the people. She took no notice of them as she passed. In her golden robes and fiery jewels she seemed to me as fair as a queen out of Avalon—Morgan le Fay appearing from her palace in the depths of the lake and vanishing again. Perhaps she could cast her spell not only on the king but on his kingdom.

❦ Nine

Elizabeth Woodville's coronation was carried out with greater splendor than Edward's own, including the customary banquet held in Westminster Hall. Nothing marred the well-ordered pomp of the ceremony or her feast. Edward had succeeded in winning the approval of his chief city, and outwardly had imposed his will on everyone in his family except his mother. She gave her retirement from public life as an excuse for her absence from the coronation, but the whole world knew how bitterly "Proud Cis" resented the crowning of a Woodville. However, Edward's brothers and sisters were present—gathered at the same table with Elizabeth's family. Two hostile groups, mingled together at the high table, keeping to the rules of good manners.

Lady Jacquetta's eyes glittered with triumph as she conversed with Lord Jacques. He and all her kindred had despised her and forgotten her and it must have been sweet to show them how high she had come in the world. Was it by her knowledge and practice of witchcraft? Perhaps. I had heard the legend of the love potion in the wine cup.

Anthony Woodville, Elizabeth's best-loved brother, was tall and well-made, with a thin, fine boned face and almond-shaped dark eyes; he was always followed by a great retinue of people, and he always wore splendid clothes—even outdoing Will Hastings. Recently, he had stirred great resentment by making a match with a rich and high-born widow, and through the lady, had taken on the title and estates of her deceased husband.

Anthony might be as greedy as the rest of his family, but I thought that his wife could have done worse. He had talents and learning, and he seemed to have some kindness in his nature. Also, she was a plain-faced silent little woman. In the midst of the Woodvilles she was like a barnyard hen among a dazzling flock of wild swans.

Elizabeth's younger sisters were present. They had grown up at Grafton, unwooed and unwed, but now they had come out of their obscurity and were either married or affianced to heirs of the greatest estates in England, causing bitter jealousy in the hearts of other marriageable demoiselles and their parents.

However, a young man might be well pleased to have as fair a wife as one of the queen's sisters. Seeing them together, it was hard to decide which one was more beautiful than the others.

At the coronation, George had acted as High Steward of England, as he was the brother next to the king in age, and heir presumptive to the throne. He followed Edward's example in wooing the people of London, and the crowds acclaimed him. Throughout the coronation ceremonies he had played his part to perfection, although he despised the Woodvilles, and was all too apt to give vent to his scorn.

His brother Richard held his tongue, but he looked unhappy. And Margaret, devoted as she was to her brothers, most of all to George, was unhappy because of the storms that had boiled up in the wake of Edward's marriage.

Edward had two sisters older than himself. They had both been married in their childhood to Lancastrian peers, one to the Duke of Suffolk, a clod without brains or spirit; the other, Anne of York, was the wife of Henry Holland, Duke of Exeter. He had fought for Lancaster, and was now in exile at the Burgundian court. Ragged and barefoot, he had become a beggar, until the Duke of Burgundy had learned his name and had granted him a pension.

My lady of Exeter had cleaved to York—and to her brother Edward. In her place I might have felt the same, but knowing her, I wondered if she would have loved Edward so well if he had lost. Her husband deserved credit for his proven loyalty, but she never had a good word for him or a shred of compassion in his misfortunes. According to the talk, she was eager for his death because she wanted to marry her lover.

As Anne of York had been venomous in her remarks about the Woodvilles, I had not expected to see her at Elizabeth's coronation, but she was at the Abbey and at the banquet. There she was—a great beauty once but now a massive woman, blinking with rubies, emeralds, diamonds, and busily stuffing herself. She was a complete contrast to her daughter, who was sitting opposite me at the board. She scarcely touched the rich dishes offered to her, and left her wine untasted. Although I had never met her before I knew she was Anne Holland, the sole heiress of all of the Exeter estates, and promised in marriage to the Earl of Warwick's nephew.

My lord of Dorset sat next to her and had been listening to what I had been saying to her. When her answers were slow, he

59

glanced at me as if inviting me to share his disdain for her. I ignored him, and he turned his attention to her, and began to flatter her. I heard him say, "I had a great curiosity to meet you," before he lowered his voice. She flushed a dull red, and became more confused than ever. She was unused to the idle jargon of the court, but I hoped that natural good sense would enable her to recognize the jingle of false coin.

As we left the Hall, Dorset suddenly appeared beside me. "Have I been unlucky enough to offend you?" he asked.

"Have you any reason to think so, my lord?" I answered.

"You gave me a cold shoulder."

I contented myself by bidding him good night.

"Spare me a moment," he urged. "I did have a great curiosity to see her."

A week after the queen's coronation, Margaret and I were together in the solar, at work on an altar cloth for the chapel at Fotheringhay when the Duchess of Exeter came to Baynard's Castle and went directly to her mother's apartments on the floor above.

"She sent word that she had business to discuss," Margaret said, and went on with her needlework, but an hour later, when I supposed that she had already left Baynard's Castle, my lady of Exeter burst into the solar before she could be announced. "They told me where you were hiding," she panted, as Margaret and I rose to greet her. In answer to my curtsey she gave me an off-hand nod, and declined to sit down. She had no time to linger for Edward had invited her to follow the hounds at Windsor.

"I leave you to make my peace," she rolled her eyes upward, indicating the Duchess of York's apartments.

Margaret suggested that her sister would do better to put off her going and make her own peace with their mother.

"What I had to say made her angry," Lady Exeter answered. "She's been upbraiding me for the last hour."

"What did you say to her?" Margaret demanded.

Lady Exeter gave a little laugh. "You might as well know it

now as later—I've decided to break off the match between my daughter Anne and our cousin Warwick's nephew."

Margaret and I stared at her. "But how can you, sister?" Margaret asked. "You've already given your word. You can't break a solemn promise of years standing."

"There's been no official betrothal, you know that, Meg!" Lady Exeter adopted a wheedling tone. "The young people aren't bound to each other."

"You were satisfied with the match," Margaret reminded her. "Why have you changed your mind?"

"I have other plans for my girl." Lady Exeter became defiant again. "I'm marrying her to young Dorset!"

Margaret turned pale, and my knees felt weak. I groped for the chair behind me, and sat down—and went on staring at Lady Exeter.

"This will be bitter news to our cousin Warwick—to all of the Nevilles," Margaret tried to plead with her. "How will you ever make your peace with them?"

"They can find another heiress for the boy." She turned to face us. "My little innocents, these days Elizabeth's son is a much greater match than Warwick's nephew! And much more to my advantage. Elizabeth came sidling up to me and promised me four thousand pounds for my consent. And she has paid—I made sure of that."

If he had wished, Edward could have upheld his sister's pledge and commanded her to disgorge the four thousand pounds. Why was he willing to offend the earl and all of the house of Neville—to please Elizabeth? Edward was no weakling; in all important matters he took his way. Perhaps the people were right when they whispered that witchcraft held their king in thrall.

"This affront makes all true Yorkists uneasy," John Dynham said to me. "The earl's anger is formidable." However, when he came back from France, the earl was fully master of himself. For reasons of his own he had evidently decided to suppress any outward show of wrath. As soon as he had discussed matters of policy with Edward and the Royal Council, he left London for

Middleham Castle, to take up his heavy responsibilities as Warden of the North. Elizabeth had won. Her victory had cost her four thousand pounds and might cost her more than money. The people muttered that she brought discord.

In the summer the court moved to Windsor, and Edward's visits to his mother were infrequent, but George and Richard were often at Baynard's Castle. "My younger sons have not changed toward me," my lady Duchess said, but in her presence they showed a deference and reserve that concealed their thoughts and feelings. Richard's disciplined and well-ordered life under the earl's tutelage had come to an end with Edward's marriage and the quarrel with Warwick. Perhaps Richard was old enough and learned enough to set up an establishment of his own as a royal prince. He had castles and manors, and in London, a house of his own, but instead of being glad to escape from arduous military training and long hours of study, his freedom seemed to sit heavily on him.

"I'm tired of being idle," he told me, in one of the rare moments when he spoke of himself.

"You've taken charge of your estates—and from what I hear, your methods are proving successful." I added, "Edward says so."

"I wish I could be of some use to him. Of course I am not old enough to hold office." He frowned a little, "I miss the north."

Richard was devoted to Edward, but he was too stiff and silent to be happy at court, or at ease with the Woodvilles.

"At Middleham, you had the company of your friends—and the earl's daughters," I said. "Anne is near your own age." At mention of Anne, his face lighted up, and he said how gentle and kind she was, and from the way he spoke of her, it was plain to see that she was dear to him. If his affection for her had taken deep root, the wrench of parting with her might still be raw and unhealed.

Richard's health and looks had greatly improved; he was brown-haired, with deep set eyes and a prominent forehead. When he was with his brothers, their conspicuous tallness and brilliant coloring made Richard dwindle into a puny boy. As he said, "Edward and George look as if the sun was always shining on them."

When I had first met Margaret she had been overshadowed by her brothers, but since Edward had won the throne, her position had likewise changed. As the King of England's only unmarried sister, the question of choosing a husband for her was a matter of grave political concern. There was talk of an alliance with Charles of Burgundy. He had offered to marry her, if Edward would aid him against the French king. But time had passed and Burgundy had not pursued the matter further.

In the past, England's wool, "the best in the world, and our chief treasure," as the earl had pointed out, had been sold in the Low Countries. But in late years, our weavers had become remarkably skillful; they used most of our wool at home, and were doing a brisk trade in exporting their fine cloth. Their rivalry threatened the trade of the rich Flemish cities to such an extent that the Duke of Burgundy had forbidden the import of so much as an ell of English woven cloth into his domains. His decree had aroused the ire of every man, woman, and child in this country. All of us were affected, even my own estates in the west country and the flocks of sheep on the downs at Shute.

"Edward is aware," George said. "He's in the wool trade himself. There's another obstacle to the match," he added. "Charles of Burgundy hates Edward."

"He couldn't hate Margaret," I said.

"He's not interested in women. He wants fame and military glory."

The earl wanted a pact with France, George explained, and the French king had promised unrestricted trade—a vast market for our goods, and other advantages.

"All he asks in return is peace with us—and the privilege of making a match for you, Margaret. He promises it would be suitable—more than suitable—brilliant."

"Who does he have in mind for me, brother?" Margaret asked, without any great show of interest.

"A French prince—or someone friendly to France," George answered.

As far as I knew, the earl was the only person who had any faith in the Spider King of France.

"Our cousin Warwick has warned Edward that if he makes any close ties with Charles of Burgundy he'll be sure to repent it."

Margaret would have little to say when it came to deciding her destiny, but then she had always expected to make an alliance for the good of the country and the best interests of her family. However, she was no cipher; she had both character and intelligence—and she had beauty as well.

"George dined with the Milanese ambassador today," Margaret told me a few weeks later. "He's promised to come to see us later."

I was glad for I knew that George was her favorite brother.

It was a still gray evening. Within the thick walls of Baynard's Castle the rooms had become filled with shadows, and the candles had been lighted in the solar, where Margaret and I were playing at cards—a pastime invented to soothe the mad King of France, who had bequeathed his madness to his grandson, Henry the Sixth.

I noted the Queen of Hearts, holding a white flower in her hand; she and the king were painted with yellow hair, and he brandished a great sword. There was the knave, decked out in bright colors. When George was announced, the cards were pushed aside and forgotten. For a moment George was outlined against the door. He wore white and scarlet, set off by the jeweled order of the Garter and the collar of suns and roses. However, as he moved into the light, I noticed his sullen look. His sister and I welcomed him, and he answered in a dispirited voice. Instead of sitting down with us as he usually did, he went closer to Margaret and stood near her. "Public announcement will be made tomorrow—the woman we must call queen is with child."

This was good news, but in deference to George's mood, I refrained from saying so. He would lose his position as the heir presumptive to the throne. The king's son, born in lawful wedlock, would be heir apparent, and oust George from his present place as next in line of succession.

"You must have foreseen that Edward would father children," Margaret said to him.

"Judging from the number of his bastards," George answered. "But Elizabeth's older than he is—by quite some years. She takes care to keep her age a secret, but she might have proved barren."

"She has two sons by her first marriage, and she isn't too old for child-bearing," Margaret said. "She's likely to give Edward a family."

"If Edward had married a king's daughter who would breed a royal family instead of Woodville's daughter," George muttered, "I'd be glad of the child."

Not glad, I thought, but less resentful—even so, the depth of his ill-feeling startled me.

"Woodville arrogance will be past endurance," he said.

I thought of all that Edward had done for his younger brothers, caring for them, shielding them—and how generous he had been to them! He had been particularly lavish to George, and in making him Duke of Clarence had given him the estates and honors of the great Clare inheritance.

For some minutes George seemed to be struggling with his ill temper in silence, frowning down at the cards scattered on the table. "They say that Elizabeth's mother understands how to find meaning in the turn of the cards," he told us. "Doubtless they reveal good fortune for the Woodvilles, or rather continued good fortune." He picked up a few cards and let them fall again. "All the astrologers and soothsayers have set to work drawing up horoscopes. They've already promised Edward that the child will be male. And in every church in England masses will be offered and special prayers will be said, importuning God Almighty to send the king a prince."

"Send England a prince," I amended.

"Of course the child may prove to be a girl," George caught at the hope. "God or the Devil might trick Edward!"

65

"He's likely to have more children," Margaret said, "and even if not, there's no law in England to prevent a woman from inheriting the crown."

George laughed. "Neither lords nor commons would ever accept a woman's rule. They're growing restive under Woodville rule!"

Margaret looked around uneasily. "I wish you would be more prudent."

"I know enough to be on my guard elsewhere, but no one's here but you and Cicely. If it's dangerous for me to speak out to my own sister and my own dear cousin who can I trust?"

George knew very well how to soften Margaret's disapproval, but his ire flashed out again. "How will the peers stomach it, how will close-mouthed brother Richard stomach it when we must kneel and swear to serve and obey Woodville spawn?" he demanded.

I could hold my tongue no longer. "You look far ahead. Edward's young and full of health and vigor. For many a year you and Richard and the Lords and Commons will give your allegiance to him, please God."

Margaret added "Amen." But not George. Instead he turned suddenly to me. "Do you believe that every mother's son in England gives Edward allegiance now? How many of his subjects pay him lip service, and give their real loyalty to Lancaster?"

This was a question which no one could answer with any certainty. During the war, our enemies had been able to bring larger armies into battle than we could muster—but now most of the known Lancastrians were in exile, or dead. What of the others? Who were they and where were they?

"The country prospers," Margaret said. "You have only to look out and see how the ships come and go. And the people seem content with Edward's rule."

"He should never have let himself be enticed into a secret marriage with a Lancastrian widow," George answered.

"Take care what you say and where you say it." Margaret looked around uneasily.

"Brought about by spells and witchcraft!" He pounded on the table with his clenched fist. The cards leaped up and some fell on the table, others on the floor. "Brought about by spells and witchcraft—and that's no secret! Who knows if the people will be content to accept the fruit of this misty marriage as the lawful heir to the crown!"

❧ Ten

Great preparations were made for the birth of this all-important child. For her royal lying-in, Elizabeth took care to surround herself with all the ceremonial observances. "Every custom used by former queens in this country," Margaret told me when I came back to London after a stay in Devon. "And her mother has introduced some of the customs of the Burgundian court. Green hangings—because it's the royal color."

"I thought purple or crimson was royal," I said.

"The Duchess of Burgundy was brought to bed in a chamber with green hangings."

As her time drew near, the highest officials of the crown went in procession to escort Elizabeth to her apartments. From then on, until after the birth of the child, she had only women to serve her. Women baked, turned the spit, superintended the laying of the table, the seating of the guests, the carving of the meat, the pouring of the wine. There was one exception—Elizabeth's personal physician. His name was Dr. Serigo, and he was installed in the palace to care for her health and to take charge of her accouchement. Custom or not, she valued his skill. Nor did she exclude Edward, Margaret told me. "He comes and goes quietly by way of a little door, hidden behind a panel of tapestry."

Five state beds had been made ready—very richly decked out, I heard. Like the London goodwives, I asked how one woman needed five, but was told that four of them were for show. Elizabeth was accused of being spendthrift, but ladies, gentlewomen, and goodwives eagerly discussed the queen's approaching lying-in, and all of the regulations and splendors surrounding her confinement. "In our time we've never known the like," my lady governess said. "Marguerite of Anjou's son was born into an unwelcoming world without much ado."

The Duchess of York again gave her life of retirement as an excuse for not paying a visit to Elizabeth, but Margaret of York felt an obligation to please Edward.

"And so I must wait on the queen, and you would do well to go with me," she said to me, and I agreed, to please Edward—and to please myself.

At the palace, horses were already saddled and waiting for the couriers who would ride north south east and west—or sail across the Narrow Seas to take the news of the child's birth to other countries. Foreign envoys, members of the Royal Council, prelates and courtiers gathered in the king's presence chamber; clerks were at hand, waiting to write proclamations.

A little group of astrologers were conspicuous because of their tall peaked hats and full dark robes, sewn with cabalistic symbols. I looked at them with curiosity, and when John Dynham met us and was leading me to the queen's apartments, I asked him to name the soothsayers to me. "The one with the fat white face who moves his hands about—is he Friar Bungay?"

"That's Master Domenico," he answered. "The Friar never joins with the others, and is seldom seen."

When Margaret and I were admitted to the queen's apartments I expected to find Elizabeth in her green-draped bedchamber, but she was in her solar. Two of her sisters were with her; Mary Woodville, now Lord Herbert's wife, was russet-haired and beautiful, with sharp wits and at times a sharp tongue. And beside her Katherine Woodville would soon make a greater match with the reluctant young Duke of Buckingham. Elizabeth was sitting close to the fire. She was wrapped in the folds of a fur-bordered crimson robe, and her hair, hanging loose, was red gold in the firelight.

Her sisters spoke of "our little Prince of Wales." "Master Domenico is certain," Katherine Woodville said. But I knew that Elizabeth had consulted the mysterious Friar Bungay, and he had refused to predict the sex of the child. Edward hardly needed to ask the soothsayers what was written in the stars; he believed in his own star, and God would grant him a son.

Elizabeth seemed calm, but as I soon noted, her stillness was like a wild animal's. The firelight put gold reflections in her eyes which looked out from covert at a hostile world.

In the icy bluster of a February day, Londoners eddied around Westminster Palace and crowded close to the gates, waiting for the bells to ring out, announcing the birth.

Margaret of York and I waited in Elizabeth's solar. Our unmarried state excluded us from being present at the birth. In contrast to the cold gray morning, the solar glowed with warmth. With nothing else to occupy me I took in every detail of the room. The tapestries caught my attention particularly because they were so joyous. One panel showed a group of children fishing in a little river, another showed the same children dancing in a flowery meadow—as the young Woodvilles might have spent a summer's day in their childhood.

In time, we heard the cry of a newborn child. We started up and went out. The door to the queen's bedchamber opened and a waiting woman spoke. "The queen is safely delivered of a fair princess."

Edward's hopes for a male heir were thwarted, but he controlled any show of disappointment. After the baby had been washed, and wrapped in swaddling bands, the head nurse placed her on a velvet cushion, covered all but her face with a velvet and ermine coverlet, and carried her to the king. He took her, acknowledged her as his, held her up for the assembled lords and prelates to see, and offered his thanks to God for giving him a living and healthy child. While he spoke, he looked down at the little face. The baby yawned and opened her eyes. Edward's expression changed, he broke off and finished in a different voice, "And we give you heartfelt welcome."

But the Woodvilles wore long faces, and Elizabeth moaned, "Only a girl!" when the midwife told her. When Margaret and I were admitted to her bedchamber, her mother and her sisters were hovering around her, trying to console her. Her waiting women had made her ready for Edward's coming. She was in a vast bed, propped up on pillows. She was white-faced and hollow-eyed, and the green hangings cast a greenish shadow, giving her the look of a wraith. The cradle was cedar wood, carved, inlaid with gold and mother of pearl, curtained in crimson velvet, topped by the three feathers of a Prince of Wales. "Take away the feathers," Elizabeth sighed as Edward came in, still holding the child in his arms. He never so much as glanced at the cradle. He went to Elizabeth, kissed her and sat by the bed, leaning close to her, and speaking to her in a low voice.

"We'll make sons and daughters too," we heard him reassure her. "Now we can rejoice in this demoiselle."

Edward had made overtures to the Earl of Warwick by inviting him to stand sponsor for the child, and the earl had sent a prompt acceptance. He and Edward met in London with every appearance of friendship, and the earl was not only courteous but affable to the Woodvilles. Perhaps he had decided to avoid clashes with them, but he had not brought his wife and daughters with him. As usual they had stayed at Middleham. "Where they prefer to be," Richard had told me. I shrank from the very thought of Middleham Castle but Richard seemed to think of his three years there as the happiest he had ever known.

When the earl was in London, crowds gathered in Warwick Lane, and Warwick House offered its bountiful hospitality to all classes. Every morning eight oxen were roasted in the kitchens, and any man who could claim even the slightest acquaintance with one of the earl's servants was welcome to dine in the hall and take away as much meat as a long dagger could hold.

The earl's greatness seemed to tower higher than ever. He had brought hundreds of retainers with him and his men were well paid and well disciplined. London was glad to see the flash of their red jackets. Peers, prelates, knights, foreign envoys, and prominent citizens paid their homage at Warwick House. Whenever the earl appeared, crowds followed him, and the cry of "Warwick, Warwick," resounded through the streets.

A group of Bohemian nobles came to London; their king had sent them to England to make a treaty and Edward gave a feast in their honor. A few days later the earl entertained them at Warwick House at a much more elaborate banquet, with double the number of courses. George and Richard had come to London, and were drawn to Warwick House. Why not? Edward and Warwick were friends again, or appeared to be.

Edward had planned magnificent celebrations to hail the birth of a prince, and kept to the same arrangements even though the baby was only a girl. She was his first born, he said, his first legitimate child, and must have her due. And for the first time in England, the christening of a princess was celebrated with as much pomp as the christening of a prince who was heir apparent to the throne.

The earl's gift was a gold cup, set with jewels, and he did his part as godfather in a happy spirit. The Duchess of York and Lady Jacquetta were the godmothers. Seeing them together, I noted the contrast between the two women. My lady Duchess had great dignity, and as she grew older her stateliness suited her. She showed the effects of sorrow more than time.

Jacquetta's face had scarcely changed since I had first seen her, but had she ever been young? It was impossible to picture her as the girl who had sacrificed her rank and state because of a consuming passion for her lover. The people called the Duchess of York "Proud Cis," but she commanded respect. Jacquetta aroused hostility and fear. To the people, she was a sinister figure.

The mother of the king and the mother of the queen would never be friends, but at the baptismal font they were transformed. They became two grandmothers, admiring their newborn granddaughter. She was the fairest baby ever seen, the most perfect in every way. For once, they were in complete agreement. And the look on Edward's face put me in mind of the young Edward that I had met at Ludlow.

The child was baptized Elizabeth—Edward had never considered giving her any other name. The bells rang, the fountains ran wine. Edward ordered food and money to be distributed to the poor. People—young and old—danced in the meadow beyond the walls, to the tune of gitterns and viols. People filled the streets and gathered around the bonfires blazing along the river's banks, to laugh and sing and eat and drink. Yorkist London had hoped for a Yorkist heir, but the crowds shouted "Long live Lady Bess," and drank her health with great goodwill.

And one person was overjoyed—the king's brother, George, Duke of Clarence. His pages scattered coins to the crowds, and George smiled and smiled, endearing himself to the citizens. He was still the nearest male heir to the throne.

When Elizabeth had recovered her health after childbirth, her churching took place, followed by a banquet at Westminster Palace. Custom excluded the king, and he had asked the Earl of Warwick to represent him. Elizabeth chose to seclude herself in a room hung with cloth of gold, with her ladies in waiting and her women. Her mother was also in attendance on her, and perhaps her sisters as well. I could not say, because as I passed by I looked, but my view was limited, and I saw only Elizabeth, framed in the arch of the doorway. She sat alone at table. She wore the trefoil crown used for state occasions. I caught a glimpse of the canopy over her head, and the shining hangings behind her.

During the banquet, lasting a full three hours, and the dancing afterwards, Elizabeth stayed apart from the rest of the company. It was not until I was in the barge with Margaret, George, and Richard that I learned how much indignation the queen had

72

stirred. She had never moved from her gold-lined room, never condescended to speak to the earl, or the Bohemian envoys.

"They were spared," Margaret's voice was thick with anger. "During the banquet she kept her ladies and waiting women on their knees. Why, for a time her own mother was kneeling to her!"

"She has vastly overblown ideas of what's due her," Richard said. "To exact so much homage is not our way—it's un-English." He added: "Can you picture our mother ever kneeling to you, Meg?"

"Not even if you were Duchess of Burgundy," George put in, and the idea of such a thing made us burst out laughing."

"Or Empress of Byzantium," Margaret finished.

"But you can be sure that Elizabeth's mother was willing," I argued when we grew sober. "She had a hand in arranging the ceremonies. I'm sorry for the rest of them, but not Dame Jacquetta." And she had a motive. "She would gladly cavort with a dancing bear if the exhibition would enhance Elizabeth's importance."

"Today's performance won't," George said. "Do you know what happened? Before we left the palace the earl asked the Bohemian lords if they would like to see the queen, and led them to the open door, where they could look at her. There she was in her golden chair. She sat alone at the board and never said a word to anyone. The Bohemian gazed at her, gazed at the ranks of silent kneeling women, and the earl didn't need to ask them what they thought of our Woodville queen. They praised her beauty, but were dumbfounded by her arrogance."

"She doesn't always behave with such haughtiness," I said, "and she could never impose such a rigid rule when Edward is present."

"He's a man under a spell, and lets her do as she pleases," George said.

"But she tries to please him," I pointed out.

I blamed her for showing no consideration for her attendants, but as for the rest, I could understand why she had been eager to avail herself of all of the trappings of royalty. Her prayers for a son had gone unanswered; the soothsayers had deluded her with false promises; her enemies offered their felicitations, but as she doubtless knew, they mocked at her for not producing a son. Edward was happy, but was Elizabeth content? I doubted it.

❧ *Eleven*

The winter of 1467 had gone and in the lengthening light of the spring days seemed gone forever. Now Lent had come to an end, and the royal court followed Edward and Elizabeth to Shene Palace for Easter. "You are right, Cicely," Margaret conceded. "Either Elizabeth and her mother have seen their mistake, or perhaps because Edward is here, she no longer plays at being Empress of Byzantium. She's remarkably gracious."

"Edward's presence endows her with life," I said.

His happy spirits had a good effect on Elizabeth and on all of us. I had yet to hear Elizabeth laugh out loud, but John Dynham had told me that "her sweet feminine smiling" had been a lure for Edward—still lured him. At Shene, she had smiles for his family as well as for her own, and made his friends feel welcome. After Easter, there would be hunts, banquets, and in the evening, dancing.

Since I had come to Shene, the Woodvilles had singled me out for notice. Elizabeth's son Dorset had brought his wife, the Exeter heiress, and the Woodvilles showed her kindness, and tried to draw her into their conversation. Their efforts only made her more than ever confused and tongue-tied.

"But you can hold your own with them!" she said, confiding in me. "I've never been taught what I should know."

"You can learn," I told her. "Why not?"

"I'll try to become learned—then Dorset needn't be ashamed of my ignorance."

"He has no reason to be ashamed of you now. Boys of his age are apt to think too well of themselves."

"He's selfish," his wife conceded, "but I want him to think well of me."

"He must—if he has good sense," I tried to reassure her.

"I would have better hope of winning him if I had beauty," she sighed. "I envy you your face and your body."

I was still taken by surprise when anyone admired my appearance, although my looks had greatly improved. I had grown tall and though I was still somewhat too slender, George could no longer call me a "scrawny little crow," as he had once. He had taken to praising my dark eyes and black hair.

"None of us can hope to outshine the Woodvilles," I said, "but they are skillful in the art of enhancing what nature has given them." As soon as I had set eyes on them, I had studied them, and in some ways had learned how to imitate them. I chose the fashion that suited me best, and followed their example by wearing clinging silks.

Dorset's wife had asked me to walk with her in the gardens, and we were following a secluded path with shrubbery on either side. I was sorry for her, and wondered what could be done to transform her. She had not inherited her mother's Plantagenet coloring, but except for her slightly protruding teeth, her features were good, and as her health became better, her looks would improve; she could learn to choose her attire to minimize her defects, smile with her mouth closed, and perhaps make use of artifices.

I told her that the queen bathed in perfumed water, then her maids rubbed unguents and lotions on her face and body to keep her skin soft and silken, then costly essences of jasmine or roses. "And she reddens her lips." I was speaking to a girl who could buy all the essences and spices of Cyprus and the East, and who listened amazed.

"I do the same," I admitted. "Dorset would approve."

"He greatly admires you," she said, "and he has fastidious taste."

75

Fastidious! That finicking boy with his excessively pointed shoes! If Anne of Exeter had married the earl's nephew he might have been well content with her goodness and her capacity for devotion, and she would have been happier as chatelaine of a northern castle, I thought. Unassuming goodness and affection—Dorset would not set store by those qualities!

The path widened out, bringing us to the greensward where there were many people. Dorset was directly in front of us, deep in conversation with a young demoiselle, but when he saw us he made his excuses to her and hurried to join us. Talking and laughing, he accompanied us to the palace, and even this much attention seemed to make his wife happy, for the moment. He always treated me with great deference, and yet now and then I had the impression that there was something more in his attitude than mere gallantry. I wasn't sure what it was.

After midday on Holy Saturday, the Easter bells rang out. The time for penitence had come to an end; flutes and viols and gitterns took up their melodies again, spinning lively airs, or sighing out love songs. Before dusk, the halls and presence chambers were crowded with guests, with more expected for the coming week, but the Earl of Warwick was not one of them. Not because his relations with Edward had worsened, but because the earl was going to France, with the king's full approval. The business of outfitting men and ships kept him from holding Easter at Shene.

At the High Mass on Easter Day, the choir of the king's chapel sang, their voices clear and pure; against the glitter of the altar the candles were golden stars. After the Mass, when the king and queen had left the chapel and the court had followed them to her presence chamber, some of the demoiselles of her entourage surrounded her brother Anthony and offered him a golden collar, set with jewels and further ornamented with a pendant, an enameled forget-me-not, the Flower of Souvenance.

This had been prearranged, and Elizabeth had chosen me to tell him the meaning of her gift. The queen and the ladies of England asked him to undertake a suitable enterprise by inviting a knight renowned in foreign tournaments to come to England and meet him in the lists. My Lord Anthony kissed the Flower of Souvenance, and vowed that he would indeed remember his knightly devoir. It seemed natural for him to word his thanks in the language of chivalry and to send a challenge to the lord known as the Grand Bastard of Burgundy, who had so far been victorious over every opponent who had been bold enough to joust with him.

"My lord, you select a redoubtable knight, but the queen and the ladies of England have entire faith in you as our champion." At the moment I was able to admire his spirit and having said what was required, I went back to my place, rather pleased with my part in the enterprise.

My Lord Anthony wrote his letter to the Burgundian, stating the terms of the tourney, and inviting him to "bring the adventure of the Flower of Souvenance to a conclusion." Chester Herald was summoned, and was ordered to sail to the Low Countries and deliver the letter.

In the afternoon, George drew his sister and me away from the palace and the gardens thronged with people to the bank of the river.

"I wonder why the queen encourages her brother to take on the Burgundian," Margaret said. "They say he is always with Duke Charles in all of his reckless doings."

"A tournament isn't a battlefield," George told her. "Anthony and his forget-me-not won't come to any harm. His Flower of Souvenance is a Lancastrian symbol, you know."

"Not in this instance," Margaret pointed out. "It's only a fanciful device."

"Without any political meaning at all," I added.

"The Woodvilles are always involved in some sort of intrigue," George said. "But never mind, Cicely, your sweet words to Anthony were gracefully spoken, and your manner all maiden demureness."

"Anyone else could have served the purpose. The words were mine, but Anthony knew what was planned, and had already decided on challenging the Burgundian. I don't know why Elizabeth decided on me to present the collar."

"Evidently you are high in her favor," George's tone accused.

Margaret defended me, "Cicely never seeks her favor!"

"No," George admitted, "but don't fall into their honey trap." He looked at Margaret. "They're trying to win your favor, Meg, but the Woodvilles know better than to ask you to have any share in offering an invitation to Charles of Burgundy's bastard brother —not after the way Charles has treated you and our family!

"The earl is leaving for France to make a treaty with the French king," he went on, "and he's likely to find a suitable husband for you, sister. A handsome prince who'll please you much better than shock-haired Charles."

Margaret smiled. "I'm in no haste to marry."

"Perhaps the earl will find a fair princess as a bride for you," I said to George.

His color deepened. "I'll never follow Edward's example and demean myself, but I might find a wife here in England."

In the latter part of May, a great crowd gathered to shout "Warwick, Warwick," as the earl's trumpeters and heralds marched through the streets. The uproar grew louder and louder as the people saw the earl himself, astride his great stallion, Roan William. A band of lords, knights, and squires, also on horseback followed the earl. Some two hundred men were in his train, besides a company of archers wearing his badge. Londoners seemed to be against an alliance with the French, but it satisfied their pride in Warwick the King Maker to have him appear in magnificent style when he went to meet the mean-spirited Spider King of France and his pinchpenny court.

The French lords complained of their Spider King's chosen associates—friends he never had—but a butcher, a barber, and a few others of lowest origin and character were the Spider's creatures. He used them to spy out dissent and to carry out his reprisals, without mercy. "But he shows another side to Warwick," George told us. The Spider was evidently keeping his low-born familiars

78

out of sight. He had summoned the highest-ranking peers of France to ride with him to Rouen, to welcome the earl, gave him a state entry into the town, entertained him at a series of regal banquets, and held long private conferences with him. Flinging aside his usual avarice, the Spider lavished gifts on the earl and the lords who had accompanied him, and bestowed gold pieces on their attendants.

Stories of the earl's triumphs circulated in London, and people were delighted to think that he had so much power in a foreign country. He was the only person who could wield any influence over the Spider, who for once in his life had behaved as a king should. "As a king doing honor to an equal," Hastings said.

While the earl was in France, occupied with statecraft, in England the court was busy preparing for the Burgundian champion. He had accepted Anthony Woodville's challenge, and had given Chester Herald his own rich cloak as a reward for bringing the Flower of Souvenance, with its message. I thought of the Burgundian as a knight errant, determined to prove his worth and win a high reputation because he felt unhappy on account of his illegitimacy; if he had a proud and sensitive nature, the bar sinister might shadow his spirits. I pictured him as the Knight of the Swan who had come back in another guise.

Crowds hurried to catch sight of the masts and sails taking shape out of the golden mists on the river. A flotilla of brightly ornamented barges set out to meet the Burgundians and escort them up the Thames to London. During their stay, the Bastard and his knights were lodged in the Bishop of Salisbury's palace, in rooms hung with cloth of gold. The June days were warm and sunny, showing London in its fairest aspect. The town houses of lords and prelates lined the river and their gardens were abloom to the water's edge. The swans went gliding up and down, past palaces and ships—the king's swans aloof and proud in their security.

Just beyond the walls the countryside was patterned with orchards and farms, green fields, and flowery meadows, with woodlands in the distance. The roads were crowded with people coming into London, eager to catch a glimpse of the contest between the Burgundian and Anthony Woodville. Before the foreigners appeared, London was already in a fever of anticipation. The last formal tournament held in England had been in honor of Henry the Sixth's marriage to Marguerite of Anjou, before I was born, and I was eager to see one. At first, George had refused to show any interest. He would be present, he had told me, but would take no part in aggrandizing the Woodvilles. However, he had changed his mind—or his mood—and entered into all plans with zest.

The Burgundian was not only the victor of every tournament in Europe, he had fought against the Infidel, and if he had lived in another age he might have been a great crusader, like his ancestor Godfrey. But when the Grand Bastard came into the royal presence chamber at Westminster, and I met him face to face, I was ready to burst into tears. He was squat and hairy.

Coarse hair bristled on his head and sprouted on the backs of his hands. He looked out from under bushy eyebrows—and had to peer up at Edward. Yet the champion, ill-made as he was—gave an impression of bodily strength. He was heavily muscled, with a bull neck and powerful shoulders. Anthony Woodville, taller, but slight of bone, might very well quail at the prospect of an encounter with this foreigner.

I managed to stammer out a few words, but my face must have betrayed me, because later in the evening, Edward asked me what I thought of the Grand Bastard. "I expected him to look the part of a hero," I answered, "and he's as ugly as a toad—a great bedizened toad!" I spoke without thinking. "There's a strong likeness," Edward agreed, "but in the lists he'll wear full armor. A helmet with the visor closed will improve his appearance. And you might find some very personable young men in his entourage." Edward glanced at a handsome boy standing nearby. "Yonder's one who seems to have found you; he's gazing at you with the eyes of a stricken calf." And he presented Monsieur de Croye to me.

The lists were built over a hundred feet long, and ninety feet wide, I heard. The timber and workmanship had cost over two hundred marks for the lists alone, to say nothing of the trappings, the decorations and the pavilions. On one side of the lists was the larger pavilion, provided with cushioned benches for the court, and gilded chairs for the king and queen, with an emblazoned canopy overhead. Opposite was another pavilion, for the Lord Mayor, alderman, chief magistrates, and most important citizens. Their robes of blue or crimson or violet or a combination of colors showed their office. The other sides of the lists, with tiers of benches, were for the people.

They came surging out of London's gates—all who could ride, walk, run, or hobble, and made their way to Smithfield. After a chill and cloudy morning, the day was fine, the crowds seemed in a merry humor. Men, women, and children were buying pasties— coney in rich sauce was their favorite, or flans made of honey-glazed fruits. Jugglers were performing, beggars were asking alms, and undoubtedly thieves and harlots were plying their trade. London prospered, and I saw many a silken gown and headdress of fine linen.

The clergy preached against vanity and worldliness; the Pope had condemned monstrous headgear and shoes made with excessively long pointed toes. My Lord Dorset said that the Pope's curse "wouldn't hurt a fly," and wore shoes with longer points than ever. Londoners followed the fashions of the court; the clothiers and goldsmiths had worked busily at costly materials from the looms of Flanders and the vats of the Eastern cities, fashioning settings for jewels, and hammering gold and silver into ornaments to satisfy an appetite for magnificence.

Heralds came and went, pages scurried back and forth. Behind the lists were the silken tents of the two contestants, and beyond a cluster of May trees showed their blossoms against the sky. And the shining green meadow was starred with daisies—as Marguerite of Anjou must have seen all those years ago when the tournaments had been held to do her honor, and the people had worn her daisy emblem. Somewhere in London Tower, Henry the Sixth was kept prisoner, while beyond his guarded doors and barred windows summer had come again.

The people hailed another king now. When Edward came, they shouted with uproarious goodwill. He was in purple; he wore the Order of the Garter and his collar of suns and roses. He had the kind of physical beauty that most impresses the mass of the people, and even at a distance had the look of vitality and strength that they needed in their prince. They likewise admired George, praising his looks, his bearing, and his manners. He seemed happy to agree to ride into the lists carrying Anthony Woodville's helmet.

Young Richard had his older brother's place in the pavilion—at the king's right. Richard held himself stiffly, and when he was not speaking or smiling he showed his usual solemn face. What was he thinking? No one would know, but he was pulling his dagger in and out of its sheath—a certain sign that his nerves were taut. How different he was from Edward, who talked with everyone near him, responded to the crowds, took wine and sweetmeats offered by the pages, and smiled at the women.

There were faces worth his notice, fair damsels, comely matrons, as well as others, less fair, but he seemed to smile at them all. Last night, one of the Burgundian lords had said that his master, Charles the Bold, took little interest in pleasure, but was eager for military renown and craved glory. "Not I," Edward had answered. "I'm content with what's rightfully mine, and only ask to enjoy it in peace." And he seemed entirely happy and at ease.

The highest ranking peers and chief officers of the crown were grouped around the king; below them were ranged knights, squires, and men at arms. At a little distance, and in the same order, the queen was surrounded by great ladies and demoiselles, gentlewomen, and lesser attendants. The Earl of Warwick was in France, the Duchess of York lived retired—others had absented themselves. More and more the Woodvilles dominated the court, looking around me, I saw how they dominated the tournament. Dorset had been quick to come forward and escort me to my place leaving his wife to the care of my Burgundian chevalier—to my annoyance, because his lack of concern for his wife doubtless hurt her and because I preferred the Burgundian.

Elizabeth's sisters knew how to adorn themselves in silks and fine tissue shot with gold or silver; the younger one wore wreaths of fresh flowers, and all of them displayed brilliant jewels. Jacquetta, mother of the Woodvilles, was present. Although Edward had made her husband "Earl Rivers" she refused to be Lady Rivers. She insisted on calling herself, and being addressed as the Duchess of Bedford, as if she had remained the widow of her first husband, the royal Duke of Bedford. He had been dead for many a year, but as he had been the brother of a king, she chose to use the title which had been hers during her first marriage, rather than the title of her living espouse.

Looking up, I caught her scrutinizing me, before her glance flickered elsewhere. She had eyes like a Romany woman I had once seen, and to find her watching me gave me a momentary sense of unease. The people said that her knowledge of the black arts had made Elizabeth's destiny. I realized why I had thought of the Romany for Jacquetta seemed to belong to a country farther away than Luxembourg, and I was afraid of her.

On the other side of the pavilion, the people crowding the benches stared at her, their faces sullen. They pushed and jostled to get a glimpse of the queen. Elizabeth wore white, embroidered all over with traceries of seed pearls, like a pattern of moonlight. A pearl-sewn headdress, heart-shaped and close-fitting, framed her face and gave emphasis to her eyes. Instead of the great golden crown, she wore a circlet of dazzling roses, made entirely of diamonds, the stones cut in the new way to wake all of their fire, and she held a cluster of fresh roses, diffusing their perfume in the heat. The flowers trembled in her unsteady hand.

The great crowd of onlookers felt the suspense. The heralds lifted their trumpets and sounded a fanfare, inviting the combatants to appear in the lists. The constable raised the white wand in his hand, and announced the tournament. Let the contest begin, in honor of God, St. George, the King and Queen of England, and the ladies. The heralds, followed by the pursuivants, advanced and cried the names and titles of the two knights, then withdrew.

First, George, Duke of Clarence rode into the lists, carrying Anthony Woodville's plumed helmet. His azure and crimson mantle and the trappings of his horse were emblazoned with England's lilies and leopards—as if he proclaimed that whatever part he took, he was not an upstart, nor a bastard. He was royal and true born.

The spectators—Londoners and Yorkists of all ranks—stood up, shouting his name.

Then the two knights rode in, from opposite sides of the lists. On horseback, the Bastard was not so underslung and ungainly. His crested helmet added height, and the visor drawn over his face hid his coarse features. But it was Anthony Woodville who held my attention. He had become transformed into a knight out of a romance or a legend, and appeared in the guise of the White Hermit. His armor was white and silver, the plumes in his helmet were black and white; his horse was covered with cloth of silver housings, the head adorned with a cluster of black and white plumes, and protected by a sharp steel horn, the chamfron, protruding from the forehead.

A squire followed, leading a second horse, with black and silver housings sweeping the ground, and on the horse's back was the hermit's cave—symbol of a life withdrawn from the clamor of the world. The cave itself was perhaps a light wooden frame covered with folds of cloth, skillfully painted to imitate a rocky ledge. I could imagine that such a cave existed, somewhere in the depths of the forest where Merlin had been held for centuries in his spellbound sleep and in the distance there was the faint glint of Camelot's moonlit towers. I could imagine the White Hermit, mysterious and melancholy, who had come to fulfill a vow, and would return to his solitude.

The opponents wheeled their horses and faced one another, then at the signal, charged. The lances were blunted, but the encounter seemed dangerous to me; the Bastard drove with his great strength, but was baffled by the White Hermit's quickness and deftness. He and his horse moved lightly, as if they followed the pattern of a dance. As he veered aside, the steel chamfron on his horse's head caught the Bastard's horse in the nostril, ripping it; the wounded horse, struggling to get free, reared and hurled his rider to the ground.

The Hermit was generous. He helped the Bastard to his feet, refused to take advantage of the accident, and insisted on going on with the combat. Edward asked the Bastard if he wished another mount. The Bastard declined—he chose to continue on foot, and to use spears. He brought his surliness into the lists, to judge from his lunging attacks, but after a time, Edward intervened. The tournament was for pleasure, he said, and he would not see his friends attack one another with such mischievous weapons. Let the outcome be decided without endangering their lives.

The Bastard and the Hermit took up battle-axes, and renewed the fight, circling, feinting, striking. As the excitement grew, women threw flowers, scarves, and gloves into the lists, tore their veils to shreds and were driven to ripping off the sleeves to fling. My hopes were on the White Hermit, but with every moment his chances grew less. He defended himself ably, but he must gain some advantage before the stronger man wore him down. The Bastard had only to wait. I saw the Hermit dodge a blow, swerve with catlike agility, and swing his battle-axe. It struck the Bastard's helmet. The sound of steel ringing against steel echoed in an almost complete silence. The spectators were too intent to shout or speak. The spur of the axe had caught on the Bastard's visor. He wrenched free at once, arm uplifted to deliver a mighty blow. With the effort, he somehow lost his footing, stumbled, and fell sprawling. The cloud of dust rose from the ground.

In a moment, he was on his feet again, but he yielded the victory. Edward gave the signal, and the most notable tournament of the century had come to an end.

"Take each other by the hand," he ordered, "and love one another like brothers in arms." The White Hermit raised his visor, and became Anthony Woodville again, but he held out his hand to the other in friendship like the "perfect gentle knight." The crowd

85

was cheering, and Elizabeth threw her roses into the lists. They fell at her brother's feet, and every lady present, with a flower left to throw, tossed them beside the queen's roses. He saluted the king, the queen, and the ladies, gathered up the roses, and left the lists with his squires.

Elizabeth smiled at Edward, savoring her triumph.

❧ *Twelve*

Edward had invited the Burgundian lords and the court to sup at Windsor. Before dusk, thousands of wax candles glittered in the castle, torches were lighted in the gardens and along the walls. With sunset the dancing began; flowers and garlands wreathed the columns in the great hall, the floor was strewn with flowers and herbs to be crushed under the feet of the dancers. My Burgundian chevalier, Monsieur de Croye, sighed because he was setting out for the Low Countries at dawn. He was handsome and courteous, and I was well pleased to have him pay me ardent homage during his stay in England, but was reconciled to his going.

He had already confessed that he loved me, but was about to be married to a well-dowered demoiselle whose lands marched with his.

"You will be happy with her," I predicted.

"Not when I leave my heart in England," he sighed again and kissed my hand, as we began the slow, stately pavan, but he could not linger with me through all of the figures of the dance. We were swept away from each other and I was too much absorbed in the joy of dancing to care.

After all, he would soon be gone, and very soon I would forget him as he would forget me.

George claimed me for a courante, and I was vain enough to be pleased when he signaled me out, but I was puzzled for I did not believe that he felt anything more for me than cousinly affection. A change of partners brought me face to face with Dorset. He took my hand and drew me into the line of dancers and into the intricacies of a gaillard, demanding agility and skill. Dorset was expert and the music was luring. Now in light, now in shadow the dancers glittered and faded, then reappeared, spinning and spiraling to complete the design, and bringing to an end all the festivities of the day and the night.

The crowd of guests were dispersing, but Margaret of York and I, with some others, including Dorset and his wife, were staying at the palace for the night. He offered me his arm to escort me to the king and queen, who were surrounded by a throng waiting to make their farewells before leaving the castle. I was anxious to escape from Dorset as my chevalier was following me. Suddenly George stepped in front of Dorset and said, in a loud, angry voice, "Where is your wife?"

I knew that tone, George was ready to force a quarrel.

"She had overtaxed her strength"—Dorset's tone was bland—"and preferred not to dance. So I put her in her mother's care."

"Her mother left here hours ago," George said. (I had seen her leaning tipsily against Sir Thomas St. Leger, laughing and pawing at him as they went out together.)

George pointed a finger at Dorset. "When I happened to come upon your wife, she was wandering about in the dark, all alone. And why? Because you berated her—called her clumsy, told her she made a fool of herself and you by shambling about—that you'd prefer to be partner to a performing bear." And added: "You forget who she is—how far above you."

Dorset was shaking with rage, and tried to speak, but George cut him short.

"I will take charge of my cousin. Come with me, Cicely," he commanded, and drew me away.

Muttering under his breath, he hurried me across the hall. He had urgent business in London, he said, and relinquished me to Monsieur de Croye. He had followed me, and when I turned and summoned him with a look, he came up to me. We went out on the terrace, and were not alone, but at this hour, no one was likely to notice me.

Monsieur de Croye startled me by asking if my guardians were likely to think that he was an eligible alliance for me.

"But you are committed to a marriage in your own country," I reminded him.

"But no promises have been exchanged."

"My guardians have no fault to find with you, but they want me to marry in England."

Sail away, and spend the rest of my life in a foreign land, the very thought of it seemed absurd. But when Philippe de Croye put his arms around me, I not only allowed him to kiss me, but returned the kiss with more fervor than I had intended.

"I will think of you—remember you always," he said, "and perhaps now and then you will have a thought to spare for me."

When he had gone with the Grand Bastard's entourage I lingered at an upper window, too restless to sleep, although it was near dawn. The room was dim lit and silent. One of the smaller antechambers, it was rather sequestered. A tapestry-hung doorway gave on to a passage and the stairs. Another door led to the rooms where Margaret of York and I were lodged, but instead of going on to my bed, I stayed here, leaning out of the casement, watching the lights on the barges flicker and fade away.

A slight sound made me turn. I was no longer alone in the room. Dorset had come in. "I'm sorry if I startled you," he said, coming nearer, and eying my face. "After dancing all night you are still as fresh and lovely as morning."

"And you still indulge in flights of fancy," I told him. "But now it is morning and I bid you good day." I made a move for the door.

"Before you go, tell me what I've done or said to offend you, and how I can make amends."

"You would do better to try to make amends to your wife," I answered.

"You heard a much distorted account, and are quick to blame me."

"It's not my place to blame you."

"But you do! No, don't go," he pleaded, standing directly in front of me. "It's not her fault, but is it mine if I recoil from her touch? From the first, I've battled to hide my distaste."

"Hide it from me," I said, "and if you have any kindness, from her."

"It's easy for you to preach kindness, and affection. Easy for Edward to clap me on the back and tell me to bed with her often. Make children."

I tried to interrupt him, but he went on, "I am virile," he boasted, "but I'll never be able to beget an heir on her sickly body."

"You were not forced to marry Anne Holland," I reminded him. "You seemed very eager. And she's in better health now than she was then!"

"Who would be fool enough to throw away such a chance? The richest and greatest match in England!"

Suddenly, he grasped me by the shoulders, pulled me to him and kissed my mouth, stifling me.

"By good luck, the tournament was held yesterday, not to-day" seemed to be the universal comment, because the fine weather had changed. The dull skies threatened and in the evening, rain was falling, but by then Margaret of York and I had returned to London, and the household at Baynard's Castle—to the real world. Margaret and I were alone in the solar, and had taken up our embroidery, working on a segment of the rich material destined for an altar cloth. It was a tedious task, I told her, and would take years to complete.

"If ever," Margaret sighed. "Here I've used azure where the design calls for green." She jerked out the threads with an impatience that she seldom displayed, and began folding the length of stuff.

"The light's too dim," she said.

From the look on Margaret's face, I knew that something troubled her, and waited.

"I'm not entirely sure yet, but . . ." she began, but before she could say what was in her mind, one of the pages opened the door to announce George, Duke of Clarence and Richard, Duke of Gloucester.

Richard spoke to us in a quiet voice, but I scarcely noticed him. I watched George. Without a word of greeting, he went up to his sister. "Well, Meg, must I wish you joy?"

"What do you mean, brother?" Margaret asked.

"Charles of Burgundy needs England as an ally, so he's come to heel, and renewed his offer to marry you," George told her. "What was the object of all the pretty mummery? To bring the Burgundian emissaries over here. While the feasting and capering was going on, and the so-called champions pranced around the lists, the treaty was drawn up, signed and sealed. Edward signed it—with the Woodvilles hovering around him."

George's announcements took me entirely by surprise, and revealed me as a simpleton, gulled by pageantry and my own fancies. The enterprise, undertaken in the spirit of chivalry, had been an illusion to hide the cold maneuverings of state policy. A clause in a treaty decided Margaret of York's destiny, and would take her away from us. She had been brought up with the idea of making a match for the good of the country and the House of York, but tears stood in her eyes, and George said nothing to soothe her by repeating, as she already knew, that Charles of Burgundy was the most quarrelsome prince of Christendom and hated her family.

"You will induce him to change his mind," I said.

"He has good qualities," Richard put in. He had retreated to a chair at a little distance, and sat frowning at the chessmen on the table in front of him. Castles, kings, queens, bishops, knights, and pawns were set out on the board. A few moves had been made, but the game had yet to be played. "The earl wants you to marry a French prince, but name me one who can compare to Charles of Burgundy in wealth and power. Edward's right to make the greatest possible alliance for you, sister."

"And how did he go about it?" George demanded. "By lulling the earl with promises."

"No promises," Richard corrected.

"Don't haggle over words." George began to pace about. "Edward gave him full powers to treat with the French king, but to himself Edward said, 'Godspeed, cousin Warwick, and a merry chase after will of the wisps!' Without warning, the earl's work—his long patient work—has been destroyed, and his wisdom cast aside! For the second time!"

None of us had forgotten the first time: his secret marriage to Elizabeth Woodville.

"Edward shows his will to make a mock of Warwick before the world." George turned to Richard, and grasping the edge of the table leaned over it. "How long do you expect a man of his stature to endure one gross insult after another?"

"A man of his stature is not so easily made small," Richard answered.

"No, but you'll have to admit Edward's heartless ingratitude." George brought his clenched fist down on the table. The chessmen tottered and fell, some on the board, and some on the floor. Only a few were left standing.

"What of your own ingratitude?" Richard asked, and seeing her two brothers confronting each other, Margaret intervened. "If you must quarrel, do it elsewhere! You forget yourselves!" Tears stood in her eyes. Richard asked her pardon, and mine. George went to her and kissed her. "I'm in a dark mood because I dread the thought of your going from us."

Margaret forgave him, but warned him to guard his tongue. "Edward and the earl will soon be friends again," she predicted. I doubted if she was fully convinced herself.

George resumed his restless pacing. "Edward'll try to gloss over matters," he muttered.

"We are gloomy," I said to Margaret, "but you will be the greatest lady in Europe. Greater than any queen."

"But I still envy you, Cicely—you won't be wrenched away from family and friends and home. You can hope to marry in England."

"To fall prey to the Woodvilles?" George wheeled around.

"All of them are married or promised in marriage."

"Not all," George told me. "Elizabeth still has a second son by John Grey."

As the boy was being educated at Cambridge, and was seldom at court, I had forgotten his existence. "He's only a child."

"That won't hinder Elizabeth when she hunts a rich wife for him. Do you think that Hastings or Warwick could defend you? You would be a tasty morsel."

"She'll stalk bigger game for her brat," I said, "so I'm in no danger."

"Elizabeth is dangerous to all of us," George said. He was overexcited, and Margaret tried to reason with him. "You paint her too black."

"You'll be making your escape from her, and the whole Woodville brood. Edward loves them because they are pliant reeds who fawn and flatter, while they plot against Warwick and Hastings and you, Richard! And me!"

"They could never touch you, or Richard," I said.

"You overrate their influence, brother," Margaret told him, and Richard agreed. "In matters of policy not even Elizabeth could persuade Edward to take any course against his will."

"Before she cast her spell on Edward, he and Warwick were friends, but not any more. Do you think that our brother the king will ever forgive Warwick for telling him the truth? He was the only man in England who dared tell him that only evil would come of his secret marriage to Elizabeth Woodville."

Charles of Burgundy had promised to open the Low Countries to English cloth.

"That's a great advantage to us, as any child can see," Dame Joan Wynant said, "and though you mope at the thought of my Lady Margaret's going, the king has made a splendid alliance for her."

"Doubtless the whole country agrees with you, and yet the earl has grounds for complaint."

I had just paid a visit to my mother. She was indignant at the treatment Warwick had received, and though she was more reasonable and less violent than George, she blamed the Woodvilles.

"To sign and seal the treaty behind the earl's back seems knavish," Dame Joan admitted.

However, when the earl came back to England, bringing the French ambassadors with him, Edward received them in state, and listened courteously, although his lack of interest in what they had to say, or offer, was plain to all present. Elizabeth's father and two of her brothers—Anthony and John—were standing near Edward during the interview.

The earl seemed to accept the defeat of his policy with calm, but as he left Westminster with the French lords, his wrath flashed out.

"Did you see the traitors who surround the king?" he asked, and the Admiral of France answered, "My lord, you will be well avenged."

Ominous words, I felt, when George reported them. He quickly added, "But it would be imprudent to repeat what was said."

His sister Margaret and I promised to hold our tongues. As if we would babble on such a matter! But for George to counsel us to be prudent made us laugh. A few angry words were unimportant, I decided, and I soon forgot what George had told us. There was no open quarrel between Edward and the earl, who made only a brief stay in London. The day before he left for the north, he came to Baynard's Castle to make his farewells to my lady Duchess. Margaret and I were expected to be present, and no one else was admitted to the room where the duchess received members of her family in private.

After the earl had greeted us, he went to Margaret and kissed her hand. "I salute the Duchess of Burgundy," he said, and spoke of the brilliant prospects ahead of her, as if he had forgotten his bitterness, or had never felt it.

"Gaining you is Burgundy's great good fortune."

"I hope that the alliance will prove fortunate for us," she answered.

"We must hope so." His response was temperate, I thought, but he directed the rest of his conversation to my lady Duchess, and while they talked together, I watched him, and remembered what others had said of him—"the finest knight now living," or "Warwick the king-maker," or "the Earl." In his bearing, looks, and manner he gave the impression of greatness. How could he have any liking for the Spider King of France? What could those two have in common?

Every country, including France, was afraid of the Spider, and though he had never showed any remorse for his sins, he was fear-ridden, and dreaded death.

I could understand why the earl commanded his respect, but the earl's attitude puzzled me, and I pondered over it during his visit. The time passed pleasantly, but when he was ready to take his leave, he spoke again to Margaret of her future, and spoke with great seriousness. "You are certain to wield some influence in your new country, and I trust your good sense. I dare to warn you of possible troubles lying in wait for Duke Charles. Do your utmost to persuade him to make peace with France."

"I will try, I promise you, but I doubt if I ever will have any such influence," Margaret answered.

"Do what you can—your destiny will be linked to his. Burgundy is strong and rich, and in England, Burgundian victory seems certain."

My lady Duchess frowned a little. "You seem to have your doubts."

94

"Yes, because Charles of Burgundy glories in being called the Bold." The earl had put aside his personal feelings or so I felt.

"Louis of France cringes." The duchess was scornful.

"But he has infinite patience, and great foresight," the earl answered, and his cool judgment spoke. "In war, there are no certainties." He seemed to forget us and had become as remote as a hawk in the sky, searching out a wider landscape than the one we knew, and seeing what was still hidden from our eyes.

The Earl of Warwick went into the north, where his wife and his two daughters lived, where his friends and his Neville kinsmen gathered to do him honor, and no one challenged his power. In London we saw what happened to another man who opposed the Woodville power. His name was Sir Thomas Cook, and he was one of the richest of the city's merchants. Unluckily for him, he had built a large house, and among other luxuries, had adorned it with a remarkably fine set of tapestries.

Lady Jacquetta had seen them, and coveted them. She offered to buy them—at less than their worth—and Cook had refused to sell them, at any price. Soon, he was accused of conspiring with Lancastrian agents, arrested and tried, but as no evidence could be found against him, he was acquitted. The verdict was no safeguard. On some legal pretext, he was fined a great sum of money. To pay it, he was forced to sell his house, and Jacquetta finally had her way. She gained possession of the tapestries, at a small price.

"Of course she wove a plot against an innocent man," George said. "The earl was convinced of his innocence, and sent him a letter telling him so, and money as well. This Cook business shows the people whom they can trust."

"For God's sake, watch your words!" Margaret begged him.

George laughed. "I do—elsewhere. I'm as much a pattern of prudence and discretion as brother Richard!"

Very likely he was telling the truth, I thought. Otherwise, we would have heard some echo of his remarks, and not a whisper had reached us.

"I promise to hold my tongue, if a vow will please you and Cicely," George went on, "but all of the other tongues will go on wagging."

London was abuzz, and I listened to the talk around me. Sir Thomas Cook was a victim of the Woodvilles—of Jacquetta's black arts. Perhaps she was a witch, but was Edward deluded and deceived by spells and magic?

"Why did he allow Jacquetta to despoil Sir Thomas Cook?" I asked Will Hastings, as soon as I had the opportunity.

"Edward has good grounds for believing that Cook was acting for the Lancastrians. Shear off some of his wealth, and he won't be able to send so much money to Marguerite of Anjou."

"But did he? Where's the evidence?" I persisted. "None was forthcoming."

"Edward has his informers, and paid spies," Hastings answered. "They report to him what they can glean, but if they showed themselves in open court, they could never be useful as agents again."

"I can understand that, but then any man might be convicted on secret information, and that would make a mock of justice!"

"Justice can and has miscarried in open court," Hastings argued. "Witnesses sometimes give false testimony. Juries might be made up of knaves or fools, judges and juries might be bought or intimidated, but it's not likely now."

Hastings defended Edward, but the case of Sir Thomas Cook made him uncomfortable. Perhaps his answers failed to satisfy him, and I went on asking myself what had become of the young king—the Edward who had filled the people's hearts with hope, and had taken his place on the king's bench to make sure that his judges were honest and impartial.

As I left London behind me and journeyed to the west country, to see to my estates, my doubts receded. On the way, we saw market towns busy with buying and selling, passed prosperous farms, and little hamlets, nestled in blooming gardens. There were new manor houses being built—more than ever in the last two years. Now even lesser gentry had their enclosed parks, stocked with red and fallow deer, but instead of strong walls and arrow slits for windows, the manors and town houses were made in the new way, with large rooms, many windows and chimneys. "In former times, only the greatest lords had windows filled with glass," Dame Joan Wynant said. "Now every manjack must have them."

We found Exeter flourishing on its waterborne commerce; the river carrying many a boatload of fish and foreign goods as well, to be sold inland. English wares and wool woven into fine serges were brought to the port. In Exeter, as in London, the people expected great things from the treaty with Burgundy for the rich markets of the Low Countries would be open to us.

The town was full of sailors, some from countries far away, and the ships sailed to Jutland and Spain and Finisterre. The weather was fair, and the restless treacherous sea glittered in the light, tempting men to venture.

My mother was unable to come with me to my estates, as she was waiting for the birth of a child, praying for a son, hoping to give Will Hastings an heir. I was thankful that Dame Joan, who had buried two husbands, was disinclined to take a third. Although I would not blame her for marrying again, a husband might take her away from me, and I would be lonely indeed without her. My mother's marriage to Will Hastings had proved a blessing for me, but his amours with other women caused her great unhappiness, and troubled me.

When I saw Shute again after a long absence, the sight of the woods and the manor house made me feel a world away from Windsor and Westminster, and I was glad to make my escape.

The west country gentry who had been loyal friends to the Bonvilles came to Shute. Most of them lived on their estates, often

97

put to sea, but only rarely if ever made the journey to London, or put in an appearance at the royal court, but they brought me news of what was happening in the rest of England since I had left Baynard's Castle.

Edward dismissed his treasurer, who was a stout friend to the Earl of Warwick, and gave the office to Elizabeth's father. Edward thought well of his ability. He had proved useful in carrying out several missions and various business transactions for the crown. But of all the Woodvilles he was the most hated.

"If he has something to gain, he's fawning, otherwise we must endure his arrogance," Will Hastings had said, but what caused most concern was his greed. The gentry and people of the west country told me that the upstart was too greedy to be honest in office. The public money would stick to his fingers.

Shortly afterwards, Elizabeth's brother John married the Dowager Duchess of Norfolk. Neither Lords nor Commons were squeamish when it came to making a match which promised material advantage, but laity and clergy cried out in protest at this one. John Woodville was a fine-looking young man of twenty and his bride was "a skittish damsel of some eighty winters," and an old fool as well as an old hag, but she had immense riches. All over England, bishops and priests protested that the marriage of a young man and an old woman was contrary to the laws of God and nature—a travesty contrived by the Devil himself.

Then a French spy was caught, and when hot irons were applied to his feet, the wretched creature screamed out a number of names. One was the name of Sir Thomas Cook. Edward had always maintained that Cook was a Lancastrian agent, conspiring with France and Marguerite of Anjou, but in the west country, as in London, the people saw him as a victim of the Woodvilles, and discounted the spy's information. It was proved worthless anyway for he had also named the Earl of Warwick.

Edward ignored the accusation, and the earl disdained to make any answer. His deeds answered for him. The luckless spy was hanged. He was one of the French Spider's creatures.

After the man's execution, honest citizens were ready to see

French spies behind every hedgerow, lurking in every shadow. There was talk that the French were planning to invade England.

"There's no truth in the rumors," I told my men, who were keeping constant watch in scanning the sea for the sight of hostile ships. "We can sleep in peace."

"Men say it's an uneasy peace," my steward answered.

In early autumn, while I was still at Shute, John Dynham sent word that he had come to spend some weeks on his estates, and would pay his duty to me. The following day he and his mother rode up to Shute Manor, and as the dark came early accepted my hospitality for the night.

"Perhaps you can tell us what to make of the wild tales drifting to our ears," Dame Joan said to John Dynham, after we had supped and were sitting by the fire. He smiled and asked which ones had reached us.

"A swarm of French spies were said to be in our midst, but I don't believe it."

"The Spider of France has always sent his agents into this country, and every other country. Doubtless the usual number are here now, but they're no more dangerous now than before."

"We've heard of unrest here and there," Dame Joan continued. "In Exeter, and even here, secluded as we are, the people seem apprehensive—without knowing why."

"The government has unearthed a few bits of evidence," John Dynham spoke slowly, "that rumors have been deliberately planted, and fears aroused, and suspect disaffected Lancastrians, but who are they? No one knows or will admit knowing anything about the troublemakers."

His mother looked up from her needlework. "The Woodvilles are the real troublemakers." She was not echoing her son's opinion, I knew, but stating her own. Lady Dynham judged for herself. "And will make trouble for anyone who stands in their way."

"You know them better than anyone," I said to John Dynham. He stared at the fire, watching the driftwood blaze up in strange blues and greens as if he expected to see salamanders dancing in the flames.

"When I fisrt saw Elizabeth Woodville in Whittlebury Chase I thought that she was one of the heathen spirits that still exist in the forest. I'm still afraid of her."

❧ *Thirteen*

Parliament had granted the necessary sum as a dower for the Lady Margaret of York, and she had appeared before the Royal Council to give her willing consent to the marriage arranged for her. Since then, time had passed, but Charles of Burgundy had made first one excuse then another to postpone his wedding, and in England Lords and Commons were grumbling at the delay. So matters stood when I went back to Baynard's Castle in early winter. Margaret's jewels and bride clothes were ordered, but her mother's elderly ladies in waiting, huddled over their needlework, sighed dolorously, and told one another that the marriage would never take place.

Margaret seemed quite content to wait at home, but George who had always been against the match, was furious at the slight offered to his sister. He had the grace to hold his tongue in her presence, but vented his feelings to me. "Charles of Burgundy goes bellowing off to make war, and leaves Margaret a puppet dangling on the end of a string." I was entirely in accord with him, but tried to soothe him. He was living in his town house—a palace in size and luxury—surrounded by his friends and winning popularity in London. Through the winter, Edward was often away from the city, and George reaped the homage.

The people admired his loyal affection for the Earl of Warwick, his filial respect for his mother and his affection for his sister Margaret—the citizens saw his barge on the river, going and coming to and from Baynard's Castle. Since I had last seen him, he had grown taller, and the added height made his good looks more impressive than ever.

"His faults are not in his face," I said to Dame Joan Wynant.

"Do you find fault with him otherwise?"

"I always did, you know."

"When you were only a child, but both of you have changed. You have become beautiful."

"In your eyes, but you are partial."

"In the world's eyes—certainly in his. I blame him for showing his feelings so plainly, before the king and the whole court."

"Do you blame me for any lack of reserve?" I took both of her plump little hands in mine.

"No, child, you never gave me cause, but I have wanted to warn you, but with young people, warnings and opposition serve to incite."

"Are you warning me against giving my love to George? I never will—and would have told you so if I had known that you were concerned."

"Of course I'm concerned! The king doubtless has his own designs for George, and he must obey, even if he loves elsewhere."

"If he loved me would he parade his feelings in public?"

Dame Joan considered his behavior in a new light. "If he's trying to cozen you out of vanity, I blame him more than ever!"

"With him, vanity would take another form, but he has some reason."

"And is making use of you?" Dame Joan was more indignant than ever.

Either cousinly fondness, or pricks of conscience, or a need to confide his secret, gave me part of the answer; on George's next visit I found out why I was useful to him. It was a rainy, blustery day, and the light waned early. In the solar, Margaret and I yawned over our needlework until George was announced. He enlivened our dullness and brought the stir of the busy world with him. He had dined with the Lord Mayor, and some of the most

101

influential citizens, which explained why he wore such rich clothes. They had expected him to appear as a prince, in velvet, ermine, and splendid jewels.

George flung himself in a chair and gave us what news he had gleaned, but in a few minutes, he left his chair, and after wandering about, came to halt by the hearth. When he held out his hand to the blaze, I noticed his rings. One took my eyes. It was a large emerald set in goldsmith's work, and I had never seen it before. Neither had Margaret, and while I admired the stone and the unusual design, she asked George who had sold it to him and how he had happened to find it.

"You're not going to find another among a merchant's wares," George told us, taking it off, and giving it to her. She examined it and passed it on to me. The emerald was beautiful, the setting was finely made, but the whole ring was massive, suited to a man, but too heavy for a woman.

"Italian jewelers make the same kind of ring," said George, "to hold poison."

I returned it to him quickly and he laughed at me for my haste. "You needn't shrink from this one, Cicely. It doesn't hold poison. It holds something of far greater value than all the gold and jewels in the world!"

George's eloquence startled me. His sister looked at him with a puzzled frown on her face. "Then what does it house?"

"If I trust you and Cicely with a secret, will you keep it?" He had become solemn and mysterious. When we nodded, he touched a hidden spring and opened the ring. Behind the emerald was a small hiding place. With an air of triumph, he drew out a tendril of dark silky hair. Margaret glanced quickly at my black braids, which were too densely black and straight to match the few coiled threads—a wisp of a ringlet small enough to fit into the hollow of the ring.

"You would be quite safe in displaying it," Margaret said. "No one could identify it." And she added: "She was not overgenerous, was she."

"I've acquired a long curling strand, but I've put it away. This is easier to wear—to have always with me!"

"Who is she?" Margaret asked, but George refused to tell her name. I did not need to ask, I could guess, and George's secret weighed on my mind. Because it was a dangerous secret.

After he had gone from Baynard's Castle, Margaret and I sat in silence for some time, and then she said, "George should have confided in us sooner."

For my part I would have been better pleased if he had kept his emerald ring in his strong box and held his tongue.

"He took me by surprise," Margaret began.

"Doubtless we should have expected him to set his heart on her," I said.

"Her!" Margaret leaned forward. "Then you know who she is!"

"One name comes to mind," I answered. "Isabel." The Earl of Warwick's eldest daughter. She and her sister Anne were well fitted to mate with princes, but there were difficulties.

"Why do you think of her?" Margaret asked.

"Not because she has dark brown hair, or because he prizes a love token."

"But if she gave it to him—" Margaret took my meaning. As she knew and I knew, Lady Isabel Neville, co-heiress of Warwick, was not to be treated lightly. I had not laid eyes on her for a long time, but from all accounts she was shy, and brought up to maintain reserve. If she had gone so far as to exchange love tokens with George, then he must be paying his court to her in earnest. He had gone to Middleham Castle last September, and had seen Isabel then, but had taken care not to mention her.

"George left most of his secret untold," Margaret said, "but I agree with you—Isabel must be the one."

Doubtless she saw George as a glittering young prince, and had willingly given him her heart. They might be happy together, but there were the two others to react—the Earl of Warwick and the King of England. The earl approved—more than approved.

I remembered what George had told us after he had been to the feast at Cawood Castle when the earl's brother had become Archbishop of York.

Edward had been unable to go into Yorkshire then, but had sent his two brothers. "And so Richard and I had the place of honor," George had told me—told me many times. "We were in the chief banqueting hall, and sat on a dais, under a canopy of state. More homage was paid to me, because I am older than Richard."

Neither the deference nor George's boasts were unusual or significant, but I remembered something else. The two demoiselles of Warwick, Isabel and Anne, had been seated at the same table—directly opposite George and Richard. "To please us by giving us companions near our own age," George had explained. The Countess of Warwick, who outranked her daughters, had yielded precedence to them, and had been content to sit at the second table. Evidently the earl had wanted his daughters to please the princes, and had succeeded.

At the time of the feast at Cawood, the earl and Edward had been friends, and George had openly extolled Isabel as the most beautiful young girl in England, and the sweetest-natured. He no longer mentioned her. Doubtless someone had urged him to be cautious.

"If you remember, George spoke of finding a wife at home," I reminded Margaret, "and had already found Isabel. Doubtless he hopes to marry her—with the earl's blessing."

"Then George does well to keep his hopes a secret"—Margaret gave a deep sigh—"and give up hoping. He is indulging in a boy's dream of love. But he must wake up."

"It would be an honorable alliance for them both," I argued. "Not only that, but they might be entirely happy together."

"But you know, Cicely, how when it comes to marriage, the king's brother must gain the king's consent, and Edward will undoubtly say 'no.' For reasons of state."

Margaret was right—and I realized why reasons of state stood in George's way. He was close to the throne, and as Duke of

Clarence, he was lord of towns, castles, manors, lands. Hundreds of men wore his livery, and how many hundreds more could he assemble if he chose? And if he married Isabel he would build up the earl's already formidable power—give him control over too large a wedge of England for the king's liking.

"There was a time when Edward might have been glad to say yes," I said, thinking of the past when he and the earl had been completely in accord.

"There was a time, before Edward made Elizabeth Woodville queen." Margaret spoke with more bitterness than I had ever known her to display.

George would be forced to give up his dream of love. He was changeable by nature, but this love of his for Isabel was interwoven with restless visions. I could only guess his state of mind but his secret troubled me. Although he knew that Edward would forbid the match, instead of being in low spirits, George had been elated. Did he intend to give up Isabel, and her share in the Warwick possessions? She had too much to offer. I suspected George of being deeply involved in making plans. He dared not let Edward get wind of a courtship which was being carried on as deviously as Edward's own.

It was a wet and unhealthy winter; in London and in the shires there was more sickness than usual, and a greater number of deaths were reported. Dorset's wife was taken ill with what some said was the sweating sickness. The physicians hovering around her bed tried a number of remedies, but she grew worse instead of better. When I saw her, I winced, and tears started to my eyes. However, she was able to talk a little and asked me to sit beside her, which I did, until she fell into an uneasy unresting sleep, muttering unintelligible words, sometimes groaning. It was the fever, her attendants said, and stood about helplessly, waiting for the queen's physician. Doubtless the heavy rainstorm had delayed him.

In the meantime, a steeping of medicinal herbs could do no harm, and might be soothing, I suggested. As I spoke, I was aware of someone standing directly behind me. I turned to see Elizabeth. She had come in as quietly as a shadow. Perhaps it was the dark veil over her head, or something in her look, but she seemed to me just as I had seen her for the first time.

"Dr. Serigo will be here shortly," she whispered, "but you are right. I have brought a potion to cool her fever and calm her sleep." And she added that her mother had gathered the herbs herself and had prepared the potion with her own hands.

Elizabeth was wintering at Greenwich Palace. She had come through wind, rain, and foulest weather, but when she mentioned the potion made by Lady Jacquetta, the waiting women glanced at one another, and hurriedly crossed themselves—behind Elizabeth's back.

When I left the bedchamber, and went into the adjoining antechamber, I saw Dorset, warming his hands by the fire. He came up to me, smiling. "It's been long months since I've seen you," he said. "First you linger in the west country through the Christmas festivities, then you shut yourself up in the vastnesses of Baynard's Castle."

"I come here, to your house occasionally. But this is the first time that I have encountered you."

Dorset's town house was a rambling palace, but I had yet to find him with his wife. However, I took care not to mention her, which seemed unnatural, but I wanted to avoid any more frankness from him in regard to his marriage. He insisted on accompanying me to my barge.

"And you need not tell me to go to my wife, I am on my way to her. She would never thank me for any discourtesy to you," he said, forestalling my objections.

As my own servants were following and the rooms, passages, and stairways were full of people, I was not alone with him.

"How do you like my house?" he asked. "It was Edward's gift."

I had an impression of rich furniture and hangings and every luxury, warmth from blazing fires, a glitter of light from lamps and candles, a parade of servants.

"A palace rather than a house," I answered, thinking that it was without the life and breath of home.

"You are not enraptured," Dorset said. "Doubtless you have finer castles in that far away west country where you disappear."

"You would find Shute Manor bleak and comfortless," I told him.

"Perhaps too near the sea for my taste. I detest its howlings and crashings. I would never willingly set foot on a ship."

By that time, we had neared the door. "You take some risk by going into the sickchamber of anyone with a virulent fever." Dorset spoke with an air of concern. "You might succumb to it yourself."

"Possibly, but it's not likely," I said. Even if I was afraid, I could not have stayed away, but it was useless to try to explain such a feeling to Dorset. "The queen is here," I pointed out.

"She never has any form of illness." Dorset seemed more indifferent to his mother's health than to mine. Certainly Elizabeth would brave worse danger to win Edward's admiration, but I had left her sitting by the bedside, holding the cup, and by using patience and skill, she induced her daughter-in-law to swallow the sleeping draught—drop by drop.

"At some time in the future, I'll entertain the whole court at a great feast," Dorset predicted, "and I hope that you'll be persuaded to grace the board."

"Your plans seem to me ill-timed," I told him, but he kissed my hand and begged me to guard my health. Perhaps it was the torchlight but his expression was sly and secretive and more than ever I sensed the indefinable mockery in his manner.

A week later, Dorset's wife died. Her obsequies were held with great solemnity and magnificence. On a fair day, full of the promise of spring, the long procession trailed into Kent, to the little church where Anne Holland, who had been niece to the King of England, heiress of Exeter, and Marchioness of Dorset, was buried with her Holland ancestors. I felt for her father, in his exile.

Although he had not seen her for years, she was his only legitimate child, and the news of her death must be a grief to him.

In her will, she had bequeathed some of her jewels to Margaret of York, and I was touched when I learned that she had thought of me. She had left me a heavy gold necklace, blazing with precious stones, and a ring set with a great ruby. I had noticed it on her finger, and had admired it. Elizabeth had treated her well; all of the Woodvilles had done what they could for her in her illness. Even Dorset had appeared solicitous—but any kindness from him came too late for her.

Elizabeth had seemed fond of her, but who would believe it? Her slyness and her greed in stealing a great heiress for Dorset were too well remembered. However, I remembered her gentleness and the pitying look on her face as she gave the sleeping draught. "As for Elizabeth's tears—she's suffered a great disappointment," Will Hastings pointed out. "Her fine son Dorset has been unlucky enough to lose his wife while she was still a minor. Her estates will revert to the crown."

Not to Dorset. Death had tricked him out of the rich Exeter inheritance.

Needlewomen and embroiderers, furriers and goldsmiths had done their work to make Margaret of York ready for her wedding. Everything was locked away in chests and caskets. At Baynard's Castle no one mentioned bridal robes to Margaret or to my lady Duchess until Edward came. He had some private discussion with his mother, then out of her hearing laughed at the elderly black-clad ladies who surrounded the duchess. They were as gloomy as a flock of moulting old ravens, he said, and advised Margaret to shut her ears to their croakings.

"Before summer's end you'll be Duchess of Burgundy, I promise you!" Edward told her. No doubt she wondered as I did what Charles of Burgundy's promises were worth, but Edward had complete faith in Burgundy's word, since he was outfitting ships to take Margaret to the Low Countries. "You'll go in great state, and the earl will act as your official escort to the coast. I've invited him and he has accepted."

At least we could be thankful that Edward had made a move to appease the earl, and even more thankful that the earl was willing to be appeased.

At last, after nearly a year of haggling and hesitating, Duke Charles declared his readiness to fulfill his promises, and sent his envoys to bring Lady Margaret of York to his domains. She and her mother exchanged their solemn farewells at Baynard's Castle, but I had a place in Margaret's entourage and was with her on the first stage of her journey—as far as the monastery of Stratford Langthorne. Her three brothers had taken other roads than hers, but would join her there, with the queen and the most important people of the court. The crowds who gathered along the way cheered when they saw the Earl of Warwick riding beside Lady Margaret at the head of the shining cavalcade.

At Stratford Langthorne a city of bright-colored tents had sprung up beyond the monastery grounds. I saw a young monk pause to gaze at us, then scurry away from the sudden onslaught of the world, the flesh, and the devil. During a stay of three days and nights, the time was given up to festivities in honor of Margaret's marriage, culminating in the banquet served on the last evening. The weather was hot, and the tables were set up in the gardens and the long colonnades of the cloisters.

In Edward's presence all quarrels seemed forgotten, and enemies wore masks of friendship. Elizabeth had made the earl welcome, and in her soft voice told him that he had been missed. Perhaps she hoped to make a truce with him. Some of his friends said that he had accepted the Burgundian alliance with good grace.

In public, Edward drank to his "good brother of Burgundy," and in private called him a madman obsessed with dreams of conquest. The Burgundian ambassador spoke at length on his master's great admiration and affection for the King of England. Actually Charles of Burgundy had invented and circulated a calumny—the grossest of lies—by pretending to believe that the Duchess of York had been guilty of adultery with a Scottish archer named Blackburn. He usually spoke of Edward as "the son of an archer."

Edward had heard the story, Hastings said, but had shrugged it off as another lie, not worth his notice, or any notice. He was armed with his own certainty that he was Duke Richard of York's true-born son. Not even his worst enemy could believe that Edward was other than he was. His mother was known for the strictness of her morals, and her devotion to her own husband, but it was Edward himself who gave proof of his lineage. In the molding of his bones, in his spirit—in the deeps of his nature he was the very essence of a Plantagenet.

Apparently unaware of any hidden conflicts, the people lighted bonfires, drank, and hailed Margaret of York's auspicious nuptials. The Burgundian envoys paid her homage, the Woodvilles crowded around her. Elizabeth praised her beauty, said how much she would be missed, but pictured the splendid destiny waiting for her.

"To my mind, Charles of Burgundy is the one who is fortunate," I said to Will Hastings, and the earl, who happened to be near, heard me and agreed. He had showed no sign of bitterness or ill feeling on the journey—partly because he seemed to admire Margaret, but while the court promised her every blessing under the sun, her cousin Warwick contented himself with wishing her well.

The earl had one ally in George. "Margaret is leaving all that she holds dear," he kept repeating to me. At the banquet, he was across the board from where I was, which was too near since Dorset was next to me and could watch him. Following the fashion, George wore a number of jeweled rings. I noted the great emerald on his finger, and then avoided looking at it. Knowing its significance, I was too much aware of it, but others were not, I told myself. Yet I was sorry to see it adding its particular fire to the blaze of rubies and diamonds and sapphires. George seemed to take pride in flaunting his secret.

Dorset was quick to drop all pretense of grieving for his wife. I had as little to say to him as good manners would allow, but he ignored rebuffs and persisted in talking to me. The Burgundian envoys were all old, he remarked. "The young lord who devoted himself to you last summer has been left to pine."

For a moment I was puzzled, and Dorset laughed. "You show a blank face! Have you forgotten him so completely?"

"He would be a fool to pine. By now he must be married."

"He is." Dorset told me.

I wondered why Dorset took the trouble to find out such a fact, but I did not ask him.

"Marriage is no sure cure for pining," he went on, "and my grandmother has told me that the demoiselles of the Low Countries are fair but more often than not lack savor."

"Then my Lady Jacquetta is very different from her countrywomen." I looked in her direction and saw her face in profile as she made herself agreeable to the highest ranking Burgundian. No one could be more agreeable, when she chose to be.

"Her family are given to foreign marriages," and with a challenging air Dorset mentioned Jacquetta's kinship to Marguerite of Anjou. "They're not so distant cousins."

Of the same blood, I remembered, and unlike as they were both were accused of practicing witchcraft. When I looked up I saw Jacquetta's bright hard eyes. She was watching me for a moment, and my scalp prickled with unease.

"Duke Charles breathes fire," Dorset went on, "but he's the richest prince in Europe. For his wedding, he'll appear covered with jewels from head to heel. He owns the Sancy and it's the largest and most perfect diamond in the world." Dorset looked across the board, not at faces, but at the display of jewels. There was the ruby in the center of Edward's crown—the Black Prince's ruby, one of the prizes of his victory at Crécy, and it still belonged to the victor of the battle.

Elizabeth's necklace, a double row of pearls fringed with pear-shaped pearls, brought another necklace to mind—Marguerite of Anjou had worn it.

George lifted his wine cup, and the emerald in his ring rippled with green lightning, attracting Dorset's gaze. He admired the stone's size and color. "I have a particular fondness for emeralds," he said.

"I have a particular fondness for this one," George answered.

"No wonder—the goldsmith's work is worthy of it. And skillfully designed—its secret use is to carry poison. You could have enough with you to put an end to some of us." Dorset spoke lightly, but I felt a tinge of mockery, of insolence lurking beneath the words. It was easy for him to strike sparks from George.

"I wear this ring as an amulet," George told him. "To ward off evil. Most of all to protect me against witchcraft."

We were crowded together in the monastery; my waiting women shared my bedchamber, but after they had fallen asleep Margaret came in to speak to me. We moved to the window and kept our voices to a whisper. Margaret hoped that I would be content to stay on with her mother when I was not in Devon, but her greatest concern was for her brother George. "Richard has more prudence, and he's more entirely devoted to Edward."

It would be useless to deny it, but I tried to calm her misgivings. "All these past months, George has behaved prudently." Until tonight, when he had mentioned witchcraft with emphasis on the word. He had turned his head and looked at Elizabeth, then at her mother—a look full of meaning. Dorset had understood. Doubtless I made too much of a small incident, but even a veiled accusation of witchcraft was a grave matter.

"I've begged him to be on his guard in his dealings with the Woodvilles. They are dangerous," Margaret said, "and his own cousin Warwick's influence is a greater danger."

"Since we've been here, they have been friendly, but Warwick has made no effort to seek him out."

"The earl is too wise to display his influence in public, but he may be tempted to offer Isabel. George still wears that ring," Margaret reminded me.

"So I noticed, but it's been a long time since he's mentioned love tokens to us," I said.

"Because he no longer confides in us," Margaret sighed. "I am afraid for George."

The ring was no talisman, I thought. It could lead George into danger. After Margaret had left me, I stayed by the window. It overlooked the Abbot's garden. The arches and columns made densely black shadows on the grass plot, but all of the other shadows were transparent in the summer night. The torches no longer burned, the music had come to an end. Voices and laughter had faded into silence. The monks were chanting, to remind us of the things of the spirit, and of a world beyond this one.

As I watched, a shadow at the far end of the cloisters moved, became a figure, the figure of a man, wrapped in a dark cape. He kept close to the columns, but as he moved again, I recognized him by his height. Edward. He had only one reason for being there at this late hour, to meet a woman, or perhaps a young girl—too easily persuaded to part with her virtue. Or a harlot, or a great lady playing the harlot. Then I saw her. She was veiled, but made no attempt to keep to the darkest shadows—stealthy and yet bold.

She held out her hands to Edward. He went to her, and they disappeared in the sheltering blackness of the colonnade, but not before I knew who she was. When Edward had come to her, she had pushed back her veil, and a wayward glimmer of light had showed me her face as she had looked up at him, ready to kiss and be kissed.

But why did Elizabeth and Edward clasp and kiss in the garden instead of in their bed? Doubtless Edward had stayed late with the envoys, and she had watched for him and waylaid him, impatient to lure him to her bed.

I waited, but they did not come. I hoped to catch another glimpse of them, but they had vanished like figures in a dream. Where? I remembered the little gate in the wall, leading not to the tents but opening to a coppice. A path wandered through the trees to a little river.

Why would the king and queen take that way? I could think

of reasons why Elizabeth would try to draw Edward with her beyond the walls—to re-create the summer nights at Grafton, when she had been his secret wife. Perhaps she hoped to renew his passion for her. The warmth, the perfume of flowers, the soft dark seemed made for the hot delights of sensual love. And yet, when I had first seen the veiled figure, I had the instinct that she was evil. I could not rid myself of that impression.

✿ Fourteen

Margaret sailed on the *New Ellen* of London, and thirteen other ships accompanied her to the Low Countries; the flotilla brilliant with silken streamers floating from the mastheads. The *New Ellen* was painted gold and azure, the sails were studded with the initials of the bride and bridegroom, Charles and Margaret. The wind was fair, the ships arrived safely, and Margaret was received with every honor.

"The good people of Bruges often include the Judgment of Paris in their pageantry," George had told me, "with three handsome naked girls to represent the three goddesses. And for good measure, they have sirens, naked, with long disheveled hair, disporting themselves in the water."

However, Charles the Bold was not so likely to entertain the English lords and gentlemen, as his father had done before him, by reserving all of the brothels in the town for the use of his guests, and at his own expense. (Duke Charles was often reproached for living too chaste a life.) His nuptial celebrations were the most elaborate and costly ever known, but from what we heard of them, Margaret must have found them very wearisome. The giant pastries, the dwarfs, the ships full rigged, the whales, and the monkeys—all must have been ugly.

On my return to Baynard's Castle, my lady Duchess showed me more affection than usual, and seemed glad to have me with her. "Although I must be prepared for you soon to follow Margaret's example and marry."

As my mother had been born a Neville, and the earl was the head of the family, she looked to him to arrange a suitable match for me. He would likely consult with my mother and my stepfather. My lady Duchess's approval would be asked, but Edward's consent was necessary. I took it for granted that he would agree to my family's choice, and I was thankful that my marriage was not an affair of state.

"Your Neville cousin has been mentioned," the duchess said, "but your mother thinks that the kinship is too close, and she's quite right."

As I was by no means eager to take a husband yet, and had never clapped eyes on the boy, I was content to give up all idea of the match. Elizabeth had defrauded him by stealing his promised wife—the Exeter heiress—from him and giving her to Dorset.

"You are young, and will never lack for offers," my lady Duchess pursued, "but perhaps the earl and your mother should be thinking of a match for you."

The earl was doubtless preoccupied with other plans, and I could expect to be free and single for some time to come. In my secret heart I yearned for an all-consuming and deathless love. How I envied Elizabeth Woodville!

At summer's end she was at Shene Palace, but I was in a mood when the festive life of the court wearied me. George went off to one of his manors in Gloucestershire, and the earl was in London, making a brief stay at Warwick House. When he came to dine or sup at Baynard's Castle, the sedate household woke to a bustle of preparation, in an effort to equal the hospitality of Warwick House. Occasionally he came without announcing his visit beforehand.

One evening the household had attended Vespers and had supped, and a torpor had settled on Baynard's Castle when the earl's barge appeared out of the hazy mizzle and drew in to the water gate. "My Lord Hastings is with him," a page told me, which was not unexpected for Hastings often came with the earl. My lady Duchess received them in her private apartments, and after some length of time, sent for me. I took the summons for granted, and would have felt aggrieved if Will Hastings, the kindest of stepfathers, had come and gone without asking to see me.

When I entered the room, my lady Duchess was sitting stiff and upright in her high-backed chair, and the two men were standing. All three stared at me. My knees grew weak. "My mother? Does anything ail my mother?" I demanded.

"Nothing—she's well," Hastings was quick to reassure me, "and in perfect health."

The room was dim, but I saw the black circles around his eyes and his rumpled hair, giving him an unfamiliar look of disarray.

"What we have to tell concerns you."

His gloom disheartened me. The earl was frowning too, his eyebrows making a straight sharp line. What had I done to offend him? Nothing! Then I realized that his wrath was not directed against me.

"I leave you to break the news to Cicely," my lady Duchess said. She held out her hand to me, then went out of the room, to shut herself in her adjoining oratory. When the door had closed behind her, Hastings drew out a chair for me, and took a nearby bench, but the earl remained standing. I clutched my hands together in my lap, and waited.

"Elizabeth has been busy," the earl said. "She has decided on a second wife for her son Dorset. You!"

"Second wife—oh, no!" I cried out. "The passing bell has just stopped ringing for his first wife."

"Did you ever suspect Elizabeth or Dorset of keeping an eye on you?" Hastings asked.

"At times," I admitted, "but I entirely failed to understand."

"How could you understand their schemings?" the earl asked. "You are too young, too innocent."

Not innocence but vanity had deceived me, I told myself. If I

116

had not been a fool, a witless fool, I would have seen why Elizabeth and her family had taken pains to cajole and flatter me. They had watched Dorset's wife wasting away, and had taken alarm. Even while they had hovered over her, they had looked around them to find another richly endowed heiress for Dorset. As they dared not aspire to any daughter of Warwick's, they had decided on me. They had undoubtedly calculated the value of my estates down to the last sheep, the last haystack. As they had foreseen, the Exeter heiress and her great property had escaped them, and they must content themselves with the Bonville heiress —a lesser prize.

"I am unwilling to have Dorset," I said.

"He's not our choice for you, God knows," Hastings sighed.

"Then you'll prevent . . ."

Hastings interrupted me. "I've done my best. I've just come from a long interview with Edward. I argued, I begged, but he's determined on the match. The contract is already drawn up. He showed it to me."

"And the terms prejudice your family's interest," the earl explained. "If you should die childless, or if Dorset found some excuse to seek a divorce, or if you try to separate yourself from him, all of your estates would revert to him."

"He'll trump up some flimsy pretext to cast me off, so that he can squander my inheritance!" I was burning with fury.

"A wife is not so easily put aside." Hastings tried to soothe me. "And I'll play devil's advocate. You can be sure that the boy has no such idea in mind."

"I mistrust him. And I deserve better."

"Much better," Hastings agreed, "but I can only advise you to obey the king."

Will Hastings was Edward's close friend, held high office, was well loved by peers and people but here he confessed himself helpless. All he could give me was tame counsel. I looked up at the earl. "Must I take Dorset?"

"I see no alternative," he answered, admitting another defeat in his strife with the Woodvilles.

The earl exerted himself to be kind to me. I must feel free to call on him, he said, but I sensed his impatience to end the interview and go. I realized how it galled him to admit aloud how little influence he had over Edward.

But I had my own bitterness. The earl had lost a minor skirmish, not a major battle, and would fight on. My whole future was involved. These two great lords of my own family—Hastings, my stepfather, and Warwick, my uncle—deserted me. It was not their fault, and yet I felt cast adrift to fend for myself.

"To be Marchioness of Dorset offers you worldly advantages, Cicely," Hastings pointed out.

"In these times, you have to scramble to make a marriage with one of the queen's family." The earl's tone was sharp with contempt. "It's the only road to royal favor and worldly success."

Hastings was ready to follow the earl out of the room.

"Edward feels strong affection for his own family, and his own friends," he said.

"Does he?" the earl demanded. "Edward tramples down any opposition from you to enrich Dorset, who is jealous of you and already plots against you. Do you still trust the king's friendship?"

"He can trust mine," Hastings answered quietly.

"Then I leave you to contend for his favor." The earl moved to the door, halted, and turned. "Edward makes a mistake if he thinks that the Woodvilles are strong enough to uphold the throne." He spoke without rancor, without personal feeling. He had set a distance between himself and his enemies—he looked down on them and appraised them with cold authority. "Edward decks them out in all of the trappings of greatness, but neither he nor any other king, emperor, or pope on this earth has the power to breathe into them what they lack—the soul of greatness."

My mother was reserved and self-controlled, but she showed something of her brother Warwick's nature in her anger, and berated Dorset, Elizabeth, and Edward with eloquence. "The marriage contract is grossly unfair to you and the children you might yet have by Hastings," I repeated.

118

"It's unjust, and very likely illegal, but my concern is for you. Your own family will lose you to the Woodvilles for Dorset is one of them."

"I will never be one of them, I promise you!"

"Marriage will change you," she prophesied. "Your interests will be bound up in Dorset's, it's unavoidable, because you will have to consider your children's interests."

"I will never change," I vowed, but I knew what my mother meant. The enmity between my own family and the Woodvilles threatened me with trouble. I felt more than ever forsaken.

The Duchess of York had been forthright in expressing her displeasure. "Once Edward would have listened to me," she said, "but that time has passed." And she advised me to do my best in the married state and to make Dorset a good wife.

"He is not seeking a good wife, madam, only goodly estates."

After my lady Duchess had talked to me at some length, I retreated to the solar. Most of my attendants had gone out to enjoy the bright evening weather, welcome after yesterday's chill rains. Londoners were playing at ninepins or tennis, practicing archery in the meadow beyond the city walls, going up or down the river in barges and wherries, or otherwise disporting themselves.

I had no heart for pastimes, and Dame Joan insisted on keeping me company in the solar. I made pretense of busying myself with needle and thread, but my eyes were heavy after a sleepless night. The design blurred and Dorset's face—his pointed chin and yellow-hazel eyes—seemed to look out at me from the pattern of leaves and flowers and fruits. I rebelled against being one more victim of Woodville greed.

The pages in the antechamber adjoining the solar opened the door and announced "The King's Grace." Edward sauntered in, gave us a smiling greeting, and told Dame Joan that every time he saw her she looked younger than before. She laughed, picked up her needlework and moved to the other end of the room. I stayed where I was, intent on watching Edward, and was unaware that I was twisting a thread of embroidery silk around my finger, drawing it tighter and tighter until my finger was numb. Even if important matters clamored for the king's immediate attention, Edward always had an air of being at leisure.

He invited me to sit down, and settled himself in a cushioned chair with his long legs stretched out in front of him. He had just come from Windsor, he said, and had stopped by to visit his mother. "And to see how you are faring. I had hoped to see you at Windsor, but since you failed to come, I must seek you out."

I thanked him for doing me the honor, and waited for him to say more. "Why do you stay mewed up here on a fine evening?" he asked. "Except for Dame Joan, you are surrounded by my mother's ladies, and they are dry stalks left to rattle in a winter wind. Are you well? You look somewhat pale."

I was quite well, I told him. He was very brown, I noticed, with ruddy color in his cheeks. His doublet was azure satin, the color of the sky, his belt was gemmed with pearls and sapphires and amethysts, and in his left hand he held a bright sweet-scented nosegay—cottage garden flowers, such as a child would gather to throw in the king's barge as he passed by. Some of my embroidery floss had fallen on the floor; Edward spied the tangle and picked it up. "A cat's cradle past unwinding," he said, and flung it aside.

Here he was, in what had been his accustomed place in times gone by. The lute on the wall, the books on the small table, the dappling of sun and shade reminded me of that time. So did Edward, leaning against the cushions, his feet crossed on a footstool. He held up the nosegay, savoring the perfume, and he reminded me too sharply of the Edward before he had been king.

This was no time to dwell on what had gone. The future loomed, and I must speak out. While I was struggling to find the right words, Edward noted the thread wound tight on my finger. "Dorset will give you a fairer ring," he said. I stared at the thread, seeing it for the first time, and snatched it off. "Of course you know that he's made you an offer of marriage. With my full consent."

"So I've been told, and thank him for the honor, but I ask your permission to decline."

"Why?" Edward's dark blue eyes scanned my face.

"As the marriage contract was explained to me, he can put me aside and keep my estates."

"That will never happen. The provision is there only to make sure that your family will not be tempted to break the marriage."

"Any rights of my mother's are ignored."

"Shadowy rights at best," Edward argued. "You have sound health, you'll live long, please God, and have many children."

"Who knows?" I sighed.

"In any case, your mother is richly dowered, and I intend to give Hastings due recompense, so that she and her children by him will be well provided for."

"If my Lord Dorset is rash in spending my substance . . ."

Edward smiled. "I commend your prudence, Cicely, but you have nothing to fear. I'll safeguard you and your inheritance. You have my solemn promise."

I thanked him for his pledge.

"Apart from what I've given him, Dorset has succeeded to the lands and honors held by his own family," Edward pointed out. "He bears a Norman name as old as your own. Bonvilles and Greys have intermarried before now. You'll have a high place in the world."

"A lower would content me better."

"Your uncle Warwick—my good cousin Warwick—has done his work and primed you to be stiff-necked!"

"The earl's not to blame—I am. My reluctance is all my own."

"In God's name, why?" Edward demanded. "It's not as if I were trying to fling you into the bed of some worn-out dotard to warm his creaking bones with your young body—if I did, you would soon have a swarm of lovers."

Neither Edward nor his friends saw any wrong in adultery.

"I would rather be an honest woman."

"Then you need a young and handsome husband to satisfy

you. And I'm not urging you to bind yourself for life to an ass. Dorset has a shrewd brain."

Shrewd enough to win the king's favor. He was greedy, and heartless, but if I ventured to say so, Edward would never believe me.

"What more do you want?" Edward was patient with me.

Want? What I could never give Dorset, what he could never give, what Edward had seized for himself. Love.

"Dorset is very eager to have you," Edward told me, and as I made no response, he asked, "What secret are you guarding?"

His question took me by surprise, and doubtless my face reflected my confusion and unease. "Have you set your heart on George?" He was watching me closely.

Almost I was startled into blurting out "No! No! No!" But the burden of George's own secret held me back. I must take care not to betray him. "He can look higher," I answered.

"George and Richard must make foreign alliances, for the good of the country." Edward seemed sure of their obedience. The king's brothers must do their duty, although the king had shirked his—for Elizabeth.

"Then, my dear, all will be well!" Edward said, sure of victory, indulgent to what he took for reasonless whims, but implacable.

Shortly after, I was married off to Thomas Grey, Marquis of Dorset, in the presence of the king, the queen, the Woodvilles, and most of the court. Out of affection for me, her goddaughter and namesake, the Duchess of York attended the nuptial Mass, but not the wedding feast. The Earl of Warwick was in the north, which gave him a reason to absent himself. However, he had sent me jewels of great value as a marriage gift.

My lady of Exeter, mother of Dorset's first wife, was conspicuously on hand. She made an opportunity to come up to me, and breathing fumes of wine, mingled her felicitations with sighings for her dead daughter. "You've taken my child's place. Oh, I don't begrudge it to you—she was Dorset's first choice." Leaning over she had hissed in my ear, "Elizabeth paid me four thousand pounds for my consent to the match, much good it did her!"

Both of the king's brothers graced my wedding. Richard with his air of being alone in a crowd, wished me well in a gloomy tone. George took care to remind me of his predictions. "You thought yourself as safe as a little mouse in its hole, but the cat with green eyes was watching you, waiting to pounce—just as I warned you."

John Dynham gave me encouragement. "Dorset is unlikely to interfere in the administering of your estates. He is interested in keeping close to Edward—to make sure of Edward's favor, and his continued bounty."

I knew that Dorset preferred to be where he could watch his enemies. He never visited his own estates in the Midlands. As for going off into the west country, I could not picture him enduring one day at Shute. He was made for the luxury and glitter of court life.

We had our apartments in all of the royal palaces, and Dorset had a house in London, where we spent the first winter of our marriage. It was the house where my predecessor had died, but had been furnished anew for my coming. There were spacious gardens, sloping to the river, recently enlarged and replanted. Both without and within, Dorset's house was splendid enough to be the palace of the king's son, rather than the king's stepson.

Edward was lavish to Dorset, and to me as well. Elizabeth presented me with the nuptial bed, carved and gilded, inlaid with ivory; the hangings were crimson satin, lined with white satin. Lady Jacquetta had ordered the tapestries for my bechamber— the Four Seasons, worked in glowing colors, and showing a happy company of lovers reveling throughout the whole year in their own joyous world.

At the time of my marriage to Dorset, he was still a very young man but he already prided himself on his skill and prowess in sensual pleasures. He chose to play the amorous bridegroom, and as I was young and hot-blooded enough, I responded to his desire, for a few weeks, a few months, but the sad ghost of his other wife came from her grave to cast a chill shadow over my marriage bed.

"He wants you as he never wanted me," I could almost hear her say, "but he has a cold heart. He is trying all of his arts to seduce you into loving him because your reluctance to marry him is a challenge to him. He is seeking a personal triumph, but if you ever love him he'll quickly tire of you!"

And Dorset waking up turned to me and bit my shoulder. His teeth were sharp, and I jerked myself away from him. He laughed and drew me to him again. "Do you still remember the first time that you ever saw my mother?" he said.

"She and Lady Jacquetta were kind enough to come to that bleak manor house where the Duchess of York and her household were held."

"And they wanted to look over you—Dame Jacquetta thought of you as a match for me."

At the time, the household had wondered why Elizabeth and Lady Jacquetta had troubled to come. Now, years later, Dorset supplied the answer.

"My mother meant well by you. Lancaster seemed victorious, your family's estates were declared confiscated, but Marguerite of Anjou would have given them to my family, so better for you to marry me. Of course the war followed another pattern." Dorset laughed again, "But with all the changes, you were destined to marry me. So here we are snuggly bedded down together." He yawned and fell asleep.

My destiny had been decreed by Dame Jacquetta and Elizabeth. No, not entirely—I vowed to exert some control over my own life. As for Dorset, I would do my best to learn how to deal with him, not out of duty, but in self-defense. He still seemed to me to be my enemy. And perhaps my enmity for him, not always concealed, added fuel to his ardor.

He came very late to my bed one night. He and others had been wandering in the city with Edward, he explained, although I had made no comment and asked no questions. It was Dorset's idea of entrenching himself in royal favor to follow Edward in his wilder diversions. Dorset was too young to slink through the dark forests of London's midnight streets in search of low pleasures, but I said nothing.

Despite the gloss of manners, at court adultery was rated as a venial sin, or no sin at all, and seduction was practiced as a game, but to my mind it was no game for Dorset to play in my own household. I had made place among my demoiselles for the daughter of a knight who had given his support to my family. The girl had a scanty dowry, but she had considerable beauty, and she caught Dorset's eye. He singled her out, and overwhelmed her with flattery, lying promises, and gifts. It was some time before I realized what was happening.

Early in the winter I became *enceinte*, but soon miscarried, to my great disappointment. I made a quick recovery but my spirits were low for some time, and in my listless mood was slow to see that the girl's smiles and blushes were for Dorset, or the significance of the necklace sparkling around her throat. However, I did notice the sudden change in her, when her smiles stopped and her tears blotched her face. In private I asked her if she had heard any ill news from her home. There was nothing wrong, she assured me. With the necklace in mind—it was too costly for her father's means—I asked if she had made debts, and if so I would pay them. She had no debts.

"Then what ails you?" I demanded, and she burst into tears. The girl was crossed in love.

It was easy to guess why. The foolish creature had listened to Dorset, I was certain, and if I had accused her doubtless she would have confessed everything, but I was sorry for her, and tried to spare her feelings. However, I must deal with the problem of what to do with her. First, I consulted Dame Joan, who had kept her knowledge to herself to avoid troubling me.

"I was angry with the girl for her light behavior," she said, "but since my lord's fancy for her has waned, it would be best to send her back to her own home."

Then I spoke to Dorset, saying that the girl's father wanted her at home. I could have spared myself the telling of a lie.

"By all means get rid of her," he answered, "and if she's with child, she need not think that I'll make provision for it."

"Luckily she's not." I had taken care to find out. "Her father would not receive her if that was her condition."

I would have been compelled to find shelter for her, then take on the child's maintenance, but Dorset did not ask what would have become of her, or of the child.

She left without a word of farewell from Dorset, and her unhappy face caused me a pang. "She didn't yield her virtue for some trumpery jewels," I said to Dame Joan. "She yielded her heart as well."

"And wore it on her sleeves. So my lord soon found her cloying."

"My lord will soon tire of a lawfully wedded wife," I said.

"Not of you." Dame Joan's round, bright blue eyes surveyed me.

"Why not?" I asked, knowing that she was too concerned for me to flatter. "He's already faithless."

"And will be, I daresay, but he's not likely to become indifferent to you—as long as your aloofness baffles and puzzles him."

She left me, and I sat by the fire, thinking. Outside snow was falling in the dark winter night. I hated the snow, but I did not see it, or feel the cold here in the warm, scented room, bright with firelight and candlelight. Dorset's voice startled me he came so silently. He came to the hearth to warm his hands, then kissed me lightly. "Are we friends again? Now that you no longer have cause for war."

"I would rather have peace, and leave you in peace, but I am responsible for the young girls in my household, as you know, and I must beg you to let them alone, instead of marauding among them."

"Why do you put all the blame on me?" he asked, watching me with curiosity. He moved a little, and I could no longer see his expression as his face was in shadow; his eyes glinted out of shadows, and the firelight gave a reddish tinge to his hair.

"Admittedly, you are the fox who robbed my hen roost," I said.

"Then your pretty little chickens shouldn't come fluttering across my path." Dorset seemed amused and pleased at my comparison. "Come to bed." He picked me up and carried me to the bed, pushing me down among the pillows. "You are something of a vixen—and so we are well mated."

A pair of wild animals coupling in a forest den might be true mates, but Dorset and I were not, and never would be. I told myself that he was no worse than others, but while I was in his arms, desire for him flickered and faded, burned out; my body refused to respond to his. Soft words, kisses, caresses, claspings failed to give me sensual pleasure, perhaps because I could picture him using the same words and caresses—and sexual skill—when he had seduced the girl who had believed him.

✿ *Fifteen*

Marriage to Dorset had thrust me into close relationship with Elizabeth and the Woodvilles. Although they had kindled hatreds and jealousies, and had brought dissension into the House of York, they were always in complete accord with one another. "Now you are one of us," Elizabeth said to me, and once I had become Dorset's wife she invited me into that magical circle which the Woodvilles drew around themselves. She used the same tactics with the others who were linked to the Woodvilles by the bonds of marriage.

"We are flies drowned in honey," I said to Will Hastings.

"To keep peace within her family," he answered, "and because every one of you is useful or might be useful in building up the family power or the family dynasty. The Woodvilles have large visions," and he added, "but never let me, or any one tempt you to disparage them. Hold yourself aloof from all quarrels and dissensions, not even in the cause of your own friends and family. No matter how strongly you feel keep your feelings to yourself. And be on your guard with George."

I thanked Hastings, and promised to follow his advice. I had not seen George in months, not since my wedding feast, as he had stayed away from London and Edward's court. The Duchess of York had wintered at Fotheringhay; very likely George sojourned with her for some time, and from Fotheringhay had gone to Middleham Castle, where the earl's wife and daughters lived. Late in the winter he reappeared in London.

"George has come back," Dorset announced, with the air of one who is first to tell a piece of news, but as George had ridden through the streets at the head of a large retinue and crowds had gathered to wish him well, his arrival was no secret. "He'll make trouble," Dorset predicted, watching me.

"Why blame him beforehand? Wait until he does," I answered, although in my own mind I agreed.

"You absolve him beforehand," Dorset accused me.

"Why should you think so?" I asked.

"Because of his handsome face, for one thing."

"Are you determined to quarrel with me merely because George is in London?" I spoke lightly hoping to end the discussion, but Dorset persisted. "I only ask you not to give him too warm a welcome."

"If I ever give you any reason to complain of my behavior or my manners, you have only to tell me."

"You needn't fly to arms! Am I finding fault with you? No—not at all—even though I learned that you were unwilling to marry me." He watched me with a sly look in his eyes, waiting for me to deny the charge, but as I said nothing he went on. "Because your family was against me—and a young girl accepts her family's opinions. But not you, my little one—you were never one of these mild as new milk girls."

"Perhaps they sour with age," I said, but Dorset was not to be deflected.

"If you had wanted me, you wouldn't have given a farthing for your family's feelings. You had a stronger motive for your reluctance to have me—your feelings for another person. He was close at hand. And he lavished enough attention on you to kindle your hopes."

"Are you alluding to George?"

"Who else? Very likely you dreamed of being Duchess of Clarence."

"You are speaking of last year, or year before," I reminded him. "At that time I was free to indulge in all kinds of thoughts and feelings—if I chose. I had no husband then, but you already had a wife."

All this while, George had been cherishing a dream of his own, and with both his love and ambition to spur him on he would make definite plans to marry Isabel of Warwick. Did George intend to ask the king's consent? If so, he waited too long, because Edward found out, possibly from one of his informers.

"He summoned the two of them to Westminster—George and Richard, both," Dorset announced, his eyes agleam with malicious enjoyment, "and berated them for daring to discuss marriage without consulting him—it seems that the earl was plotting a double alliance. He hoped to marry his two daughters off. Isabel was to be George's wife, and Anne was to be Richard's."

"It could be a happy arrangement," I said.

Dorset stared at me. "Have you gone wood-wild? Edward would never consent. It would be against the interests of the crown—of the whole country!" Dorset went on to explain what I already knew—what anyone could grasp—the various reasons why Edward would never consent.

"Richard was repentant, it seems, but George was defiant," Dorset told me. "Edward ordered him to stop talking like a fool and go. This time he's really brought trouble on himself."

Dorset's complacency irked me. He had not been present,

and might have heard an embellished account, but it was doubtless true. "The trouble will soon blow over," I spoke with more confidence than I felt.

George must accept his lot. He and Richard must make the sacrifices demanded of princes, so their family and their friends said. I could understand their feelings, and felt sorry for them. Less sorry for the earl's daughters. Anne doubtless had some affection for Richard, and might be happy with him. Isabel loved George, but she scarcely knew him, and to know him well was not to love him more, but less.

To my surprise, George asked Edward's pardon, and promised to put his cousin Isabel out of his mind. I had not expected him to yield so quickly. Edward forgave him at once, peace was restored in the family, and the three brothers seemed on affectionate terms with one another. But I wondered.

Elizabeth gave me a high position in her household. I would have declined the honor, because it restricted my freedom, but Dorset insisted on my accepting it, which meant that I not only followed the court, but was brought into daily association with the queen. By spending many hours with her, I learned to know something of her private life. I had always thought of Elizabeth as the enchantress, triumphantly sure of her power to hold possession of Edward's heart. This was the general opinion, but as I found out Elizabeth was by no means as sure as she seemed, and she was not always happy.

Early in April the court took up residence at Windsor. Saxon kings had hunted in the woods at "Wyndlesore," and William the Norman had built a wooden fortress on the hill to dominate the countryside. Through the years his rude fortress had become a great castle, built of massive slabs of hard, polished heathstone, formed of some substance that gave the stone a crystalline glint.

Although it was a stronghold, the long walls enclosed a palace, said to be the finest in Europe. During the sad reign of Henry the Sixth the state apartments had fallen into disrepair, but with his hazy wits and unworldliness, he had taken scant notice of the decay in his palaces or in his realm.

Edward loved Windsor; he had brought the finest architects and artisans to restore and embellish the castle and the grounds. This year he was adding his Vineyard of Pleasure to his gardens, and rebuilding the chapel of St. George. The most noble Order of the Garter had been instituted here at Windsor, and Edward had announced that he would hold a Chapter of the Order at Windsor on the feast of St. George.

Great preparations were under way for the ceremony, and for the entertainment of the knights, their ladies, and the court. There would be hunts, tournaments, balls, banquets, outdoing the famous Feasts of the Round Table which had celebrated the founding of the Order. The people would not be forgotten; Edward would always include them; he would provide them with meat and drink in plenty, various sports and amusements, and the sight of royal and courtly pageantry.

In the chapel, each knight had his stall, with his helmet, sword and emblazoned banner above. The rules of the Order compelled them to have a helmet burnished in fine gold; the mantlings must be cloth of gold lined in sarcenet, the tassels must be gold and silver, intertwined with silk in the main color of the knight's arms. The sword, with gold pommel and cross, was sheathed in a cloth of gold scabbard. For the solemn ceremony on the feast day the knights would wear velvet mantles bordered with miniver and surcoats powdered with little garters done in silk and goldsmith's work—very costly as the motto of the Order was embroidered in each one.

The queen would play her part as chief lady of the Order. Her ceremonial robes, like the king's, were velvet in garter blue, widely bordered in ermine. The robes for the ladies who had the privilege of being Dames of the Order were the same blue bordered in miniver, and were a gift from the king. He had presented the knights with their swords—the pommels and hilts gilded with pure gold. He had also given each knight an embroidered saddle.

131

Seamstresses, tailors, embroiderers, furriers, jewelers, and gold-smiths had been toiling for months. The royal purveyors had been busy throughout the countryside, and all of the carts available were laden with provisions and came creaking up to the castle. Ships from foreign lands had brought almonds and wine, a variety of spices, and fruit—dates grown in the East, and sweet Spanish oranges. Every year the trappings had become richer, and more costly, and the festivities more elaborate, but where was the spirit of chivalry?

Within the walls of a royal palace rumors were born and flourished and faded, but the queen lived sheltered behind a wall of deference and flattery, and seemed unaware of the feeling against her and her family which had become so widespread among the people. Because I showed interest, Elizabeth was glad to speak to me about her childhood, when she and her brothers and sisters had been happy together at Grafton. "But we were blessed in having such parents as ours, devoted to one another and to us." She pictured them as self-sacrificing, unfailingly cheerful in adversity. A mother who had proved herself a capable house-wife, expert at contriving to make a little go a long way, combining domestic skills with learning and courtly graces. Both parents had taken great pains to educate their children. How well they had succeeded!

Affection colored Elizabeth's account, but she had told the truth—as she saw it. And yet the people believed that her mother was a witch and hated her father. They saw his hardness, his coldness, his greed, his lack of honesty. Elizabeth thought the great lords disliked him because they were jealous of his success, but during the winter a mob had broken into the grounds of one of his manors in Kent and had despoiled his gardens, killed his deer and carried off the carcasses.

"Why should they destroy my father's property?" Elizabeth had asked, completely bewildered. "What harm did he ever do those Kentish ruffians?"

If he was too harsh a landlord—if he had gained possession

of that manor by trickery—I could think of several reasons why a certain number of men had banded together to vent their anger, but I could not say so to Elizabeth. Edward had recompensed her father for his loss. None of the mob had been caught, and doubtless never would be.

Elizabeth had other causes for anxiety. However, she said nothing until we were at Windsor.

Edward and most of the court were following the hounds in Windsor Chase, but Elizabeth stayed in the palace. Her sister Katherine and I were with her in her private apartments. It was no sacrifice for me to give up the day's sport, or any day's sport. What Elizabeth knew of the chase she had learned by hearsay, or from the pages of a book, and she had studied the art of falconry until she was word perfect, but she had a positive aversion for hunting and hawking.

Her children had been brought in—the two eldest. They were beautiful, healthy children, but they were girls. "I love them, God knows," Elizabeth said after their nurses had taken them away again, "but I long for a son." In the royal nurseries, rockers and wet nurses and servants tended a baby, a third girl, as promising as her sisters, and Edward had given her a fond welcome, but she was not the much-desired prince. There was George, who still claimed to be heir presumptive to the throne. Doubtless the people, or most of them, agreed with him.

"You are certain to have a son," Katherine Woodville said, "when the stars are right."

"When! I am growing impatient," Elizabeth answered. "You and Cicely are still very young."

Katherine said nothing, but picked up a mirror, and after studying her face, put it down. Her reflection should have pleased her—she had her share of the Woodville beauty. The youngest of Elizabeth's sisters, Katherine had made the greatest match of all, with the Duke of Buckingham. He had been a sullen bridegroom, boasting of his Plantagenet blood, and brashly declaring that a low-born Woodville was not good enough to be his wife. Perhaps his words had never reached the ears of the king and queen; if so they ignored them. Buckingham was gorged on royal favor and Woodville flattery. He seemed to be drowned in honey, and doubtless well content with a beautiful and loving wife.

However, Katherine was not always happy. In the light of this fair spring morning, her eyes showed traces of recent tears. "What troubles you, Kate?" Elizabeth asked her.

Katherine struggled for composure, but she was in the habit of confiding in Elizabeth. "I waited all night, but my husband never came to my bed!"

"Neither did mine," Elizabeth told her.

"Was Buckingham with him?"

"I did not ask," Elizabeth said.

"Buckingham came back only in time to make ready for the hunt. I asked him where he had been. He turned on me and berated me."

"You make too much of his passing moods, Kate. Buckingham is only a boy, with a boy's odd humors. Be patient, and give him soft answers. Welcome him when he comes and never question his goings," she advised. "Wives might do well to practice the arts that courtesans use. Forswear tears, Kate, and avoid any display of jealousy."

"I will try to school myself," Katherine said, "but you are fortunate, sister, Edward loves you."

After her sister had left the room, Elizabeth's face turned somber. "And I must school myself to hide my own." She seemed to be speaking her thoughts aloud, but then she spoke directly to me. "Yes, I am jealous—and always at war with my jealousy."

I heard her and was bewildered. "No one could suspect it, madam. I can only admire your self-command."

"I have had long practice," Elizabeth said, "but in my heart I rage against every woman in England who might attract my lord's desire—I scan every face at court. Which ones will he notice—and seek out."

She picked up the mirror but put it aside after a glance at her reflection. "Last night was only one of many nights. Instead of coming to my bed, he went elsewhere—to waste himself on bawds and harlots. Or does he go to a mistress?" Elizabeth demanded.

Since Edward's marriage, I had never heard of his keeping a mistress. Perhaps he wearied of his women too soon for any of them to acquire the name.

"I have less to fear from many women than from one," Elizabeth said. "One woman who might become dear to Edward and who might win some share of his heart."

"You command his heart, madam," I told her.

She seemed to think over what I had said, and when she spoke it was in a different tone, "And I will do battle now and always for what is rightfully mine!"

Late in the day, when the clamor heralded Edward's return, Elizabeth went out on the terrace to meet him. She was fresh from the hands of her tiring women, and she had with her all three of her children—the royal children, rosy cheeked, and golden haired. They clustered around her, their small faces showing their joy at the sight of their father. As Edward rode up to them he saw a happy, smiling group to welcome him home from the hunt.

In the evening, the eve of St. George's Mass, Edward held a great feast in the Round Tower. Beforehand, the court gathered in the presence chamber. The Earl of Warwick had come to take part in tomorrow's ceremonies. I had not seen him since last summer, when he had appeared at Baynard's Castle to tell me that Edward had decided to marry me to Dorset. My uncle Warwick talked to me for some little time, then Will Hastings and John Dynham, who were standing beside me, drew him into a discussion of the recent troubles in the north.

Early in the spring, news had come of a minor uprising led by a man called Robin of Redesdale. The disturbance had been easily quelled and he had vanished. A few weeks later, another disturbance broke, even more easily suppressed than the first.

"I wonder who is behind these rebellions," said Hastings.

"There are disaffected Lancastrians in England," the earl

pointed out. "Robin of Redesdale is probably a dispossessed Lancastrian who has turned outlaw."

"If he really exists."

The earl frowned, "How do you mean, Dynham?"

"His complete disappearance is puzzling," John Dynham answered. "Either he has many more friends than we've been led to believe, or as the people in Yorkshire believe, he's not flesh and blood." John Dynham was Devon-born, and found it easy to believe that an unappeased ghost or a heathenish spirit might assume the guise of a man and stalk the northern shires, sowing dissension.

"It might be," Will Hastings conceded, who for all of his air of cheerfulness, frequented astrologers and soothsayers.

"How else can you account for his fading into air before the people's eyes?" John Dynham asked.

The earl had listened intently, then looked toward the opening door as Elizabeth's father made his entrance with his usual air of arrogance. Even great lords were expected to bow before him, but he could never exact the deference freely accorded to the Earl of Warwick—he stood aloof from the "upstart" Woodville, and after one glance, ignored him.

"The damage done to Woodville's manor is something of a mystery," Hastings said. "Whoever led the attack has also vanished into air."

"Perhaps the spirit of Robin Hood is astir again," the earl spoke with great seriousness, "to redress the people's wrongs."

After the banquet was over and the boards were cleared, Edward left his chair of state to move about among his guests, and his brothers followed his example. When George came up to me, he said, "You've changed since I last saw you. But are you always as grave and silent as you are tonight?"

He saw me glance at the emerald ring on his finger.

"I went openly to Middleham to see Isabel, and Edward found out," he said.

"It was not a secret that could be kept forever," I answered.

Although the music and the noise in the hall prevented anyone from overhearing, I moved closer to the wall, to prevent a possible eavesdropper from coming up behind me.

"You've heard how Edward stormed."

"I'm sorry he opposes you," I said.

"I have not changed, either in heart or mind."

A page came up, offering wine, fruit, and sweetmeats. George took a cup of wine, and watched the boy scurry away before saying anything more. "Edward commands me to forget Isabel, but I made no promises to him. I love her, she loves me, and we have her father's blessing. I am promised to her, and I'll never give her up!"

"Take care." I glanced over my shoulder to make sure that no listener was lurking in the shadows.

George drank his wine, and flung his empty cup away, careless of its value. I winced as it struck the floor, but a page saw its golden shine and retrieved it before it was trodden underfoot.

"Let the Woodvilles take care!" George muttered. "But I forget—you're Dorset's wife now, and perhaps I would do better to be on my guard with you."

"With me, with everyone," I whispered, looking to right and left.

George laughed. "I'll take that much of your advice." He looked at me. "But I can tell you this—I am not so easily thwarted as you think. I still have secrets and know how to hoard them."

The wine was telling on him, making him excitable and boastful, and yet something in his manner rather than his words gave a sense of disquiet.

"As for Elizabeth," George said, "she's only a summer queen."

Edward held out his hand, she took it, and they led the dancers in the pavan. Elizabeth had too much wisdom to yield her place as Edward's first partner to another woman. Seeing them together I felt certain that she had reasserted her power over him, and would not lie alone tonight.

"Your comparison is inept," I said to George.

"Is it? All England celebrates the May, but some of the

villages in the north, and in your west country too, select a queen to reign from May Day until the end of the summer, but no longer."

I knew the custom; the fairest girl was chosen, as elsewhere, but wore her flower crown and received homage from the whole village, until the harvest was in, then no more crown, or homage or glory for her.

"And summer ends," George said.

❧ Sixteen

St. George's Mass and all of the ceremonies of the Order of the Garter were celebrated with the greatest pomp, as Edward had planned. After he had left the chapel he discussed the new rebellion. Robin of Redesdale had reappeared, this time in Lancaster, and the officers of the crown in those parts had sent word that they were unable to deal with the trouble, and asked the king's help. Edward seemed unperturbed, but decided to put down the rebellion himself.

The Earl of Warwick had the responsibility of beating off any attempt to invade the country from the sea for the Spider King of France might be scheming to land men on the coast while the Lancastrians stirred rebellion in the north. George was being sent to Dover. His task was to outfit the king's ships, although older and more experienced men would be in charge. What did George know about ships? Less than I did! However, he would have the opportunity to learn. As he and the earl were going in the same direction at the same time, it was only reasonable for them to set out together. I wondered what they would say to each other on the journey.

Richard had been chosen to ride north with Edward, and was hoping to gain military experience.

"You're likely to be disappointed," Edward told him. "These

rebels are a raggle-taggle band of outlaws, and as soon as they hear of any army at their heels they'll fade away as they did before."

Edward was taking only a small force. "And Richard doesn't add much to its size," I said to Will Hastings. "He's still small and thin."

"But he's a royal prince," Hastings pointed out. "It's a good thing for the people to see one of the king's brothers riding with him to offset the queen's two brothers, and her father, and her son Dorset."

Too many Woodvilles for the people's taste, and Edward had also invited Elizabeth to accompany him as far as Fotheringhay Castle, to wait for him there while he gave chase to the rebels. When he had restored order, he would escort her back to Windsor again, or perhaps to Sheen or Eltham.

The Duchess of York was in residency at Fotheringhay. It was not part of her dower, it had belonged to the house of York, and now belonged to Edward, or rather to the crown, but his mother had always preferred it to any other castle. She stayed there often, and queened it over the entire countryside until it seemed to be hers, the domain of "Proud Cis." I could picture her anger when she read Edward's letter, and learned that he was bringing his wife with him for a stay of weeks. My lady Duchess would not linger, she would make haste to move her establishment elsewhere. No castle ever built was large enough to hold Edward's wife and Edward's mother under the same roof.

I asked Elizabeth to dispense with my attendance until her return. She gave me leave, and urged me to guard my health.

"You have been somewhat wan since your mishap," she said. "But you are young and will regain your strength."

She and Edward intended to visit the shrine of Our Lady of Walsingham, and pray for a prince.

"May God answer your prayers," I said, "and grant you a safe and happy journey."

The journey would be entirely safe, Elizabeth assured me.

Edward would make the country safe, "Edward, and my own father and my brothers and Dorset."

She ignored the men who had helped Edward win the crown. If we had to depend on the Woodvilles for our security God help us! I thought. Outside, grooms curried the war horses, squires were busy polishing armor, messengers came and went. Edward had ordered new banners, their bright colors were as yet unstained by sun, rain, dust, and war. A long line of sumpter mules and baggage carts were waiting, and servants were loading them with the queen's gear. All of these preparations seemed more in keeping with a pleasant *chevauchée* in summer weather than with a military campaign.

Elizabeth was in her bedroom, her loosened hair falling over her shoulders. In the garderobe, her women were folding silks and satins, regal mantles and gleaming tissues; they had packed lotions and unguents, essences of jasmine and roses, and all of the various cosmetics that Elizabeth used with such skill. Her jewels were locked away in caskets. Elizabeth was taking her own arms and armor.

"It will be a happy journey for me," she said, and asked me to describe Fotheringhay Castle, which would be Edward's headquarters. The old keep, built in the twelfth century, looked out on a fertile landscape, and was reflected in the nearby River Nen, I told her. In the distance there were the miles of flat, wet fens reaching out to meet the sea.

"It'll be pleasant there in summer," she said. "It will seem to me like the first summer of my marriage."

Fotheringhay would be crowded with armed men, but she did not think of them, she was deep in visions of the time ahead, a sojourn to a far-off castle with Edward; he would leave her to make a brief foray against the rebels, but would come back to share her bed and lie in her arms, just as he had found his way to her when she had been his wife in secret. This summer of 1469, full of disquiet for the rest of us, might grant her all that she desired—might bring back that other summer's ardent June.

Dorset had chosen to follow Edward against the rebels, and

in public tried to ape young Richard's very real zeal, but when he was alone with me he was gloomy about having any share in the undertaking.

"But if I hang back," he admitted, "Edward will think less of me."

I had intended to go to my own estates, but I had agreed to do as Dorset wished and go to Astley. "It would be well to find out if my lazy steward and my rascally bailiffs are sending me all of the money due me. The castle's old-fashioned, but habitable or so the steward reports. If your stay becomes too wearisome, you can join the queen at Fotheringhay."

"Have you often been to Astley?" I asked, and Dorset astounded me by saying that he had never been there at all. As I knew, his early childhood had been spent at Bradgate, and when he and his mother and brother had been disinherited they had taken refuge at Grafton throughout the lean years. With Elizabeth's marriage to the king, her eldest son had been restored in lands, rank, and honors, but he had stayed close to the king for fear of missing Edward's lavish gifts.

"It would be better if you would visit your estates and judge for yourself," I pointed out.

"I'm only interested in the revenues collected," he said. "I could never endure the tedium of rural existence—not for a day. Besides, I have more important matters on hand."

He seemed to thrive on the jealousies and intrigues, the jostling for place and favor that infested the court. I asked him if the yield of corn and the wool clip compared favorably with other estates, if the arable was tilled in strips, if all of his tenants were free and paid their rent in money, or if some still owed boon work and the various fees exacted in the past according to the custom of the manor. Dorset clapped his hands over his ears and called me a busy goodwife.

"I hope to earn the name," I told him. "Edward has gone into trade, you know, and busies himself buying and selling. Why shouldn't we do what we can on our lands? It's only good management." I had been brought up to believe that a woman should look to the ways of her household.

Dorset laughed at me, but gave me permission to do as I thought fit, and said he would thank me if I could devise ways of extracting more money from his Midland estates. I promised to do my best. On my own lands I had the advantage of wise guidance and trustworthy officials. I was thankful that Dorset was too preoccupied to interfere, and that Devon was far from the court.

Costly armor hid Dorset's qualms, and made him look as brave as the next man when he rode off with Edward's little army. News of the rebellion was scant, but some of my women were afraid to leave the security of London's walls. We were traveling with a number of armed men to guard us, I told them, and Astley Castle was as safe from Lancastrian rebels as London. Kenilworth was near and the town and castle of Warwick were only ten miles from Astley. By the end of May, a damp murky heat settled on London. The people were troubled by dreams and portents, and went running to soothsayers. I was glad to be out of the city.

Traveling with a large retinue, as well as a great number of sumpter mules and carts laden with household plenishings made progress slow, but I took pleasure in the long days of riding through the countryside. As I had often heard, there had been many more people in England before the Black Death than could be counted now. In every shire forest and waste had crept back to take land that had once been tilled, but the Midlands were more thickly settled than the north or the west. From the looks of them, the people prospered, and thronged the roads to Chipping Norton, Chipping Camden, and Coventry, where the great fairs were held. The inhabitants of Warwickshire seemed intent on their crops and their trading. To my eyes, the gentle Cotswold landscape seemed to offer contentment. In my part of Devon, we were always aware that beyond the lushness and brilliant flowering there was the sternness of rocky headlands, and the tameless sea.

Turning off the highroad we followed a narrow tree-shadowed lane with glimpses of fields on either side until we came to the church and Astley Castle. Built of Cotswold stone, the castle was honey-gold in the afternoon light. On one side the ground falls away to the moat, and beyond the moat was the chase. On the other three sides there were fields, pastures, orchards and gardens, then the village, hidden by trees. The ground was level, and the castle's outer walls were low. It was not a fortress, it was a lord's house, meant to be lived in.

My men eyed the low walls, but said nothing. A few of my women murmured that any foe could cross the moat and climb over the walls with ease.

"If we are attacked we take refuge in the keep," Dame Joan Wynant told them. She was stouthearted herself, inclined to scoff at timorous fancies, and I wondered why she gave a serious answer.

"What enemy?" I demanded. "No one will attack us, nothing will happen!"

Just then I saw my lord's tenants converging on us to greet us, and put a smile on my face. And I tried to keep intrusive memory at bay of another time and place. The wood, the bridge, the moorland and Sandal Castle, gray in the Yorkshire grayness.

Our coming was an event, stirring curiosity and excitement, and we were duly welcomed. For the time being, I gave very little thought to what might be taking place elsewhere, and set myself to the task of seeing to Dorset's affairs. The steward was a short round man with a round face. He had been in charge for many a year and was doubtless lazy, but he was shrewd, and I found him helpful and willing to tell me what I needed to know.

During the years of warfare, armies had swept by, but "had not come trampling here." Some of the young men who had marched behind their lord's banner had been killed in battle, the others had drifted home again—or had taken the opportunity to stay away. Here as elsewhere, the people had known loss and grief, but the turbulence of the time had left no outward mark.

Warwick town and castle were nearby, "But the earl's retainers let us be," the steward said. "They never so much as burned one haystack or made off with one pig."

The Yorkist leaders had always kept strict discipline. They were mindful of the hatred Marguerite of Anjou had aroused because she had permitted her armies to ravage the countryside on her southward march. The steward spoke of Dorset's father as a brave knight, and regretted his death. As far as I could judge from watching, listening, and asking questions, the people here were well content with Edward's rule. Certainly none of them were likely to join a Lancastrian rebellion.

"We are still agape at my Lord Dorset's sudden change of fortune," the steward said.

Dorset himself seemed unreal to these people. If he wanted their loyalty, he would have to earn it. So would I, and I resolved to gain their good will.

Astley was like most of the estates in the midlands. The tenants paid for their acreage in money instead of in services and dues to their lord. The terms of payment were recorded in the manor court roll, according to the custom of the manor, and if the terms were met, neither the tenant nor his heirs could be dispossessed. Men were no longer bound to the soil. They and their children were free born.

The steward complained that some of the young men chose to put on a great lord's livery—only to laze and brawl—or else slipped away to the towns, seeking adventure. Many were no longer content to stay and till the soil. However, Dorset had a good number of tenants here. The soil was fertile, and markets were within easy reach. The majority were good farmers. The steward at the castle and the bailiffs impressed me as being honest, and after studying the manor rolls, I concluded that the estate was paying Dorset what he could rightfully expect.

However, the breed of sheep could be improved, and the

flocks should be larger. Wool was a source of riches, as even Dorset knew.

In this quiet corner of Warwickshire, rebellion seemed far away—non-existent. However, there were lesser problems. The priest came to me to bemoan the wickedness of his flock. The people here were loose-living, he told me. The girls and women were given to wantonness. I thought of some great ladies who were the same. The priest was scandalized because the villagers made use of amulets and potions; they put their faith in fortune-tellers and portents and magic. Like the men and women of Edward's royal court, I thought. "They kneel to the power of Satan and ignore the power of God," the priest sighed.

I sent Dorset word that I had arrived safely with my retinue, and that if luck held his revenues would be forthcoming when the harvest was in. I asked after his health, and begged him to send me news. If I tried to give him any account of my daily life at Astley, he would yawn and toss my letter aside unread. His answer, when it came was even briefer.

There was a dearth of news. The countryside was peaceful, and if I was weary of Astley, I could join the queen at Fothering-hay. Edward planned to remain there throughout the whole of June, and early in July, march against the rebels. "If he can find them."

In the torpor of a late afternoon in July, Dame Joan and I were sitting in the privacy of the castle's parlor. The great hall was long and wide, with windows filled with painted glass, a minstrel gallery, and a chimney piece, richly carved. The solar, the principal bedchambers, and the parlor were of good size, and the windows were glazed. The rooms were sparsely furnished, but I had been prepared for that and had brought enough to serve our needs. In the parlor, hangings brightened the walls, fresh rushes covered the floor, and fresh flowers gave a pleasant perfume.

Word from Dorset was long overdue. Even if the king's army was still hunting the elusive rebel Dorset should have sent some message.

From the parlor I could hear the usual sounds, a dog barking, cattle lowing, voices in the castle, someone laughing, a cart creaking, but in the distance I thought I heard the thudding of hoofbeats. Dame Joan likewise listened. From where we were sitting we had no view of the road, but when we heard the horse clatter over the drawbridge, we both ran out into the hall. Dorset had sent one of his men to bring me strange and unexpected news.

On the fifth day of July, Edward had marched from Fotheringhay, but as soon as he had entered the town of Newark, his scouts had come panting to warn him that Robin of Redesdale was nearby, and advancing with an army much larger than the king's small force. Instead of dealing with a raggle-taggle band of rebels, headed by a Lancastrian fanatic, as all had assumed, Edward had found himself confronted with a well-equipped, well-disciplined military array. A trap had been set for him, as it had been set for his father at Sandal Castle.

Edward had avoided a battle by doubling on his tracks and by pushing on in great haste he had reached Nottingham Castle without any losses. The castle was a royal stronghold, and no rebel bands would dare to attack its solid ramparts. Edward was prudent enough to shut himself within its walls and wait for reinforcements. Dorset was with him, and had sent a few lines to bid me to stay where I was, until I heard from him again because at present the country was in an unsettled state and it might be unsafe for me to travel.

Dorset seemed to me too fearful, but as I preferred to stay where I was, I was very willing to obey his wishes. Elizabeth was still at Fotheringhay, or so the messenger thought, but seemed vague and uncertain. Edward and his Council had greatly underrated the strength of the rebellion, but he had seen his mistake and would be quick to right it, I thought.

"The king has sent for his brother George, Duke of Clarence," the messenger told us, "and for the Earl of Warwick, and their men to come from Dover without delay." As usual in time of trouble, Edward called on the earl, not the Woodvilles.

"This crisis may bring them together again," I said to Dame Joan.

The messenger was not wearing Dorset's livery, we noted, and when I asked why, he said that he thought he would be safer in clothes that would not cause him to be noticed. When he had nothing more to tell, I sent him off to have food, wine, and a bed for the night, but ordered him tomorrow to convey my letter to Dorset.

"He promised to deliver it, madam," my servant reported later. "But if you want my lord to have it, you would be better advised to send me."

"Why do you say so, Giles?" I asked.

"I doubt if he intends to go back to Nottingham, madam. He's afraid."

News came seeping in from all directions—much of it could be disregarded, but when the constable of Kenilworth Castle sent a courier to me to tell me what had happened, I was forced to believe his account. Instead of advancing to join Edward, the earl and George had sailed for Calais, in secret—not a secret long. The earl's wife and his two daughters had been conveyed on board, and a number of lords and knights had chosen to take part in the exodus.

Shortly after they had landed, a throng of French nobles had joined them, and all had assembled in Calais Cathedral. There George, Duke of Clarence, brother to the King of England, had married Isabel Neville, the Earl of Warwick's eldest daughter. George and Isabel were cousins—within the forbidden degree of kinship, but the Pope had granted the necessary dispensation, and had obviously granted it some time ago. The other preparations had likewise been made in advance.

Years of association with George should have found me better prepared. He had proclaimed his intentions often enough, but I had refused to believe his wild words. What would George's marriage cost? And who would pay for it?

From Calais the earl and George signed an open letter; in it they stated the king's loyal subjects had called upon them to save king and kingdom from "seditious persons." The letter heralded their return. Landing at Dover, the earl's great popularity among Kentishmen attracted hundreds to his banners. Gaining adherents on the way, he and George made for London. The city opened its gates to them, crowds welcomed them, the mayor and magistrates received them courteously, "But were perhaps glad to see them go after twenty-four hours," Dame Joan commented.

They moved boldly across England, and the people cheered them on their way. The constable at Kenilworth kept me informed, and on a still and sultry day, his messenger came to Astley to report what the constable had just learned. Edward had left Nottingham and had marched southward to join expected reinforcements under Lord Herbert's command. But before he had ever left the fortress, Edward had ordered the Woodvilles to seek their own safety and go into hiding, rather than risk falling into the hands of their enemies. They had obeyed, creeping out of Nottingham Castle in the night and had taken to their heels.

As Edward had led his scanty force into Olney, he had met a few stragglers in full flight, survivors of the long-awaited reinforcements. "Robin of Redesdale had swooped down on them, and after a fierce battle, had cut them to pieces," the messenger told me. The two lords in command had been taken prisoner, and both had been beheaded.

"By whose orders?" I demanded.

"Robin of Redesdale's," the messenger answered.

"And who is he?" I saw him as a malign spirit bringing the vengeful cruelty and bloodshed of the past to life again.

"They say that he is kinsman to the Earl of Warwick." The messenger spoke reluctantly, but I remembered the bitter enmity between the earl and those two lords. The earl had taken the opportunity to be rid of them, and had ordered their execution—as Edward undoubtedly knew. Edward was not likely to forgive the death of his friends.

148

It was obvious now that the earl and George had gathered a strong army, and Edward's men had deserted him. He had seen two of his knights fling down the leopard banners of England, and display the bear and ragged staff of Warwick. Edward had counted the few who were faithful to him, thanked them, and ordered them to leave him. His brother Richard, Will Hastings, John Dynham and others—I could guess who they were—had refused to go. Edward had set out to subdue "Lancastrian unrest" and had found himself facing a rebellion, led by his brother George and his cousin Warwick.

He was a king without an army, seemingly without friends, except for those few loyal ones, but Edward was always cool-headed in a crisis. He accepted his plight, and had made the best of it. He lodged at a little inn, and when the landlord had stammered excuses for the lack of comfort and fine fare, Edward had put the man at his ease by saying that the accommodations and the food suited him very well. He ate with good appetite, then went to bed, advising the others with him to do the same.

In the middle of the night, Warwick's red-jacketed men came into the town. They knocked on the door to rouse Edward, and "with great courtesy" asked him to dress and ride with them. "The earl sent certain lords who were with him to escort the king." Edward went with them to the encampment where the earl and George waited for him.

I tried to picture that meeting, in the depths of the night, with the rusty glow of torches ringing them around, and beyond the light, the shadows swaying tall. Did George stay in his tent or was he bold enough to speak to Edward?

The earl welcomed Edward as an honored and willing guest, but neither deference nor fair words could gloss over the reality. Edward was a prisoner. He knew it, the country would know it—and the rest of the world as well.

The messenger paused, and I was aware of the steward's keys clicking and clacking together, and a bee buzzing around a pot of flowers in the room. "Where are the other lords who were at Olney with the king?" I asked.

"The earl made no effort to detain them," the man said. "They could go where they pleased."

"What of the queen?" I asked.

She had left Fotheringhay and had gone to London, to take up her residence in the Tower "Obeying the king's instructions." No harm would come to her, but the Tower's high walls could not keep out her fears.

George had likewise set out for London, we heard, "to supervise the work of the Royal Council in governing the country," which made me smile. He had with him the Archbishop of York, the earl's brother, who was very learned and astute. The earl would rule the country—for the time being, until Edward regained his freedom and his power. Perhaps the earl had hoped to win over Will Hastings, who was his brother-in-law and who hated the Woodvilles, but Hastings had made his choice. There was Richard, the loyal brother. Doubtless he seemed too young and insignificant to be worth watching.

One morning my servants came running to tell me that the road leading to Warwick was aswarm with the earl's men, steel glinting and scarlet flashing as they had passed by in a haze of dust. "They're taking the king to Warwick Castle," the steward panted. In his excitement, he spoke his thoughts aloud. "What does the earl intend?"

After dark, a sudden commotion broke out to disturb the quiet. My women, already nerve-strung, were huddled together muttering prayers and gazing out at a line of flickering lights on the water of the moat. "Corpse candles," someone murmured. The moat ran into a stream, and the stream joined the River Avon. Trees grew too thickly to see where the lights began, but the long chain of little greenish fire wound along the surface of the water and disappeared. Corpse candles were said to follow the steps of a person who was destined to die next twelvemonth. "Or within two years," someone amended. "Never longer."

Warwick Castle was on the Avon, the lights were moving in that direction. "The king took that way," my tirewomen whispered. "A great number of men took the road to Warwick,"

Dame Joan said sharply but she lingered with me at the window watching the procession of pale corpse candles until they faded and were lost in the dark. At the time, I never thought of the earl, and no one mentioned him, and yet he had also taken that way.

Kings had been deposed, and had disappeared from the world of men, but the great Earl of Warwick would never blacken his soul and his name with murder. Edward was safe enough. He was kept at Warwick Castle for a short time only before he was hurried away, in the night, and in secrecy, to Middleham Castle, far to the north. There the earl's power was centered, and there Edward's friends would have difficulty in any attempt to free him.

Elizabeth was free to stay in the Tower's royal apartments, or to go where she pleased. She was safe, but must endure her fears and her suspense as best she could. The constable at Kenilworth offered me the refuge of the castle if I felt myself endangered, and the earl's seneschal at Warwick sent me word that he could spare men to guard me and my household if I needed protection. I assured them both, my own retinue was sufficient for our safety. But I could well understand Elizabeth's state of mind. I had heard nothing from Dorset since he had left Nottingham, and I became more and more concerned for his safety.

August came, with still hot days and a haze of pale sunlight on the fields. No one seemed able to give me any news of the Woodvilles. On a Sunday morning, as I was going to Mass, I saw the paper fastened to the church door. One of my servants tore it down, but I took it and read it. The proclamation denounced the Woodvilles as greedy vermin who were sucking the lifeblood from the realm, and bringing ruin.

Who had nailed it there? I could not read the faces of the village people or learn anything from their manner to me.

"It would be easy for someone from Warwick to come here and fix it to the church door," Dame Joan pointed out. "In any case my lord Dorset is too young to be a target."

151

Too young and too unimportant to his enemies, I thought. The proclamation was aimed at Elizabeth's father and her brother John. They were the "vermin."

"Very likely Anthony and his father and brother and Dorset made for the coast, found a ship and are now safe in the Low Countries."

Dame Joan was silent, and I persisted, "But you don't think so, do you?"

"I doubt it," she answered. "There are too many difficulties unless they could count on enough staunch friends to help them."

"With Elizabeth helpless, and Edward held in Middleham Castle, where would they find friends? They only have enemies."

"Somehow they must have taken cover," Dame Joan said.

A farmer and his son went to market in Warwick, and came back with a tale to tell. The steward heard it and came to me panting with excitement. "My lady Jacquetta, the queen's mother, has been openly accused of practicing the black arts!" he began. She was in London, with Elizabeth, and George was likewise in London, exulting in his power and position. He had gone so far as to label Jacquetta a witch, proclaiming in public what he and others had been repeating in private for years and what the mass of the people already believed.

"There's no evidence for the charge," I spoke up in her defense, but the steward told me that the Earl of Warwick's men had searched Grafton Castle and found a great store of books and all kinds of implements used in sorcery. They had also come upon a puppet made of lead, only a few inches long, representing a man in full armor. Small though it was, it was recognizably the Earl of Warwick, and was wrapped in a piece of red silk, embroidered with the bear and ragged staff.

Most damning of all, the figure had been deliberately mutilated. A sharp bodkin was thrust through it. That meant a violent death. Jacquetta's enemies were already crying out that she had planned to do away with the earl through sorcery, perhaps hoping to contrive his murder.

I had sent my women to their beds, but was too wakeful to go to my own, although it was late. Dame Joan was likewise unable to sleep, and sat with me in my bedchamber, talking in lowered tones.

"The earl's not likely to persecute a woman," I argued.

"He's not in London," Dame Joan reminded me. "She is, and so are her accusers."

"Would they dare proceed against her? She's too highly placed."

"But doubtless she is thinking of the fate of another woman, Duke Humphrey's wife. At the time, she was the greatest lady in England."

"I've heard of her, and how she was accused of practicing witchcraft."

"Long before you were born," Dame Joan said. "Duke Humphrey's enemies accused her of making a wax puppet in the likeness of Henry the Sixth, with the aim of causing him to sicken and die. She was brought to trial and compelled to do public penance. Afterwards, she was incarcerated on the Isle of Wight, and died in her prison."

Jacquetta was a resourceful woman, but witchcraft was a dread charge. "In the morning, I will assemble my entire household," I said to Dame Joan, "and remind them that you and I, and most of them, have stayed at Grafton, and that I have seen the famous Tower Room, and that it hold books in foreign languages, and rare manuscripts—some very old, also maps and charts—evidence of Lady Jacquetta's superior learning, but nothing else. I will forbid any man or woman in my service to say otherwise. Of course it's merely a gesture on my part."

"Nevertheless, order them to hold their tongues," Dame Joan advised.

"I balk at swallowing this so-called evidence," I said to Dame Joan. "Because if my Lady Jacquetta did make a puppet in the likeness of the earl, if she did commit herself so far, neither the earl's men nor any other foe or friend will find any trace of her handiwork. Not at Grafton, not elsewhere."

"Not until the Day of Judgment," Dame Joan agreed.

In London, George was proclaiming that the king's marriage was the work of witchcraft, and perhaps he believed it. But neither all of the angels in heaven nor all of the demons in hell could have induced Edward to take a wife against his will.

❧ *Seventeen*

It was high summer, but the days were growing shorter, and the farmers were busy in the fields, hoping to harvest their crops before the weather changed. The church bells rang, summoning me to Vespers and I made my way alone to the church near the castle gates. Around me were the tombs and effigies of the Astleys, long dead and turned to dust, but the village people still brought flowers to deck their tombs. In the dimness I failed to notice a shadow darker than the rest emerging from behind the altar until a faint sound made me look up. I rose from my knees and stood trembling and staring at the outline of a face taking form out of the dusk. Then the phantom whispered my name. It was Dorset.

I went to him but before I could reach him he sank down on the chancel steps, leaning against the communion rail. Was he wounded? Was he hurt? I knelt beside him trying to support him. In answer to my question he shook his head, but he was weak, from hunger he whispered. The sight of him with his bloodless face and his clothes hanging in tatters told me what hardships he must have endured. He huddled on the steps, limp and boneless but when I offered to go for help, he shook his head and struggled to his feet.

"Are you able to walk further?" I asked. "The castle is hard by."

"It's daylight. I'll be seen." His voice was hoarse but he had regained the use of it. He was beyond any concern for his looks. "The people in there—they'll give me away."

I tried to soothe his fear. "Not any person in my household. The others are your own people."

"Pack of treacherous knaves—like all the rest."

"Where else can you go for shelter?" I asked.

"Nowhere."

The sentry at the gate stared at me as I came out of the church, leading what appeared to be a wild boy of the woods. He had never laid eyes on Dorset before, and seemed dazed when I said, "Here is your lord, who has come." He was quick to understand for doubtless he had seen fugitives before. I ordered the drawbridge raised and the gates closed, but even after he was within his own walls, Dorset kept glancing over his shoulder. When my servants came, he shrank back, although he knew them well. However, he allowed them to lead him up to my bedchamber, and ordered them to rid him of his stinking rags.

They bathed him in warm water, washed and combed his matted hair and wrapped him in a clean robe before he would eat. Dame Joan would allow him only a limited amount of food and wine to appease his sharp hunger; if he took too much it would sit ill on him, she warned. He was too weary to protest, and as soon as he was abed, he fell into a heavy sleep.

I sat by his bed all night, keeping vigil. Dame Joan, likewise, watched over him, alert for any signs of fever, but none developed, although at times he moaned and tossed. After midnight, he slept more peacefully. His lips were cracked, his face had thinned and sharpened, but was no longer ghostly.

"He's young, and has sound health," Dame Joan said. "All he needs is good food and rest."

"And peace of mind," I added.

"All of us need that, but despite all troubles and turmoil, he will always land on his feet."

By morning, when Dorset woke, he seemed well recovered. It was useless to try to keep his presence here a secret, I told him. What was known in the castle was known in the village. "And will soon spread through the countryside," he said, and agreed to show himself occasionally in the great hall. However, he refused to set foot beyond the castle's walls, and asked us to keep the drawbridge raised at all times, during the day as well as during the night.

"I was too bold," Dorset said the next day. He had dined in the hall but immediately afterwards had shut himself up with me in the parlor and had locked the doors. I looked at him, noting how gaunt he had become. The clothes that he had borrowed from a young squire in my household hung on him.

"Bold?" I echoed.

"To come here, only ten miles from Warwick Castle and town."

"The earl is far away, in the north," I pointed out.

"He hates me," Dorset said.

"He has no intention of doing you any harm." I grew impatient with Dorset's excessive fears.

"George hates me even more," he said.

"He is in London."

"His men are swarming through the Midlands."

"They won't come here," I assured him and asked him to tell me how he had made his way from Nottingham to Astley.

Dressed as servants and on foot, the Woodvilles had stolen out of Nottingham at midnight. Dorset, Elizabeth's father, her brothers, Anthony and John. Two of the four separated at once, but Dorset and Anthony had set out together. They had a little money with them, but were afraid to make use of it. In any town or village or farm, their speech and manner would arouse suspicion. They had gone into hiding during the day, in a coppice or ditch and had trudged through the night, seeking little-used lanes, stumbling across rough fields.

They had lived on wild berries and what fruit they could steal from orchards, sometimes they had come upon a nest of eggs, and once they had seized a stray chicken. "We were ravenous enough to dare kindle a fire when we discovered the hot ashes and embers left by woodcutters, or outlaws."

They had skirted Stony Stratford, and had finally reached Grafton.

"Why? Why did you go there?" I asked. "It has become too conspicuous."

"We'd agreed to meet there, because of the money. We had to have money to make our escape to the Low Countries."

The older Woodville had secreted a sack of gold coins at Grafton, and had given Anthony and Dorset instruction to enable them to find it. "We intended to share it equally, then each one of us would try to reach the coast on his own," Dorset explained. "My uncle Anthony and I were first to reach Grafton." He gave a long sigh.

"You succeeded in evading the earl's men," I said.

"They had been there, the steward told us, but had gone."

"What did they take with them?" I asked.

"Not the gold," Dorset went on. "It is—or was—buried at the foot of a tree in the garden. We intended to look for it after nightfall, but had no time. The steward warned us to go at once. The townspeople in Stony Stratford were hostile, and our servants were not to be trusted. We snatched up a little food to take with us."

Anthony Woodville had insisted on parting company with Dorset. "Because if I went alone, I would have a better chance of escaping notice. He approved of my coming here, and so I pushed on, and after long miles, I saw what I knew to be Astley Chase."

Dorset had spent the greater part of yesterday in a hollow tree.

"Once I was beyond the chase, I was in full view but no one questions a beggar's right to go into a church. I could count on your being there for Vespers. If you had not gone alone, what would I have done?"

"The sentry would not have turned away a poverty-stricken wayfarer," I said.

Dorset was no longer the arrogant young lord, he was the hunted fox.

"Until I had put your charity to the test, how could I be sure that you would extend it to me?" He reached for my hand and studied the marriage ring on my finger. "Now I know."

The window gave a view of the fields, turning gold as the sun westered. I heard a cart creaking along to the village. Later Dame Joan knocked on the door and asked to speak to me. I went out of the room, leaving Dorset crouched in his chair.

"Ill news is written on your face," I said to Dame Joan.

"Yes, but not everyone will think so."

We were alone in the great hall. In the distance a shepherd boy was piping his song. The sound came faint but clear in the evening stillness. And Dame Joan spoke in a whisper.

She began by telling me that a market had been held in Coventry yesterday. Near midday, a great crowd of armed men had come up to the town's gates, bringing the queen's father and her brother John with them—the two most hated Woodvilles. Just outside the gates, the mob had halted and built a scaffold. An executioner had appeared. He had beheaded the Woodvilles, doing the work quickly, while the citizens had lined the walls to watch. The mob had been orderly throughout and immediately after the executions had gone away as suddenly and silently as they had come.

So far, Anthony had escaped.

"Where were they taken?" I asked.

"At Grafton," Dame Joan answered. "What possessed them to risk going there? They must have known the danger."

"They knew," I told her, "but they were desperate to get their hands on the gold secreted in the garden."

Now I faced the dreaded duty of breaking the news to Dorset. I was beginning to realize how lucky he had been.

After the lawless executions at Coventry, the rebels seemed to think that their task was done, and drifted away to their own homes. By September, Edward was free. He had word that Richard, and Will Hastings, at the head of an armed force, were waiting for his orders. He summoned them, and they escorted him to London. Anthony Woodville and Dorset came out of hiding and joined him. The peers of the realm set out to meet him and accompanied him into the city. The mayor and aldermen, in scarlet robes, and two hundred craftsmen, in blue, welcomed him.

Edward came by way of Chepe, to give all citizens the opportunity of seeing him and seeing his brother Richard, riding beside him, at his right. There were lords, knights, and squires, numbering over a thousand horsemen, but the earl and George were not in the cavalcade. Edward forbade them to set foot in London.

As soon as I reached London, I went at once to Elizabeth. Westminster Palace was astir with life and bustle, the Royal Council was assembling, clerks laden with documents hurried here and there, pages were shepherding a group of merchants into the king's presence chamber. Edward had taken the government of the country into his own hands again. In contrast to the swirl of activity elsewhere, a hush prevailed in the queen's apartments. All of her attendants wore deepest mourning, and spoke in whispers. The bright tapestries were concealed under black hanging, and in Elizabeth's bedchamber, where she received me, not only the walls but the windows were entirely covered over, shutting out the daylight. The fire had burned into ashes, and a few candles in the far corners of the room only deepened the gloom. I felt as if I had come into a burial vault, and the doors were shut behind me, leaving me with the dead for company. At first, I could scarcely see the silent motionless figure, swathed in black, until Elizabeth raised her head and looked at me.

Her eyes were set in dark shadows, and her voice was hoarse from long hours of weeping. I had not seen her since last spring—on the eve of her journey to Fotheringhay with Edward. I remembered how she had exulted in all that the summer had seemed to promise. As I knelt to kiss her hand, she put her arms around me and held me. When we were both calmer she made me sit near her. "You have proved yourself a true wife to Dorset," she said, and thanked me for contriving to send word to her that he was alive and well.

I had chosen one of my own servants to ride to Kenilworth, and find out if the constable had any means of conveying my message to London. At the time, a courier, with an armed escort —disguised as a group of traders—had been ready to set out. He had promised to deliver my message and had kept his word. Elizabeth had never doubted that Edward would regain his power, but his triumph had come too late to save her father and her brother John.

"My father and my brother, victims of a brutish mob, so I'm told. Am I expected to believe it? I know the enemies who tracked them down and slaughtered them," she faltered, struggling to find breath.

It would not be the first time that a mob had become inflamed and bloodthirsty, and Elizabeth seemed unaware of the people's ill feeling against the Woodvilles. But I had also listened to an eyewitness straight from the scene of the beheadings at Coventry. His account had turned me sick and filled me with forebodings. The mob had been too well disciplined.

Elizabeth stared at the shadows. "The murders were carefully, ruthlessly carried out," she said. "The earl and George are the murderers."

Both of them had been far from Coventry, and not so much as one witness—not one person—had come forth with evidence against them. What did Edward believe? He did not confide in his friends. He offered a general pardon to all who had taken part in the recent rebellion. The earl and George were included. The people seemed glad to return to their allegiance. Publicly, the death of the Woodvilles was glossed over.

Elizabeth and her mother stayed in seclusion, and Edward had decreed official mourning for the whole court. "At Westminster we must wear long faces," Hastings said, "but whoever contrived the death of those two Woodvilles did Edward a service—

even though nothing rouses his anger to a hotter blaze than for his subjects to take the law into their own hands."

While Edward had been at Warwick and at Middleham he had been treated as the king paying a royal visit of his own free will. On his side, he had kept up the pretense; he had behaved as a guest. Apparently in good humor, he had agreed to all of the earl's demands. When he had regained his power, he disavowed his promises—they had been extracted from him, he claimed, and had no validity. London was glad to see the earl's red-jacketed retainers thronging the streets and taverns again. Foreign envoys and London officials hurried to Warwick House. The banner on the highest turret displayed the white bear and ragged staff, as if confronting the leopards of England. The earl took his usual place on the Royal Council.

"Edward speaks to him as if they were friends again," John Dynham told me. "Both of them are being politic."

I was no longer as gullible as I had been. I knew better than to hope for any lasting truce.

My lady Duchess came to London. Abetted by her daughters she made every effort to heal the rift between her sons. At last Edward agreed to meet a seemingly repentant George at Baynard's Castle. I was with Elizabeth when Edward came back from the interview and told her why he had consented to a reconciliation. The country needed peace. Elizabeth had resigned herself to accept the news with what calmness she could muster. But I asked myself if she would have enough self-command to put her personal feelings aside. I underrated her.

"I am always for peace and pardon," she said, and praised Edward for his generosity and his large-hearted willingness to forgive.

"George begs me to recognize his marriage," Edward told her.

"Has he persuaded you?" Elizabeth asked.

"No"—Edward hesitated—"not yet, but my mother and sisters are besieging me."

And doubtless expected Elizabeth to undermine their work. But she refrained.

"A valid marriage can never be undone," she said.

Edward watched her face. "George wants more. He wants to bring Isabel here. Would you be willing to receive them?"

"If you are ready to welcome them, so am I," she answered.

Elizabeth needed all of her skill as a dissembler, and I wondered if she could play the part required of her and meet George face to face without betraying her unforgiving enmity for him. Her mother found excuse to avoid him by claiming illness, and keeping to her bed. There was no longer any danger that Lady Jacquetta would be prosecuted for witchcraft. Edward scoffed at the evidence.

Elizabeth was not taxed with the earl's presence. He had left London for the north. Dorset walked more boldly now, although he stayed close to Edward, who seemed sorry for him. Unlike his sister and mother, he was not overwhelmed with grief. I knew that because Dorset was frank with me; he had learned to trust me. Once in London again, he went seeking women, and he still taunted me for my supposed fondness for George.

"You will be glad to welcome him back to the fold," he taunted.

"Where we hope that he will remain," I answered.

I had no desire to see George at present, but there was no escape for me, as Edward had asked me to be on hand to welcome George and Isabel.

On the appointed day, a drear winter rain was falling, bringing an early dusk, but the king's presence chamber, with wax candles and the great fire blazing on the hearth, was a background to make mourning garments conspicuous. And the brilliant light revealed us too clearly at a time when we must guard every look and word. Even before George came, we were a discordant and ill-assorted group.

Elizabeth's father had been Constable of England, and after his violent death, she had hoped that her brother Anthony would inherit the office. Instead, Edward had appointed his own faithful brother Richard—making him Lord High Constable for life, with a great increase of authority and responsibility. Although Elizabeth accepted Edward's decision with her habitual air of docility, in private she brooded over her disappointment. Edward had learned that in time of crisis the Woodvilles had proved to be more hindrance than help. They lacked the stuff of greatness.

The doors opened and pages announced the Duke and Duchess of Clarence, and George led Isabel into the presence chamber. He wore crimson, satin embroidered and re-embroidered, cloth of gold, ermine bordered, and many jewels. Instead of showing constraint, he had a triumphant air as he presented Isabel to the king and queen. He must have fortified himself with wine, I thought, to make him so bold—or perhaps the boldness covered qualms of conscience. Elizabeth maintained her composure, spoke a few words to him, gave him her hand to kiss, and she was all graciousness to Isabel, who needed to be reassured.

Edward took pains to put Isabel at her ease, and draw her into conversation. It was not long before she lost some of her timidity and responded. When it was my turn to speak to her, she seemed glad to find me here, although it had been many years since we had met. She was very much as I remembered her, small and slight, with soft dark eyes, and dark hair, now covered by a matron's headdress and the jeweled coronet of a royal duchess. Her jewels seemed too heavy for her size, and her long state mantle weighed her down and made her seem even smaller than she was. Compared to her, I was as brown and sturdy as any west country farm wench.

Richard also made an effort to renew the friendship and affection of the past. They were able to talk to each other freely enough for Richard to ask her about her sister, Anne. Here was the loyal brother, deprived of his Anne when the disloyal brother had contrived to win Isabel.

I gave George credit for loving her, as well as he could love anyone, and doubtless she had given him her heart. Very likely she saw him as the daring lover who carried her away and had risked all to marry her. As for his behavior toward Edward, she would believe what George and her father the earl told her that the sole aim of the rebellion was to curtail the power of the Woodvilles. This indeed is what the people believed.

George came up to me. "As you see, I kept my vow," he whispered. "I swore to marry Isabel, and marry her I did." Edward was nearby, and perhaps he had heard, because he turned and gave George a long searching look. "Take care of your wife, George," he said. He spoke in earnest, and in his voice and the way he put his hand on George's shoulder there was some trace of the old fondness and a hint of warning, "She's not made for rough weather."

🌹 *Eighteen*

As the Year of Our Lord 1470 came in, England seemed quiet, and foreigners called London the busiest city in Christendom. But by the end of winter, a new disturbance started up in Lincolnshire. It began when a former Lancastrian, who had sworn allegiance to Edward, attacked and despoiled a manor belonging to an officer of the crown—a serious crime under Edward's government. Edward decided to deal with the lawlessness himself. With anger spurring him, he was soon ready to march.

"In this harsh weather," Elizabeth sighed, listening to the boisterous wind. Her mother and her sister Katherine had just left her and I was alone with her in her private solar. She still wore her black draperies, but her apartments were no longer shrouded. The solar's six lancet windows overlooked an angle of the garden, planted with roses and lilies, but it would be a long time before they bloomed.

Elizabeth sat near the fire, embroidering, the three leopards on a length of silk—a scarf for Edward. "He will not be able to wear it when he goes in the morning," she said. "My work is not finished."

"It will be ready for him on his return," I told her.

"When will that be?" she sighed.

"Very shortly, madam," I answered, with more certainty than I felt.

"So he says and I must believe him, but I have learned to dread any parting from the ones that I love."

I had nothing to say. I knew that parting might be forever. Through the archway leading into her bedchamber I had a glimpse of her great bed, with its emblazoned hangings. Every night she waited for Edward to come to her, sometimes in vain.

However, throughout the autumn and winter, although Edward had his amourettes, Elizabeth had lured him to her bed night after night. "To make a prince" his friends said. And because he had an enduring passion for her, I thought. Now Elizabeth would lie alone and wakeful until Edward came back to her.

After I had left her, I met Edward. Instead of greeting me and going on, he insisted on accompanying me to my barge. Although he was setting out at next day's dawn, he seemed in no hurry, and sauntered along with a leisurely air. "I seldom have a chance to speak to you without a swarm of people about," he said, taking the private staircase. As he knew, I was in the habit of using it to come and go, leaving my servants to wait for me in an antechamber on a lower floor.

Edward thanked me for my constant attendance on the queen. "Your company is good for her."

"She longs for your company," I said.

"I'm sorry to go away," he said, "but less than an hour ago a courier brought word of more disturbances, and the good people in Lincolnshire are gibbering in terror because a rank crop of rumors has been started. I'm said to be on my way to hang most of the population."

"They're fools to be so easily gulled!"

"But it's best for me to go myself and set their fears at rest."

"Who sowed the crop?" I asked.

"Who would you say is trying to turn the country against me?" Edward asked.

"A Lancastrian malcontent first broke the peace," I answered.

"When last summer's trouble began it was called Lancastrian unrest. This new ferment seems to be following the same pattern."

"God knows I hope not!" I spoke with fervor.

"I was easily gulled then, but as my cousin Warwick and my brother were in rebellion last summer, do they hope to lead another this spring?"

In the shifting light and shadow, the steps in front of me seemed to spiral down and down. My knees threatened to give way. Edward drew my arm within his and took a firm grip on my hand.

"You must never go down this staircase alone, Cicely," Edward warned me. I had been up and down countless times without giving a thought to the possibility of falling.

"I am unusually surefooted," I assured him.

"And move with grace but your trailing skirts could entangle you and make you lose your balance."

"Not my skirts but what you said knocked me off balance."

"I mentioned a possibility. I have to weigh it, but you need not think of it. I might have become too distrustful."

Immediately after he had presented her at Westminster Palace, George had taken Isabel to Warwick Castle, and there they had stayed. The earl was still in the north. He had promised to join Edward in Lincolnshire.

"You and my mother and sisters form a league to defend George," Edward accused me, but without anger. "Because of your fondness for him."

I looked up to see Edward smiling at me, and this time he halted, waiting for me to speak.

"I am not spurring to George's defense," I said. "Because I no longer know his mind."

"He has given his word to come to the appointed place at the appointed time." Edward was no longer smiling. In the light of a torch set on the wall, his face had turned hard. "If he fails me—"

In time, messengers came from Edward as he marched into Lincolnshire, but without the earl, and without George. Why the delay? It was ominous, even though they had sent letters to Edward, still pledging their support.

"He'll get no help from them," Elizabeth said, after the messenger had gone. "This rebellion, like the other, is all their work."

Edward lost no time. He pushed on, met the rebels and overwhelmed them. "As I knew he would," Elizabeth said when his letter came. He had taken a number of prisoners. Some wore the earl's device of the bear and ragged staff, or George's blazonings. And the others who managed to escape by taking to their heels quickly enough had torn off their telltale jackets. Edward had named the scene of the clash, Lose-Coat Field.

The rebel leader was executed, after he had declared that the earl and George had planned the uprising. They had hoped to wrest the crown from Edward and make George king. Edward had freed all of his other prisoners, "And am content to let the men who ran away from me so nimbly go back where they came from . . ."

The people of Lincolnshire had returned to their senses, since they no longer believed that the "king was coming to destroy the commons." They were busying themselves thinking up long speeches to welcome him. As spring had come to the fens, doubtless the women and girls were weaving garlands. If they were like women elsewhere, they were hoping to catch the king's eye.

Edward sent John Dynham to London to transact some matter of business for the crown, and he found time to come to Dorset House, where he could talk freely. Edward had written letters to the earl, and to George, ordering them to disband their army and meet him at once.

"They promised, they declared their loyalty, but never came," John Dynham told me. "Then Edward ordered one of his squires to go to George with a final summons. 'Tell him that I command him to come at once, or by the Body of God, he will repent it through every vein in his heart!'"

Edward's Plantagenet wrath was all the more startling because it was so seldom displayed. Even his friends quailed before it.

"The poor devil of a squire fell on his knees and begged Edward to send another messenger, because he dared not repeat those words to George. And so Edward sent England's herald, Garter King-at-Arms—"

"As if he were declaring war on his brother," I said.

"Yes, and without waiting for an answer, he's marching with a strong army to track down those two rebels—George and the earl."

"Have they earned the name?" I asked.

"You know the evidence against them," John Dynham said. "When the earl began the uprising last summer I think that he set out to destroy the Woodvilles, I doubt if he intended to depose Edward, but the plan grew."

"And failed."

"It's an ill-starred venture for them," John Dynham said, and so it proved.

Their men deserted them, slinking away to find cover. With a scanty following, the earl and George made for Warwick Castle, where Lady Warwick, Isabel, and Anne were waiting, only to learn that nothing was left for them except exile. They must ride for the coast and leave England behind them.

Again the earl's ability showed itself. Outdistancing Edward's pursuit, he led his family and several hundred retainers, to Exeter. The seamen of the Devon ports admired him too much to think of him as a traitor. He gathered enough ships, and sailed for France.

When the news reached London, the citizens seemed dazed. I saw a fisherman standing at the water gate, gazing at Warwick

House. Locked, barred, lifeless, it had become a mass of stone. Doubtless the watcher thought of other mornings, when the doors had been flung open to admit him and hundreds of others into the court, to eat and drink their fill in the midst of a friendly swarm of red-jacketed servants and retainers.

The earl had chosen his way, aware of the hazards, but his wife and daughters were victims, and with all my heart I pitied them. They had known sudden twists and changes of fortune, like many other women, but Isabel and Anne seemed particularly unfitted to endure bodily hardship. Isabel was a delicate girl, and she was in the eighth month of a first pregnancy, in no state for exertion. Yet, with the others, she had made the long ride on horseback from the Midlands to the coast, without rest, with scarcely a halt on the way. Then she had been hurried on shipboard, to be tossed and buffeted again.

The earl had hoped to add to his flotilla at Southampton, and seize the flagship, *The Trinity*. But Edward had sent Anthony Woodville to command the port. He was on the watch, and sailing out of the harbor with part of the Royal Navy, attacked the earl's ships and forced them to draw off. Making for Calais, the earl was attacked by Burgundy's ships, but routed them. He was still Captain of Calais, and as he had appointed the lieutenant, he expected a welcome. Instead, as the earl's ships neared the harbor, the guns protecting Calais opened fire, forcing the earl to cast anchor outside the harbor. His lieutenant was "acting under the King of England's orders."

While his little fleet was at anchor off Calais, Isabel felt the pangs of childbirth. There was no physician or midwife on board, and everything in the way of necessities was lacking. Her mother and sister doubtless did what they could, but Lady Warwick was not the woman to be useful in such a case, and Anne was a young girl who had never before so much as seen a woman in labor. They became more and more frightened for Isabel's life, as the labor went on all day and into the following night.

The earl determined to find some help for Isabel, and sent a boat to Calais asking for wine. His lieutenant at least granted that favor, and sent several casks of the best to be had. At last Isabel was delivered, but the poor infant never drew breath. Lady Warwick and Anne wrapped the dead child in a piece of sailcloth for the burial at sea. For several days there was scant hope for Isabel's life, but finally she rallied.

Setting sail for Honfleur, the earl was again attacked by ships of the Royal Navy, with Anthony Woodville in command.

"A sharp encounter," we heard. The earl lost men but gave the English fleet a battering, and made port at Honfleur. The Spider King of France did much more than grant refuge to a group of fugitives; he sent the greatest French lords to offer them royal hospitality and pay them homage.

"He seems to be wreathing them with laurels, as if they had come in triumph," Elizabeth said.

She had exulted when the royal courier had brought word of Edward's victory, but had felt great anxiety for her brother Anthony in his sea battles. He had come out unscathed, and was no longer in danger. "He has earned laurels," she said. In her palace she did not hear what Londoners were muttering to one another.

Even with Lord Howard as second-in-command, Anthony Woodville was no match for the earl, either on land or sea, and would do better to keep to the tiltyard. In the Cinque Ports, the sailors jeered at the Woodville Admiral.

"The French lavish every attention on George," Elizabeth told me. I had heard that he had left Honfleur and that Isabel was with him.

"I wonder that she still lives," I said.

"The French provide her with every luxury, and doubtless she will soon recover her health," Elizabeth tried to reassure me.

"But not her child."

"A male child yes, after such long suffering the loss of her son must be a great grief to her." Elizabeth could feel compassion

170

because the child had died. Would she have been glad if George's son had lived and thrived when she had yet to give Edward an heir?

"I'm still able to give Edward a prince," she said, showing the direction of her thoughts.

"A Prince of Wales and a Duke of York," I answered.

Edward was on his way home to London, and was expected in a few days. With the good news the somnolent palace woke up, and after months of tears and melancholy, Elizabeth had decided to leave off her mourning and banish all outward signs of grief so as to please him on his return. As I saw, she was again interested in making use of every art to enhance her beauty.

Dorset seemed glad to see me again, and approved the changes that I had made in the house and the gardens. He ordered magnificent clothes for himself, new liveries for his servants and retainers, and enlarged his household, but he could only stay a few days in London.

"Edward will soon be off to Canterbury and the Cinque Ports," he complained. "That means endless miles of hard riding, as well as coarse fare, flea-ridden beds and raw-boned, blowsy girls."

Edward was going to inspect the coastal defenses. "You have summer weather now," I pointed out, "and you are sure to find handsome wenches."

"Edward will be sure to pre-empt those. And your good stepfather Hastings," Dorset said, and told me to do my best with the estates. As he had little hope of being in London, he was willing for me to make a visit to the west country. After his victory, Edward had re-established order, and even during the disorders and rebellion, the west country had remained quiet. Dorset left the administration of his own lands as well as mine to me, which had great advantages, but also gave me problems to solve.

A bridge had fallen in and must be repaired before winter

rains made the ford impassable; a quarrel between a prosperous tenant and his shiftless neighbor must be settled; a miller overcharged the village people for grinding their corn, besides other complaints and grievances usual on any estate—these were small problems and could easily be set right. But other matters were beyond my control. In the Midlands, bad weather threatened the harvest, and Dorset's tenants would be unable to pay him as much as he expected, unless conditions improved.

In the west, good weather had favored the farmers, and the crops flourished, but here, as everywhere else, the wool was not fetching as high a price as last year because the treaty with Burgundy was proving a disappointment. The Low Countries were not taking as much of our cloth as Duke Charles of Burgundy had promised. The people had other reasons for discontent. Lords and commons alike complained of the heavy taxes, and when my neighbors came to welcome me, they discussed the king's burdensome demands. "He orders us to be ready at all times to defend the realm," one of them grumbled. "At our own expense, too."

The others present agreed. They also agreed that Anthony Woodville, commanding the king's ships, could never keep the Earl of Warwick mewed up in France, if the earl chose to sally out. However, the earl would never bring foreign troops to England.

When I listened to such talk, I asked, "Then what will happen?" It was the question that everyone in England was asking and no one could answer.

However, I had too many daily duties and tasks to occupy me to give much thought to the future. I had rebuilt and refurnished my grandfather's town house in Exeter. In his name, I had enlarged the Almshouse and Hospice that he had built and maintained, but I had made a few changes at the old manor house at Shute. At a little distance, it seemed an outcropping of rock, but Dame Joan Wynant and I were content within its rough-hewn walls.

"How can you endure the discomforts and isolation of that place?" Dorset asked when I returned to London in the fall.

"It was necessary," I answered, which was partly true. Actually I was always reluctant to leave Devon.

London seethed with rumors—one tale contradicting another. "The earl's spies are everywhere," Dorset told me. "Working to undermine the government." He looked over his shoulder, as if he felt pursuers hard on his heels.

The rest of us had other worries. My mother was one of those who was pulled this way and that. She was married to Will Hastings, and loved him, but she was the Earl of Warwick's sister, and had a great affection for him. In her view, he had been driven into exile by the Woodvilles and by Edward's ingratitude.

She had declined to accompany me into the west country, for fear of missing her husband's visits. "I would have done better to go with you," she told me on my return. "Hastings was traversing England with Edward, and when he is in London, he finds scant time for me or his children."

"He has scant time to call his own," I said.

"Like you who are with the queen day and night. But her favor brings luck in all worldly matters, so they say."

"In our times no one can say how long luck will hold," I answered. "But Elizabeth has been kind to me."

"Kind? What does her so-called kindness cost her? Have you forgotten her trickeries?"

"On the contrary, I remember all too well."

"Hastings is the king's man," my mother said, her eyes filling with tears.

"I understand your feelings," I told her, "and his—it was no easy choice." The earl's rebellion and exile had destroyed her peace of mind, and threatened the somewhat precariously maintained peace of her marriage. By birth and upbringing my mother was a great lady, and in some ways reminded me of the Duchess of York, who was a Neville too, but the pattern seemed to be outmoded in Edward's court, and in Edward's England.

When I left my mother, I went to Baynard's Castle. The Duchess of York was likewise unhappy. The rift between her sons preyed on her. She had recently taken up residence in London again, and I made haste to pay my duty to her. Perhaps because my spirits were low, or perhaps it was the pallid winter sun, but Baynard's Castle seemed a gloomy mass of stone. Even the state apartments, which had once impressed me with their magnificence, seemed dim and cheerless. Doubtless I had acquired a taste for the Woodville palaces—but even the fairest palace would have no effect on my mood.

My lady Duchess looked old and gaunt, her face reflected her troubled mind and heart. She met me with more fondness than she usually allowed herself, but at first we spoke to each other with constraint. I was wary of saying too much. Ever since my marriage, she always offered me a chair, but after a few minutes I asked her to let me have my old accustomed place. I drew up a cushioned footstool—known as mine because I had embroidered the cushion—and sat down close to her chair.

"No one else can ever take your place," she said. "Now if Margaret could be here, sitting beside me—" My lady Duchess broke off. "A letter from her reached me today."

From a recent letter to me, I could gather what she had written to her mother. Margaret's greatest anxiety was for her brother George. He was young—a boy in love—easily led astray.

As my lady Duchess was about to speak again, Edward came in, smiling and untroubled. He settled himself in one of the tall-backed chairs. "Barbarous chairs" he called them, but not in his mother's hearing. After he had asked about his mother's health, he talked to me, showing accurate knowledge of conditions in the west country, although his arduous journeys had taken him in every other corner of England, but not there.

"The west seems tranquil," he said, "but the people grumble about taxes and the state of trade. My good brother of Burgundy must keep his word."

"He's turned cool to us," my lady Duchess said.

"Not cool—angry. Margaret feeds him conserves of roses and violets to calm him, without much effect."

"Margaret does her best, but the disunity in our family makes foreign courts wary." My lady Duchess was doubtless quoting Margaret's opinion.

"Charles of Burgundy won't break the alliance," Edward told her. "He's too deeply embroiled with the French Spider." He eyed his mother. "You and Margaret want me to be reconciled with George."

"A house divided—" my lady Duchess began.

"All of us are aware of the danger," Edward said, "but these days the French show scant consideration for George. They give their homage to Warwick, so George may be weary of cooling his heels in exile."

"And if you were to offer him terms—" My lady Duchess leaned forward in her eagerness. She had greatly loved and admired the earl, but she had cast him off for the sake of her sons, and the dynasty and for what she felt was the good of the country.

"Margaret would use her influence to persuade him," she said.

"How could she reach him? The Duchess of Burgundy would not be permitted to go into France. France and Burgundy are in a state of war. She has no way of communicating with George. Letters or messages would be intercepted and would be useless even if they were delivered."

"Then send some entirely loyal person, someone with the necessary tact, and someone who knows George," my lady Duchess suggested.

"How am I to find such a person?" Edward asked. He turned to me. "The Marchioness of Dorset would be too conspicuous," he said. "Otherwise you would be well suited to take the part of the dove bearing the olive branch. It would have to be material reward to dangle before his eyes."

"You credit me with more power than I have," I answered. "And no one could be less suited for the part."

"Why?" Edward studied my face. "You know him, you might induce him—"

"To desert the earl?" I spoke before I thought.

"George deserted me and I am his brother," Edward reminded me, and turned away.

❧ Nineteen

Over a month had passed since I had seen Edward at Baynard's Castle. He had gone into the Midlands, but was back in London. I had met him, and we had spoken a few words to each other. Even if he found the opportunity, I doubted if he or his mother would again mention any hope or plan to bring George into the fold. Both the Spider of France and the earl would be on the alert.

In the spring of that year a group of Kentish seamen mutinied, and Edward sent the Earl of Worcester to deal with the trouble. He had always been a friend of the Woodvilles, partly from self-interest, but he was doubtless drawn to them because he shared their taste for books and learnings. Then too he had traveled to Venice with a large retinue and had made the long and dangerous pilgrimage to the Holy Land.

My Lord Worcester had other talents as well. Edward valued him as a military commander. The people had a different view. Some years ago, Edward had sent him to Ireland, but was compelled to recall him because he was too harsh. I had heard accounts of his cruelty here in England. In Kent, he gave the mutineers quick trial and hanged the lot. Doubtless the men were guilty of treason according to the law. They had declared for the Earl of Warwick, and had intended to take their ships over to him, and my lord of Worcester was not for softening the rigors of the law. In this case, he went beyond the law, and impaled the trunks and heads of the executed seamen on stakes.

"The people are not squeamish, God knows, but this turns their stomachs," Will Hastings said.

In Dover, in Kent, in London, the people cursed Lord Worcester and muttered threats against him.

Elizabeth knew that the mutiny had been suppressed, but I doubted if she knew how her friend Worcester had gone about his work, and as she lived secluded within the palace, she was unaware of the outcry here in London. It was not her fault. Edward did his best to spare her by keeping disquieting news from reaching her ears, but as soon as I saw her, I spoke of the mutiny, and said that I knew how little she could approve of the Earl of Worcester's methods of quelling it.

She was in her solar, sitting by the fire. "My brother Anthony is in command of the ships," she reminded me. "The mutiny put him in danger." Her eyes filled with tears.

"I well understand your concern for him, madam, but my Lord Worcester's cruelty makes him hated, and the people's hate is dangerous." As she and her brother Anthony and all Woodvilles should have learned.

"Kentishmen are always unruly," she murmured, and went on to praise Worcester. She picked up a book and showed it to me. "This is his work." It was a translation of Cicero's essay on friendship.

"The people know his other work," I answered, "and if you had seen bodies thrust on stakes—"

Elizabeth put her hands over her ears. "Not another word! I pity them—but they were traitors—put them out of your mind!"

"If you would use your influence with the king," I ventured. "Impalement may be legal in Padua, but not here."

Edward would have to do what he thought best, she said, and she could not allow herself to think of bloodshed and treacheries. "It would do harm in my present hopeful state— this child must be protected from all evil influences."

Elizabeth was *enceinte*, and called on me to share her joy. The birth of a prince, she said, would make the people happy, and end all dissension. And she went on planning the future of her son.

Edward could again cherish hopes of an heir, which should have softened his heart, but on the contrary, he seemed more ruthless.

The Earl of Worcester came clattering into London, ignoring the crowds who shouted, "Kill the foul butcher." In the evening he appeared at the palace and was ushered into the queen's presence chamber. Edward and Elizabeth showed him the same friendship as before, but when he turned his bulging eyes on me and came up to me, I could not bring myself to speak to him or give him my hand to kiss. I moved away from him without a word of greeting.

Dorset had sharp words for what he called my uncouth behavior. He never chose to show anger by storming, but came into my bedchamber with a sauntering gait and stood in front of me staring at me before he spoke. "You turned your back on a great lord high in Edward's good graces. You showed yourself an untaught wild creature, more fit for your rude house in the west country than for a royal palace!" His scornful tone gave his words more emphasis. He may have succeeded in wounding his first wife, but I wore heavier armor.

"You are quite right," I told him, "and I often think that it was a mistake for me to leave my rude house for any palace or lord's castle."

I looked around the room, entirely changed since Dorset's first wife had died here, and furnished to my taste, but at times, I felt stifled here.

"At my house, the air is cleaner."

"And the winds howl through it!"

"I would rather listen to the wind than to lies and rumors and malicious talk. If you wish it, I will go back to Shute Manor for whatever length of time you please."

"I do not wish it . . . You are forever seizing on some excuse to fly away to your estates."

"Or to yours—on your orders," I reminded him.

"I know, I know. Stay." Dorset had abandoned his disdainful manner. "But remember, Lord Worcester is a friend. Treat him with courtesy."

"He's no friend of mine, and your friendship for him is likely to do you harm."

As the following day was mild and sunny, Elizabeth went out, and strolled in the garden with some of her ladies. Edward joined her, and after a time, he offered to show me the new fish pond, and drew me away from the others, who lagged behind. Edward's silence showed his anger. So did his face.

We reached the fishpond, but Edward did not look at it, he looked down at me. He seemed twenty feet tall. "Last night what possessed you to insult Lord Worcester?" he demanded.

"If I had spoken to him I might have called him by the name that the people give him—foul butcher."

"Do I need to tell you that the safety of the country depends on the navy? Or the danger of a mutiny? The mutineers were Warwick's men."

"Accustomed to his leadership," I said. "Lowly sailors, confused and puzzled by the changes of this last year."

In the past, Edward had been willing to pardon such people, but not any more. I saw how rebellions and betrayals had hardened him.

"Blame the Earl of Warwick for their death—he incited them to mutiny."

The earl was partly responsible, and I wondered if he blamed himself.

"Lord Worcester did his duty," Edward said.

"Did his duty include devising such an obscene spectacle as impalement?"

"A warning to other traitors and would-be traitors!" Edward was taut with anger, but I was reckless. Had he forgotten Wakefield and its aftermath—the row of heads withering on the gates of York?

"You are the king—you can uphold or condone or forbid useless cruelty—but I am making my appeal to Duke Richard's son."

Edward's face went bleak, but at that moment Elizabeth and her ladies came up to us. After a few words to them, he left claiming that he had messages to send. When I saw him again, he was perfectly courteous, but I felt a definable change in his manner to me. Edward had never resented plain speaking, but he seemed unwilling to forgive me my boldness. Why? It was as if I had flashed a mirror before his eyes. Did he catch a momentary glimpse of what he might become in future. A ruthless king, feared and hated?

A few weeks later Will Hastings told me that Edward had "drawn rein" on the Earl of Worcester, and the clamor died down. The queen's pregnancy was publicly announced, and prayers were offered in all churches. Londoners showed no signs of jubilation, and Elizabeth found the suspense harder to endure than before. Her enemy was Time. When Edward was present, she exerted herself to please him, by seeming to be in good spirits, and boasting of her health. She always spoke of "our son" to him.

Edward wanted the expected child to be born in London, to please the citizens, and at Westminster Palace preparations were begun for the queen's lying-in. However, trouble broke out in Yorkshire. "Summer heat lightnings," Edward said, but as the earl still had power in the north, Edward decided to march in Yorkshire and take control himself. For greater security he thought it best for Elizabeth and her children to move from Westminster Palace to the Tower's royal apartments.

To please Elizabeth and himself, no expense had been spared to refurnish and embellish the apartments for her use. The ill news from Yorkshire seemed to make him all the more determined to celebrate the child's birth with sovereign pomp, to dazzle his restless subjects, and to impress foreign courts, particularly the

French. Kings and queens had lodged in the palace of the Tower but none of them as luxuriously as Elizabeth Woodville.

Dr. Serigo, the queen's chief physician, had fixed the date of the child's birth at the end of October, or the earliest days of November, and seamstresses were at work on velvets and cloth of gold for the queen when she recovered from her confinement. Hundreds of the finest ermine skins from Russia had come on a ship out of Norway, costly furs to make a regal mantle for the queen's churching.

Elizabeth had kept to her bed, suffering from a fever. She was desperately afraid of losing the child, and even more afraid of danger to Edward and her son Dorset and her brother Anthony in the forthcoming campaign. Her anxiety was doubtless responsible for her illness.

On a hot day in September I went to the window of the queen's solar for a breath of air. Looking out, I could see a mass of walls and turrets. The Tower was a palace, a fortress, and a prison. One prisoner who was still there had once been crowned and anointed as Henry the Sixth.

A slight sound startled me; I turned and saw Friar Bungay. The queen had summoned him, he told me. He had the privilege of using the private stairs to her apartments, and had come in the narrow, tapestry-hung door. For a moment, I believed that he had taken shape by magic, until I had exchanged a few words with him. He wore a plain black robe, without any cabalistic signs. No one knew his early history, but his gnarled hands and the furrows in his strong-boned face gave him the look of having once known toil and hardship—and doubtless he had known grief too.

The queen would be disappointed, he said, because he had failed to cast a horoscope for the child, and refused to make any predictions.

"I know how intensely the queen longs for a son," he said. "Marguerite of Anjou likewise longed to be the mother of a prince, but her son is doomed to be the child of sorrow and misfortune."

It was night, and Dorset had come into my bedchamber. He flung himself into a chair, yawning, and propped his feet, encased in long pointed shoes, on a cushioned footstool. His widely distended sleeves were slashed to show cloth of gold, and around his neck he wore the collar blazing with golden suns and shining with the White Roses of York. The door to the garderobe was open, and Dorset sat up suddenly. "There it is, waiting for me."

It was his armor, bright steel, embossed in gold. His squire had polished it, assembled it and arranged it on a stand in readiness for Dorset to put on and ride off with Edward in two days' time.

"Edward's taking a scant force," Dorset complained. "He seems to have no misgivings, but I remember last summer all too well."

I thought of Dorset, hiding, hunted, slinking into Astley church. Good fortune had come again, but the fear lasted.

"This expedition will be very different from last summer's," I told him. "Edward is alert, and all England is on guard."

When Dorset was in bed with me, I tried to respond to his desire, but sensual passion offered him only brief escape, and afterwards he clung to me.

"Perhaps I will be killed," he sighed, "and you will not be long a widow."

"I am content to wait until I am one before I think of taking a second husband."

"You were reluctant to have me for your first."

"You had a first wife—your unkindness to her made me wary of you—"

Dorset laughed. "You dealt me some stinging rebukes, I remember, but it's too late for us to quarrel on her account. She was not the real reason for your reluctance—neither was your family's wrath—you were sighing for George."

"If so, it's too late for us to quarrel on his account," I answered.

"Edward knows that most of the people around him give him only a lukewarm loyalty and suspects you of being drawn to the earl—"

"Why?" I asked, angered by Edward's doubts.

"Because of your family. Your mother resents seeing her brother's greatness so diminished. Also because you hold a grievance against Edward for putting an end to your hope of marrying George."

"I never nursed any such hope—"

Suddenly, outside in the dark, a voice shouted, "A Warwick! A Warwick!"

Dorset groaned and buried his head in his pillow. The cry came again, nearer. The earl still had a friend in Edward's London—perhaps many friends in the nighttime city. Dorset's whole body tensed with listening.

"Warwick's in London, coming here to find me!"

"He's in France—far away," I said.

Eventually I succeeded in calming Dorset. He sighed, sank back on his pillows, and soon fell into a quiet sleep. But I was wakeful. Now and then I heard rain pattering down; between showers the waning moon hurried through ragged clumps of cloud. It must have been near day when I finally slept.

Toward evening of the following day, Elizabeth was waiting for Edward to come from the Council chamber where he was discussing his plans for the ride north with his lords and chief captains. She was in low spirits, but was outwardly composed, and only her constant glances at the door betrayed her impatience at his delay. To divert her thoughts, her sister Katherine persuaded her to see Master Domenico, who was sought after as an astrologer.

Neither Elizabeth or Lady Jacquetta had any faith in him. In serious matters they quietly consulted Friar Bungay, but for the moment Master Domenico served to deflect Elizabeth's gloomy thoughts. While she and her mother and sister listened to him, I took the opportunity of paying a visit to the chapel. Before I left the room I heard the astrologer promise Elizabeth a fair prince, who in time would have a long and glorious reign. It was written in the stars that the future would bring triumphant success and perfect happiness to Elizabeth and Edward.

The day had been overcast, with a dull murky heat, but at sundown the Tower showed dark against a band of sultry red in the western sky. I hurried to the chapel, dedicated to St. John, and found it empty and deserted. Once the door was closed behind me, I no longer heard voices and tramplings and clattering.

A faint chill always lingered here, and the pungence of incense. The Sanctuary lamp glowed, and candles were kept burning on the altars, but beyond the range of their light the columns cast deep shadows. The sunset made the windows blaze with crimson, deep azure, green, and purple, but the prophets and martyrs depicted in the painted glass seemed to be staring at me with grim faces. Halfway to the altar I knelt down.

In my prayers, I asked God to protect Edward—to save his life and his kingdom, and to grant him the grace to save his soul from the Devil. Long ago, a Plantagenet had made a pact with Satan, and had exchanged his soul for the kingdoms of this world. "From the Devil we came and to the Devil we must go," Richard the Lionheart had said.

The door opened and closed, very quietly; I neither turned nor raised my head, but I heard the clink of spurs on the stone floor and listened to the footsteps echoing in the silence. Whether he was shod in velvet or leather or steel, I knew his step. He was on the other side of the chapel as he went up the aisle. My head was veiled and I was in shadow, but Edward was sharp-eyed. However, he took no notice of me, and went on to kneel at the rail of the main altar.

In a few minutes he rose, turned from the altar and came toward me. The candlelight touched his tawny hair with gold and made a radiance around his head, giving him the aspect of a warrior archangel. Without speaking, he gave me his hand to assist me to my feet. He stood directly in front of me, with his right arm thrust out, and his hand flattened against a nearby column. The swinging folds of his cloak brushed against my shoulder, imprisoning me in shadow. His silence oppressed me, and when he moved his head a little the light slanting across the upper part of his face showed me his deep eye sockets. I could also see his heightened color—a stain of fire on his cheekbones, and I was aware of his anger.

"You seem absorbed in your devotions," he said and the harshness of his manner made me flinch. "Were you praying for Warwick's success? Or for George?" Edward gave me no chance to answer. "News has just come—"

"From the north?" I asked. It must be dire news to rouse Edward's wrath. My knees shook and there was a roaring in my ears.

"No, from France. Are you as ignorant and as innocent as you seem? How can I tell?" Then he grasped my hands and held them, "Forgive me, child. God knows I should never doubt you."

"My prayers were all for you," I told him.

"I need them, the country needs them," he said. "Warwick and Marguerite of Anjou have met. They have agreed to forget the past. They have made an alliance, signed a pact, and celebrated a wedding. In Angers Cathedral, the Earl of Warwick gave his daughter Anne in marriage to Marguerite's son."

As I listened, the light drained away from the windows, the candle flames blurred and went out; the shadows began to swim and whirl and darken. "Cicely—" Edward's voice brought me to myself. His arms were around me, holding me close, warming me. I heard his heart beating quick and strong. We did not need to speak. When I looked up at him, he bent and kissed me on the mouth. I clung to him, responding, and our ardor grew.

He was the first to leave off kissing. "No—not with you. I must keep you safe," he said, "protect you from any harm."

"And count me as your cousin and your friend."

"You were a child then but you once promised me your

friendship, through all time and change. Will you make the same promise now?"

"Now and always."

His lips touched my forehead, to seal the bond. "Remember that you are near and dear to me always."

"God go with you, Edward. And one day I will bring your son to you to ask for his father's blessing."

❧ Twenty

The Spider King of France had brought about the meeting between the earl and Marguerite of Anjou. That much was certain and as the facts became more fully known, it was not too difficult to trace what arguments the Spider must have used. Now the earl's friends and well-wishers were forced to believe that he had hoped to make George king, but had failed. Either the once mighty Earl of Warwick must forswear all ambitions and endure the dreary lot of an exile, while Edward reigned triumphant, or be reconciled to Lancaster. If the English people refused to accept Henry the Sixth, there was Marguerite of Anjou's son, now a boy of sixteen. The Lancastrians viewed him as heir to the throne. Why not swathe him in scarlet and ermine, marry him to Warwick's daughter, and put a crown on his head?

Urged on by the Spider, the earl had agreed to the plan. But for a long time, Madame Marguerite declared that she could not and would not pardon the earl who had been the greatest cause of Lancaster's downfall.

But the Spider had pleaded, promised, flattered, argued with all of his tireless patience and tortuous skill, always holding before her the hope of England's throne for her son. In her interview with the earl, she had kept him on his knees for a quarter of an hour, and "at the request of the King of France" had granted him pardon, and had promised never to reproach him.

How could he so debase himself as to kneel to that woman? Even my mother—his devoted sister—who had always defended him, could find no excuse for him. She could not forget the past, nor could I.

Marguerite's son had plighted himself to Warwick's daughter Anne, but as I understood it, the marriage had not as yet been solemnized or consummated. However, by the terms of the treaty, Anne was to be in the hands of Marguerite, the cruel evil queen of Anne's childhood. Would she be a kindly mother-in-law? Before a great crowd of people, the earl long ago had accused Marguerite of being a vile whore and had declared that her son was a bastard. No matter how long he stayed on his knees, she was the last woman on earth to forget the slur.

"No good can come of that unnatural marriage," my mother said.

"The boy is a suitable age for Anne." I tried to find some good in the match. "He's well educated and handsome, and is said to be in love with Anne."

But I knew that a long shadow darkened Anne's ill-omened marriage to the Lancastrian prince. Edward's shadow.

How did George stand to gain by the alliance with Lancaster? When he had rebelled and fled, his Duchy of Clarence had been declared forfeited to the crown. However, the pact with Marguerite of Anjou offered him all of his former estates and honors. More, he was to have the Duchy of York, with its great wealth, and if Anne's marriage to the Lancastrian prince proved barren, then George was to succeed to the crown.

Nebulous prospects, I thought, because Edward's navy, reinforced by the Burgundian fleet maintained a strict blockade, preventing any invasion of England. My lady Duchess of York, still at Fotheringhay, wrote that she was thankful to know that George had held himself aloof from this treaty with the enemy, which I took as a guarded allusion to her hope of seeing him reconciled to Edward. Was George content to have his claims to the throne thrust aside to make way for the Lancastrian prince? Not George!

Edward reached York without opposition; the rebellion had subsided as quickly as it had sprung up, but he found the shire wracked with lawless violence. He had offered pardon to all who had taken any part in rebellion, but he stayed on in York to check the crimes and bring the guilty to justice. As I knew from Dorset's letters to me, Edward had not told Elizabeth all. There was also the threat of new uprising to keep him in the north. And the confusion seemed to be spreading through the country, with a surge of rapes, robberies, extortions, and murders. Travelers banded together for protection. Women, if unaccompanied, stayed close to home, and no man dared stir without being fully armed.

Londoners were uneasy—the king's authority was needed, but at summer's end Edward was still in the north. The first days of September came and went, without a word from him or from his army. I felt as if he and his men had vanished in the mists somewhere in the secret dangerous north.

Toward evening, I left my house to go to the queen. The warm calm weather had changed. Clouds had formed and darkened. Chill gusts of wind were rising to fret the river, more than ever crowded by a number of fishing vessels and luggers. The threat of a storm had driven them into port, and they were seeking their usual moorings as quickly as they could. My oarsmen needed all of their skill to avoid colliding with them, and to bring the barge safely to the Tower's water stairs. The tide was already sweeping through the arches of the bridge and flooding the Tower wharf. A sea gale was in the making.

Men at arms in York's livery of murrey and blue were everywhere, pacing the ramparts and posted at every door. Edward had left well-equipped disciplined soldiers to guard the queen. Her antechamber was deserted except for a group of pages lolling by the fire, enjoying a haven of warmth and luxury. In contrast to the troubled city, the noisy buffeting wind, and the military sternness of the rest of the Tower, the queen's apartments seemed quiet and safe.

For a time, Elizabeth and I played at chess, but we only made a pretense of playing, our thoughts wandered elsewhere. The noise of the storm became louder and louder. Elizabeth shrank from the sound; she and her mother were afraid for Anthony Woodville, Admiral of England's fleet. It was a night for shipwreck. I did not need to be told that the gale had scattered the navy and had doubtless broken the blockade. Reports came in—some ships had been lost—most had reached port, but nearly all had suffered some damage. The earl was no longer mewed up in France.

A mud-spattered messenger on a lathered horse brought Elizabeth word from her brother Anthony. The storm had battered his ship, but he had succeeded in making port at Dover. He was riding north in haste to join the king—to avoid being made prisoner by the earl's partisans. Kent was disaffected, the messenger said, now that the earl had set sail from France. Depending on wind and weather, he could be expected to land in England.

No one could dismiss the news as another rumor. The earl always made careful preparations. He had been ready and waiting for the autumnal winds to rise and fling the blockading ships away from the French coast. The wind had spent its force by morning, but rain was still falling and the seas were rough. He would not wait for calm. He would take the opportunity that the storm had given him. Warwick was coming to England as an invader.

Elizabeth and her mother controlled any display of fear, but as they knew, Anthony Woodville was no longer safe ashore until he reached Edward's protection. Edward had taken care to strengthen the coast defenses, and the earl's attempt to land, of course, might fail. Dover Castle was a royal fortress, and could withstand assault, but the port remembered the Earl of Worcester's cruelty to the Kentish sailors—and Dover would welcome Warwick.

After midday swarms of people—farmers, traders, women, and children—people who lived beyond London's walls were streaming into the city, seeking refuge from wild Kentishmen who had taken to the road and were massing on London. By nightfall, they had surged up to the walls. On their way, they had been joined by a drunken rabble. They smashed into Southwark, setting fire to the Dutch and Flemish taverns. London closed the gates, and citizens patrolled the walls. The Kentishmen and their followers rioted through the night. By morning the tumult had quieted but they had not gone away. They were still encamped on the other side of the river.

The earl landed in Plymouth. "Unopposed," Elizabeth told me. "The Spider of France provided him with money and ships."

"But not with men, so he must have brought a scant force with him. What of George?"

"He has come—to take part in the invasion." Elizabeth's tone revealed her bitterness.

"Traitors contrived these mysterious rebellions in Yorkshire," Elizabeth said, "to draw Edward northward and make it easy for Warwick to land."

And as she knew, he had chosen Plymouth because many of the great landholders in the west country were either openly or secretly for Lancaster, and he expected to gather adherents on his way.

As for those families who had been friends and allies to the Bonvilles, and had proved their friendship to me, they would not join the earl, but I doubted if any of them except the Dynhams would be with Edward on this.

However, in the west country and elsewhere, bands of men gathered to fight for the king, but they were leaderless, and they failed to impede the earl's march to the Midlands. We heard that by the time he reached Coventry he had gathered a great army.

During Edward's reign he had improved the roads and kept them in good condition, he had also established relays of official messengers at various points, with horses always in readiness. News could be brought quickly from the shires to London and from London to the most important towns and fortresses in the realm. As the earl moved on, he made use of this system to send word of his progress, either to overawe London, or to inform his partisans in the city. There was still no news of Edward and his friends became more and more troubled by his silence.

"The storm must have alerted him," Elizabeth said. "He must have turned south as soon as he learned of the enemy invasion," and she added, "I hold the Tower for him."

She had a clear understanding of the danger menacing Edward, but she showed a valiant spirit. She ordered the victualing of the Tower, conferred daily with the constable and the captain of the guard, and every evening accompanied them when they inspected the garrison and the soldiers on watch. I often went with her, and as I followed her out on the ramparts in the chill dusk, I found myself admiring her as I never had before.

I was standing behind her one evening when she paused to speak to the men patrolling the walls. She was wrapped in a violet velvet mantle furred with ermine, the wind fluttered the light veil of her headdress, and a strand of her hair had escaped to sparkle and shine purest gold in the torchlight. The sight of her, and the sound of her soft voice would undoubtedly influence these men, I thought. They might decide that the Woodville queen was worth what she cost.

London felt the lack of the king's firm government. The news of the earl's landing brought the Lancastrians out of hiding, to clash with the Yorkists. The aldermen did their best to keep order, but brawlings and knifings, robberies and murders made the streets dangerous even in daylight, and at night, no honest person dared venture out at all. I went back and forth from Dorset House to the Tower, but always by barge and with my well-armed servants to protect me, in case of trouble.

Once a wherry drew alongside and someone shouted, "Where's whoreson Dorset now?" but that was all, and the wherry faded away in the mist on the river. Whenever my barge neared the banks, I noted ratlike faces peering out, then vanishing in the shadows. The city's scum was rising and the Londoners who had something to lose were afraid for their lives and their possessions. They muttered, "Let the king or the earl come, and come soon."

Instead of a royal courier in a stiff and brilliant tabard, the man who appeared quietly at dawn and claimed to be the king's messenger was not even in the Yorkist livery. However, he showed Edward's signet ring and was admitted to the queen's presence at once. Her mother and I were summoned to hear what he had to say, and the sight of him spelled disaster. He was a soldier in Edward's army and had evidently exchanged the telltale blue and murrey for rough homespun to avoid being recognized as one of the king's men.

He told us that Edward had swung southward, commanding Percy of Northumberland and Montagu to follow him, and reaching Doncaster, had halted there for the night. Some hours before cockcrow, Edward's sergeant of minstrels had roused him from his rest to urge him to get up at once for his enemies were upon him.

Northumberland, still Lancastrian at heart, had never moved. But my lord Montagu had come stealthily in the dark—not to the king's aid but to the earl's. Many of Edward's own men had gone over to Warwick, or had deserted. It was not the first time that an army had left him, and this time only a few had proved loyal—the same few who had been loyal before. Edward had seized his sword, and only partly dressed, had mounted his horse, rallied his little band of friends and had galloped for the coast.

"Some of his men," the messenger said, "found horses and followed him. He got clean away from Doncaster and made his way to the northern shore of the Wash—but found only small boats, and not enough for all, or I would have gone. The storm had made rough weather, and the seas were running high, but the king decided to embark. He knows me well, and called me to him, commanding me to come to you, madam, to give you a true account of what happened. He intended to head for Norfolk, when I last saw him."

"And then where?" Elizabeth asked.

"To the Low Countries, madam." The messenger added: "And will find means of sending you word of his safety."

The little boats had vanished from sight, and we must wait to learn if they had ever reached shore again. Elizabeth thanked the man, ordered her servants to provide food, drink, and lodging for him, and when he had left the room, she sat huddled in the cloak that her women had flung over her shoulders, saying nothing. She held Edward's ring cupped in her hand, and went on gazing at it. Her women had not yet arranged her headdress, and her hair fell loose over her shoulders. The chill gray of the autumn morning filtered through the window and touched her face in its paleness.

Lady Jacquetta whispered to me: "This shock might bring on premature labor," but Elizabeth was stronger in mind and body than her looks indicated. She put the ring on her finger, closing her hand into a fist to keep the ring from falling off, and gave orders for the Tower's officials to meet with her. When her women had made her ready, her natural color had returned. She wore scarlet and ermine, a royal mantle and a jeweled crown. With all the dignity of a queen, Elizabeth swept into her presence chamber to make it clear to the group awaiting her that, in the king's absence, she would uphold his authority. "Your prince will soon be born, here in London, in your midst. I will defend his rights."

In a few hours, Londoners were repeating the news to one another. One of my servants, who had gone into the street, reported what the people were saying. They knew that the king's army had deserted him, and that he had fled from Doncaster in the night, and then embellished facts with rumors.

The people were discussing Montagu's sudden defection. He had always been devoted to Edward, and had never taken any part in rebellion, but he was the Earl of Warwick's own brother, and when put to the test of making war on the earl, loyalty to his brother Warwick was stronger than loyalty to his cousin Edward. If Montagu had become a traitor, it was only after long conflict with himself, but his choice had cost Edward dear, and as the day waned, the queen's servants spoke in frightened whispers of the king's flight.

The aldermen did what they could to keep order, the Tower's constable told Elizabeth, but London was in an uproar. She sent commands to keep the gates locked against the Kentish rebels, and to call up a special guard, but mayor, magistrates, and sober citizens were powerless to quell the mobs rushing through the streets. Not only Lancastrians, but every thief and murderer had come out of hiding. They joined the mob, and broke open the prisons, letting loose a horde of cutthroats to prey on the city.

Across the river, Kentishmen and watermen had renewed their burning and pillaging. Armed with clubs, scythes, and axes, they were making ready to batter down the city gates, the constable said. "They're drunk on what they've swilled and in a mood to kill." And within the walls, the rioters were drunk and might be as murderous.

London was devoted to the king, but the king had gone, and the Earl of Warwick was advancing with an army, and the people cowering in their locked and shuttered houses were praying for him to come soon. At nightfall, this malevolent London was unrecognizable as Edward's city. As Elizabeth admitted, she had lost hope of defending it against the earl, but she was still determined to hold the Tower.

The black autumn night closed in. Elizabeth waited for the constable and other officials to come and escort her to the walls to inspect the soldiers on duty but the constable burst in unannounced. He was alone and looked harassed. In his haste to speak, his words ran together. The soldiers had left their posts— left the Tower. Their captains had gone with them. They had taken care to wrench off their Yorkist badges. And the constable was frank to admit that he would surrender his keys to the earl. "He would never make war on ladies, madam, but until he comes with his army, there is danger. The rioters are armed, and already raging through the streets nearby. If they learn that the walls are unmanned, God knows what they might do—"

Make an assault on the Tower, force the doors, surge up the stairs, batter their way into the royal apartments—find Elizabeth and her mother—the hated witch. Who was to stop them? The constable was an old man, the wardens were too few. Elizabeth's servants and Lady Jacquetta's as well had crept away, the constable told us, every man and woman, even the pages.

"The children"—Elizabeth's voice was faint—"the king's children must be taken to safety."

How? I thought as I went running to the nursery. Anterooms and presence chamber glittering silent and deserted—the royal barge rocking at the wharf—without oarsmen. Where could we take them—three small children? In the passage, I collided with Dame Joan Wynant, who was looking for me. She was solid, dependable, and reassuring. She had just come from the nursery, the children's attendants were still with them, and had no thought of leaving them. My own servants were waiting for my orders, and my oarsmen had my barge in readiness. As she pointed out it was less conspicuous than the royal barge.

Elizabeth agreed to make use of it, and the constable insisted that all of us should go. So it was decided, and Lady Jacquetta bestirred herself. "I will gather only what is necessary," she said, already moving briskly to the queen's bedchamber, bidding me to come. I followed her into the bedchamber and on to the garderobe adjoining it. She went on her knees to unlock and open the great jewel coffer. It was too heavy to be taken—its weight would encumber a crowded barge. Jacquetta scooped up rings, bracelets, brooches, necklaces, the pearls, the crown, gold, and precious stones. She was quick at her work, and soon emptied the coffer.

Under her direction, I found lengths of cloth and helped her to tie up the jewels into bundles. As she bent over the glittering hoard, folded the cloth, and knotted it, she had the furtive air of a thief making off with stolen goods. A Romany crone, clutching the larger bundle, and hiding it in the folds of her cloak.

What if the rabble on the banks caught sight of the barge,

and hurled stones enough to sink it? We could hope to evade notice, but how and where would we find haven? Baynard's Castle? But only servants were there. My lady Duchess and her household were at Fotheringhay, thank God, or she might be in danger. I thought of my own house—but it was known as Dorset's house, and if the palaces on the Strand were attacked, his would be a target. Elizabeth was far advanced in her pregnancy and her children were small and helpless, but we must be off before the mob made an assault. The Tower no longer seemed a strong fortress, it could prove to be a trap.

Elizabeth was wrapped in a dark cloak and was heavily veiled. All of the women had followed her example. Dame Joan shepherded the nurses who came carrying the children. One of my servants reported that the barge had drawn up to the landing. The constable turned to Elizabeth, "Madam, where will you find refuge?"

"In the Sanctuary," she said.

🌹 Twenty-one

The night of October the second was moonless and starless. A chill wind roughened the river and brought smoke sharp with the stench of burning to catch us by the throat. The glare from the fires was reflected in the sky—London huddled dark under the menacing scarlet. Once outside the Tower's walls we heard the noise in the street, but it lessened as the barge moved upriver toward Westminster, the cries and screams and curses became the howling of wolves in the distance.

The Sanctuary stood at the end of St. Margaret's churchyard, and was unchanged since Edward the Confessor had built it hundreds of years ago. Political offenders evaded their foes and criminals eluded the gallows by seeking Sanctuary and claiming its privileges. Dark, massive, with a church in the form of a cross, I doubted if even the noonday sun of a summer day ever lightened its gloom, and it was forever shadowed by its dark associations with the desperate and the lost.

The Abbot of Westminster was aroused and came himself to open the doors to Elizabeth and her family. Never before had any great lady, much less the Queen of England, asked admittance until Elizabeth Woodville registered herself, her three daughters and her mother as Sanctuary persons. I kept myself free of its regulations, with the right to come and go as I pleased, but I stayed for the rest of the night, although when I first set foot within its dank walls, I doubted if I could endure the place until morning.

The place stank vilely of its former inmates, the rogues and felons who had rushed out to take part in the rioting. "For myself, I would rather brave the mob," I whispered to Dame Joan, trying to control my retching, caused by the noisome odors. My concern was for Elizabeth, who was overcome with weariness and shivering with the cold.

Westminster Sanctuary had been built centuries before chimneys had come into use, and none had been added. In the center of the hall there was a circular stone hearth, and the smoke could only find its way out through the opening in the roof. Any fire would have been welcome, but we found only ashes and a few charred bits of wood. However, the Abbot immediately sent an army of servants and lay monks to build up a fire and sweep out the filthy rushes. They threw out the verminous straw mattresses, and brought fresh. I overheard the Abbey servants talking together as they went out, and one said that for the queen to hide herself in Sanctuary meant disaster for York. All was lost.

The earl entered London by way of Newgate, so I was told, and George rode with him, at his right, his armor inlaid with gold, and his ducal coronet brilliant with rubies, emeralds, and diamonds. A fine figure of a prince, smiling at the crowds and generous in distributing money.

As soon as the earl's army was sighted, the mobs dispersed, and the criminals took care to slink away. Once he was in the city, he restored good order, and the people could again go about their business without fear.

"He's given his allegiance to Lancaster," Dame Joan said to me, "but he keeps Yorkist discipline—and the people are accustomed to think of him as a leader, but you know those proud Lancastrian lords—they were always his foes. They're likely to grow restive in harness."

"How can he be content in their company?" I asked.

The earl went straightway to Wakefield Tower, to release a prisoner, and hail Henry the Sixth as "my sovereign lord." Henry was arrayed in velvet and ermine, and lodged in the Tower's royal apartments, in the gilded luxury of the rooms which had been decorated and adorned for Elizabeth's lying-in. So the earl had restored the crown to a Lancastrian king, but it was beyond any man's power to restore Henry's wits. He signed what was put before him, without any knowledge of what was done in his name.

"He's as limp and helpless as a sack of wool," someone told me, and one of my servants who saw him as he was led in procession to St. Paul's described him "A shadow on the wall."

As London was now safe, and the earl had assured Elizabeth that she was free to go where she wished, without interference, I expected her to leave the Sanctuary and go to Westminster Palace, and I asked her when she intended to leave, but she shook her head.

"I know that Edward and those with him have weathered the storm and have landed safely in the Low Countries. He will soon send word."

How could she know? She could only hope, and yet it was as if she had seen it all—the storm-wracked ships and the safe landing. She led me to believe in the same vision.

"I will wait for him here until he comes for me, and he will come to wear the crown again and reign over all England."

A few hours later we learned how Edward had succeeded in reaching Lynn, on the Norfolk coast. They were in desperate haste, and crowded aboard the fishing boats in the harbor. There was not enough transportation for all of the men who were willing to follow Edward into a foreign country, and he was forced to leave some of them on shore. The seas were running high, and the captain of the Dutch smack that Edward had boarded, warned him of danger, but Edward ordered him to set sail for the Low Countries.

Off the coast of Holland the storm had abated somewhat, but a worse danger had threatened. A flotilla of the Hanseatic towns had given chase to the defenseless little boats, and were closing in, but the Seigneur de Gruthuyse, governor of Holland for the Duke of Burgundy, saw the plight of the English, and sent his own fleet to beat off the attackers.

As Edward had not a penny, he gave his cloak, lined with sables, to the Dutch captain, to repay him for the voyage. Edward had contrived to send a letter to Elizabeth by the Burgundian envoy, a few lines written in his own hand to reassure her. He urged her to guard her health and promised on his return to reward any and every person who had proved to be her friend.

Doubtless his brother Richard had faith in the future, and the friends who had been with Edward through good and ill fortune, such as John Dynham and Will Hastings, lived in hope. But here in England, known Yorkists had scattered, or were in hiding. In London, the earl's red-jacketed men were everywhere, and Lancastrian badges were flaunted in the streets.

"My lord of Warwick is well pleased to rule in the name of a king who has neither wits nor will," Lady Jacquetta said. The earl had gathered the power into his own hands, but he used it with great ability, taking for himself only what had been his before he had rebelled against the crown. He adopted Edward's policy of reconciliation rather than revenge.

However, the people demanded the death of one man, the Earl of Worcester. He was captured in a forest, where he was found hiding in the branches of a tree. He was tried and condemned for crimes of injustice and cruelty, and on his way to execution the people would have seized him and torn him asunder if the earl's soldiers had not guarded him. He faced death with courage and declared that if he had acted harshly, it was for the good of the state.

"Edward has lost a loyal friend," Elizabeth lamented, with tears. "And the world has lost one of the most learned men of our time," Lady Jacquetta added, which to my mind made his lack of compassion all the harder to forgive. Edward was well rid of such a friend.

The earl found time to send me a message, assuring me of his protection and his readiness to be of use to me. I thanked him, but I had no intention of asking him for any favor and no desire to see him. It was of no importance to him if I held aloof, but perhaps he felt a pang of disappointment when my mother, his favorite sister, who had always showed her affection for him, refused to meet him, and sailed away to join Will Hastings in the Low Countries.

When Elizabeth fled to the Sanctuary, she had her jewels with her, but no other possession, and she was in want of everything. She and her mother found themselves penniless. The revenues from the queen's dowry and from Jacquetta's estates no longer reached them.

"They are not likely to be forthcoming for some while," Dame Joan said to me. "The queen is dowered on crown lands, now taken over by the present government. And Lady Jacquetta's tenants will spend her rents as they please. Who will compel them to pay her?"

Jacquetta had amassed riches, but if she had money stored away, it was out of her reach now, and she dared not reveal where she had hidden it. As she was fond of telling me, I was fortunate that the earl would not hand over my estates to a Lancastrian, but for the time being, I was pinched for money. Word had come from Shute that Lancastrian enemies of the Bonvilles had come back to England and were abroad in the west country. It would be imprudent to attempt to convey a sum of money from Devon to London. I had the same report from the Somerset manors.

In his behavior to Elizabeth, the earl was courteous and considerate. He paid some of her servants to return to her, and paid the wages of the nurses, who had accompanied the children. Elizabeth had an able physician in Dr. Serigo, and Mother Botts was the most experienced midwife in Westminster. The Abbot did what he could, and I provided bedding, linen, wine, oil, and candles from my own house.

With winter coming on, the family in Sanctuary needed warm clothing. I brought woolen stuffs and furs for them, and Elizabeth urged me to save what money I had on hand.

"I can always borrow," I said. As I knew, she could not, for the risk of lending money to a queen in Sanctuary was too great. She would not hear of selling or pawning any of her jewels, not so much as a ring or a brooch. I could not accuse her or Jacquetta of greed. Both of them were saving their entire store for Edward's use. He could convert pearls and diamonds and goldsmith's work into weapons and soldier's pay. Elizabeth expected me to contribute money and jewels to his needs too.

While they were in Sanctuary, Elizabeth and her children found friends in the people who lived and worked nearby. One was a butcher, John Gould. Although he knew that the queen and her mother were unable to scrape up a penny between them, he supplied the inmates of the Sanctuary with half a beef and two muttons weekly. The goodwives of Westminster were touched by the plight of the queen and her family. Elizabeth in Sanctuary, dependent on charity, won the goodwill which she had never had before.

Existence in Sanctuary was harsh. The building itself was dark, cold, and comfortless. The windows were narrow and unglazed, with ill fitting wooden shutters. Sunlight never came in, but the chill of autumn came. However, Elizabeth and Lady Jacquetta endured hardships and inconveniences without complaint, and with good grace.

"If Lady Jacquetta had always been as gentle-tempered as she is now," Dame Joan said to me, but did not need to say any more.

When the Earl of Warwick appeared at London's gates, asking to be admitted, that same Sir Thomas Cook whom Jacquetta had despoiled of his tapestries, had used his influence and London had opened the gates. Had injustice driven Sir Thomas to give his help to the king's enemies? Or had he always been a Lancastrian in secret? I would never know, but the people said that Woodville greed had cost Edward his London.

But the Woodvilles were paying for their sins. Elizabeth waited for news, waited with a heavy heart for the child to be born. I found a few white roses blooming in my garden and took them to her. "You see how well they have survived last night's wind and rain."

She held them close to her face to catch their fragrance, and it saddened me to see how much she valued them. Again, I asked her if she would not consider going elsewhere for her lying-in. Dr. Serigo was afraid for her health.

"And I am afraid to leave," Elizabeth answered. "Not for myself, my fears are for my mother."

She was thinking of the charge of witchcraft brought against Lady Jacquetta.

"I will never desert her," Elizabeth said. "And if she ventured out of Sanctuary, she would be in grave danger, if not from the earl, then from George. He would be quick to renew the charge."

The river ran black and cold, and by dusk the lowering cloud bank threatened snow. During the day I had spent a few hours in my own house, but returned to the Sanctuary before nightfall. Elizabeth was too near her time for me to leave her again. The news from abroad was too discouraging to tell her.

Margaret of York, now Duchess of Burgundy, was making every effort to help Edward, but Charles the Bold was not only at war with France, he had embroiled himself in a quarrel with the Swiss, and showed a marked lack of interest in Edward's cause. He even spoke with scorn of a king "too easily toppled from his throne." But the Spider of France was giving Marguerite of Anjou money and ships. She was gathering a great army, and when her preparations were complete, she would sail for England. And in this country, the people seemed to accept the Earl of Warwick's rule.

Elizabeth went early to her so-called bedchamber. Dame Joan Wynant and I sat by the fire, using its uncertain light to mend the children's clothes. Lady Jacquetta was brewing a posset, a mixture of wine, herbs, and spices, she said, and doubtless some other ingredient which she preferred to keep to herself. She stirred it over the fire, and as the fumes rose I grew drowsy.

Jacquetta took the posset to Elizabeth and came to the fire again. She sat down and set to work mending a worn and much loved doll for her granddaughter Bess. I could picture her using her unholy knowledge and her skillful fingers to mold a puppet in the likeness of the Earl of Warwick—the leaden maumet pierced through the heart to bring about his violent death.

In St. Margaret's churchyard, the stark trees rattled in the wind. Now and then snowflakes sifted through the hole in the roof and fell hissing into the fire. A great gust of wind sent the smoke eddying through the hall.

Dame Joan looked around, and crossed herself. "In the northern shires many believe that on winter nights my Lord Clifford spurs his black stallion across the moors with banners unfurled."

On this Allhallows Eve of the year 1470, his vengeful spirit could exult. Now his enemies, the hated Yorkists, had turned against one another.

Hallowmas was a drear day, with snow and wind. Dr. Serigo predicted that before another day had passed, the queen would be brought to bed. Before dusk she felt the first pains. Elizabeth was not as fragile as she looked, but this time her labor was prolonged. After midnight, in the blackest and coldest hour of the night, the child was born. Elizabeth called out "Edward" to come to her, and his son. The baby's cry was lost in the sound of the wind. The hangings screening Elizabeth's bed billowed in the draft, and the smoke spread mingling with the shadows. Then the wind sank to a long wailing before it rose again.

The king's son was christened on the day of his birth, without feasting, or music, or laughter, without a great company of people assembled to bid him welcome as heir of England. The nurse wrapped him in swaddling bands and muffled him in coverlets to keep out the cold.

In the Abbey the shadows made a dense gloom. The candles burning on the altar seemed as distant as the stars. Thomas Melling, Abbot of Westminster, was godfather, Lady Jacquetta was godmother, the subprior administered the sacrament and gave the child his father's name. No crowds, no splendor, no acclaim, but the baby would not feel the lack. What he needed was Edward's presence and protection.

✿ *Twenty-two*

It was March and the first faint gloss of green showed in fields and gardens. Through the winter the baby had thrived under the experienced care of Mother Botts, but his eldest sister had become thin and listless. Hoping to raise her spirits, I took her and the other children out into the Abbot's garden, which was within Sanctuary grounds. As the sun was shining here, and the wall sheltered the garden from the wind, Mother Botts brought the baby.

His sisters hovered around him, murmuring endearments. Little Mary ran off, found a newly budded daffodil and offered it to him. "He can look at it," the grave older sister explained. "He's not able to hold it."

Dame Joan smiled, and turned to me. "When he's out of swaddling bands, doubtless he'll be as eager to reach for a scepter as any of his forbears entombed yonder in the Abbey."

"Not all of them were able to hold it," I answered, looking up at a row of windows, the Abbot's private parlor, the state apartments and the Jerusalem chamber, with its tapestries, depicting the Crusaders' conquest of the Holy City. King Henry the Fourth had died there. He had seized the throne and murdered his cousin, Richard the Second, by starving him to death in Pontefract Castle.

"Henry the Fourth held what he had grasped," Dame Joan said, "but you know they say that on his deathbed he cried out that Richard's ghost had come to accuse him. They're saying now that Edward couldn't hold what he had grasped."

"I don't believe it!"

"Nor I," Dame Joan agreed. "He does not belong in our list of fallen kings."

I wondered how many others shared our faith in him. I spent most of my time with Elizabeth. When I went to my own house my barge took me up and down the river, and the river not the streets reflected the true state of London. As the winter had dragged on into spring, I saw the city's life ebbing away. Only a few ships were making for the sea, taking English wares to foreign ports. The Burgundians and the French were at war, and as the earl upheld the Spider of France, trade with the Low Countries was cut off. Nor was trade with other lands thriving. Our wool and cloth glutted the warehouses.

"Merchants and traders, doubtless most of the people, would be glad to have Edward back in his palace," my bargeman said.

"And all the women would be overjoyed," Dame Joan added.

The sunlight had left the garden. It was time for the children to leave. Mother Botts carried the baby, and Dame Joan helped to shepherd the little girls. The sky was still bright and I lingered in the garden, reluctant to go into the gloom and cold awaiting me in the Sanctuary building.

The dusk was already deepening in the churchyard. I started in fear as a shadow detached itself from the rest and came toward me. I was about to turn and run when I recognized Friar Bungay in his black robes, with a hood drawn over his head. He often came at this hour to hold long discussions with Lady Jacquetta and Elizabeth. When he came up to me he spoke in a low voice, giving me the news that I had longed and yet dreaded to hear. Edward had come back to England.

When Elizabeth was told, she caught my arm for support. I

noted that her grip had surprising force. Her belief in Edward's coming had sustained her. Now she woke up to full awareness of the hazards confronting him and was wild with terror.

"The king tried to put a landing party ashore nearabouts Cromer. His men were met by arrow fire and forced to put to sea again, with some losses. The king then steered for Yorkshire."

But the Earl of Warwick held Yorkshire; his men scanned the roads and watched the ports, his brother Montagu had gathered a formidable army to bar invasion. During the night, a storm had churned the sea, sending Edward's ships flying in all directions. With morning, he had looked in vain for the ships under his brother Richard's command, and by nightfall had found no trace of them.

Edward had managed to land finally at Ravenspur, with a fragment of his scanty fleet. In a few hours Richard and his men had appeared. The wind had flung their ships on a deserted headland some miles away.

"What has happened to them since then?" Elizabeth demanded. "Where are they now?"

The Friar was unable to tell us, but he said that Edward had an army of less than fifteen hundred men, including a few Flemish gunners, provided by the Duke of Burgundy, who had also supplied the ships and weapons, and perhaps a certain amount of money. The richest prince in Europe had not been overgenerous.

Lady Jacquetta held a low-toned conversation with Friar Bungay at the other end of the hall. I did not see him go—he seemed to vanish in a blur of smoke. Elizabeth sighed, and then spoke of Dorset. He was her first-born, and I think that she loved him as well as she did Edward's children. If I could not love him, I remembered that he was my husband and was concerned for his safety.

Edward was on English soil. His ships were gone, there was no retreat for him. Ravenspur was nothing but a fishing village, without walls or defenses of any kind. He could not linger there.

In the morning my servants came to me in a state of great

excitement. The earl and his army were leaving the city. As I should have realized, Warwick would not stay in London once Edward had set foot in England. "And my Lord Duke of Clarence is going too, with the whole of his company." The earl was expected to turn northward and make for Warwickshire. It seemed that George had spoken very freely of his own moves. "He has promised to gather a great fellowship from his own estates and join the earl again."

George and the earl rode out of London together. A flood of people watched them as they passed, but I shut myself up in my own house, in no mood to be with Elizabeth. To her, the earl had always been an enemy, but I remembered when young Edward had looked up to his cousin Warwick as the finest knight in all the world. Inevitably, he and Edward would meet.

The earl had placed the government in charge of his brother, the Archbishop of York, who administered affairs with skill. There was no recurrence of riots. London was described as calm.

"Lancastrians strut through the streets and gather in the taverns," my servants reported. "They roar out songs telling of victories in France."

Elizabeth knew—all knew—that the odds were against Edward. "And Marguerite of Anjou is bringing an army," Lady Jacquetta reminded me, when Elizabeth had moved from her place by the fire and had gone to be with her children.

"Madame Marguerite has been expected all winter. She and her son have yet to appear," I said.

"She is also bringing the earl's wife and his daughter Anne, as well as the prince." Lady Jacquetta was busy with her needlework while she talked. "But not on the same ship, as she does not permit her son to bed with his bride. Evidently she keeps the boy in leading strings."

"And keeps Anne as hostage!"

"She wants to be sure of the earl, I think." Lady Jacquetta held up her needle to the fitful firelight so as to thread it. "However, now it's spring, and we can look for her to sail with her army."

"Lancastrians are boasting of a 'mighty army,'" I said. "But doubtless they are lying."

"Discounting their extravagant claims, she has gathered a sizable force, financed by the King of France."

Another threat to Edward, but he would be aware of all the dangers facing him.

"Lady Jacquetta never sets foot beyond the doors of the Sanctuary," I said to Dame Joan later, "and yet she seems to have information."

"She gets it from the Friar, where else?"

He could go anywhere and escape notice.

"And by casting a spell, the Friar can doubtless see what is taking place at a distance." Dame Joan lowered her voice, and crossed herself.

He came nearly every day, after sundown, and so I watched for him, lingering in the Abbey garden until dusk to waylay him, I knew he sometimes kept discouraging news from Elizabeth. If I had not been watching for him, I would not have seen him—or would have taken him for one of the monks—an elderly lay monk.

"What I have to tell will soon be known in London," the Friar said one evening.

Instead of hiding out, Edward had suddenly appeared at the gates of York. Storm battered, weary from long marching, he and his men must have had the look of a band of outlaws to the citizens gazing down at them from the walls.

"Who has joined him?" I asked, thinking of barons and knights.

"A group of country folks out of Holderness trailed along," the Friar said. "One a priest is called Martin of the Sea, some are beggars, some doubtless have homes and occupations."

I could guess why they were drawn to follow Edward—to escape from the drabness of their existence, or because they had a formless hope of bettering their lot, or because they were impelled to seek adventure.

"They wouldn't add to Edward's strength," I said.

"On the contrary! The mayor and aldermen saw him surrounded by a cloud of uncouth people and refused to admit him."

They had seen a throneless king, who had no followers in England but a group of raggle-taggle wayfarers.

"If he was turned away from York—" I began. "His own inheritance—"

"He claimed his inheritance. He declared that he asked only for his Duchy of York, and ordered the city officials to open the gates. The Bootham Bar's portcullis had lifted for him. He and a few of his friends walked through the streets, crying out long live Henry the Sixth."

Edward would think it a cheap price to pay. I could hear his voice, see him strolling through the town, smiling on the inhabitants, eying the women, as if he had put aside thoughts of the dangers ahead.

"Were the townspeople so easily gulled?" I said.

"They knew, but Edward is their lawful duke. Since they could not deny it, they could not deny him the right to enter his own good town of York."

Elizabeth had grown very thin; she scarcely ate or slept. Friar Bungay had brought her a map, and she studied it by the hour. Edward must veer southward. "He will come this way," she said to me, her finger tracing his road from York to London, as if he could march unimpeded. The map did not show the hostile armies waiting for him, their strength so much greater than his.

A courier came from the earl's headquarters in Warwickshire to bring reports to his government in London. He spurred through the gates, his red jacket a streak of scarlet, his horse in a lather, but the bystanders were accustomed to seeing the messengers and retainers and soldiers clattering in and out on the earl's business. However, what this man had to tell seeped through London before nightfall, and caused a great stir. Edward had eluded Montagu's army drawn up near Pontefract to intercept him. Edward's friends thanked God for a miracle. Edward's enemies, forced to admit what they had always declared was impossible, said that his escape was due to sorcery.

"The Lancastrians are saying that my lord Montagu's scouts were tricked by witchcraft," Dame Joan told me. "Their eyes deceived them. They looked for Edward in the wrong direction. A mist distorted the landscape and concealed him. He passed to the west of Pontefract and bypassed Montagu's army."

The talk of witchcraft pointed to Lady Jacquetta and Friar Bungay. If Elizabeth's enemies had seen her brooding over the map they might have believed that she had the power to direct Edward, and defying all hazards he would come to her.

He was pushing on, we heard, and halted for the night at Sandal Castle. After Yorkist victory, it had become a royal castle, but never a royal residence for Edward. He kept it in repair, and had left a small garrison to guard it. The village of Market Wakefield gave him a loyal welcome, and the countryside supplied him with horses. Edward's stables had been famous throughout Europe and these were sturdy plodding farmhorses, paid for with the money grudgingly doled out by the Duke of Burgundy.

"If only I could have some direct word from him," Elizabeth sighed. "But of course it would be too great a risk to send a messenger."

"However, news does come, even if slowly," her mother pointed out.

Lady Jacquetta had become an old woman in these last months but when she moved or spoke, her quickness and energy revitalized her. Elizabeth had lost some of her beauty, her eyes seemed too large for her thin face. In her plain dark woolen gown, with a black veil covering her head, she was wan and wraithlike— as Edward had first seen her when he had met her in Whittlebury Forest. He had loved her then; he would love her all the better now.

Edward pushed his way into the Midlands. Will Hastings had estates in Leicestershire, and had rallied his retainers. Perhaps Dorset had been able to recruit men from Astley and Bradgate, but

I doubted if he had inspired his tenants to follow him. However, other Yorkist landowners had brought their men, and Edward's army had grown.

Once in the Midlands, he discarded the pretense that he had landed in England only to claim the Duchy of York. He and his lords had put on full armor; his men were outfitted in Yorkist colors, with the patch of gold—badge of the sun. The leopards and lilies of England, and Edward's banner of the sun flared at the head of his army.

He drew men to him, but a great number of lords, knights, and squires stayed aloof, and waited to see what the outcome would be. Some I could name had no heart for the struggle between Edward and Warwick. Edward was outnumbered by the earl, who was at Coventry, with a strong army, which would be still stronger when Montagu and Oxford brought their troops. The earl was also waiting for George.

"He's recruited seven thousand men in the southwest," Dame Joan told me. "Or so they say." It was very likely true. And soon Marguerite of Anjou would come with her army.

In London, the earl's friends were quiet, but the Lancastrians exulted. Edward would be trapped in the steel ring of three armies converging on Coventry from different directions. Elizabeth was aware of Edward's danger but she seldom mentioned the situation. April had come, but in Sanctuary it was always winter.

Now that George as well as the earl had left the city, would there be any danger to Lady Jacquetta? I asked Elizabeth one day.

"We still have enemies in the city. They are not only a threat to my mother, but to my son."

"Who would harm a little baby?" I began, then remembered who this baby was—Edward's son—heir apparent to a disputed throne. "Marguerite of Anjou undoubtedly has her agents in London, they are not to be trusted."

"London must be full of them," Elizabeth said, "but I was not thinking only of Lancastrians. There is George.-He is not to be trusted."

Trust George? No. But did she think that he would send secret assassins to do away with his nephew? He was not a monster and yet it was monstrous for him to be leading an army to make war on his brother.

"You are concerned for us, Cicely," Elizabeth was saying, "but I am thankful to have this safe refuge for my son until his father comes." She looked up to greet Friar Bungay. I knew he had entered by way of the door at the end of the hall, but he seemed to materialize out of the smoke. He had brought some rare medicinal herbs to Lady Jacquetta, or so he said, but perhaps he had another motive as well. She drew him aside and they talked together in an undertone for some time. Before he left he told us that he could foresee good news on the way to us.

The next day, a horseman clattered up to the Sanctuary gates. Shouts and cheering echoed in the streets when the people recognized the royal arms of England emblazoned on his tabard. He was Edward's courier, bringing a letter to Elizabeth first. Then he would deliver letters and messages to other important people in the city. I had a few lines from Dorset. He was well, he wrote, and the courier would explain what had happened.

"The lines waver before my eyes," Elizabeth whispered to herself. The paper rattled and shook in her hands, but she scanned the page quickly, then reread the letter more slowly, lingering over each word. At last she looked up to tell us that Edward was near. He would make his camp at St. Albans, "This very night, and make his entry into London tomorrow. Edward, Dorset, Anthony Woodville." She repeated their names several times. Clutching her letter to her breast, she sighed, "Tomorrow."

But how had Edward brought his army to St. Albans? A scant ten miles from London? Where was the earl? Lady Jacquetta, not Elizabeth, asked the questions, and the courier answered in a rush of words. George had moved out of Banbury, and Edward had moved forward. The two armies had come in sight of each other, then had drawn near, facing each other in battle array. Archers, foot soldiers, squires, knights and lords on both sides had been braced and waiting for the leaders to order the assault. Then

George had appeared alone in front of his own lines and had galloped toward the opposing army.

Edward and Richard, on horseback, had gone out to meet him. Flinging himself from the saddle, George had knelt down. Edward had dismounted, raised him up, and kissed him. Richard had likewise kissed him. "They talked together," the herald said, "and their knights mingled as friends. My lord Duke of Clarence called on his army to acclaim King Edward, his squires distributed the White Rose to his men. They tore off Lancaster's badge, and put on York's badge; then the trumpets blew and the minstrels played.

As I knew, the Duchess of York and her daughters, most of all Margaret, had done all in their power to bring about this reconciliation. "Why destroy your own family to give the throne to Lancaster?" was their argument. But while his brothers were in exile and when Edward's attempt to regain the throne had appeared to be a rash adventurer's madness, foredoomed to failure, George had stifled his bitterness against the Lancastrian alliance, and the earl for making it. When Edward had swept into the Midlands and had gathered an army to his banners, George had begun bargaining with him in secret—at least, that is what I assumed from what the herald admitted. Messages had passed back and forth. I could guess their tenor. "What will you give me for turning traitor to Warwick and bringing you the seven thousand men that I have promised to him?" What had Edward offered? Evidently enough.

Until the last, George had gone on lying to the earl. "Avoid a battle until I bring you reinforcements." And the earl had waited in Coventry instead of attacking Edward. After his reconciliation with Edward, George had offered to act as mediator and peacemaker for the earl. The herald repeated the earl's reply, and how he had cursed George.

Edward had also sent messages, perhaps hoping to detach the earl from Lancaster. "The king promised good conditions, profitable to my lord the Earl—" The herald sighed. "But he would not accept them."

George's treachery was useful to Edward as it left the road to London open for him. He was coming by way of Watling Street and forced marches had brought him near enough to see the spire of St. Paul's. George had chosen a crucial hour to abandon and betray the earl. I wondered if he felt any qualms when he thought of encountering Isabel's tears and reproaches. She was the earl's daughter. What would she think and feel?

It was the Wednesday of Holy Week when Edward came within sight of London. The Earl of Warwick, who was pursuing him, had sent orders to his government in London to hold the city, and lock the gates. At any moment now Marguerite of Anjou, with her son and her army, would land in England. If Edward could be kept outside the city long enough, two armies would close in on him, but the earl's strategy depended for its success on London. Would the city close the gates to the king or not?

Throughout Wednesday confusion grew. After I had heard Mass at the Abbey, I went to Elizabeth, who was bitterly disappointed when I told her that Edward was unlikely to enter London this day. There was fighting in the streets as Yorkists came out of hiding and brawled with groups of Lancastrians. There was fear of the mob becoming riotous again. The Archbishop of York, acting as head of the earl's government, tried to arouse the people's fervor for the cause of Lancaster. He put Henry the Sixth on a horse and led him through the streets. One of my servants who had seen him reported that the procession was scant, "And the sight of him pleased the people only as much as the fire painted on a wall warmed the old woman."

By morning the mayor and councilmen had agreed to open London's gates at the king's command. "How could they dare do otherwise?" Elizabeth said, with a touch of her old haughtiness, but she was right. The citizens would undoubtedly open the gates themselves as soon as Edward was near enough for them to recognize him, not because he had an army at his back, but because he was Edward.

He was near enough for Elizabeth to become the queen again, I thought, but when the Abbot of Westminster pointed out that she and her family could leave the Sanctuary in perfect safety now, and go to the palace to welcome the king, she declined to stir.

"The king knows where to find me," she answered. "My mother and my children and I will wait here for him to come." The Abbot's thin-lined face wore a puzzled expression as he bowed and left her. He failed to understand why she chose to remain in the gloom of the Sanctuary building, but Lady Jacquetta knew and I knew why. Edward had encountered dangers and had danger waiting for him, while she had suffered agonies of fear. She wanted Edward to see her in these grim surroundings; then he would realize how much she had endured.

She asked for a mirror. All these months, she had not so much as glanced in one. Now she studied the blurred reflection of her face. "The light is too dull here," I said. "You see only a dim outline."

"Yes, but I see the truth, I have become dim," she sighed. "The color of a corpse candle. But what do my looks matter?"

Her waiting women brought out the rich gown and embroidered mantle that Elizabeth had worn on the night when she had fled from the Tower to Sanctuary.

"Madam, you can appear as queen again," the woman said, but Elizabeth refused to change her plain woolen gown.

"I am only a Sanctuary person until the king takes me away," she said, "and makes me a queen again."

She went to the open door, apart from everyone else, and called me to her. "Today is for meeting the ones that we love. I will try not to look beyond to partings. Or the battle. For the next few hours, be happy."

She covered her face with her hands. At the sound of trumpets in the distance, Elizabeth looked up, listening. She gathered her daughters around her. Lady Jacquetta stood behind her.

Mother Botts held the little prince. All of us were silent, tense, and rigid with waiting.

There were crowds in the streets, I knew, and the people had adorned their houses with lengths of cloth and tapestries.

I could picture the officials in their robes, blue, or murrey and scarlet. And the women of London, leaning out of windows to catch sight of the king—their king. In the Tower's palace Henry the Sixth still wandered, or knelt, mumbling his prayers, perhaps unmindful of Edward's trumpets.

When the trumpets sounded close by, I asked Mother Botts to give the little prince into my keeping. She put him in my arms. He woke but made no outcry, only stared at me out of his round bright eyes, then as I rocked him in my arms, he smiled. I looked up to see Edward coming in the door. I saw him through a blur of tears. He seemed to fill the dark place with the burnish of steel and the glow of scarlet as he went to Elizabeth and took her in his arms.

She lifted her face to his, he bent to kiss her mouth—for a moment it was as if they had made their escape from all the rest of the world and were alone beneath the great oak in the forest. I felt a pang for them, because they could not stay there. When he turned from Elizabeth to his children I carried his son to him. "My lord, the Prince of Wales welcomes you, and asks you to give him a father's blessing."

❧ Twenty-three

After our long separation, Dorset seemed glad to see me, although he had only a little time to spend with me, or to discover the pleasures of London again. Edward had made his state entry into the city on Holy Thursday, in bright April weather. He had taken over the government, and was marshaling his army.

"He keeps us all on the run," Dorset complained, when he

was with me behind the shelter of the bed curtains. After making love, he was too nerve-strung to sleep, and was disposed to talk, describing his misery during the storms at sea, his boredom during the months of exile, the hardships of forced marches, until London had opened the gates to Edward.

Elizabeth and her mother and her children were freed from Sanctuary, and lodged in the Tower's palace, surrounded by luxury and homage. Elizabeth was no longer the Sanctuary person of yesterday; the goodwives of Westminster who had gathered at the gates to glean news of her and her children, and who had praised her patience, would not follow her to her palace. They would always be eager for news of her, but she was the queen again, and had returned to a world remote from theirs.

When she had offered Edward the casket of jewels for his use, I had seen tears come into his eyes. "If you had sold them you could have bought what you needed but here I find you threadbare, depending on charity. Yet you clung to these gawds for my sake!"

"Our sake," she had answered. "All I have in this world comes from you and belongs to you," and she had added in her softest voice, "Without you I am nothing."

"And you included yours, or were willing to sacrifice them," Dorset said to me later. "Luckily, the Duke of Burgundy supplied Edward's needs, so you've won great credit, and at the same time you can keep your diamonds and pearls."

Edward had thanked Mother Botts, and the butcher, and Dr. Serigo—thanked every man, woman, and child who had been of any use to "his Elizabeth" in her need. He had paid all debts, been liberal with gifts of money, and promised further reward in future. Later I heard two of my waiting women discussing the king's generosity. "He will keep his word," one said, and the other answered, "If it lies within his power."

I said to Dorset, "So the Duke of Burgundy proved liberal after all." Evidently Margaret of York had really influenced her husband.

"For a long time he refused to do anything for Edward,"

Dorset told me. "He ranted and shouted and cursed, called Edward a witless fool who had been flung out of his kingdom because he was too lustful and lazy to control his subjects. Margaret argued with him night and day until he disgorged some of his riches. If he hadn't, Edward would never have landed in England."

"He would have found some other way," I said, thinking of Henry the Sixth who had been removed from the royal apartments. I asked Dorset what had become of him.

"Edward clapped him in his prison. First the guards brought him to Edward. What a contrast! Henry's a small, thin shrunken creature.

"He's out of his wits," Dorset said, "but he recognized Edward at once. 'My cousin of York,' he said, 'you are very welcome, I know that with you I will be safe.'"

"And how did Edward respond?" I asked.

"He thanked Henry for giving him welcome and added a few courtesies. Edward's never at a loss for words. He ordered Henry to be kindly treated, but kept under lock and key, of course."

I winced, but Dorset was uninterested in Henry, and was concerned with other matters.

It was the night of Good Friday, and in London and throughout Christendom, the bells were silent. In every church the altar was stripped bare, and the tabernacle was open, and empty. I thought of the words, repeated again and again, in the liturgy of the day, "Jerusalem, Jerusalem, be converted to the Lord thy God." The warning was meant for us, but we went our way.

The sound of Edward's trumpets, woke the sleeping city. Dorset groaned. "Edward held a war council tonight."

"What was decided?" I asked.

"In the midst of it, Edward's scouts came in to report that the earl's approaching London. Edward's glad of it. It suits him to force Warwick to do battle before Marguerite of Anjou lands with yet another Lancastrian army! For all anyone knows, maybe she has already landed."

I had prayed that by a miracle the battle could be avoided, but it loomed near and inevitable. Edward's truest friends, such as

Hastings were unhappy because they must take the field against the earl. John Dynham was being sent to guard Calais, a post of great honor. When I had felicitated him, he had admitted that he was thankful to avoid meeting the earl in hand-to-hand combat.

"Edward's army seems half-hearted to me," Dorset said. "They deserted before, and might desert again."

"They're not the same men," I said, although I knew nothing about them.

"This time we have the high and puissant prince, George of Clarence with us. You'll have to grant that he's slippery—"

"The earl would scorn to have him back," I said.

"And who do you think Edward has appointed as his second in command? His little brother Richard!" Dorset burst out. It was the most important post of all next to Edward's own, and usually entrusted to a veteran captain.

"Londoners will think we have no chance to win when they see that undersized boy leading the van!"

"His cousin Warwick took charge of his military education," I reminded Dorset. At Middleham Castle, Richard had learned something besides the use of weapons. He had learned to love his cousin Warwick's daughter Anne, and had given her up. Even so, if he thought of her, and remembered the happy years that he had spent under her father's care, Richard must feel many a pang now on the eve of battle.

Dorset's grip tightened on my shoulder. "I have no stomach for this battle," he confessed.

"Neither have I."

"The King-maker would take pleasure in skewering me on his sword."

"He won't seek you out, Thomas."

"Nor I him! But I must not seem to avoid him. George and Hastings—all of them would take very great pleasure in branding me a coward!" Dorset clung to me, and I tried to soothe him. He would not be asked to expose himself to needless danger, I told him.

"In the *mêlée* there's always danger," he muttered.

"I will never blame you for being afraid."

He seemed to find some comfort in admitting his fear to me. "You are the only creature on earth who shares my shameful secret." Dorset laughed a little but he was in earnest. In our world, it was considered shameful for a great lord to display any sign of cowardice in war, and so he must take the risk of battle. It was the price exacted for being Thomas Grey, Marquis of Dorset, stepson to the king.

"Why does the earl come so close to London?" I asked. "He could have veered westward and waited for Marguerite of Anjou to land before he challenged Edward."

"He can do without her help, he has a strong army," Dorset explained.

"Perhaps he would rather do without her arrogance," I said. The earl showed his mastery of men by welding his adherents, who had once been Yorkists, and Lancastrians, into a well-disciplined army, but I had heard of incidents—hints that ill feeling among former foes still smoldered within his ranks.

"He feels confident that he can gain the victory," Dorset said, "and his chances are too good for my liking."

In the morning, the scouts reported that the Earl of Warwick had reached Barnet. It was Holy Saturday, and shortly after midday Edward led his army out of London. I saw him with his brothers before they rode on. Richard wore white armor, highly polished. He was mounted on a great war horse and undoubtedly looked small. His badge was a white boar, derived from Ebor, which had been the name of York in ancient times.

As I had stayed in my own house, I had been able to avoid any meeting with George. Handsome, and debonair in manner, wearing armor overlaid with gold, outwardly he was a fine figure of a prince. Perhaps the people would believe that the House of York was united.

Dorset was encased in steel, and outwardly appeared as brave as any lord in Edward's army. Edward had not yet put on his helmet—he wanted the crowds to see his face clearly. He was twenty-nine years old, but when he smiled, he seemed eighteen. Then he was gone in a blare of trumpets and music, his highest ranking lords followed him, their banners flickering. Elizabeth leaned out of the casement watching until they were out of sight.

Edward was meeting the main body of his army near the city walls. As he rode through the streets, the women would watch him, following him with their eyes, wishing him success, and he would smile at them as if he loved them all. Even at such a time, he would notice a fair face.

Although I would have greatly preferred to keep to my own house, Elizabeth had summoned me. She needed me, she said, particularly as her mother was ill. However, she was well enough to receive Friar Bungay. Doubtless Jacquetta wanted him to predict the outcome of the battle, but later, when she came into the room where Elizabeth and I were waiting for the hours to pass, she kept whatever she may have learned to herself. Edward had made his own predictions. He had promised Elizabeth, promised his army, that he would be in London again tomorrow, with victory won. Doubtless he believed it, and Elizabeth seemed to find comfort in quoting his promise, although he knew and she knew the dangers and uncertainties of tomorrow. And I tried to keep at bay a nagging fear that Edward might be gone longer than a day, a month, a year. He might be gone forever.

Before sundown low-lying clouds and mist blotted out the light, bringing sudden chill and sudden darkness. Some ten miles away, two armies, shrouded in blackness, endured the night.

When morning came, London had disappeared in a dark mist. After several hours dim shapes began to swim in the murkiness, then faded. But as I watched, the mist thinned. Houses, trees, turrets, spires, London Bridge emerged in wavering outline.

It was Easter Sunday, 1471. Crowds coming out of the churches gathered in the streets and near midday fugitives from the battle galloped into London. They were Hastings's men, crying defeat, Yorkist defeat. The news spread through London and reached the palace. The lieutenant of the Tower brought the report to Elizabeth.

"Where is the king?" Elizabeth demanded, but the men who had made their escape were not able to say. The Lancastrians had suddenly appeared from out of the dense mist, and had charged Hastings in great strength. His line had crumbled, then had broken. Struggling in the mist, they had lost sight of Hastings, their own commander, but they had fled, had managed to find horses, and had pounded all the way to London. From their evidence, the Yorkist army was routed, and Hastings might have been killed. They did not know what had happened to him and I could still hope. These men had not seen the king at all, for the rest of the field was hidden in the murk.

As the lieutenant pointed out, the fugitives had taken to their heels early and were croaking disaster from their own limited knowledge. "They seem befuddled by the mist," Elizabeth answered, but fear had turned her ashen. Her women had reddened her lips, and adorned her with a jeweled headdress, making her face look all the more haggard.

"The battle is not yet fought," I reminded her. It was what Edward had said at Towton, when defeat had seemed inevitable.

Later in the day, we heard a faint thunder, growing louder and nearer—the crowds were cheering as Edward's own herald spurred his horse through the streets to the Tower, holding up the king's gauntlet to proclaim his victory.

It was true that the Lancastrians under my Lord Oxford had broken Hastings's line, killing many of his men, and giving chase to the survivors all the way to the town of Barnet. In the meantime, Hastings who was neither killed nor wounded, rallied what men he had, and Richard came to his help. "The king fought like a dozen men," the herald said, "beating down all who stood in his way." When Oxford and his Lancastrians returned to the field, they intended to come upon the Yorkists from the rear, but the battle had swung in another direction, and the Lancastrians came up on Warwick's men.

Oxford's banners displayed his blazonings—the silver star with rays of light. In the mist, the star had a great likeness to Edward's own emblem of the sun, and the Earl of Warwick's men, thinking that a new Yorkist army was attacking them, let fly with a volley of arrows. The Lancastrians were confused and cried "Treason, treason." Warwick, with his brother Montagu and Oxford, did their utmost to restore order, but Warwick's men, mistrusting their Lancastrian allies, felt that they had been betrayed and took up the shouts of treason. Montagu was killed, and the soldiers under his command were disheartened.

Then Edward flung his scanty reserves into the battle, every man. The earl fought on; his friends and retainers refused to desert him. They fought beside him and fell around him. At the edge of Wrotham Wood, a band of Yorkist foot soldiers closed in on him. Edward sent orders to spare the earl, but the order came too late. Warwick the King-maker was dead. The dark mist dissolved, the sky cleared, and the sun came out.

The news transformed Elizabeth and gave her back her beauty. Dorset and Anthony Woodville had come through the battle unscathed. Edward and his army would be in London before sundown. He would soon be with her, as he had promised—and his victory had saved the Woodvilles.

Lying in open coffins, and naked to the waist, the bodies of the Earl of Warwick and his brother Montagu were exposed in St. Paul's Cathedral for two days.

"I am thankful that my mother is still in the Low Countries," I said to Will Hastings. "I know how bitterly she grieves for her brothers. She would feel it as a twist of the knife if she saw the crowds tramping into St. Paul's to gape at her brothers' corpses!"

"You seem resentful," Hastings noticed, "but Edward knows only too well how rumors can start and flourish. He wants the people to see with their own eyes that Warwick and Montagu are dead."

Hastings had come to my house to give me news of my mother, who was sailing for England shortly. Hastings and I were walking in the garden. "Edward's not heartless," he went on. "He was—and is—sorry for Montagu's death, and tried to save Warwick."

"For what?" I asked. "It was better for him to die with his sword in his hand."

After two days Edward gave Richard Neville, Earl of Warwick, and his brother John Neville, Lord Montagu, honorable burial in Bisham Priory, near the tombs of their parents and their brother Thomas, who had been killed at Wakefield, near the father and brother who had fought and died for the White Rose of York. I had Masses said for the repose of their souls. After the violence of their living and their dying, I prayed that through the mercy of God, they would rest in peace.

London was glad of Edward's victory, but I soon became aware of an undercurrent of rumors pervading my household and asked Dame Joan Wynant what was being said. "Only what all London is saying. They are discussing the strange mist that hung over the battlefield and proved fatal to the earl. And Lord Montagu." Dame Joan glanced at the door. It was closed, and I urged her to go on. My household was whispering, but elsewhere the people were talking openly that the queen's mother had consulted the sorcerer—Friar Bungay—and he had caused the dark unnatural murk to delude their enemies.

While the battle was being fought on Barnet Heath, Marguerite of Anjou had landed in England. Her son and Anne were with her. A dire homecoming for Anne and her mother. Lady Warwick had sailed on another ship, and had made port at Plymouth. When she had heard that the earl and his brother had been killed, she had taken sanctuary at Beaulieu Abbey.

"Where is Anne?" I asked Dorset. He had just heard what Edward's scouts and spies had to say.

"Still with Madame Marguerite."

The spies had barely mentioned Anne. They had watched Marguerite of Anjou. When the news of the earl's death and the Lancastrian defeat was broken to her, she had been speechless for hours—in a stupor of despair.

"Later, when she did speak, she declared that she would

much rather die than live on in such a state of wretchedness and no good would come of fighting another battle at this time."

"She's afraid for her son," I said.

"She wanted to take her son back to France at once, but the lords of her party are tired of exile. They refused to go, so did the boy." Dorset sighed. "They've persuaded her to stay and you know what that will mean."

"More bloodshed."

"And this time it might be my blood!" Dorset was sitting hunched in his chair, leaning his elbows on the table in front of him. He had survived the battle at Barnet Heath with a whole skin. I had not heard of his displaying any particular daring, but no one accused him of cowardice. Perhaps he had taken advantage of the mist to evade notice.

"Who knows?" he went on. "Once a battle begins, anything can happen."

I thought of Edward. He always plunged into the thickest of the fighting, and was always the most conspicuous target. He might risk his life once too often.

All of the scouts brought in the same report. The Lancastrian commanders had convinced Marguerite of Anjou that the battle at Barnet had weakened the Yorkist army, and victory was hers if she would only take it. Edward had lost men, but he was able to fill the gaps in his ranks. Ready to march, he waited to learn which road the enemy would take. As soon as certain information came, he gave chase.

As Edward foresaw Marguerite of Anjou's strategy, she would try to reach Wales, to join Jaspar Tudor, who had landed there and had collected a sizable Lancastrian army to reinforce hers.

Edward's task was to prevent her from joining Tudor. To go into Wales, she must cross the Severn, and she would undoubtedly make for the Severn bridge at Gloucester. Edward would have to drive hard through the Cotswolds to overtake her. He had sent strict orders to the governor of the town to bar Gloucester's gates against her, denying her the use of the bridge. Then she would be forced to attempt a crossing elsewhere.

"The governor is the king's man," Lady Jacquetta said, "but the test of his loyalty will come when the Lancastrians appear and pound on his gates."

"I know." Elizabeth answered absently. She was holding the little prince in her arms, and had taken off one of her jeweled bracelets to dangle before his eyes. As he crowed and laughed and struggled to reach the shining object, he stole Lady Jacquetta's attention and mine. Suddenly Elizabeth clutched the child to her breast. "Why did Madame Marguerite yield against her will and reason! If I were in her place I would drag my son on shipboard and sail away."

"You would never have set sail for England in the first place," Lady Jacquetta told her.

"The whole country is tired of war, and more war," I burst out. "Sick of endless slaughter!"

"So am I." It was Edward's voice. He had come in by the little door hidden beneath the tapestry, come without making a sound. "And determined to make an end of it."

Edward and his captains held the Feast of St. George at Windsor, and on the following day led the Yorkist army in pursuit of the enemy, through the green and flowering countryside. Edward sent his couriers to London, but by the time his messages reached us, he had pushed on, not sparing his men.

The Lancastrians were predicting a quick and decisive victory, and when they reached Exeter, the gentry of Cornwall and Devon came to offer their services to Marguerite of Anjou. Most of these men were young, and many of them were the sons of knights and squires who had lost their lives or their lands in her cause. I could see how, if the story of her life was told by a partisan, she could emerge as a persecuted heroine. To the citizens of Exeter, however, she was no persecuted heroine, she was the "French whore." They detested the proud lords with her and were heartily glad to see her go.

Marguerite went from Exeter to Taunton, then to Wells. She had allowed her army to burn, pillage, and commit murder

as she had before. At Wells, her soldiers sa
Palace, and when the country people heard th
they fled from their houses and hid in the w

"She has spent ten years in exile," I
"And what has she learned? Nothing! She
same pattern, making the same mistakes in
London in 1461!"

🌸 *Twenty-four*

Yorkist spies dogged Marguerite of Anjou. Her army marched through the night, not daring to halt because of the desperate need to reach Gloucester, but they found the gates of the town locked against them. Madame Marguerite sent her commands to the governor; he chose to obey the king, and her herald was received with a volley of arrow fire from the ramparts to warn her off. She had neither the siege engines nor the time to attack the town. Her scouts had undoubtedly brought her word that Edward was closing in on her, forcing her tired army to take to the road again.

She would march northward—she had no other choice—and try for the next river crossing, the lower Lode ferry at Tewkesbury. The river was high from spring rains, the current was quick and dangerous, but the ferry offered the Lancastrians their only chance to make their escape and get to the other side of the river. Without sleep, or rest, they must toil on.

I knew something of the countryside between Gloucester and Tewkesbury. The road was rough for travel, and ill-suited for an army, with thorny woods on either side, or stony tracts of wasteland, broken by deep lanes. I thought of Anne, no longer of any value to Marguerite of Anjou, merely a helpless girl being dragged along with the Lancastrians on their march to Tewkesbury.

Marguerite of Anjou was aware, Edward was stalking her, ays drawing nearer. His soldiers suffered as much hardship as heir enemies, perhaps more. For long hours, they went without so much as a mouthful of food, and found no forage for their horses, but their greatest misery was thirst.

Edward compelled his army to march without a halt until he made Cheltenham, but he paused only long enough to order rations served—the first in twenty-four hours—and moved on. His spies kept watch, and were able to report the enemy's every move. When he neared Tewkesbury he learned that the Lancastrians had reached the outskirts of Tewkesbury at near four o'clock in the afternoon, but instead of making use of the ferry, the foot soldiers had flung down their weapons and sprawled on the ground.

Madame Marguerite herself and her captains had argued, exhorted, commanded, and pleaded with the men to make the effort and try to cross the Severn while they had time, warning them of the danger of staying where they were, but lack of sleep and long marches had sapped their strength and dulled their wits. Nothing could rouse them. They could not and would not stir. Edward found it hard to believe, and his brother Richard spoke up. "You would stir them, and so would I!"

However, the Lancastrian leaders did induce their soldiers to take a position in some fields in front of the town, and to dig trenches, making the place more difficult to assault.

Even without the trenches, the Lancastrians had chosen a strong position, "An evil place to attack," as Edward's scouts told him. On every side there were narrow lanes, deep dikes, hedgerows, hills, and valleys. Behind the Lancastrian encampment was the Abbey, with its square tower, a landmark for miles around. To the left was a stream, the Swillbrook, and not far off a line of trees marked the course of the Avon as it flowed through the fields to meet the Severn.

A few Lancastrian ladies, who had been in exile, returned to England with Marguerite of Anjou. With a battle impending, they were sent out of the town, and because her captains insisted, Marguerite went with the other women. A boat took them across the river to Little Malvern Priory, not one of the great religious houses, but a poor and modest place. Anne was one of the travel-worn, frightened group, and yet she did not belong among them.

Edward had encamped three miles from Tewkesbury, and that night wrote a letter to Elizabeth, every word showing his love for her and their children. His only mention of the battle was to tell her that he would send her a full account of it. When the little town was still huddled in shadow and the sky was taking on the color of brass, promising another sultry day, Edward's trumpets sounded. For his second-in-command he had come to rely on his brother Richard and gave the "undersized boy" the honor and danger and responsibility of leading the Yorkist van.

At Tewkesbury, during the first hour or so of battle, the Lancastrians could hope for their easy victory. They halted Richard's advance, forcing him back, threatening to crush the Yorkist van. Seeing an opportunity for quick success they swept down from a slope and charged the Yorkist right wing, but Richard rallied his troops to Edward's support, and Edward swung his men around to meet the enemy attack. He had taken care to keep a reserve of spearmen hidden in a wood. Obeying a trumpet's signal, they came up. The Lancastrians were surrounded. Some fought their way out, but more than half were killed.

Natural obstacles had made their original position an "evil place to attack," but after they had left it, the lanes and ditches and streams impeded them when they tried to break out of the Yorkist trap. When I heard how the field of battle had been lost and won at Tewkesbury, I found traces of a pattern—promise of victory, then total defeat—it had happened before to Lancaster, at Towton.

A band of knights and squires had pledged themselves to defend Marguerite's son, but at the last they were among the dead, and Lancaster's prince was trapped and killed in a meadow.

Later, the monks came out and asked for his body; they buried Marguerite's son in the Abbey, beneath the choir.

In the rout, the Lancastrian foot soldiers and archers had far better chance to escape than their leaders who were weighed down by their armor, and some survived, if they could outrun the pursuers, and if luck favored them. Men plunged into the current of the Avon, or even the Severn, and some succeeded in getting to the other side. Others ran for the town, and the people hid them until night.

The Lancastrian commander, with twenty-three lords and knights, and thirty or more foot soldiers had made the seven hundred yards from the battlefield to the Abbey, and ran in by the west door. At the sight of them the people who were hearing Mass stared, rose from their knees, and left the Abbey, by the east door.

The Abbot left the altar and went down into the nave to give what help he could, but he halted when he heard the din outside. Voices shouting, trumpets braying were ominous sounds. The main door was flung wide and Edward came striding in, gripping his unsheathed sword. Will Hastings, Dorset, Richard, George, and other lords followed, their soldiers crowding behind them. "They're in here. Find them and finish them off." Edward's voice rang through the dim spaces, starting echoes as if ghostly voices answered him.

The Abbot was an old man, gentle and unworldly, but he went forward to face the king. "My son, I forbid you to do your killing here, or to harm anyone within these walls."

In his crested helmet, the king seemed all of seven feet tall.

"My lord Abbot, you will please make way. I am in command here."

The Abbot had carried the Host from the altar when Mass was interrupted. "Remember who holds command over you—over all of us"—he lifted up the chalice—"here and everywhere."

Edward stepped back and fell on his knees, and all of his men in the Abbey knelt until he ordered them to go. Before he followed them out, he promised to spare the lives of the

Lancastrians who had taken refuge in the church—or so people said.

The monks brought food and drink to the Lancastrians, and cared for their wounds, but they knew that Edward had set a guard around the Abbey, and when the Lancastrians came out, they were seized and held prisoner. Edward gave the common soldiers their freedom at once, and full pardon, but their leaders were tried for treason, with Richard as their judge. Doubtless he granted them a fair trial, but they were guilty of making war against the king, and as they were defeated, they were traitors. Richard ordered their immediate execution, and some dozen or more lords and knights, including Edmund Beaufort, Marguerite of Anjou's captain general, were beheaded in the town's market place.

Tewkesbury Abbey had no special privilege of Sanctuary, Dame Joan reminded me, noticing my gloomy mood.

"But you know what is being said—he lured them out by promising to pardon them."

"No matter what he did or did not promise, they could not stay any longer, they had to come out. They knew it, Edward knew it."

"Why did he execute all of them? He's become too ruthless."

"He was harsh," Dame Joan conceded. "And yet if he had spared Beaufort or any of the others, we could look forward to more rebellions and battles and bloodshed."

Londoners had cleaned their streets and decked their houses with lengths of arras, and silk and fine cloth, until the city seemed to flow with bright colors in honor of the king and his army. Green branches and garlands of flowers wreathed windows and doors, and on Ascension Eve, London was astir before dawn. People lined the streets, crowded in doorways, hung out of windows. Boys perched on rooftops, and from a distance had the aspect of gargoyles.

The weather was fair and springlike, and while the crowds waited for the king, the people ate eel and coney pasties, laughed at the antics of a juggler, pushed their way into taverns or became drunk on the free red and white wines flowing from the fountains in the squares. Vendors cried their wares, women chatted with their neighbors, pickpockets agile as eels slithered through the crowd, whores plied their trade, beggars asked alms. Londoners were glad that the war had come to an end, thankful for a Yorkist victory. They could hope to flourish under Edward's rule. Already the goods heaped in warehouses were being loaded on ships. A favorable wind was blowing, quickening listless hulls to life, filling idle sails, sending the ships to sea again.

The mayor and aldermen in scarlet, the most important citizens in bright violet robes, were ready with their welcome. Trumpets, clarions, and drums sounded, clearer and louder, banners flared in the sunlight. Richard, Duke of Gloucester, rode at the head of the army, preceding the king. George was somewhere to the rear of the procession. Last of all, a dark unadorned chariot, guarded by soldiers, followed in the wake. At sight of it, the good tempered crowds left off cheering to curse and hoot and yell, "French whore—witch—kill the witch!" Women and children who had thrown kisses and scattered flowers for Edward, picked up stones to hurl at the woman in the chariot. The soldiers pushed them back, and prevented the mob from doing her any harm or even catching a glimpse of her.

Dorset had seen her once, in his childhood, had kissed her hand, and had become one of her worshipers. He had seen her again on the way from Tewkesbury to London. "But only once," he told me. Once was enough. Dorset was no longer the little Thomas Grey who had worshiped Queen Marguerite—he had turned cold-hearted. However, his voice was unsteady as he went on speaking. He had been prepared to find her changed after what she had endured. "But not into what she is now. Her eyes used to be brilliant, now they are dull and sunken and always inflamed—" He added: "They say that the inflammation is caused by her incessant tears. And some malady encrusts her skin with a kind of scaliness, and has left deep-pitted marks on her face. She's become hideous. A hideous hag!"

Edward had sent Sir William Stanley to find her after Tewkesbury. Stanley had brushed aside the frightened nuns, and had burst into the room where Marguerite of Anjou waited for news of her son. He had shouted, "Madam, your bastard's dead!"

"Edward should have chosen a kinder messenger," I said to Dorset. "No one but Stanley was capable of delivering the blow with such gross brutality!"

"The soldiers took Marguerite of Anjou to the Tower and thrust her into a prison," Dorset told me later. "But only Edward and her jailers know where."

Before dusk, the palace flared with lights as the Yorkist leaders and the city officials gathered for the banquet to celebrate victory. Instead of armor, the king's captains wore silks and satins, gold embroideries, gold tissue, jewels. Instead of trumpets, they heard soft music, instead of following the uncertain fortunes of an adventurer, they thronged the royal presence chambers. In a few hours, warriors had become courtiers.

The queen was asking for me, one of Elizabeth's pages told me, and ushered me into her solar. Edward was with her, sitting near her. I had seen and spoken to him briefly earlier in the day, and yet I felt stiff and constrained at finding him here. I wondered why Elizabeth had sent for me when she could have had a little time alone with him before they must make their appearance at the banquet. However, she had her reasons, I knew.

Edward rose, kissed my cheek lightly, led me to a chair and praised my looks. In a few minutes my constraint had gone, but in its place I had a sense of unreality. Edward was brown and lean from his campaigning, otherwise he showed no signs—outwardly at least—of what had happened to him during the last year. It was hard to believe in the account of his ruthlessness.

I took advantage of his happy humor to ask him what would become of Lady Warwick and Anne. The earl's estates had become confiscated to the crown, but it seemed to me grossly unjust for Lady Warwick to be deprived of her inheritance. However, I guarded my tongue, and only said that she was harmless and was not to blame.

"Let her stay where she is," Edward answered. "Retire from the world—take the veil. I have no intention of restoring her estates, for a reason—George would manage to wrest everything from her in a week!"

It was useless to plead for poor Lady Warwick any longer. She lacked the spirit to defend her property against George, and Edward refused to be her champion.

"What of Anne?" I asked. Stanley had brought her with Marguerite of Anjou to Edward's camp at Tewkesbury.

"Poor child," Edward said, "I sent her to Isabel."

"Where else could you send her except to her sister?" Elizabeth asked.

Unless she retired to a convent, Anne had nowhere else to go. In her place, I would rather take shelter in the greenwood than under George's roof, but in such a great household as he maintained she could contrive to avoid him, and Isabel would give her sisterly affection.

"And—and what of Madame Marguerite?" Elizabeth ventured, with one of her timid, sidelong glances—and this time her timidity was entirely real for Edward's face had darkened.

"I will soon put her where she'll do no more harm."

"But she is powerless now." Elizabeth's voice was scarcely above a whisper, "What do you intend?" She put out her hand.

"To get rid of her."

Elizabeth knew what he meant. "But you would never order her death. Not that way!"

He shook off her hand, and stood up. "You are too soft-hearted. Think of all the deaths that she caused!" He looked at me as he spoke. I remembered the dead, but I could no longer share Edward's implacable hatred for Marguerite of Anjou.

"Tewkesbury gave you your revenge, my lord."

"It's not a question of vengeance. The woman is a malign witch."

234

"Please—for my sake—please, Edward—be lenient." Elizabeth took his hand in both of hers and covered it with kisses.

"You waste your pity on her, my Bess." He unwound her clinging fingers and held her close, with his right arm around her. "She proclaimed that your sorrows and misfortunes would rival hers!"

I realized that Marguerite of Anjou could say what she pleased as long as she only reviled Edward, but she had enraged him by foretelling dire things in store for Elizabeth.

Edward turned his attention on me. "I never expected you to show concern for Marguerite of Anjou!"

"My concern is for you—she has nothing to live for, but she may make you angry enough to put her to death. If you did you would only harm yourself."

"Cicely is right," Elizabeth murmured.

Suddenly, he yielded.

"Be content, I'll grant what you and Cicely ask—she can live on until the Devil comes for her," Edward said. "Now you can forget her."

But when Elizabeth left the room to rearrange her disordered headdress, and I was following her, Edward asked me to wait. I obeyed, and after a moment's silence, he told me what he had left unsaid before Elizabeth.

Marguerite of Anjou had prophesied that no son of Edward's would reign, but would die young—die a violent death.

After the victory banquet that night, Dorset disappeared without a word, and I assumed that he chose to be with one of his bawds. Just before I fell asleep, I heard a nightingale singing in the gardens, and knew a pang of loneliness and longing. It must have been hours later when I was awakened by the touch of icy fingers on my bare skin. I cried out in fear, but it was only Dorset, who had come in without making a sound. "Why do you give a shriek and turn away from me?" he demanded, and even though half asleep, I was dimly aware of sharp urgency in his voice. "Because your hands are cold," I answered in a drowse. "Oh, is that all?" He laughed. "Then you can warm me."

In the morning, Dorset told me that Henry the Sixth was dead. His jailers had found his lifeless body. I asked what caused his death. "News of Tewkesbury," Dorset answered. "The official account states he died from pure melancholy." He spoke glibly, but the flicker in his eyes betrayed his uneasiness.

"No one will believe it," I said, but I asked no more questions. The corpse was carried out of the Tower at dawn and taken to St. Paul's, where it was placed on a black-draped bier, with candles burning, and monks chanting a dirge for the last Lancastrian king.

What I surmised kept me silent. There had been no reason to do away with Henry before the battle of Tewkesbury, because all of his claims would have devolved on Marguerite of Anjou's son. But after Lancaster's prince had been killed in battle, Henry the Sixth's life was soon snuffed out. Why? Because in the recent rebellion, he had been an unresisting puppet in the Earl of Warwick's hands. Because other rebels might make use of "our sovereign lord King Henry the Sixth."

From now on no one would dare to make an attempt to wrest sovereign power from Edward's grasp, and if he gave the people peace and order and prosperous times they would be satisfied, but from time to time he might remember Henry's greeting to him. "My cousin of York"—Henry had held out his thin strengthless hands—"you are very welcome because I know that with you I will be safe."

❧ Twenty-five

Early in June, George brought Isabel to London, and Anne was with her. It had been years since I had seen Anne, and I could not count on her childhood fondness for me now. I knew how easily ties of friendship could wither, and bonds of kinship had no meaning in our time. She might have forgotten that I was her cousin Cicely Bonville, and think of me only as Dorset's wife. She might class me among her enemies.

However, I wrote to Isabel, asking her if she would receive me, and the answer assured me of a welcome. I took care to choose a time when George himself was most likely to be elsewhere. He and Isabel, with the hundreds of people who made up their household, were lodged in a palace, on the outskirts of London, overlooking fields, farms, and the river. It was called the Herber, and had belonged to the Earl of Warwick. It was part of Isabel's inheritance, and as George was her husband, he had a legal right to claim it. Did his treachery to the earl ever cause him a pang of remorse? Or was he entirely carefree when he rode out on the earl's horses, hunted with the earl's staghounds following the scent, hawked with the earl's favorite falcon on his wrist?

The Herber was only a minor possession to George. He was claiming—in right of his wife—not only part of the earl's inheritance, but Warwick Castle and all of the estates which had belonged to Lady Warwick's family and which she had inherited.

At the Herber, George's banner was displayed, retainers and servants wore his liveries, but as I went in, I saw that it was not easy to obliterate all signs of the earl's ownership. His famous cognizance of the bear and ragged staff was too deeply carved in the stones of this house. Though he had seldom stayed here, he had left his imprint in the sober grandeur of the hall, and the rooms above.

I saw no trace of Isabel's occupancy until I reached her bedchamber. She was propped on pillows in a vast bed, and seemed more than ever to be no larger than a doll. When she saw me, she dismissed her women and held out her hands to me. Thanking me for coming, she asked me to sit beside her. I took her cold little hands in mine, and asked about her health. She was *enceinte*, she told me, and her physician had advised her to take precautions.

"God grant you a happy hour," I said—the usual phrase, but could a child born of George and Isabel come into this world and find a happy hour?

"I come to you empty-handed," I told her. "I tried and failed

237

to be of any use to your mother." I could not tell her why. She was George's wife and it would be better if she never learned that in return for betraying the earl her father, George had demanded her mother's estates.

"You are good to interest youself in my poor mother's plight." Tears came to Isabel's eyes. "Cicely, do you know where Anne is?"

"Anne! But she's here—with you!"

"She was, but she left this house sometime before daybreak. No one saw her go."

Doubtless she went by the small postern door, but where were the guards who should have been posted at every door?

"Was she unaccompanied?"

"No one in this household went with her, so I'm told."

Whoever had told Isabel might be lying, I thought. She did not know every person in this household. "Did she give you any hint that she might go?"

Isabel hesitated. "Not in words, but last evening when she came to bid me good night, she begged me over and over to take care of myself and not to be troubled about her. How could I help being concerned about my own sister!"

I said what I could to soothe her, found a flagon of wine, poured some in a cup and when she raised her head, I persuaded her to drink a little. Anne had done just what I would have done in her place, and yet I was aghast to think of her alone and unprotected. Another thought struck me, had she gone of her own free will?

"You need rest," I said to Isabel, and offered to call her woman.

"No, no, keep them out. I need to talk to you. Anne seemed well enough in health, but in spirit, she shut herself away—even from me—"

And no wonder, I thought, since she had to remember that her sister was George's wife.

238

"I scarcely saw her after that so called marriage to the French prince."

"Did, did she love him?" I ventured.

"Love him? Oh, no—at least she was spared that misery!"

"Anne will be found," I said. "There is one person who will scour the country from one end to the other until he does find her."

"Do you mean—"

"You can guess his name, but it is best not to say it. Not yet."

"Why do you think that he would make such a search for her?" Isabel sighed. "He is greatly changed, I hear."

"I think that he still yearns to marry Anne."

I was glad that I had not mentioned Richard's name aloud, because the tapestry near the bed swayed and the little door behind it opened to reveal George, standing in the narrow arch.

"How you startled me," Isabel told him. "You were not due until tomorrow!" Her words offered scant welcome, but her eyes brightened.

"Concern for you brought me back today." He walked into the room and kissed her before he turned to me and kissed my hand. These days, when we happened to meet, George and I observed a cold formality.

George sat down on the edge of Isabel's bed and put his arms around her. From the expression on her face and the eagerness in her eyes, she took pleasure in the sight of him.

"See what I've brought you." George held up a bracelet, a wide band of gold set with rubies, diamonds, and sapphires. Isabel thanked him, but her manner was listless, and his smile faded. To ease the constraint, I admired the bracelet.

"You see Cicely thinks well of my choice, and she's a good judge." He used a coaxing tone to Isabel. "Try it on."

Isabel passively held out her arm, but as she moved her hand her wedding ring slipped from her finger and fell on the floor. George stared at the ring as it winked in a patch of sunlight. "An evil omen," he whispered.

George insisted on escorting me to my barge. On the way he

thanked me for coming, and invited me to come again. "Isabel needs her friends to gather around her."

I said, "She needs her sister."

"No!" George halted in the doorway, then went on a little to be out of earshot of the guards. "Anne had a bad effect on her!"

"In what way?" I asked.

George flushed. "She scorns me, and turned Isabel against me!"

"Anne would not disparage you to your wife," I said, "you must be mistaken."

"Even in exile, Isabel and I were happy together, but she has changed."

"If so, it isn't Anne's fault."

George had planted himself directly in front of me, and I realized he had taken too much wine. It would be useless to expect him to see reason.

I was shaking with a kind of fear—afraid of him and as in other times, afraid for him. Wine made him reckless. "We would do better to discuss Anne's disappearance. Where is she?"

"Why do you ask me?" His sullen anger flared out. "Why?"

Richard made every effort to find Anne, but several weeks had passed, and his people had failed to give him any news of her.

He lingered on in London, more than ever close-mouthed and solitary, avoiding Windsor where the king and queen were unless he had business with Edward. Though I saw him from time to time, I had no opportunity to speak to him in private. However, it was easy enough to make the opportunity.

The next time he came, I went into the garden and strolled along the path that he would take to reach his barge. He soon appeared, and in the clear afternoon light, his face wore an unhappy look, making him seem much older than his years. Catching sight of me, he hurried to meet me, and motioned his servants to go on.

"I am anxious to go north," Richard said. "I'm not needed at Westminster or here, but first I must find out what has become of Anne. I've had another interview with George. He said that if she chose to run away and hide rather than have me, it was no concern of his."

"Never believe it! He was only taunting you."

Richard drew the dagger at his belt in and out of its sheath. He knew very well why George was trying to prevent the marriage. If Lady Warwick's rights were ignored, and he claimed her estates in Isabel's name, then Anne, as co-heiress, was entitled to half.

"Then what's become of her? Where is she?"

I hesitated before saying what was in my mind. Edward was making every effort to keep peace within his family, and yet I plunged on. "George knows where she is. I have no proof at all, only his manner when I asked."

Richard's voice was quiet, "I must find a way to wring the truth out of him."

"How? He will only deny everything all the more vehemently. Doubtless she felt herself unwelcome to him, and he may have persuaded her to go into hiding. Does Anne know that you are her friend? That you are eager to marry her?"

"I had no opportunity to tell her so."

"And you have carried on your search very secretly. Too secretly, I think."

"Anne's disappearance affords too much scope for talk, but I will disregard all of that, and announce—proclaim that I'm searching for her—in hopes of marrying her. At least the din will make George nerve-strung." He added: "But what if he's right? What if she hates me?"

"First find her, and she'll tell you otherwise," I said.

He thanked me for my sympathy and went on. I knew how Richard shrank from baring his inmost feelings but he would never rest until he found Anne.

When Richard's quest became generally known, all kinds of rumors and speculations circulated, until one day the citizens of a certain neighborhood in London must have wondered to see my Lord Duke of Gloucester and a dozen or more of his retainers crowd into the narrow street. The Duke of Gloucester himself dismounted, knocked on the door of an inconspicuous house, and was admitted. After a little time, he reappeared, and led a girl out of the house. Someone whispered that she was nothing more than a servant, but he wrapped her in his silk cloak, and showed her the greatest deference. One of his men brought up a lady's palfrey, decked with rich trappings. He put the girl in the saddle, mounted his own horse, and they rode away.

Later, the people who had gaped at the scene learned that the servant girl was the Lady Anne Neville, and were more astounded than ever. All the while that the city and whole country were being turned inside out to find her she had been a cook-maid in the kitchen of that house. How did she happen to be there? How did the Duke of Gloucester know how to find her in such an unlikely place? The questions went unanswered; but the house where she was found belonged to George.

Richard took Anne first to the sanctuary of St. Martin Le Grand, then to the house of the Archbishop of York, her uncle and mine as well. It was there that I saw her again. She still wore deepest mourning, but a little color had come into her face. She seemed glad to see me, and greeted me with fondness. As there were other people present, we had to content ourselves with superficial conversation. Perhaps she preferred to keep her story to herself in any case, but I gathered that she was quite willing to marry Richard. He loved Anne for herself, but he saw no reason why he should give up her share of her inheritance to George.

Naturally, Edward was all for Richard, but was anxious to settle the dispute legally and permanently. At last a decree of Parliament divided the Warwick possessions between the two brothers. In order to conclude his marriage to Anne without further delay, Richard accepted slightly less than his due, and George had slightly more than his share. The Countess of Warwick was no more considered than if she had been dead.

Richard and Anne were married, very quietly, and immediately left London for Middleham Castle. Shortly afterwards, Richard sent an escort for Lady Warwick, and brought her to Middleham. So Anne and her mother were again living in their former home, the massive castle overlooking Wensleydale and the moors. And there, too, Richard had spent the three happiest years of his life.

In the summer of 1471, Anne's mysterious disappearance and her marriage were still the subject of discussion, and Elizabeth's sisters were full of questions.

"What did cooks and scullions make of her in their midst—a creature so different from themselves?" Katherine Woodville whispered.

"How did Richard think of looking for her in such an unlikely place?" Katherine asked next.

Elizabeth knew the answer. "She found a way to send him a message, telling him where to come."

By the summer of 1472 England had been at peace for a full year and I had given Dorset a son. The birth of my son brought me a new happiness. I glanced at Dorset, handsome in brilliant green and white, embroidered in gold. He took great pride in having an heir, and was satisfied with me because I had given him a son. But I thought of the child as *my* son.

I loved my child too well to allow him to become another Dorset, and I was determined to do all in my power to prevent it. Perhaps Dorset sensed what was in my mind. He had said, "By all means name him Thomas—oh, not for me!" he had laughed, "for those stalwart ancestors of mine in Astley Church. If he has any likeness to them, you'll be glad of it." And Dorset had gone on to calculate how much he could expect in the way of gifts from the king and queen.

Edward had intended to endow my son with several manors which were part of Lord Oxford's confiscated estates, and I had declined them.

"Why?" Edward had demanded. "Do you refuse Oxford's manors for your son?"

"Lady Oxford is living in great poverty, trying to support herself by her needlework. And she is my mother's sister, my own aunt." And Edward's near cousin.

"You've never laid eyes on her," Edward had pointed out. "Are you and your mother sending her money and gifts?"

"To keep her from starving."

"And you scruple to take what was formerly her husband's even though I'll never restore any part of the Oxford estates."

"The heir is still a child; in time, you might restore him. Then he and my son might be enemies, because of those manors."

Edward's face had turned grave. As he had learned, his decree could transfer estates, but not long established loyalties. "Have your way then; I'll give small Thomas certain manors of my own."

I was heartily grateful to Edward, not only for the lands, but for his silence in regard to his first offer. He never mentioned that he had made it, or that I had refused it. Dorset's mouth watered for a share in the Oxford estates, and if he had known that I had let such an opportunity slip he would have never stopped berating me for my folly. However, he was well pleased with the substantial grant crown lands for his heir. Dorset would enjoy the revenues during the child's minority. Also the Oxford estates were still in the family, as Elizabeth had induced Edward to deed most of them to Dorset's younger brother.

This boy, called Lord Grey, had lived quietly at Oxford during the troubled years and was just beginning to make his appearance at court. He was present at the queen's banquet, and glancing at his dark face, with the heavy mouth and narrow black eyes I was struck by his likeness to dead John Woodville, who had aroused so much hatred and had been beheaded without trial outside the walls of Coventry. By whose orders? The Earl of Warwick had been involved, but Elizabeth held George directly responsible.

❧ *Twenty-six*

In the autumn, I accompanied the king and queen to Oxford, and took pleasure in riding through the country under the changeable sky. On our way, the people came out to cheer the king.

The visit to Oxford redounded to the glory of the Wood-villes, as Elizabeth's brother Lionel, who had taken Orders, had been made Chancellor of the University. I could picture him as Bishop, Archbishop, perhaps Cardinal—a wordly prelate—but I granted him intellect and a real love of learning. "I would be happy here," Anthony Woodville said to me, and I realized that the life of a scholar might suit him very well. Exile, war battles, and executions had changed him. He had turned to religion, and his tendency to melancholy had grown. Shortly after the battle of Tewkesbury, he had gone on a pilgrimage to St. James of Compostela.

"How dared you set off when there's work to be done here in England?" Edward had thundered at him on his return. "Wait until the country's pacified before you amble off to any shrine, no matter how holy!"

Anthony had been quickly forgiven—too quickly his enemies said—but doubtless Edward understood him better than they did.

"In a few years, you are likely to be a teacher, or so I understand," I said to my Lord Anthony. As I knew from Elizabeth, when the little prince was older, Edward intended to send his heir to Ludlow to be educated, and would appoint Anthony Woodville to have charge of him.

"If so, it will be a heavy responsibility," he answered. "In the meantime, you are in charge."

Recently, Edward had appointed me lady governess to his children. It was an honorary position, but I had the duty of supervising the children's household, and selecting the right persons to do the actual caring for their needs.

"I have an easy task," I said, "and will be sorry when the little boys are out of the nursery. Ludlow is far away."

"But it's a strong place, and a good choice for a Prince of Wales, near the border."

Royal princes had their own household early in life—when they were scarcely out of swaddling bands. I was thankful that I could keep my own son with me longer, heartily thankful that he had no royal blood in his veins. In our times it was all too often a fatal inheritance.

Edward's first concern was for the safety of his son—and he could trust Anthony Woodville, who seemed to me a logical choice, but as I could foresee, the choice was sure to cause a whirlwind of jealousy and indignation at another instance of Woodville aggrandizement. Of course there were others who had earned Edward's trust, and already I had heard this person or that asking why not appoint the king's brother Richard to undertake the education of the prince instead of the queen's brother Anthony. But Richard was already burdened with heavy responsibilities in the north and Edward's friends—the ones capable of being guardian to princes—were likewise fully occupied with the business of government.

Lady Jacquetta had never been in good health since her stay in Sanctuary, and by autumn her family were uneasy about her condition. However, she insisted on making the journey to Oxford. As she traveled in a kind of charrette, a little larger than the usual horse-drawn litter, with the curtains closed, the people had no opportunity to catch a glimpse of her. She remained invisible, which made her more than ever mysterious to them.

Once at Oxford, she seemed to recover, and was well enough for the court to hold the usual Christmas celebrations at Westminster. She had her apartments in the palace, and I dutifully visited her, sometimes with Elizabeth, sometimes alone, and on the day after Christmas, I went alone. I was admitted to her bedchamber, and found her sitting by the fire, wrapped in the thick folds of a black velvet robe bordered with black fur. She was studying the cards spread out on the table in front of her, and it was a moment or more before she turned her attention to me.

"I'm glad you have come," she said, and offered me a chair near her own.

Lady Jacquetta seemed small and shrunken, crouched in her chair, her face dark yellow in the firelight and her nose like a beak. She showed me the cards, pointing out one. "This means—" she began, then halted, without telling me what it meant, and swept all the cards together in a heap.

"Do you seek to know what the future holds for you?"

"I'm not bold enough to peer into it. Sufficient to the day is the evil thereof."

"I can give you examples of too many men and women who were forewarned and yet rushed headlong to meet their fate." She looked at me. "You at least will never have to look back and see that you have brought destruction on yourself or on those you love. You can hope for serene and happy years ahead."

"Will I be so lucky?" I doubted if Lady Jacquetta's ideas of happiness coincided with mine, but from the way she spoke she seemed to have become aware that man does not live by bread alone.

"It's well for Dorset that you are his wife, and well for him that he's half a Grey. The Woodvilles are unlucky."

They had endured griefs and misfortunes, but unlucky?

"All the world envies them, madam."

"But I am afraid for them, afraid for my daughter—for the queen." Lady Jacquetta's voice seemed tired, and the foreign intonation was more pronounced. Her hands, once so plump and smooth with delicately tapered fingers, had now shrunken into claws.

Jacquetta looked old and ill and afraid. Against the color and gleam of the hangings her hunched shadow was witchlike. I left her, and never saw her or spoke to her again. During the night her condition worsened, and she died a few days later.

The years were moving faster now. It was spring again and the court had moved to Windsor. Soon the chase was green with new leaves, and the gardens began to bloom. I had a second son now, still a baby in swaddling bands, but in time, the two brothers could be companions, and I prayed every day and every night that throughout their lives they would love each other.

Our little prince had already gone to Ludlow, in the care of Anthony Woodville. The boy was young to be separated from parents and sisters and home, but it was customary for a prince certainly a Prince of Wales to have his own establishment. Two

247

years ago Elizabeth had given Edward and the country another prince—a Duke of York, to insure the succession. And a fine strong child he was.

The Woodvilles, most of all Elizabeth, mourned Lady Jacquetta, but otherwise, no one regretted her. "When she died, it was as if a shadow had lifted," Hastings said. In her will she had been more generous to me than to Dorset, which irked him somewhat, but Lady Jacquetta had died three years ago, and he had forgotten. Also, Anthony Woodville, now a widower and childless, had made Dorset his sole heir. "In time, I'll be the richest man in England," he had boasted. "Except for the king."

Since the peace, Edward had been building up his own estates; he had bought ships, and traded with foreign countries as shrewdly as any merchant. Some of the great lords said that for a king to engage in trade was "beneath the dignity of a great prince," but Edward laughed at their criticism, and went on accumulating a private fortune of his own. Now he was likely to lose what he had, and the rest of us would be losers with him, because he was taking a great army to make war on France.

When he told Elizabeth, she had begged him to keep the peace with the French king. "You have won nine battles. Haven't you had your fill of glory?" She had spoken with more vehemence than I had ever heard her use to him. I had held my tongue, but I entirely agreed with her. And England had suffered enough from civil war to relish peace. However, the whole country had gone mad, Lords and Commons were urging Edward on. They were possessed by a wild dream of reconquering all that we had lost in France, and they hated the French king, the Spider, who was still weaving plots against us.

The Spider's plotting was not a real threat, but we had a treaty with Burgundy. "And even more binding, Charles of Burgundy helped me to regain my kingdom," Edward had explained to Elizabeth. "He supplied the money and ships for me to come back to England. In return, I gave him a solemn promise to give him what help I could, if and when he needed it."

"Duke Charles gave you only a few ships, only a little

money," Elizabeth had pointed out. "You regained your power by your own efforts—send men and money if you must, but spare yourself any further risks!" Elizabeth had forgotten all her zeal for the Burgundian alliance.

"It would be ruinous for us if we wait until the Spider swallows up the Low Countries. For one thing, we would lose all of our most important markets."

Parliament had voted a large grant to carry on war; Edward thanked Lords and Commons very heartily, but invasion would be a costly business. Already the people were heavily taxed for the war. With the help of a little advice from a shrewd clerk or lawyer he invented a devious plan to extract money from his prosperous subjects. He asked them to contribute what he called "benevolences"—according to their means.

Edward had gone out into the shires. He had journeyed all over England, and a few days ago had reappeared at Windsor, having plucked the feathers of his magpies without making them cry out. When the people on his lists were summoned to "come before the king" they looked as if they were going to the gallows. When they went away they were perfectly happy, saying that they had spoken to the king, and he had talked with them so benignly that they didn't regret their money. If a man of money offered a good sum—appropriate to his station, and his means— the king thanked him heartily, shook him by the hand and sometimes added a promise of speedy victory over the French.

"And if a man preferred to give very little, what happened?" I had asked.

"Edward knew how to deal with him," said Hastings, "by telling him 'so and so who is poorer than you paid such an amount; you who are richer, can easily pay more.' So with fair words he brought the reluctant ones up to the mark."

Edward knew how to coax and cajole the women with smiles, flattery, and an air of chivalrous courtesy. In one town, he had asked a rich old woman what she would give him to help him with the war, and she had answered, "For your handsome face you shall have twenty pounds." That was twice what Edward had expected, and to thank her, he had put his arms around her and kissed her. She immediately promised him double.

I was sitting on a bench on the other side of the fishpond, partially hidden by a screen of shrubbery when Edward suddenly appeared. He looked up, greeted me, and in a few minutes joined me. He walked back to the palace with me while the nurses herded the children on ahead of us—all but Bess, who walked with us, holding onto Edward's hand and listening to him with grave attention.

He had just signed a treaty with Scotland, he said. Peace with the Scots was a necessity or they would swarm over the border as soon as Edward and Richard sailed for France. To secure the treaty, Edward had promised his second daughter to Scotland's heir. She was much too young to be married.

"But in time she will be a queen." Edward added. "And so will you," he said to Bess.

"I would much rather stay at home," the child sighed, echoing Margaret of York, who had resigned herself to her marriage with Charles of Burgundy. A few months ago Margaret had written me a gloomy letter. I asked Edward if he had heard from her in the last day or so.

"Not directly, but the Burgundian envoy told me only a few hours ago that the state of things is growing desperate. I must think of Margaret. I'm in debt to her."

I knew that Margaret had influenced Duke Charles to part with ships, money, and cannon for Edward's return to England, and I could understand his sense of obligation to her.

"The people want war, and they will have it," Edward said. "But they delude themselves if they think victory will be easy. Whatever his sins, the Spider of France is too formidable."

In June, Edward sailed for Calais with a great army. Both of his brothers took part. I saw them briefly when they came to London. Richard was happier than he had been at any other time in his life; he and Anne now had a son, named for Edward.

I had never pictured Richard as a doting father, but so he was, and forgot his reserve as he talked of the boy, and of Anne.

George, likewise, had a son, but did not mention him, and I hesitated to ask because I had heard rumors that the child was "too listless" for his age. Also there was talk that George was drinking heavily, which was only too likely. When I met him face to face in daylight, I noticed how he had changed; he was growing fat, and the beauty of his features was already a little blurred.

My conversation with him was short. Isabel was "ailing," he told me, and he seemed genuinely concerned about her health. Otherwise we had nothing to say to each other, and he was plainly uneasy with me. When he made his escape, I watched him as he threaded his way through the crowded presence chamber.

Edward had come up, and was watching him too. "I'm taking George with me to keep an eye on him," he said, "if I left him here, he might take advantage of my absence to concoct some mischief."

These last years George had been living mostly at Warwick Castle, but he had answered Edward's call to arms by bringing two hundred or more foot soldiers and a thousand archers.

"He seems glad to go," I said, hoping that my Lord Duke of Clarence intended to act the part of the king's loyal brother.

The royal courier had brought letters to Elizabeth from Edward's headquarters. Apparently the Duke of Burgundy had delayed his meeting with Edward. At last Duke Charles had appeared—but without his army. "The truth is," Edward's letter had explained, "that the only army he has at present is broken, badly equipped, and disheartened. He lost four thousand men in the siege of an unimportant town. It will be months before he can recruit and equip another army. What he has in mind is for England to fight his war for him."

Elizabeth folded the letter, then unfolded it and read it again, and after meditating over it, her eyes grew bright. She said that from the tone of Edward's letter, he had no intention of fighting Burgundy's war without Burgundy's help, and I agreed with her interpretation of Edward's words. The English army was strong enough to challenge the French, and any number of hot heads would urge Edward on, but they would never influence him. Doubtless he was glad to have an excuse to avoid war.

Dorset's next letter to me said much more. "We are encamped in wet muddy fields," he wrote, "and suffer great discomfort, but a week ago a Frenchman came secretly into our camp while Edward was at dinner. He left the board at once and had a long private conversation with this person. It was easy to guess that he was a messenger from the Spider of France himself, sent to try to negotiate with Edward, who listened very willingly.

"As it is no secret now, I am free to tell you that the Spider had made large offers. I have not yet learned all of the terms, but in plain words he has already bribed Edward and all of the English lords well and handsomely—all but one. Richard turned stiffnecked and refused to take any money for what he calls a dishonorable peace. Hastings had a few qualms, but not so many. He salved his conscience by whispering 'put the money in my sleeve,' and averted his face while the coins were poured in. You know how spacious his sleeves are. Without doubt he has taken his share.

"Edward will get 75,000 crowns in fifteen days, and 25,000 crowns every Easter and Michaelmas as long as he and the Spider are both alive, so he can honestly cry, 'Long live the Spider.'

"The treaty includes the promise to make a marriage between the Dauphin and one of Edward's daughters. Of course he has chosen Bess, and is elated at the prospect of her becoming Queen of France. Of course the French are elated at the prospect of getting rid of the English army.

"The Duke of Burgundy quickly caught wind of what was in the making, and came roaring into our camp. His face was a very dark plum color, and for two days he kept up a violent quarrel with Edward, demanding to know how England dared make a private treaty without Burgundy's consent. The bystanders heard everything because he sneered, snarled, and hurled insults in English. Edward invited him to join the treaty too and advised him to make peace, since Burgundy evidently lacked the strength to make war.

"Some of our soldiers are disappointed—they had looked forward to looting French towns, but most of them are willing to go home without killing so much as one Frenchman."

At a later date, Dorset wrote again, describing the meeting between the two kings, at Picquigny, on the Somme, at a point where the river was narrow. A bridge was built over the river, roofed in against bad weather, with strong bars across the center, to satisfy the King of France. "He lives in deadly terror of assassination. And has been in danger from traitors. Edward has had considerable experience with them too, but goes about without any fear at all, he laughed at the iron grating."

Leaving their attendants at a little distance, the two kings met on the bridge, talked to each other through the iron bars for sometime. They seemed to have a friendly conversation, and laughed together, but as they were alone, no one knew what they said.

Before Edward and his army came back to England, there was some grumbling from people who had paid largely for the king to wage war. "Our money was used for a soldiers' frolic," one London merchant complained. At Amiens, our soldiers had so disgraced themselves by their drunken debauchery that Edward had commanded his captains to fling every one of his men out of the town. The English had not covered themselves with glory. However, when Edward came back to this country, the people acclaimed him as heartily as if he had conquered all of France and had brought the Spider with him as a prisoner.

Edward was quick to placate any discontent by promising not to collect the rest of the money that Parliament had voted, and not to impose any new taxes. He won the merchants by explaining what they had to gain by the peace treaty. "Free communication and interchange of merchandise with the French," and ships were made ready to sail for French ports to trade our wares for wines and silks and linen.

I asked Will Hastings if the "benevolences" should be refunded to the donors. "Not a penny of it," he had answered. "But they won't be cajoled into contributing the rest of their money to a long-drawn-out and doubtful campaign—so they can console themselves." He had added, in a lower voice, "As there's no hint of unrest, George is allowed to go where he pleases." He had already gone, but Richard, and some of the other great lords still lingered in London.

Edward had entertained them at supper and afterward, Elizabeth had received them in her presence chamber.

Outside a cold wind was blowing, and rain was falling, but the palace blazed with lights. In the queen's presence chamber, there was a fireplace at each end of the room where great logs burned and kept out the cold.

Richard came up to me and asked me if I had heard that Edward had accepted a ransom for Marguerite of Anjou. In the stir and excitement of the army's return, that clause in the peace treaty had attracted very little notice, but Elizabeth had mentioned it to me.

"And the Spider of France had paid the ransom," I said, "as her father was too poor. But it seems unlike the Spider to part with money out of kindness for her."

"She signed away whatever rights she had inherited from her mother, and what rights she would inherit at her father's death in Anjou and Provence," Richard told me. "The Spider has an eye to the future. And she has renounced all claims in England—all past claims too. The document merely states that she was 'formerly married in England.'"

In the presence chamber, the minstrels were making music, and singing. I glanced at Elizabeth in her chair of state beside Edward—receiving the homage due to the Queen of England, and thought of that other woman, "formerly married in England."

"Her ransom came to fifteen thousand crowns," Richard told me.

Enough to soothe Edward's rancor. "I am glad she's free at last," but I pictured Marguerite of Anjou as a dark huddled figure vanishing in the cold and wind and rain.

"You look grave and sad," Richard said. "You and I are the only solemn ones here."

"Then we had better seem as cheerful as the others," I whispered, as the music came to a halt. Edward's face was flushed; he had taken a fever while he had been encamped in France, and perhaps it still lingered, although he claimed he was rid of it, but he was in the best of spirits. In Elizabeth's eyes, and in his own, he had come home in triumph.

"You are the only person in the world who ever succeeded in getting the better of the French king," she exulted, smiling up at Edward.

"She always spoke of him as the Spider," Richard muttered, "Now he's elevated into 'The French King.'"

The music began again, and Richard could say what he pleased without being overheard, but only the strongest feelings could impel him to break his usual reticence. "Edward is obsessed with the ambition of making Bess Queen of France," he said, "but then I am opposed to the whole peace treaty."

"I am thankful for peace," I answered, "but for the King of England and all of the greatest lords to be the Spider's pensioners —all but one. I admire you for refusing."

"Edward has won nine battles," Richard said, "and has lost one—his contest with the Spider of France."

❧ Twenty-seven

By the summer of 1476, Englishmen no longer dreamed of reconquering France. With peace and trade, England had waxed fat.

George was living in state at Warwick, and a merchant from the Midlands who brought me messages from the steward at Astley, had other things to say. As Dorset was out hawking, I could ask questions, and though the man guarded his tongue, he

255

had stayed in the town of Warwick, and in veiled words repeated what was common talk. George's guests at the castle were former Lancastrians. "They have now given their allegiance to the king," I said, "and it's the king's policy to forgive the past and unite the country. Doubtless my Lord Duke of Clarence follows it."

The merchant—I knew the man quite well—agreed politely but believed not a word of my explanation, nor did I, but I would not have seen any great significance in the gossip if Will Hastings had not told me in strict confidence that George had been in communication with some of the exiled Lancastrians. "Edward has conveyed a warning to George—I hope he'll heed it," Hastings said. "I need not tell you to guard your tongue."

"Tell Edward to guard his tongue with Elizabeth," I said. "He does not see that Elizabeth hates George—she hides it too well."

"When will he see her as she really is?" Hastings demanded.

"For his sake, I hope never," I answered.

Edward had sent his eldest son to Ludlow, but we still had the little Duke of York with us. When he was a forward two years old, another princess had been born. In the autumn of 1476, after the court had returned to London, Elizabeth had provided the House of York with a fifth princess. Her birth was celebrated with bell ringing and bonfires, and Edward took delight in her, and showed Elizabeth the greatest consideration and tenderness.

"Duke Charles would do well to make a son," Elizabeth said, one afternoon. "Margaret is young and in sound health, but has never had a child!"

"She may have children yet," I answered.

"Isabel's child is due," Elizabeth went on. "Perhaps she has been brought to bed—I hope without difficulties."

Isabel was at Warwick Castle, with physicians and midwives and servants to care for her, but her health was anything but sound. Elizabeth was able to feel sorry for her, but she would hate George more than ever if he sired sturdy sons.

She turned silent and abstracted. I was sitting close to her, and saw her face in the light from the window. Her eyes, her smile, her voice expressed whatever she had in mind—and intended to express, but at the moment she was not on her guard and I noted the hint of guile in her face. Her long habit of suppressing her feelings and dissimulating had left their mark. Suddenly she was alert as the tapestry at the farther end of the room was pushed aside and Edward came in by way of the private door. He moved at a slower pace than usual and the firelight showed his gloomy look. George's herald had just come from Warwick Castle with dire news. Isabel was dead.

All Christmastide festivities were abruptly ended; the court went into mourning, and the passing bell tolled for the Duchess of Clarence. Isabel was virtually unknown in London, but the people knew her history, and she had been the great Earl of Warwick's daughter. They remembered him, and still spoke admiringly of his exploits.

Isabel died in childbirth. The baby, a boy, survived, but was sickly, and not likely to live long. George was wild with grief and gave his wife perhaps the most magnificent funeral ever seen in England, "As if she had been queen—as he wished her to be." In winter weather, the funeral cortege wound along the road from Warwick Castle to Tewkesbury Abbey where Isabel's corpse, after lying in state, was buried.

In mid-January the Burgundian herald—Toison d'Or—brought an account of disaster. Duke Charles had disdained all advice and arguments and pleas—all warnings—and in the depths of the severe winter had laid siege to the capital of Lorraine with a small army. His enemies had swarmed out of the city, his Italian mercenaries had betrayed and deserted him. The Burgundians fought with him, but they were too few; they had been beaten twice before, which had weakened them. In this battle, fought in the snow beneath the city walls, Burgundy had gone down in a final defeat.

257

And Charles the Bold had not been found until the next day. The searching party had come upon him in an ice-glazed swamp with other corpses around him, and had some difficulty in identifying him as the plunderers had stripped him of jewels and armor and everything that would proclaim who he was.

The duke's body had been mangled by wounds and had become locked fast in the ice.

He had ruled the richest and most flourishing part of Europe, and had ruled with almost unlimited power. He had left only one child, a girl of not more than thirteen. She was fortunate in having Margaret of York as a stepmother. Margaret was now Dowager Duchess of Burgundy, and would do everything possible to rally the people, but with a broken and leaderless army, with most of the nobles killed or taken prisoner, and with a horde of enemies swooping down on the Low Countries—how could a woman and a girl stave off ruin?

Margaret had great courage, I knew, but already the Spider of France was sending his troops into Burgundian territories, and she sent desperate pleas to Edward. He must help her— England was Burgundy's only hope—only ally. As she pointed out, the rich cities of the Low Countries were most important to our trade, and without trade England's prosperity would wither away.

Edward summoned the Great Council, summoned his brothers, who came to London in haste. At Westminster, lights burned far into the night as questions were debated and decisions made. Messengers came and went, envoys set out for Burgundy or France. I asked Dorset if we would go to war against the Spider of France, but he thought not—Edward hoped to help Burgundy, and at the same time keep the truce with the Spider.

"How can he do both?" I asked.

"The Spider will gather up some choice morsels, but he will avoid provoking Edward into invading France again," Dorset said. "We will send aid to Duke Charles's wife and daughter without coming out in the open against the Spider."

Edward and the lords of the Council—all but Richard—clung

to their pensions from the Spider. Even more important to Edward was the plan for a marriage alliance. However, he dispatched reinforcements to the English garrison at Calais. And who was to have the vastly important post of Captain of Calais?

Elizabeth had no doubts—her brother Anthony. "He has greater experience in sea battles than anyone else you could name," she pointed out to Edward, "and you can be sure of his devotion."

"Anthony has other duties," Edward answered. "I've decided on Will Hastings."

"But he is given up to his revels and his wanton pleasures." Elizabeth's voice shook. She hated Will Hastings because he encouraged Edward to join him in his revels, and because he was Edward's closest friend.

"He has military experience, you know," Edward reminded her.

"What about his ability as a leader?" Elizabeth persisted. "Because of him, Barnet would have been a defeat. Fortunately you were in command to gain the victory as always."

"Hastings was not to blame, and the victory was largely due to Richard," Edward told her, then changed the subject, and after a few minutes' conversation, left the room. Once he had gone, Elizabeth went into one of her long brooding silences.

She was not the only woman who nursed great ambitions for a favorite brother. Dorset came late one night from a meeting of the Council. "A courier arrived from Burgundy bringing Edward a letter from the pen of his sister Margaret."

"What did she have to say?" I asked. "Not more bad news?"

"No, but Edward only discussed her letter with a few of us and we were startled when we found out what she has in mind." Dorset stood with his back to the fire, but I could see his face and the sly mocking look I knew. "But perhaps you can guess," he said.

"How can I?" I was puzzled. The Dowager Duchess of Burgundy lacked the time to keep up a correspondence with friends.

"She is eager to make a match between my Lady Mary of

Burgundy—greatest heiress in Europe—and her dear brother George. Edward sent his answer at once—'No.'"

As I learned later, Margaret had found a few arguments to support her hopes, but her real aim, I felt, was to spirit George out of England—out of reach of his enemies and satisfy his gnawing ambitions. She had last seen him in France, nearly two years ago, and, of course, did not realize how much he had deteriorated in these last months.

George was only a few months widower, but his grief for Isabel would never prevent him from snatching at the chance of wearing the coronet of Burgundy. Unfortunately, he learned that Edward had refused it for him, and was furious. As Mary of Burgundy was as quick as Edward to say "no," I hoped that we would hear no more of the business, but Elizabeth cherished a plan of her own, and took the first opportune moment to draw Edward into it.

On an evening late in February, Edward came into the solar. Elizabeth had expected him, and while she had waited, she had played the lute, as she sometimes did when her sister Katherine and I were her only attendants. The room in its glow of lights and the swimming reflections from the fire on the hearth, banished the cold and the dark. And Elizabeth making sweet music—bittersweet and sad—had a look of softness and gentle melancholy, in harmony with her music. It was hard to believe that she was ambitious or greedy or scheming.

Edward brought good news. The Burgundians had rallied, the French armies had halted their march into the Low Countries—the crisis had eased. "Thanks to your skill at statecraft." Elizabeth's voice and eyes flattered more than her words.

"Doubtless the Spider is merely being cautious," Edward said, and made himself comfortable in the chair near hers. Elizabeth took his hand in both of hers. "He's afraid of your power. But Mary of Burgundy needs a husband to defend her and be entirely loyal to you."

"And you see Anthony as her knight and champion." Edward disengaged his hand, but he wound a tendril of her hair around his finger, obviously taking a sensuous pleasure in the color and texture.

"Her true knight and champion, but always your true subject, ready to obey you and serve you," Elizabeth pleaded.

Although George was unsuitable—and Edward would never dare to trust him—at least he was of royal blood. But Anthony Woodville—for a Woodville to aspire to Mary of Burgundy! Elizabeth was unaware of any presumption in her ambition for her brother. She was Queen of England; let Anthony be Duke of Burgundy.

"He is part Burgundian," she reminded Edward. "He has the princely blood of Luxembourg in his veins."

I understood Elizabeth's point of view, but not Edward's indulgent attitude, and when he yielded to her soft insistence, I was dazed.

The next evening he was in the presence chamber, and with the music and talk making it possible to speak without being overheard he said, "You stared at me like an owl when I agreed to the queen's wishes." He smiled. "It's easy for me to consent to this great marriage for her brother, but nothing will come of it. Lady Mary of Burgundy has no intention of accepting him. Or any Englishman. She and her councilors are seeking a prince who has his domains in Europe and who is capable of leading armies."

As Edward had predicted, Lady Mary rejected Anthony Woodville with scarcely veiled scorn. George should have been appeased, but obviously was not. On one of the rare occasions when he appeared at Westminster Palace, he was in a lowering mood. He had been drinking and reeked of wine. The Woodvilles goaded him with their formalities and their sleek courtesies; he gave them short answers or none and made contemptuous remarks about them in their hearing.

We could all guess the immediate cause of his behavior. He was seething with a sense of grievance—Edward had immediately refused to allow his own brother, a royal prince, to offer for Mary of Burgundy, but had lent his support to Anthony

Woodville—in George's view a deadly insult. How had he found out? I suspected one of the Woodvilles, perhaps Dorset, had put George on the scent, because Edward had tried to keep the matter quiet. He distrusted George too much ever to help him to gain more power.

At table, George took his rightful place, but wherever he looked he saw Woodvilles, or the men and women who were bound to Elizabeth's family by marriage. Course after course was served, and George waved away both food and wine. Elizabeth watched him slyly, and Dorset's face sharpened with malice. Buckingham turned to me and whispered that George must be afraid of poison. As George doubtless knew, the poison had not been added to the meat and drink, but it would lurk in Elizabeth's sighs and complaints as soon as she saw Edward in private.

"The venom will be well disguised in the honey," I found myself whispering before I could check my words. Fortunately, Buckingham failed to catch my meaning, and merely looked puzzled.

George took his departure as abruptly as he had come. I left the hall by another door and caught up with him before he started down the steps. His gentlemen who were following him halted, and waited where they were. He was walking slowly, his head bent, and when I spoke he wheeled around. "Why"—I began, hesitated, then rushed on—"why must you play into their hands?"

His expression changed, and in the wavering light, he regained his good looks. His face was its natural color, his frown had gone and he was entirely sober. He listened intently, one ungloved hand adjusting the clasps of his cloak, and the emerald ring flickered and flashed. "Thank you for your concern," he said.

"Take care, please. Margaret would tell you to take care."

"My poor sister has troubles of her own. I will try not to add to them. Goodbye, Cicely." He then kissed my hand and went on.

Dorset's estates in the Midlands needed my attention, giving me good excuse to absent myself from the court for a time, and by mid-March, I was at Astley Castle, with my two little sons and my household, but without Dorset. He was willing to be buried there after he was dead, he told me, but unwilling to bury himself there while he lived.

My sons grew and thrived at Astley, and it was well for them to be known here from their childhood. I had a number of tasks and duties to occupy me, and time passed quickly enough. George was again at Warwick Castle, I knew, and when I found out what happened there, I thought he must have gone mad.

In the middle of the night, he had sent eighty or so armed men to break into the house and seize one of Isabel's former waiting women, Ankarette Twynyehoe. In the morning she was dragged before the Justices of the Peace and accused of having given Isabel "a venomous drink of ale mixed with poison." Isabel had died in childbed, and her waiting woman was entirely innocent. Isabel's child had lingered only a few weeks, and a serving man was likewise arrested and charged with poisoning the baby.

George's men threatened justices and jurors with loss of their goods and lives unless they brought in a verdict of guilty. Cowed, they dared not disobey. Ankarette and the serving man were hanged without delay. By the time the news reached Astley, they were dead. Otherwise I would have set out for Warwick and pleaded with George—and made enough stir in the courtroom to disrupt the trial.

"If only I had known in time," I said to Dame Joan.

"If only the king had known in time," she answered.

"And when he does—" We looked at each other, picturing Edward's wrath when he learned that George had flouted the royal authority by taking the law into his own hands.

"He must have been drunk, in a drunken frenzy," I said to Dame Joan, "but that gives him no excuse for this senseless cruelty."

"No, and perhaps the influence of the wine only nerved him to show that in Warwick, he was king and ruled supreme, defying the king in London."

The morning brought further news; George had accused a third person as abetting his two victims in poisoning Isabel and her child, but this man—a knight of the shire—had been in his manor house, at a little distance from Warwick. Friends had warned him in time for him to escape. He reached Kenilworth, where the constable gave him protection in the king's name. And Edward would undoubtedly grant him a formal pardon—wiping out the indictment. But what would happen next?

For a time, nothing happened. In May, I left Astley, and went into the west country to spend the greater part of the summer on my own estates. At Shute, I could go out on the walls and look at the sea, but even in Devon, my neighbors were uneasily discussing the trouble between the king and his brother, and the steward at Shute said that if my Lord Duke of Clarence could hang people at will, then the old lawless times might come again.

"There's no danger of that," I told him. "The king's government is too strong."

He seemed reassured, but like the rest of us, was puzzled by George's violence. "I always heard of him as a most pleasant prince. Perhaps some enemy mixed a noxious potion in his wine to induce a fit of madness." And he added, "Such things can be done by means of witchcraft."

Some of my servants went to a fair in Exeter, and came back with a vague story of an Oxford clerk arrested for making magical images to commit murder. This much was true, as I learned when a letter came from Dorset, giving me the facts. An Oxford clerk had been arrested on the charges, and had been "brought to confess" that they were true, and he had named a certain Thomas Burdett, who was a trusted member of George's household. So he was the one who was important! And the charge against him was even more damning. He had worked and calculated by art, magic, necromancy, and astrology the death and destruction of the king and the prince. Burdett had not confessed, but that was not necessary, as his papers had been found, and magical instruments for making images, giving complete proof of his guilt. And he had boasted of his finding; he and the other clerk had openly announced to a number of people that Edward and his eldest son would soon be dead.

If Dorset's version was true, the two men were certain to be condemned. They were given a fair trial, or so it appeared as the witnesses against them were honest people, and found guilty. Both were hanged, Burdett declaring his innocence to the last. Nothing in the trial implicated George, but after the hangings, he made for Westminster, accompanied by a Dr. John Goddard, and stormed into the Council Chamber. Edward had gone to Windsor, but the Council was in session. George forced Dr. Goddard to read Burdett's statement of his innocence, to the councilors.

I could admire him for trying to defend a gentleman of his household, even against the evidence, if George had gone directly to Edward. Instead he had appealed to the councilors urging them to turn against the verdict of judge and jurors, which meant against the king's justice. Worse, he had dared drag Dr. Goddard with him—the preacher who, in the year 1470, had proclaimed Henry the Sixth's right to the throne, during the Earl of Warwick's rebellion. This seemed a gesture of contempt directed at Edward the Fourth. No wonder Goddard had to be forced to read, then he must have scuttled away like a hare.

On that same day, there was an uprising in the vicinity of Cambridge, but it was a spark without fuel to sustain it, and had flickered out long before we had news of it. George had ordered his retainers to arm themselves, and perhaps they obeyed, but if he expected to amass an army, he failed. Not even his own men would follow him now, and yet he chose this precarious moment in his life to launch his attack against Edward's marriage and claim again that it was brought about by witchcraft.

George had begun by saying it in private, to his sister Margaret, to Richard, and to me, and we had begged him to hold his tongue. Later, when it seemed as if rebellion had succeeded, and the crown was within his reach, he had publicly proclaimed it, but that time was over and done with. "And yet he's repeating what he dared to say then," I said to Dame Joan.

"If I heard him, or anyone, question the king's marriage, I would clap my hands over my ears and run," she answered. "Take to my heels as fast as I could go."

These days, it was dangerous to openly cast doubts on the marriage but many of the Lords and the Commons believed that it was the work of "magical practices, sorceries and incantations." From what I heard, they seemed to feel a troubling sense of something mysterious, as if the secret wedding veiled a deeper secret, still unrevealed.

Before the end of summer Edward summoned George to appear before him at Eastminster. "He came bold and defiant," Dorset wrote. The Lord Mayor of London, and the aldermen were present and heard Edward charge his brother with behavior "derogatory to the laws of the realm, and most dangerous to judge and jurors," and he sent George to the Tower.

❧ Twenty-eight

"You may have wondered why I saw fit to put George in the Tower," Edward said to me. It was the first time that he had mentioned George to me since my return, and the first time that he had made the opportunity to speak to me in private. I was in the queen's solar, waiting for her, and Edward had come in unexpectedly. We were not alone, three of Elizabeth's women were also in the room, but at a distance where they could see but not hear.

"I am sorry to tell you that if George could have married Mary of Burgundy—or rather her duchy—he intended to use his position to arm the Lancastrian exiles and lead them to invade this country, with a band of mercenaries at their back to stir up rebellion."

266

Edward's face was in the shadow, but his eyes were brilliant, and watchful. He spoke quietly, as if he were stating the truth.

"But Margaret would never—"

"Of course Margaret had nothing to do with his schemes," Edward said.

"I am puzzled to know how any of this came to light," I said, since the scheme had never been hatched.

"The French king employs shrewd men as spies; they gave warning, and offered proof. George was in touch with several willing conspirators in the Low Countries."

"The Spider is renowned for making trouble and for spinning a web of lies. Can you believe his word this time—or any time?" I asked.

"Can I believe George's word this time or any time?"

As there was only one answer, I was silent.

Gentle rustling made me look up. Elizabeth had come from her bedchamber, and as Edward's back was turned and I was engrossed in what he was saying, neither of us were aware of her presence until she was quite close to us. Although Edward must have already given her a full account of the Spider's report, she had overheard something that pleased her, to judge from the sly satisfaction on her face, before her expression changed.

The Holy Days of Christmas were at hand, to be celebrated at Westminster Palace and in London with all of the old customs and with new lavishness in the way of feastings and revels. Then there was a royal marriage to take place on the day after Twelfth-night. The little Duke of York, aged four, was to marry Lady Anne Mowbrey, aged six, heiress of the Norfolk estates. The palace was astir with the preparations for the wedding, and the tournament to follow. The great lords with their retinues gathered in London, and a fever of excitement spread through the city.

The Duchess of York came to London, to Baynard's Castle, to try to reconcile her two sons; I saw her often, and pitied her with all my heart. "Edward has become hard and unrelenting," she told me, blaming Elizabeth and her family for their "malign work," accusing them of spreading slanders against George to destroy him, which was likely true, although they could have left him to destroy himself.

I had come direct from the Duchess of York to my attendance on Elizabeth, and watched her with critical eyes while she gloated over the quality of ermine skins and glittering fabrics. She slipped a diamond ring on her finger and held up her hand to catch the light in the stone. She was not as carefree as she pretended. I noticed that it cost her an effort to keep on discussing jewels and apparel, and after the merchant had left, she never glanced at the diamond or the other rings that she had bought. She dismissed her women and lapsed into one of her brooding silences. When she heard Edward, she started up, clenched her hands together, and seemed to nerve herself before she turned to meet him.

He lingered a few minutes, apparently enjoying the fire, and spoke of his little son's wedding, and said that Richard had set out from Middleham to be present. I was glad to hear it; Richard had very little love for his brother George, but would try to defend him against the Woodvilles. Elizabeth knew it too, and I saw the flicker of fear in her eyes. Edward's face no longer looked young but showed signs of the strain that he was undergoing.

Elizabeth watched him, hesitated, then went to him and flung herself in his arms—and his arms held her close. Hiding her face from him, she burst into tears.

"What ails you?" he demanded, doing his best to soothe and comfort her; as she did not answer, he asked me what troubled her, but I had no answer to give him. At last she raised her head and whispered, "I am afraid—for our sons."

"Why? Why?" he insisted, "There's no reason—"

She was playing her part well, I thought, for even in the firelight she was pale and the tears glittered on her lashes and rolled down her cheeks. Edward wiped them away.

"Tell me."

"The prediction," she sighed. "The astrologer foresees grave danger for them—from someone whose name begins with G."

She had done her work well! But could she command her tears at will? She was artful enough. Perhaps she could contrive to turn white, and yet her fear was real. She had never forgotten Marguerite of Anjou's prophecies, and now this sinister prediction. Who had made it? I blamed Friar Bungay. If he had seen some future danger in the pattern of the stars, he should have held his tongue. What was more disquieting, for the first time in his life, Edward was afraid. He had always disregarded soothsayers, and would hardly believe in this cloudy warning. He must have some more definite base for his fears.

Dorset too was nerve-strung these days. I suspected him of being the one who sent spies to gather every rag-tag bit of fact or surmise that would discredit George.

"Why?" I asked Dorset. "And why does Edward suddenly see George as a menace to the children?"

Dorset was startled, and at first, evasive, then told me what he knew. There was a secret, he thought, and it involved Edward's marriage. Not the stale accusation that Elizabeth Woodville had used witchcraft. George had unearthed something else.

Since Lady Jacquetta's death, Friar Bungay came less to the palace. I had not seen him for a great while, but he was still in London, and I sent a messenger asking him to come to Dorset House. I chose my most trusted servant to take my message, as I was anxious to avoid talk in my household. When the Friar agreed to come at a certain hour, I admitted to Dame Joan that I felt a twinge of unease.

"You are in no danger of being accused of magical practices," she assured me. "You have no enemies."

"I would not dare make an enemy of him," I answered.

The Friar arrived after dusk, and was escorted by the private stairs to my private solar. Some of my people had doubtless seen him, but would hardly have recognized him as the renowned sorcerer. Even to me he seemed only an elderly scholar or clerk, and once face to face with him I forgot most of my fear. He seemed very old and when I asked after his health he admitted that he lacked strength. He consented to sit down by the fire, admired the beauty of the room, and accepted some wine offered by Dame Joan, who then retreated to a bench in the shadows and busied herself with her rosary. I thought she was probably much busier listening to what was said.

"I am glad that I have this opportunity of seeing you, madam, as I am leaving London tomorrow," the Friar said.

"And when do you intend to return?" I asked.

"I think—never," he answered.

"Perhaps you will go back to your turret rooms at Grafton."

"My Lord Anthony Woodville kindly offers me hospitality there, but Grafton is not for me—not any more. My Lord Anthony has greatly embellished it recently, and from time to time stays at the castle, but not for long."

"Doubtless my Lord Anthony feels that a shadow has fallen on Grafton."

"He would do well if he never set foot in those fair gardens or in that splendid house."

Perhaps the old man was thinking of Anthony's melancholy temperament. The shadow of the dark forest, the darker shadow of violent death, the stories of witchcraft practiced at Grafton would sink his spirits. I was sorry that I had ever mentioned the place.

"The queen will be sorry if you go far," I said.

"Madam, I knew Elizabeth Woodville from her childhood, and she honored me with her friendship, and so did her mother, but now how can I be of any use to the Queen of England?"

"With wise advice," I said. "She—she's afraid."

"I know," the old man watched me steadily. "Too frightened to listen to any advice, wise or not."

"She has taken a soothsayer's prediction to heart—that her children, particularly her sons, are in danger from a person whose name begins with a G."

"I doubt if any soothsayer in England made such a prediction," the Friar said. "It would be too dangerous."

"Then she was not quoting you?" I asked.

"I would never say such a thing to her or to anyone. I think that she invented it—out of her own fears."

"Perhaps," I agreed, and the more I thought of it the more likely it seemed. "But I took it for granted that she had consulted you."

"She did, and I begged her not to meddle with the affair of the Duke of Clarence. She hinted at some secret and might have told me what it was, but I refused to hear a word on the subject. As I pointed out to her, if it is important, keep it quiet. Tell no one."

"You gave her what I think is wise advice," I said.

"She's in no mood to listen to temperate counsel." The old man rose to take his leave. "I will send you word where I can be found, madam, if in any small way I could possibly be of use to you. From what I can forsee of the future, you will find great happiness, and will know how to keep it. As to the queen—she should know that the Duke of Clarence is not the only person in the world whose name begins with a G."

The day of the royal wedding was cold, with snow falling, but the Chapel of St. Stephen had a magic brilliance; the walls were hung with cloth of gold, and blue velvet strewn with golden suns, glittering in the light of more than eighty wax candles.

This marriage between young children could not be consummated for many a year, and in a few days, she would return to her family, and the groom would stay on with his. But he was bound to this small bedizened puppet, and I was sorry for them both as they knelt under the canopy, their heads bowed. At four years our Duke of York was anything but a puppet. He had Edward's happy nature, and a will of his own. Now and then he raised his head and looked around with great curiosity.

A sturdy, healthy boy, active in body and mind, and like all of Edward's children, beautiful. He was not a Woodville, he had the look of a Plantagenet, but as I watched him I saw a startling likeness to George, as he had been when I had first met him. He had been older then this child was now, but the likeness was unmistakable, and must strike others who had known George in his early years.

A banquet followed the Nuptial Mass, and dancing lasted late. I made excuse to leave, and the next day, I absented myself from the tournament. So did others, including Richard of Gloucester. I happened to meet him at Baynard's Castle, where I went to pay my duty to the Duchess of York, and bid her goodbye, as she was setting out for Fotheringhay. Richard, too, was taking the road north, where he was needed to protect the border from Scottish raids—better work than applauding Anthony Woodville gathering easily won laurels at the tournament.

Parliament would meet tomorrow to decide George's fate.

"Only the king dared accuse the king's own brother of high treason," Buckingham whispered, giving me an account of what had taken place. Only Edward had spoken against his brother. The charges were true. George had been a traitor, had won forgiveness, only to conspire and betray again. But it seemed to me that Edward in accusing George of recent plots to stir up yet another rebellion had veiled a more dangerous treason that must not be revealed.

No one answered the king except his brother, and George did answer. He stood up, declared himself not guilty, offered to do battle if his words were not enough. With his own right arm he would fight it out with Edward. In his defiance he sounded like a true Plantagenet. But he was condemned and Edward chose Buckingham to pronounce sentence. It was the sentence of death.

Although reason told me that I could do nothing, I ran out of the antechamber and through the solar—now deserted—then out of the little door behind the tapestry. Edward was too preoccupied to notice me until I spoke.

"Why are you here?" he cried.

"To beg you—" It was useless to plead, but I stumbled on: "Beg you to give me some hope that the sentence will not be carried out."

"Think of all the lives his rebellions and treasons have cost—"

Suddenly, the door behind me flew open. I was leaning against it, and lost my balance—would have fallen if two hands had not grasped me by the shoulders. Small hands, but they were strong, with sharp nails, like the claws of a wild animal. "Out of my way, girl," and Elizabeth thrust me aside. She flung herself at Edward, falling on her knees and covering his hands with kisses, then she urged him to listen to her—not to me. "My son, our son—will never have the throne unless that traitor dies. He's been condemned. Order his execution now." Her rush of words, spoken in a hoarse voice, halted as she paused to regain breath.

Edward looked at her with a kind of wonder as if she had become a stranger to him. "I never expected you to demand any man's execution." He detached his hands from her clinging fingers, and she grasped at his sleeve.

"How can you hesitate?"

"He is my brother."

"I had a brother, and a father. Do you think that I could ever forget or forgive how he dealt with them? He has their blood on his hands—" Her face had become sharp, distorted. "Now George will know what it is to be dragged to the scaffold and feel the sharp edge of the axe!"

Edward drew away from her. "I never knew that you hated him so much, or nursed such a vindictive spirit. I will do what I must—but not for your father, or your brother, not for you, or even for my children—but to have peace in the country." He turned and went down the steps.

A cold sunless day followed by a starless night, and during the day or more likely in the black night of February the eighteenth, 1478, George was killed. The date seems certain because on the nineteenth his body was carried out of the Tower, with all honors, to be buried beside Isabel under the high altar of Tewkesbury Cathedral. The funeral was as magnificent as if he had died in his bed, and had not been put to death in the Tower, by order of his brother.

Everywhere in London, and doubtless everywhere in England,

people asked how had George, Duke of Clarence, died. Only a very few persons knew, and they held their tongues, and would never divulge the secret. The facts were buried in the Tower.

"Some say that he was drowned in a butt of malmsley," Dame Joan told me. It was possible, even probable. Malmsley was his favorite wine. He was well supplied with it, and while he was drunk, it would have been easy to push him into the wine cask, and hold him under until he drowned, but I never learned the truth. Neither did Edward's closest friends and neither did the Woodvilles. Elizabeth might have kept silent, but Dorset would have told me, just as he told me that other "secret matter"— why George had been a danger, not only in Elizabeth's view, but in Edward's.

I came back to Dorset House late one night to find Dorset waiting for me in my apartments, perhaps because the snow was falling. As he knew, I had not been in attendance on the queen, and he asked me what had kept me, and I explained that our little Duke of York was ailing, and that I had stayed by his bed until his fever had lessened and he had fallen asleep.

"You've succeeded in winning his affection," Dorset said.

"He's succeeded in winning mine," I answered. "But I love all of Edward's children."

"Then you should be glad that George of Clarence is where he is."

"I can never be glad because of the way it was done. Why wasn't he allowed to drink himself into his grave? It would not have taken him long!"

"Too long. Wine loosened his tongue. He would have talked. And that could not be allowed."

"Who would listen to his drunken fantasies!"

"Certain people in this country and elsewhere would have listened very eagerly to what he had ferreted out. You will understand why if you so much as hint at this you would be guilty of high treason.

"A month or more ago the Bishop of Wells was placed under

house arrest, charged with making statements detrimental to the interests of the realm."

"I heard something of it, but he was soon released—" I said.

"Warned to keep his mouth shut. And he will as long as Edward lives."

"What does the Bishop have to do with your story?" I asked.

Dorset left his chair and locked the doors before coming back to sit close by me and unburden himself of the secret that George had threatened to disclose.

When Edward had been very young, sixteen, or seventeen, he had fallen in love with Lady Eleanor Butler, a high-born widow a few years older than he. She belonged to a Lancastrian family, and Edward of York had gone through a solemn ceremony of betrothal to her, pledging himself to her with a ring, and in the presence of a priest. Because the times had become stormy, he had kept the trothplight a secret, and had induced her to keep it secret. At the time, he doubtless had intended to marry her. As she was by birth a Talbot, daughter of the Earl of Shrewsbury, it would not have been unsuitable for Edward, who was the heir of York, but then had no prospect of being King of England.

However, war had come, separating him from her; Edward's love faded, and she was forgotten, before he had ever encountered Elizabeth Woodville. After she had been deserted, Lady Eleanor retired to a convent and had died there. Before her death, she had told her story to the Bishop of Wells, and had given him proof that she had been solemnly and officially betrothed to Edward. Trothplight was not marriage, but it was a bar to marriage with anyone else unless it had been formally dissolved by the Church. Edward had never admitted that he was bound to Lady Eleanor, and unfortunately had never troubled to go through with the necessary procedure of freeing himself from his tie to her. So in the eyes of the Church he had still been committed to one woman when he had married another. Lady Eleanor had not died until 1466, and she had not entered the convent until after Edward's secret wedding to Elizabeth. If this story of the trothplight became known,

275

questions could be asked. Is the king's marriage valid? Do his sons have the right to succeed to the throne?

From the first, George had been trying to find some flaw in Edward's marriage, and had found it, and had threatened to disclose it, and doubtless sooner or later would have disclosed it publicly. A betrothal before witnesses was legally binding; this was the reason for Elizabeth's terror and why even Edward had been afraid. He knew that the country had never been reconciled to his marriage, and that Elizabeth and her family had made a host of enemies. The Bishop was a placid man, and had doubtless been warned to keep silence. Edward would certainly have exacted an oath of silence from him, which the Bishop would take care to obey, but no one had ever been able to curb George.

"Now you can understand why George's treasons and his constant plottings were so dangerous," Dorset finished.

The court was officially in mourning for the death of George, Duke of Clarence—a travesty, but at least we were spared festivities. However, Edward was receiving a foreign envoy, and Elizabeth was waiting for Edward to escort her to the presence chamber.

As always, she had taken the greatest care of her appearance; she wore black velvet, with a silvery bloom along its flowing folds, and a trailing mantle lined with ermine. In the weeks since George's death, Elizabeth had treated me with great reserve, but as soon as she had sent her women from the room, she talked to me without constraint, and spoke of Will Hastings, who had recently returned to England. As Calais was no longer endangered, he expected to stay in this country and act as Lord Chamberlain.

"There are rumors that my Lord Hastings is on fire for a woman here in the city," Elizabeth said.

"And Dorset also has his eye on her." I never spoke of his amours, but as he and Will Hastings were enemies, their rivalry over a woman would only sharpen their antagonism.

"What do you know of her?" Elizabeth asked with a sudden intensity.

"Why, nothing, madam. Only that she exists. And what rumor

276

says. It seems that Hastings and Dorset exchanged some heated words because of her."

"Has my lord seen her?" Elizabeth asked, suspecting Edward.

"Oh, no—" I began, then added, "at least I very much doubt it." But I was not certain. However, I thought that Elizabeth was too quick to take alarm. In the firelight, her eyes glittered, but there were shadows around them—marks of sleeplessness and tears; her women had reddened her mouth, but her face had become thin.

In public, Edward's attitude to her was unchanged, but I was with her constantly, and knew that since she had revealed her vengeful spirit to him, he had avoided sharing her bed. It was not the first time that he had neglected her for other women. What was more ominous, he no longer came for private conversations with her, or discussed important matters with her.

Elizabeth moved her hand, and her marriage ring slipped from her finger and fell on the floor, to shine and wink in the fire's glow. She stared at it and whispered, "An ill omen."

"It's become too big for your finger." I picked it up and handed it to her. She spoke in the same low whisper, "He no longer loves me."

❧ *Twenty-nine*

In the autumn of 1482 the towers of Windsor gleamed against a pale azure sky, in the gardens the roses bloomed and the grass was green, but the woods were burnished with russet and tawny hues. The leaves had already begun to fall, and lose their brightness on the ground. To my ears, the hunting horns blowing in Windsor Chase had melancholy echoes.

Edward no longer followed the hounds with his former zest but today he had invited the Lord Mayor of London and the aldermen to hunt, and to "be merry with him." At the end of the day he would offer them good cheer in the castle, and send presents of venison and other game to his friends in the city.

"Our king has brought us justice, and prosperity," a great London merchant said to me, "but the people are apt to value a little courtesy more than a large benefit. Too many princes who have had a long sovereignty become arrogant, and I marvel at our king, he is more than ever benign and familiar with all of his people."

I had spent the greater part of the summer on my estates with my children; I now had two daughters as well as two sons. The court seemed more brilliant than ever, but more corrupt. Or perhaps the months spent at a distance had sharpened my perception. I had paid a visit to the Duchess of York at Fotheringhay before my return to Windsor, and doubtless her unhappiness had darkened my mood.

The day was fading, although the sunlight still lingered on Windsor Palace as I went in. At the head of the stairs, I saw a woman standing at a window, looking out of the open casement, watching for the huntsmen to come in from the chase, watching for Edward. She paid no attention to the people passing to and fro but they noticed her. Some years ago, Hastings and Dorset had contended for her favor. Hastings had taken care not to let Edward see her, but Edward had discovered her. He had desired her, and she had yielded at once.

Her husband was a goldsmith, a man of substance, but she had been married to him when she had been too young, and had never loved him. Doubtless her wanton behavior made him suffer, but he had made no effort to keep her once the king had bedded with her. Not that she would have ever thought of going back to him.

"How did Edward find her so quickly?" I had asked Dorset.

"I told him she was Will Shore's wife," he had admitted.

"If you had held your tongue, his curiosity would have soon died away."

"He would have found her sooner or later," Dorset had argued. "By providing him with diversion, I earned more favor with him." Dorset had laughed a little. "Then too Mistress Jane Shore was showing a tendency to prefer Hastings to me. He won't dispute possession with Edward!"

At the time, Jane had merely been one more mistress to satisfy his sensual appetite. "Now I have three concubines," he had told his intimates, adding her to the "wiliest harlot in the realm," and the other, "the holiest harlot." He described Jane as the "merriest" of the three.

He had become tired of the others, and Elizabeth waited for him to tire of the new mistress. She waited in vain. Because Edward demanded it, Elizabeth forced herself to tolerate Jane Shore's presence at court, wherever the court happened to be. Instead of fading, Edward's passion for her had deepened. His feeling for her was more lasting than desire. He seemed to need her with him. She had her lodgings in the palace, and would not only appear, but would have her place at the high table. All the world knew that Jane Shore was the king's mistress, and no one felt any ill will for her, except Elizabeth.

It was dusk when Edward brought the Londoners into his presence chamber, where the queen and the court were gathered. Elizabeth received all of the respect and homage due the queen, then, the courtiers moved away to crowd around Jane Shore. "There was nothing you would wish changed in her except to wish her somewhat taller," one of her admirers had said of her. She was plump, but not too much so. Her breasts were round and high, as her low-cut bodice revealed. Her face was likewise round and full. I had seen her hair hanging loose; it was dark yellow, almost brown in the shade, but in the sun it seemed powdered with gold dust.

There was a harmony in her features, coloring, and proportions, but men were not only drawn to her because of her beauty, but because of her pleasant behavior. I saw her laughing and thought how happy she seemed. "Mistress Shore can read and write very well," an elderly alderman said to me, "and has a proper wit. You see her merry in company, quick and ready to answer, neither mute nor full of babble."

Hastings and Dorset had joined the group around Jane, and it was not long before Edward found his way to her. When the leopard comes, the lesser animals go slinking to covert.

Elizabeth showed an admirable dignity, I thought, and I doubt if she ever made any complaint to a member of her own family. Her brother Anthony was in Ludlow, supervising the education of England's heir, her sisters had their own troubles and Dorset could offer no help. He would only have advised her to be content, as Jane Shore was free from ambition and harmless to the Woodvilles. Elizabeth had seldom mentioned her, but she did that night, when I was in attendance on her.

"She's young," Elizabeth sighed. "And has a ripe beauty, overripe for her years, and in a few years it will decay."

Doubtless Elizabeth was right, and to my mind there was no comparison between the two women. Elizabeth was taller, her bones more finely put together, her face was more expressive. A face unlike all others. No one could equal her graceful bearing, or her elegance or her luring voice. No woman on earth would ever again have her power to ensnare Edward's imagination and even to invade his soul.

Jane Shore had a cheerful countenance, reflecting her nature. There was nothing mysterious about her, nothing subtle, and doubtless her very lack of artfulness endeared her to Edward. He would never permit a mistress to influence his policies, but Jane was well known to have a kind heart, and did her best to soften his. Many a time she had induced him to show clemency, and the people, who seldom had a good word for a royal mistress, had affection for her. She was neither arrogant nor mercenary; she had no horde of greedy kindred, and, above all, she was not an enchantress endowed with a knowledge of dark magic.

"She is carefree," Elizabeth said. "She's deserted her husband without a qualm—but I cannot throw off my cares or my sorrows and be merry."

Edward and Elizabeth had lost their second daughter over a year ago. Mary had been a beautiful girl, some thought her even lovelier than her sisters, and her sudden death brought sorrow, a lasting sorrow to her family. In their shared grief, Elizabeth and Edward had been drawn together for a time, but he had not parted from his mistress, and his former love of his wife had not reawakened.

Elizabeth was well aware of what was lacking, although he did his best to spare her feelings, and he had not entirely deserted her bed. Two years ago, another daughter had been born to Elizabeth's disappointment for she had hoped for a third son.

Since then, there had been no more children, and I doubted if there would be another prince or princess. At Windsor, Elizabeth's bed was of vast size and length, with heavily embroidered hangings lined in cloth of silver but Edward would not share it with her.

"The nights are endless when I lie alone," she said. "He blames me for George's death."

"He blames himself," I answered. As he must. But even if George had never been a rebel and a traitor, even if he had never harmed a Woodville, Elizabeth would have been his enemy. He had been too near the throne. And at last, Elizabeth's fears and her overwrought nerves had betrayed her to Edward.

"We could have been happy together to the end of our days," she sighed.

I was sorry for her, she seemed so lonely and forlorn—all the more to be pitied because she knew in her heart that she herself had destroyed Edward's love.

In London, many fine houses had been built in recent years.

Dorset had moved his establishment to one of the houses on the Strand. The gatehouse opened into a forecourt, and the house was built around an inner court. The great hall looked out on a terrace, with flights of steps leading to a fair garden, with plots of flower beds, expanses of turf, intersected by paths winding between clipped hedges. Another flight of steps led to the water gate and the river. Dorset's apartments and mine were above the great hall, and from my windows I saw fleets of ships and at times fleets of swans moving by.

In December, John Dynham came from Calais to discuss important matters with Edward, Hastings, and the Royal Council. I had seen him and talked to him at Westminster Palace, but he chose a day when I was not in attendance on the queen, and paid me a visit. I was happy to welcome him in my own house, where with only Dame Joan present, we could carry on a conversation at length and at our ease. London was rejoicing because we had won a great victory over the Scots, thanks to Richard's military skill. He had captured Berwick, which put an end to any troubles on our northern borders. Little Richard had proved himself a great commander.

"The problem now is what will Edward do to stop the Spider of France from devouring more and more Burgundian territory," John Dynham said.

For a time, the Spider had seemed willing to make treaties and alliances, but the young heiress of Burgundy had met her death when her horse had fallen with her. She had been pregnant, and in her state, the accident had been fatal. She had left two small children, and her widowed husband was doing what he could to defend their inheritance, but the Spider was making claims to towns and counties, and backing up his claims by outright seizure. As I knew, Margaret of York had been urging Edward to send help, and to declare war on France, but so far he had sent only a few soldiers.

"Edward has changed," John Dynham said. "He's still vigilant in whatever concerns the government, but he's unwilling to make decisions—at least in his policy toward France. We all know why—the money and the marriage between Lady Bess and the Dauphin."

The marriage was more important than the money from the Spider, and yet Edward who had now amassed a fortune was most unwilling to give up the pension paid by the French. Poverty had been the ruin of other kings, he said.

"The Spider of France is seriously ill—or so we hope," Dame Joan said. "If he were to die soon—"

"Then Edward's difficulty would be lessened," John Dynham finished. The Spider has had several seizures, but his brain is as busy as ever. He seems able to hold death at bay for some little time yet."

"Edward is still young, with sound health," I pointed out.

"He hasn't shaken off the fever he acquired in France—not entirely." John Dynham frowned a little.

"He eats and drinks too much," I admitted.

"Yes—but the great change is the loss of his joyful spirit. Or perhaps I am mistaken," John Dynham told us.

"No, you're right." I had noticed the same lack of Edward's former exuberance. "At times he seems unhappy."

"And not because of some political matter," Dame Joan put in. "We all know what preys on him."

John Dynham said, "Remorse."

"For George's death," I said. "And all those friends turned foe he was forced to destroy."

Throughout the Holy Days of Christmas, the city's dark streets were illumined every night with bonfires and torches. Yule candles flickered in windows, and even the poor had a yule log blazing on the hearth.

The older princesses took part in the Christmas festivities. On Twelfth-night they wore yellow velvet gowns, the sweeping skirts bordered with seed pearls, and they made all of the celebrated beauties of the court seem somewhat tarnished.

As was usual on Twelfth-night, the King Cake was brought in with flutes and singing. The Lord of Misrule was proclaimed, dancing began and the revels took on a feverish excitement. Near the end of the festivities I made my excuses to the queen and went to the chapel, open at any hour of the day or night. When I saw the doors ahead of me, I paused and turned aside to a window, leaning my elbows on the sill.

The window was one which had plain glass, and I could see out. It was a cold night, but still and clear, luminous because of the snow, and the brightness of the stars. I was too absorbed to notice the sound of the chapel doors swing or to hear Edward's footsteps in his velvet shoes until he spoke, and asked me if I had intended to go into the chapel. I said yes, but had allowed myself to be deflected. I had not expected to see him here. I had assumed that he would be in Jane's arms by now instead of praying in solitude.

He had put on a long dark mantle, which concealed cloth of gold and jewels. He need not wear armor now. Joining me at the window he looked out at roofs, snow-crowned towers and icy river, glinting under the stars.

"A proud city," he said, and I understood how well he loved his London.

"And a proud England," I answered.

"I hope to leave it strong and flourishing and at peace for my eldest son."

"At some date far in the future," I said. Edward was not yet forty-one, in the very prime of life for a man as vigorous as he was. Sometimes the tertian fever recurred, but he shook it off easily.

"Who knows?" he said. A torch was burning nearby, and its light showed his hair tawny bright, without a touch of gray and his face was unlined, with a healthy color.

"I hope that my sons will feel for each other as brothers should." He hesitated, then asked me if I had ever noticed a likeness between his son York and any other person. "I had seen it before," Edward went on, "but tonight it struck me with full force. In his looks and bearing, the boy put me in mind of George, when he was just that age."

"But only in his looks," I said. "In every other way, he is wholly unlike George."

Three years ago, Marguerite of Anjou had died in a remote château on her father's estates. Perhaps there were men and women in England who still felt loyal to her and her cause, but if so, I never encountered them. For the most part, former partisans had become reconciled to Edward's rule, and her former enemies no longer hated her. It seemed as if England had forgotten her existence, and news of her death had stirred very little interest, but in the winter of 1483, Edward and his Council was waiting—and hoping to hear of another death.

The Spider of France was ill beyond hope of recovery. He had lost the use of his legs and his right arm. "He's shut himself up in an inner room of one of his gloomy fortresses," Hastings told me. "He's surrounded himself with medals and relics. All his life he's been in terror of death, and he's now in real danger. He's making extravagant vows, calling on Our Lady and all the Saints to save him. At times he cries out because he sees the Devil waiting to carry him off."

However, the Spider was still keeping up his harassing warfare against Burgundy, and Edward still postponed sending any real help.

"Let him throw the Spider's money in his face, and make an alliance for Bess elsewhere," I said.

"The Spider can hardly last much longer, and by waiting Edward can hope to let the Devil—or Providence—solve the problem. We are trying to avoid a war with France."

Edward had built up our navy, and was always adding to its strength. In midwinter he went to Dover to see a new ship, and Jane Shore quietly followed him. "He's even become faithful to her," Hastings said, and to Elizabeth this was an added bitterness.

On Edward's return, she met him with smiles and kisses, and looked so beautiful that I wondered if he would not bed with her rather than with his mistress, but he chose Jane. When he and Elizabeth were sitting side by side, with their children around them they appeared to be as happy as any family could be, but night after night he chose Jane.

And so the winter wore away. The court would move to Windsor in April, and Edward made plans to hold a meeting of the Chapter of the Order of the Garter on the feast of St. George with great pomp, to be followed by festivities more lavish and magnificent than ever.

By the end of March, we had days when the sunlight brought

Londoners out of their houses, and beyond the city's walls to seek the open countryside. A sunny afternoon tempted Elizabeth to venture into the palace gardens. As she walked along the path ahead of me, the leafless twigs and branches above our heads wove a shadow net over her moving figure. She was wrapped in a dove-colored cloak heavily furred, pale and soft as smoke, and though the sunlight was hazy, she held her veil over her face to protect her complexion. How quickly and quietly she went, without any waste motion. At the end of the path was an open grass plot, and I knew why she had come to the garden. Edward was standing by the sundial, not looking in her direction; he was looking up, and listening to a bird's song—I heard the rippling joyous notes.

That evening we learned the disastrous news.

Burgundy had been forced to sign a peace treaty with France, and the Spider, without scruple, had broken his word to Edward by ignoring the betrothal contract. Solemn pledges had no meaning for the Spider, but it was a flagrant insult to cast our princess aside so abruptly. By the time Edward heard, another marriage had already been arranged for the Dauphin, with Mary of Burgundy's daughter, a child scarcely four years old. With her, the Spider demanded the rich provinces that he coveted as her dowry.

Edward summoned his Council, and in the palace all of us went warily and spoke in whispers, although as one of his servants said, "The king keeps his wrath for the people who have offended him." The English people shared Edward's anger. He had called Parliament together and intended to discuss a war with France.

"It's not an opportune time," Hastings said, "but Edward is mad with rage. Still he'll be slow to act I think. Edward is hot-blooded, but not hot-headed."

"Bess is dearer to him than anything in this world," I said, "and to see her rejected strikes at his heart."

"He thinks of her—and the crown she's lost," Hastings agreed, "and not of the yearly tribute of fifty thousand crowns of French gold."

"Bess seems quite content to give up the prospect of becoming queen of France," I told him. "She's sorry for the little girl who has been handed over to the French."

The child had been in the care of Margaret of York, who was most reluctant to part with her.

✿ *Thirty*

Easter Monday had a particular brightness in its weather and Edward must have found promise in the day. Instead of shutting himself up in his Council Chamber as he had done these last weeks, he had put aside affairs of state long enough to go out some distances from London, to follow the river and perhaps to fish. He had lost all interest in hunting and hawking. It had been a long time since the hounds had given tongue and the horns had echoed in Whittlebury Chase.

During the day the sunlight became fitful and intermittent, the clouds darkened, rain spattered down briefly, but brought a change in the wind, and the evening turned chill. Shortly after he returned to the palace, Edward collapsed in his chair. His servants carried him to his bed, and Hastings sent for the king's physicians. As Edward had gone to his own apartments to change his clothes, and only a few of his friends were with him, Elizabeth knew nothing of his sudden illness until a page brought her word. She went running to his bedchamber, tearful and distraught, but at the door Dorset met her and tried to persuade her to wait until Edward regained consciousness.

She would have insisted on going in if the physicians had not arrived just then, and she realized that she had no place at Edward's sickbed. They promised her a full report of his condition, and she consented to go to her own apartments to wait. It was not my turn to be in attendance on her; I was at my own house and had heard nothing until Dorset's messenger came to tell me what had happened, adding that the queen needed me.

Except for the occasional touch of fever, Edward was never ill. I was unable to picture him lying inert and helpless. When I got to the palace, the crisis seemed to be over. The king had rallied and was himself again, clear in his mind and speech. The physicians had been reassuring. The seizure had apparently left no ill effects.

Through the rest of the night, Elizabeth kept vigil, and when morning came the physicians seemed uncertain as to the nature and cause of Edward's illness. All of them agreed that he was in no danger, and would make a quick recovery. Elizabeth swept into his bedchamber, and undoubtedly he showed her courtesy in making her welcome. She soon came away and shut herself in her own apartments. I was often with her, but she told me very little. Edward had mentioned only practical matters, she said.

I asked her what she thought of Edward's state. The physicians were baffled, she thought, and were trying to hide their ignorance, but she relied on Edward's hardy constitution to restore him. I dared not venture any more questions, and she was silent.

After three days, Edward was still unable to leave his bed. Faces reflected anxiety, talk was muted, and for the first time since Edward's reign had begun, not a note of music sounded in his palace. Prayers were offered for the king's recovery and the throngs gathered in the streets prayed too. Edward's friends and a number of other people went in and out of his bedchamber, but he never asked Elizabeth to come, and according to Will Hastings, never mentioned her.

He wanted to see his children, and asked to see me. A few of his personal attendants were in his bedchamber, but no one else. As the day was warm the fire burned low on the hearth. Opposite the bed was an oriel window, and an open casement let in a flickering dance of sunlight. Edward's servants had propped him up on pillows, and in contrast to the whiteness of the linen his face looked strangely dark—not his usual healthy, sun-browned color. Even in so short a time his illness had changed him. He smiled at his children, and spoke to each one of them in turn, but it cost him an effort, and all of them were aware of it. The little girls were puzzled and uneasy, young as they were, and their brother, with his quick wits and quickly aroused feelings, was troubled and unhappy.

"Grow up to your brother's right hand," Edward said to the boy. "As my brother Richard has been mine." He then blessed the children, and the younger ones left the room, shepherded by their brother Diccon—Richard, Duke of York, who had the look of George.

I would have followed, but Edward held out his hand to me. "Stay a little, if you will." He gestured to the cushioned bench on the dais. "Sit here, Cicely, and we can talk together." His two older daughters were still in the room, and he asked Bess to play an air on the lute. "We have a dearth of music these days."

One of the attendants went to fetch a lute and brought it back. Bess and her sister moved away from the bed and settled themselves in the oriel, beneath the windows. Bess had considerable skill, and consulting her father's taste, chose a rollicking ballad, but the gaiety of the music was jarring to her overwrought feelings, and at first she made only discords.

Edward asked after my children, then spoke of Dorset, and his feud with Hastings. "I blame myself for allowing their ill will for each other to go unchecked."

"You have checked any display of it," I said. "They are under your rule, you have forbidden them to quarrel, and they will obey you."

"While I rule—"

What did he mean? From his sickbed he governed the country, and he would soon be well, so the physicians said, and yet my heart sank.

"I must think of what will happen when I am gone. My sons are still small." He spoke quietly, with a calm certainty. "Gone" echoed and re-echoed, with the sound of a knell. I bit down on my lip to stifle my tears, and turned aside until I could school my face, but failed to hide any feelings.

Edward put his hand over mine. "I am leaving too many tasks unfinished, and I did many things that I regret. The crown has cost too much."

"Who else was as well fitted to wear it?" I asked.

"If I had it to do over, I would never win the courtesy of men's knees with the loss of so many lives." He sighed, "And now I fear God's justice."

"His mercy endures," I reminded him.

"I put my trust in it," Edward said. He was silent for a little; as he listened to the lute playing he was looking toward the open casement and the limited view beyond. From his bed he could see a bit of sky, the curled edge of a glistening cloud and a green branch, spangled with light.

"The people will soon be bringing in the May," Edward said, and I wondered if his thoughts turned to a momentous May-day morn at Grafton Castle, but he spoke of riding through the countryside, and what a pleasant sight it was to see the towns and villages decked with woodland greenery and wildflowers. Listening to him, I realized that of all his loves, his greatest love was England.

He turned to me, and leaning over, kissed me on the mouth, then reminded me of that long-ago time when we had first met, at Ludlow. "You were only a child when you entered into a pact with me. Other friends and some of those nearest and dearest to me became enemies, but you kept your word. Remember that I have set great store on your long enduring affection, 'Through fortune and misfortune, time and change—'"

And I answered, "Always and forever."

The physicians admitted that the king was weakening. We had no hope. Crowds filled the churches, massed in the streets and pressed close to the palace gates in deepening anxiety and gloom. Edward sent for the leaders of the two discordant factions that divided the court. Anthony Woodville was at Ludlow, and Dorset represented the queen's family, and Will Hastings personified their enemies. And how many enemies they had made! Woodvilles ranged themselves on one side of the king's bed. Hastings, and his friends—the great lords of the ancient nobility— were on the other side.

Edward had not asked Elizabeth to be present, but he could not exclude the ghosts—Warwick, Montagu, George—cousins and brother, once loved. Doubtless Edward thought of them when he spoke to the men who had assembled around him.

"God forbid that you should turn against each other," he said, "and yet it can happen. And nowhere can you find such deadly hate as among those who by nature and law should agree together. Immoderate ambitions have led to years of warfare, and you know what losses and sorrows war brought. Now, thank God, that time is past, and all is quiet, but my sons are young, and if you carry on your feuds in a child's reign, many a good man will die."

Edward's strength of will lent him strength. "And so in this last time that I will ever have with you, I tell you it is not enough for you to love my children unless you love one another. These are the last words that I will ever speak to you—your grievances and feuds are not worth what they cost. I exhort and require you to forget them. Live in concord. I trust you will, if you have any regard either for your God or your king, your families, your own country or your own safety."

With that, Edward could no longer endure to sit up, and sank back on the pillows, but he still watched the faces around him. Grief stamped every face. Will Hastings clasped Dorset's hand, and both swore to love each other. All the lords and gentlemen present did the same. Edward saw and heard, then dismissed them. They filed out of his bedchamber, deeply moved. Even Dorset had tears in his eyes. When he came into the room where I was, he described the scene and repeated Edward's words, with many pauses as he struggled to control his voice.

"I will keep my promise," he told me, "and live on good terms with Hastings."

"He will do his part," I said.

Edward sent for the prelates and lords who were entrusted with the execution of his will. Before he had set out for France long ago, he had made his will, and had discussed its provisions with Elizabeth besides naming her as one of the executors. Now he did not summon her. He had omitted her name from the list of executors, and had appointed my Lord Stanley in her place, leaving her shorn of any power in the government. Edward turned to one of his own blood; in a codicil he gave England's heir, and England to his brother's care and protection—to his only brother, Richard, Duke of Gloucester. And Richard was far away, in the north.

Jane Shore had apartments in the palace, and from the beginning of Edward's illness, had kept out of sight. I had forgotten her very existence until she sent a servant to ask news of him. I was sorry for her because she loved Edward for himself, but she was young and desirous—and desired. She would soon warm another man's bed. As far as I knew, Edward had not asked to see her. The presence of his mistress at his bedside would have been considered unseemly, but I doubt if that would have weighed with Edward.

As every person in the palace knew, he never once asked for Elizabeth, sent her any message, or mentioned her name.

The ninth day of April was fair and sunny, flowers had begun to bloom in fields and gardens. Edward had been ill less than a week, but the bells were tolling. In three weeks he would have been forty-one years old. Mayor, aldermen, the heads of the Guilds—all who had official position—came in solemn procession to the palace, with all of the lords and prelates in London. They came to look once more at their king. Before dawn he was taken to St. Stephen's Chapel; Masses and dirges were sung, and by day and by night his lords and the gentlemen of his household kept watch.

For a week the rites went on, while the bells tolled and the city mourned, but London must say farewell to the king, and so must I, and before his body was taken away to Windsor I nerved myself to go to the chapel. Black hanging covered walls and windows, hiding the jeweled luster of the glass. The ranks of kneeling black-clad figures merged with the shadows, but the candles burning around the bier showed the brilliant figure of the king, lying in state arrayed in his royal robes, in gold and crimson and ermine, with his crown on his head and around his neck the collar of suns and roses.

Perhaps it was the candlelight that gave his face warmth and color, but it was as if he still lived, as if years of furious living had been smoothed away. When I was seeing him for the last time on earth, I saw young Edward again, as he had been when I had met him for the first time at Ludlow.

EDITOR'S NOTE

Autumn had come for the Summer Queen but she refused to admit it. Elizabeth rallied her Woodville relatives in one last desperate attempt to gain possession of the twelve-year-old Prince of Wales, crown him at Westminster, and appoint his mother Queen Regent. Richard was too quick for the Woodvilles. Perhaps he realized that another boy king had no chance of ruling England, perhaps he wanted the crown himself. In any case more Woodville heads rolled—Anthony's and Lord Grey's. Dorset fled to the Low Countries.

Elizabeth rushed back to Sanctuary with most of the royal treasure and with the ten-year-old Duke of York and his sisters. She stayed there for ten months and then gave in to the pleas and promises of the Archbishop of Canterbury and allowed the little Duke to join his brother in the apartments in the Tower. Elizabeth never saw either of them again. But soon she had made her peace with Richard and she and her daughters were re-established at court.

Richard's reign came to an abrupt end at Bosworth Field and now Elizabeth Woodville made her last maneuver. She pulled all the strings she had with the House of Parliament to petition Henry the Seventh to marry her daughter, Edward's beloved Bess. Henry acceded to this request for the marriage brought together the Houses of Lancaster and York and put an end to the War of the Roses. Better yet from Elizabeth's point of view, the Woodville blood was carried into the great Tudor Dynasty.

If she was worried about her two sons in the Tower, Elizabeth never said so. In all probability they were still alive when Henry acquired the throne. Who murdered them will always be a mystery, because the case against Richard has developed more and more holes with the passing of time.

Henry the Seventh was a cautious man and, although he had married Elizabeth Woodville's daughter, he knew that the Summer Queen was still capable of weaving her spells and stirring up intrigues and rebellions. He banished her to Bermondsey convent with a pension of four hundred crowns a year and there she lived the last five years of her life in lonely ignominy.

As for Cicely, Marchioness of Dorset, her journal on which this novel is based stops just after the death of Edward the Fourth. One may only surmise that she was too despondent after Edward's death to continue her record of the harrowing years which followed. We do know that she married the Earl of Wiltshire very promptly after Dorset's death and that she peppered Warwickshire and Devon with churches, schools, and hospitals. Presumably the latter part of her life was a very happy one, but possibly it was haunted by what she knew about the murder of the two little princes in the Tower.

Cicely lived long enough to see the end of her medieval world and leave behind her lovely effigy in Astley Church.